Dwarf Girls Don't Dance

Terry Newman was a research lecturer, working on heart and lung function, who one day happened to find himself in the BBC's Broadcasting House writing comedy. He is still rather vague about how this happened, but after he decided that writing was more fun than sitting at an electron microscope in the dark, he has gone on to write comedy and drama, with some success, for TV, film, radio, Internet, games and the stage.

His first novel 'Detective Strongoak and the Case of the Dead Elf' which introduced the well-dressed, axe-wielding, Master Detective Nicely Strongoak was a #1 Kindle Epic Fantasy Bestseller. This new adventure takes Nicely across the miles, and the years, on one dwarf's search for a hidden truth, and to find it out he must be the best dwarf in his world and a good enough dwarf for any world.

Terry now works in a nice bright room with a view of the Sussex Weald, where he also helps write musicals, but he does sometimes still miss his microscope.

Other books by this author

Detective Strongoak and the Case of the Dead Elf
The King of Elfland's Little Sister

The Resurrection Show
(with David Alter, as Dalter T Newman)

For children

The Duke of Delhi

Tarquin and his Troop
(with Tarquin Taylor)

Dwarf Girls Don't Dance

TERRY NEWMAN

MB
MONKEY BUSINESS

MONKEY BUSINESS
An imprint of Grey House in the Woods

www.greyhouseinthewoods.org

This paperback original 2020

Copyright © Terry Newman, 2020

Terry Newman asserts the moral right to
be identified as the author of this work

A catalogue record for this book
is available from the British Library

Paperback ISBN: 978-1-909295-19-3
ebook ISBN: 978-1-909295-20-9

This novel is entirely a work of fiction.
The names, characters and incidents portrayed in it are
the work of the author's imagination. Any resemblance to
actual persons, living or dead, events or localities is
entirely coincidental.

Set in Adobe Garamond Pro

1 2 3 4 5 6 7 8 9 0

All rights reserved. No part of this publication may be reproduced,
stored in a retrieval system, or transmitted, in any form or
by any means, electronic, mechanical, photocopying, recording
or otherwise, without the prior permission of the publishers.

CONTENTS

Book One
1. The Happy Hobgoblin — 9
2. The Rage — 20
3. Clean-Up Work — 32
4. Kingley — 43
5. The Wizard's Clinic — 56
6. The Seneschal — 65
7. Kellisgrund — 85
8. Diamond — 98
9. The Hat-Check Girl — 106
10. Grundrund — 115
11. The Night Shift — 132

Book Two
12. Skragsrealm — 153
13. The Nine Idlers — 165
14. The Foreshadowing — 179
15. The Eagles — 191
16. Skavernslager — 201
17. The Day of the Long Sun — 211
18. Dunkiln Delvedeep — 225

Book Three
19. Torfull Haflaxen — 243
20. The Vigil — 250
21. The Bequest — 266
22. Diamond Again — 273
23. Retirement — 280
24. Huldre — 290
25. The Snow Queen — 304
26. Captain Royalwench — 310

27	Answers	326
28	Red	339
29	The Boscomere Feast	345
30	Kellismarsh	363
31	Goodbyes	375

BOOK ONE

1

The Happy Hobgoblin

I was in a nightspot in a part of town where the name over the door changes more often than an elf queen changes her lacies. This week the club was the *Happy Hobgoblin*. Last week it was probably the *Tipsy Troll*; next week, who knows? I guess it all depends on how much *The Citadel Guide to Everyday Alliteration* can help out.

At the moment it was the *Happy Hobgoblin*, and you knew it was the *Happy Hobgoblin* because there was a colourful sketch of his ugly smiling chops drawn large on the wall by the entrance. Look, he's happy, you will be too!

The name spinning is all to make you believe that it's a wonderful new place you've never been to before, which is going to provide you with everything your little heart could ever desire in life. All the excitement, all the romance, all the sex – everything most folk secretly believe that they deserve, even though there's little evidence to suggest why this might be true.

In fact, *The Happy Hobgoblin* is the same old duck-and-dive you visited the last time you had one too many with the boys, or girls, at the end of a busy working week. But now there's a new name, new lights and a fresh lick of paint on the walls that will wear off quicker than the hostess's smile when your purse is empty. And you'll go home vowing never to visit the *Happy Hobgoblin* again and you won't... because by then it's the *Prancing Pixie* or the *Drunken Dragon* – it's only the air of enforced jollity and the stink of quiet desperation that never changes.

I'd already lost count of the number of *Happy Hobgoblins* I'd visited that evening. They had lost any pretence of individuality and all blurred into one continuous episode of too much drinking, too much pipe-leaf and too few clothes. Considering that there was a good half-thumb covering of snow outside on the Citadel cobblestones – which is what passes for blizzard conditions in this mostly sub-tropical part of the world – I just hoped all these young ladies had bought a good warm vest to go home in. A half thumb of snow in the Citadel is enough to cause the news scrolls to froth into fits of excitement, and the more fashion-conscious, and less compassionate, to go skin a member of an endangered species. Back home in New Iron Town, it wouldn't have been enough to put off young courting couples from pursuing the sort of courting activities that really require open air.

I hadn't bothered to check in my coat and hat, as I didn't intend to stay long. Not even the advertised charms of 'Diamond the Dancing Dwarfess' were going to prevent a hasty departure if I didn't dig up some treasure this time – my 'treasure' being a low life by the name of Gabby Guttersnap. His goodwife was very keen on his safe return to the bosom of the family because she had found out that he had been busy being hugged to the bosom of a completely different family. This had not endeared him to his legally married spouse, but she was willing to take him back if he truly valued his wife. My client, however, happened to be the forgiving Mrs Guttersnap's older brother who was rather less forgiving, but equally keen for Gabby to return to Mrs Guttersnap – if he valued his life.

As a master detective, I don't normally get involved in marriage guidance, but times were tough that winter and I liked to think this was less about infidelity and more about homicide prevention.

I bought my drink – these clubs are funny like that – and I looked the crowd over with no success. It was the same crowd I'd seen in all the other nightspots – men mostly – loud men and their loud women in loud clothes. As I looked around, I saw that these men were actually a cut above most of the customers I'd inspected at the other night haunts I had frequented that evening. Maybe it was a better grade of flesh-market, but it was still a flesh-market nonetheless.

I wondered why this form of evening entertainment seemed to have so little appeal to the other Citadel folk. Elves would rather gouge their eyes out with dragons' teeth, gnomes wouldn't get past the door-check, and most of us dwarves would never pay the drink prices – mine were going on expenses. You'd find a few of the more housebroken and presentable goblins knocking around alongside the men and women, but by and large, they'd either be running the place or supplying muscle. Men and women do seem to like to get together in very confined spaces where they can't work out whom they are shouting at – or why.

I finished the drink because it was in my hand and pushed through the gyrating folk on the crowded dance floor towards where the 'Way Out' light flickered. Not an easy job, even though I'm tall for a dwarf – easily the height of many small men – with a shoulder width that negates the need for padding.

Just as I hit mid-floor, the band, a three-piece that sounded in need of a fourth, struck up an intro fanfare. Hemmed in at all sides, it seemed that I was going to see "Diamond the Dancing Dwarfess" after all.

Oh goody.

I didn't anticipate that this was going to be the highlight of my evening. How wrong I was, and how different life would have been if the trumpet player had gone for a comfort break and given me the extra two minutes I needed to get to the door. But his bladder was under control, and his lips were nicely moistened, so he did his big welcome for 'Diamond the Dancing Dwarfess' and my heart sank.

You see, the Citadel's constant need for novelty has always provided an opportunity for shorter women to pass themselves off as, admittedly rarely seen, Dwarfesses. They can thereby earn themselves some corn, carrying out what is euphemistically known as 'amorous dancing'. This provides much amusement for us dwarves of the male persuasion, who know one thing for certain: Dwarf girls don't dance.

The lights went down, the three-piece managed to agree on the same tune if not the same tempo, and the curtains on the small stage opened. On came 'Diamond' and down dropped my jaw. Diamond wasn't cheap cut glass; she was the real thing after all. She was a dwarfess, and she could dance, really dance – in the fashion proscribed by the Citadel Guild of Amorous Dancers and Associated Divesters.

So, firstly, let's clear a few things up.

For those of you who have yet to make the acquaintance of one of my sisters, there are a few things I should point out. Number one, as the male dwarf is to masculinity, so the dwarf woman is to femininity. We have muscles that would shame an ape, and shoulders you could balance anvils on. They have curves and a bust that would make a hobgoblin blush. Dwarf women have everything it takes to make the habitual trouser wearer's wildest fantasies come true, and it's all present in the compact version. Best things come in small packages, was not a phrase coined just to describe us male dwarves.

Secondly: dwarf women don't have beards. In fact, dwarf women have remarkably little body hair, because it all grows where it should do – on the top of their heads. To say a dwarf woman's hair is her crowning glory is an understatement along the lines of 'trolls get hungry', 'goblins have personal hygiene problems', and 'elves require humility lessons'. More care and attention is lavished by a dwarf girl on her hair than anything else in her life, often up to and including whoever shares her bed. From the simplest beehive to the most complex of knots and plaits, a dwarf woman will, without any shadow of a doubt, try them all at some stage of their lives. Her hair is in a state of constant flux, akin to something that normally requires a dozen scholarly equations to summarise. They say there are now more hairdressers in New Iron Town than axe makers, although I think a few may double up on occupations by some of the cuts I've seen in recent years.

Here's another thing most Citadel folk aren't clear about – although many rumours do abound – whatever those crazy chemicals are that the female of the species produce to attract the male, dwarf girls hold the patents. And they don't just affect dwarf men either. Oh no! Hence the appeal of the dwarfess dancer for anybody wanting to attract paying customers to their night-time entertainment establishment.

In all that particular evening, Diamond took off: one pair of evening gloves (elbow length), a neck choker (velvet), a belt (silver chain), and a single silk garter. And there wasn't a single one of those aforementioned habitual trouser wearers present in the *Happy Hobgoblin* that evening that wasn't ready to fight dragons with a fruit knife and howl naked at the moon; simply for a snap of that garter.

Diamond earned herself five enthusiastic rounds of applause from everybody present, even the ladies, and I had to admit I was similarly… intrigued. Nothing more, of course.

A small runt was guarding the door leading to the dressing room corridor. If he was the *Happy Hobgoblin*, he'd had a bad day, and I was expecting some backchat, but he melted when he saw me. There was a crystal 'diamond' sparkling on the dressing room door, which was kind of cute, and raised the *Happy Hobgoblin* up in my estimations. Mind you, there was not a lot of room left to go in the downward direction. I knocked and waited.

Finally, I received a 'Yeah, what?' shouted in a tone of voice that translates better as 'I've got a shooter in my hand, so what are you going to do about it?'

I entered, very carefully. She didn't have a shooter in her hand, she had a pewter ash cup, and even though I was prepared, it only missed me by the width of an insurance salesman's smile.

'Get out!' Diamond added, 'I told those petrified worm turds that I'd rather get shafted by the Horde of Hasged than listen to their advice. Let alone take it!'

Diamond's accent was pure Rust Hills and none the worse for that. The lady herself was now attending to her make-up in the dressing room mirror.

'Good evening, Mistress Diamond,' I said, taking off my hat because my mother made sure her sons knew exactly the right protocol for talking to amorous dancers in their dressing rooms. 'Very pleased to make your acquaintance.'

I picked the ashcup up off the floor and smoothed out the dent in its side that, thankfully, had not been made by my noggin. I continued my introduction speech.

'And may I offer you congratulations on a riveting performance, if that isn't too forward? Or should I conclude that that particular mark has already been over-stepped?'

She turned back towards me. She considered, blinked a couple of times, flapped eyelashes that on anybody but a dwarfess would probably have been almost comically false and pursed lips that you wanted to nibble like ripe cherries. Pulling her robe tighter across a front-back with curves that could have kick-started a cardiac casualty, she looked me up and down before concluding: 'So the greybeard brigade didn't send you?'

I shook my head.

'I was purely here on business when I caught your rather awesome act. I thought I'd just pay my respects.' I handed her a card. She did me a big favour and took it from my hand.

'Nicely Strongoak, Master Detective and Shield-for-Hire,' she read carefully, betraying just the slightest squint which somehow only added to her cute quotient. 'What business brings a Master Detective out to a dive like the *Gay Grunt* on a snowy night?'

'Matters pertaining to a wayward heart.'

'In my experience,' she observed, 'it is not the heart that goes wayward – that just follows on behind, on account of it being connected to the wayward bit.'

Diamond poured us both a drink. You can tell a lot about women of any race by the way they pour a drink and Diamond had done it before. She poured generously and didn't spill a drop. She also poured from a bottle of 'Black Star'. Dwarves are renowned for liking their spirits strong and sticky. They don't come much stronger or stickier than 'Black Star'. In some dwarf circles, the glassful she gave me was enough to warrant a marriage proposal. I took the proffered drink and toasted her, before adding, 'Women have been known to go rambling off-road too.'

'Yeah sure,' she shrugged, 'and worms have been known to fly, but most times when I look out the window, it's birds that I see fluttering by.'

She knocked back her drink in one, not fazed in the slightest.

'You're a long way from the Rust Hills, Diamond,' I mentioned casually, approaching my drink with more ceremony.

The drink was good, like a fresh linen shirt with gold buttons. I knocked it back, and she offered refills.

'Sounds like you're a long way from New Iron Town, Master Detective.'

'Hey, don't we both know our dwarf diaspora?'

'That's a fancy word for a cluehound.'

'I buy them by the dozen, just for occasions like this,' I explained.

'So what took you from those old slag heaps of home – bleach lover, are we?'

A 'bleach' is a derogatory term for an elf, which is only slightly more insulting than 'doorstop' is for a dwarf. Given some of my more recent romantic adventures, the name just might have some justification – not that she was to know that and not that I was saying.

'Why? Been dancing around the forest maypole yourself?'

This won me a grin and another top-up. We were both on good form that evening, shame someone had to go and spoil the party just as we were getting into our groove.

The door opened behind me and, to my surprise, a male voice I recognised, but couldn't immediately place, asked: 'Everything okay here, sweetness?'

He wasn't talking to me.

I turned and saw the familiar curly blond mop of hair and the handsome face of Roland Seneschalson, heir to the last inheritable position of any consequence in the Citadel. Roland 'Roli' Seneschalson – well-loved playboy, womaniser and notorious gambler who had papered the Citadel with his promissory notes. Roli Seneschalson – bad-tempered drunk, danger-seeker and dwarf.

By that, I don't mean he was of the race that is known in the common tongue of Widergard by this designation (what we call ourselves is our business, thanks), but that he was affected by the medical condition men call dwarfism. Good looking guy and as rich and powerful as a dragon with a trust fund.

'Master Strongoak is just paying a social call, Roland,' Diamond said, with regard sufficient enough to inform me that whatever position Roland Seneschalson might hold in the Citadel, his position with regard to Diamond the Dancing Dwarfess was much more interesting and enviable.

'That's right – just a social call. Now back to business.' I finished my drink, put my hat back on and tipped it at the lady.

'What business would that be, Master Strongoak?' said the son of the man who was probably one of the ten most influential folk in the Citadel. You can't buy that sort of connection, or if you can, not in any currency I have ever had in my pocket. So I smiled my best 'hire me, I'm honest' smile as I handed across another card. This smile is the same as all my other smiles, but I raise the corners of my mouth.

'Detective, eh?' He pocketed the card carefully. I had the feeling that despite his reputation, or maybe because of it, Roland Seneschalson was a careful man. 'Never know when you might need a good detective.'

'So I like to tell people.'

'And are you a good detective, Master Strongoak? It's just that I find so many people, of every race, so often fail to live up to their reputations. Now I, myself, I have taken every opportunity to ensure that I live up to, or down to, my reputation. Usually down, as it's so much closer.'

A self-deprecating height joke – there wasn't really much I could add to that. So I tipped my hat at Diamond again, because I'm good at it, and I was all out of snappy exit lines.

'Off so soon, Master Strongoak? We must do it all again some time!' He waved at me in a manner that was not going to ever make him friends, but I had a feeling he never, ever, went looking for them.

Diamond looked at my card again as I left. I knew that she would never call me, not unless…

I made my way out along the dressing room corridor, squeezing past the suited up goblin grunt who now occupied so much space that air particles were queuing ahead of me to get through.

'You were lucky this time, doorstop,' said the grunt, who I took to be the Seneschalson's minder.

'I was born lucky – it's why they call me Lucky Loopy Longlegs.' This only confused him, so I let it ride. It was a work evening.

I checked my mental list for the next nightspot and made my way to the *Blissed-out Boggart*. It wasn't far, but for some reason, the walk felt like a thousand miles. A thousand miles in the wrong direction. I thought I would probably never see either of them again. Unexpectedly, I saw Roland Seneschalson the very next week.

2

The Rage

There's a body shop I visit round the corner from the converted armoury that I like to call home. No membership required because if you have to ask you can't come in. It's not got anything fancy: weights, bags, a couple of sparring rings and a room where a dwarf can keep in shape by swinging his axe in peace – without taking off the heads of any innocent bystanders. The bloodstains on the floor are all self-inflicted, or so the story goes.

I was towelling down in the changing room when I became conscious of a certain absence of sunlight. I mean it's not exactly a well-lit room at the best of times, being in the basement, but even the frosted glass at street foot level was being obscured. The goblin-shaped reason was standing in front of the afore-mentioned frosted window, to one side of the entrance, and to the other side of him was Roli Seneschalson. It's unusual to have social visits in the changing room. I let him speak first, so I could calculate just how social this visit was.

'Diamond's my girl, Master Strongoak.'

Oh, straight to business then – not very social at all.

Dwarf Girls Don't Dance

'That makes you a lucky man then, Seneschalson.'

'I think so.'

'As long as Diamond is of the same opinion, naturally.'

'We're going to get married – the full three volumes – no jumping of broomsticks.'

Well, that was news from the old bird and no mistake. The Seneschal's son marrying out, and not to some elf either, but to an actual spade-wielding, ore-digging dwarf. Not that Diamond did much of either I'm sure, but the breeding was there. I could probably sell this titbit to the gossip scrolls and not have to work for the rest of the year. The fact that then I'd probably never, ever actually get to work again, certainly not in the Citadel, was a given.

'You must tell me where you are placing your wedding slate,' I commented, tying my hair in the family knots. 'You don't want to get too many chicken bricks.'

'It's the Seneschals' tradition to hand out presents at such occasions, not to receive them.'

Roli sat on the bench next to me; the goblin just got on with glowering.

'The dwarf side of the family are going to love that!' I observed.

I packed my bag carefully, especially the hand axe. Roli now shifted along closer, and his goblin shadow shifted almost imperceptibly forward too.

'That's good, my sleuthing companion, because I'm now going to give you something for nothing – some good advice.'

I put on my jacket and hefted my bag onto my shoulder.

'You would be surprised just how much of that you can accumulate in the Citadel, Seneschalson. There's always some body willing to offer another body good advice. Why, if it only had a resale value, I could have opened a market stall.'

'You don't talk to Roli Seneschalson like that!' said the grunt, who I recognised from the *Happy Hobgoblin*.

'I can take care of this, Cluff,' the Seneschalson said angrily, slapping down the goblin. He stood and came close enough for me to smell his skin-freshener, which is too close in my book.

'My advice is solid gold, Master Strongoak because it'll keep you healthy, if not wealthy. Keep away from Diamond. We don't need no ex-Cit dwarf poking their hairy nose into our business.'

I let out a disappointed sigh.

'Now that's not going to endear you to the bride's family at all, Seneschalson. Anyway, I think Diamond is probably old enough to choose her own friends, don't you?'

I made for the door, but the goblin mountain got there before me and, wonder of wonders, strung two sentences together: 'I don't think you heard Master Seneschalson. He was being nice, but I don't do nice,' he said, reaching down with one huge paw of a hand.

'It's not Master Seneschalson, you big lunk!' I said, swatting his hand away. 'Seneschalson is his title. It's like saying, Master Master.'

The big goblin grunt chewed this over for a moment, decided he didn't like the taste and this time made his hand into a fist that could have driven in pit props.

Roli Seneschalson shouted a hasty, 'No, Cluff!'

However, still pumped up from my workout, I was now well out of Cluff's reach. And I don't do nice either, not when I don't have to. I didn't have to now. I'd just been minding my own business and working up a thirst, and now all that good work had been wasted. Honestly!

I'm no scholar, and I've never looked at a dead body for pleasure or knowledge, except to establish how it came to that estate. One thing I have noticed, whether you are dwarf, elf, goblin, man or wizard, we all share very similar knees. Teeth, ears, hair and lips are up for grabs, but knees are pretty much straight off the shelf. Size can vary, naturally, but in terms of hinges located mid-way down the leg, good for kicking, walking and running, a knee is pretty much of a given construction. And knees do not like going sideways. I moved Cluff's left knee sideways.

I could have kicked harder. I have kicked harder, but I wasn't harbouring any grudge – it was one professional to another. I let the goblin writhe and turned to Roli Seneschalson.

'I hope you run a good employment health plan for your staff, Seneschalson, because he's not going anywhere at a run for half a year or so.' I took a step towards the smaller man. 'I also don't know what's pothered your pony, but I'll say this, for the last time – there was nothing more sinister about my visit to Diamond's dressing room that evening than one dwarf getting the urge to dig the dirt and share a drink with another, got it?'

Roli Seneschalson met my gaze; I'll give him that. He looked me in the eye and said: 'I wish now that I had spent slightly more time with the dwarves with beards.'

'It's always an education, or so they tell me, as long as you understand them. Do you understand me?'

Roli nodded like he meant it and I left, treading carefully over the writhing Cluff and hoping I never saw the Seneschalson's smiling face again. I didn't. He did send me a bottle of something very sticky and very expensive the next week, along with a hand-written and signed apology note. I thought about pouring the drink down the drain, but as I said, it was a tough winter that year.

The note, I folded carefully and filed for future reference. That's what detectives do.

The winter passed, eventually, and we all shed our overcoats, and most got on with the serious job of looking fabulous and getting an all-over tan. Like that matters. I eventually found Gabby Guttersap, and with only a small amount of financial persuasion, he returned to his wife and family. Within a month she had battered him to death with a marble rolling pin after discovering him in the marriage bed with her own sister.

A return to his own family indeed, just not the right branch of it.

You may see this as a somewhat hackneyed response to spousal infidelity; she dealt with her sister much more imaginatively, which is why she was currently facing an appointment with Master Cleaver – the nickname for the approved local method of terminating a miscreant's life.

You do your best and look what happens.

Spring brought me more satisfactory employment in the guise of a fraud investigation that involved the import of fake dragon whangers. The supposed aphrodisiac properties of dragon whangers is said, by some, to be the main reason for the dragon's decline – well, that and the development of the automatic machine shooter, which made heroics with swords rather redundant.

This story could be true, which is a shame of epic proportions, because, for a start, there really is no logical reason to suppose that the ingestion of a bit of over-aged chewy muscle is going to do anything other than give you heartburn. More relevant is the fact that the male dragon does not have a whanger.

Yes, dragons are whangerless – how about that?

Dragon reproduction is an act that involves an even greater amount of intimacy, not to mention some discomfort. This has been suggested as being the reason why both male and female dragons are notoriously bad-tempered and the real reason that there are so few of them. It also supplies the answer to the riddle: How do mummy dragons and daddy dragons make baby dragons? Answer: carefully.

This hasn't dented in any way the popular belief amongst dunderheads that something as large and powerful as a 'traditional' dragon, must simply have an equally impressive one-eyed ploughman. Boy, are they barking round the wrong family tree. The fact is that your dried, powdered or fillet of dragon whanger, is more likely to be mutton and blasting powder.

This particular assignment of 'whangers', when I finally found them, had been fashioned to resemble what somebody's fevered imagination most imagined a dragon whanger to resemble. No way could male dragons have even got off the ground carrying that mighty a whanger around with them!

Lots of people weren't happy about the dragon whanger fraud – with the exception of the gnome pocket-mastermind behind the whole venture, who I finally apprehended in bed with a trio of young lovelies from Canning Town. As I observed at the time, he was not in need of his own medicine.

I mostly forgot about Diamond and Roli Seneschalson, except to occasionally check out the social scrolls when I was visiting my tailor's. I never saw any marriage notice, and by summer, my mind was elsewhere. And then one sunny morning in my office at the *Two Fingers*, with the birds singing and the sun beaming down, I got the call I knew I was never going to get, not unless…

'Nicely Strongoak, Master Detective and Shield-for-Hire. If you've got the gold, you don't go on hold.'

I'd been working on that. Not bad, I thought.

I happened to be sitting in my favourite thinking position: both feet on the desk and the chair tipped back as far as possible without contravening one of those pernickety laws of nature they go on about nowadays. I heard one small noise, somewhere between a gasp and a sob and I was already halfway out of the door.

'Where are you, Diamond?'

The reply barely bothered the horn earpiece. It seemed to come from somewhere else, someplace where birds no longer sang, and the sun was just a big burny ball of combustion put in the sky because whoever is in charge of that sort of thing never got round to building a decent fireplace.

'Small coffee lodge, north of the Wizard's Gate – the name of Gallgot's. Know it?' she whispered.

'I'll find it – just don't move.'

I got there in record time, even though I had to make a major detour while the Citadel Guard cleaned up after rival 4th and 5th Level goblin gangs. They had apparently decided to have a knife party to resolve who exactly was most capable of senseless violence. As the infirmary wagons got busy carrying away the prone combatants, I guessed the answer was a draw. Date for return fixture to be decided, subject to anybody being still capable of locomotion.

Diamond was a faint ghost, a face just visible through the lodge window. She looked like she had been sitting there since the founding of the Citadel in the Olden Ages and maybe they had built everything else around her. Whatever she was wearing had been thrown on with no thought for fashion or practicality;

not that she gave a pixie's fart. Even her hair was all mussed up, which was enough to place very bad thoughts where they shouldn't be at a time like this. She nursed a cup of something milky that had developed a skin so thick that you could have banged out a paradiddle on it. Next to her were the remains of what must have once been a mighty big pile of pan-fried cakes. On her engagement finger was a ring blessed with a large shiny rock that was as magic as fine gem-craft can make.

As I walked in, the proprietor was paying her way too much attention. I sat down at the table, opposite her.

'Laugh,' I said.

She looked at me blankly, as if I had just invented language and she wasn't sure if it would catch on.

'Laugh,' I tried again. 'Laugh like we had a bust-up and you've now forgiven me on account of me being such a swell sort and there is now nothing in the world to be worried about – especially for coffee lounge owners.'

She took her cue this time and let out a laugh that convinced the proprietor that everything was swell too. I signalled for two coffees, and he got to business with the proper apparatus.

'Nicely, I have to tell you…' she began.

'You have to tell me nothing. Not until you sign this.' I took out the contract that I had grabbed on my way out of the office. I placed it in front of her. 'This means that you are my client and as such, I have certain obligations to you that make it impossible for me to divulge sensitive information to certain third parties – such as the Citadel Guard – that could be interpreted as being detrimental to your continued legal status as a free citizen.' I paused and pushed the paper and a quill in her direction. 'It's not essential, but it might prove helpful – yes?'

She nodded and signed and pushed the contract back towards me.

'Roli's dead,' she added. The news I really was hoping not to hear.

'Where?'

'The rooms he bought for me, about two streets up from here.'

'You told anybody?'

She shook her head.

'Good girl, keep it that way for the moment. Got the key?'

She actually took out a couple of keys that must partner some real fancy pieces of lock-work and slid them across the table to me. I looked at her hands, nice nail work; metallic blue and engraved with tiny dragons. 'Don't you want to know what happened, Nicely?'

'I will do, but it doesn't have to be now. Now, I want us to drink our coffee, and laugh again. I'm guessing the Seneschalson isn't going anywhere.'

She shook her head slowly.

'No, his sort of dead don't go anywhere.'

'Time for another laugh, Diamond.'

She managed it, just – in time for the arrival of the coffee. I fed the owner some corn, and we both gave him our best smiles. She didn't have many left in her. I could see that.

I sipped at the coffee. It was better than it had any right to be.

'Was it the Rage?' I asked her finally. She nodded again, slower this time. 'Do you remember anything?'

This time a shake followed by: 'Not a thing.'

'How do you normally manage? When you're dancing?'

'Practice and control.'

She looked at her coffee and then looked at me, really intent, as if desperate for my answer.

Dwarf Girls Don't Dance

'How do you manage? I mean, when you're on a case or something, there must be times when you get... angry, worked up... doesn't the Rage take you?"

'Practice and control, Diamond. Like you said, practice and control.'

'Yes... guess that's all it takes.'

I stared out of the window.

'I can't remember the last time the Rage took me, and I've been through some interesting times. Bury it deep enough and it may not be at hand, not even when you need it.'

'But sometimes I guess deep isn't deep enough,' she said bitterly.

I nodded – sometimes deep doesn't do it at all.

We both knew this.

The Dwarf Rage, the subject of more talk and gossip than almost any other aspect of dwarf life – apart from the speculation surrounding certain aspects of male dwarf anatomy. The Rage – the anger that turns an over-muscled axe-wielder into an unstoppable dispenser of death; an indomitable destroyer rampaging through armies without any thought for personal safety. Of course, it's added considerably to dwarf reputation and mystique, but we seldom talk about it – especially to other races. The Rage, which we dwarves also call 'the Curse'.

The general public does not know that dwarf women have their own particular version of the Rage – not even as the most whispered of secrets. And that is because the Rage takes dwarf women at the most intimate of moments. Such secrecy has only added to dwarf women's somewhat notorious reputation and mystique.

'It hasn't been a problem between us, the Rage. He's a good man, Roli – was a good man. A kind and generous lover too.'

She looked at me accusingly, but I had nothing to add. 'I'm sorry that he got a bit overprotective. I was cross when he told me he'd paid you a visit.'

'Don't feel sorry for me, Diamond,' I said, with a shrug. 'Feel sorry for that big protection detail he trails around with him.'

She looked blank for a moment before continuing: 'Oh, Cluff! He's not Roli's employee – that's all down to Roli's father, the Seneschal. He doesn't place much trust in Roli – always worried about… his safety. Roli doesn't even really like Cluff – didn't like him.' Her voice broke a bit, and she sucked up some coffee.

'So, last night?' I said, finally.

'Last night was different. Maybe I let my guard down a bit, I don't know. Roli was supposed to be attending some function, on behalf of his father.'

'Recall the details?'

She shook her head. 'Sorry, something for the White and Wise, way up the Hill. He cut out early and came home. Then… well, it must have come out of nowhere. One minute I was pouring drinks for the both of us and the next – it was morning, I was exhausted, and Roli was lying there… all beaten up and bloody, with his neck… broken.'

Dwarf courtship can be kind of physical. I guess nature did its best to safeguard the future of the dwarf race by ensuring the most desirable of dwarf women only went with the toughest dwarf men – even if the women had to do some whittling down of the population. Not that this is generally a problem – male dwarves are not built like men with dwarfism.

'I didn't know what to do, Nicely. I had to get out of there, get something to eat, before I could even think – post-Rage comedown, you know?'

Dwarf Girls Don't Dance

I nodded. The low blood sugar you get after the Rage turns you into some kind of starving demon. To be honest, food doesn't always get... cooked; which explains another part of the dwarf reputation.

'Then I remembered you... phoned... from the street horn opposite. I kept your card,' she added, unnecessarily.

I looked across at the horn shelter – nice and secluded. Hopefully, she had not been seen.

'That was a good move, Diamond.'

Fear and apprehension came upon her in a rush.

'What am I going to do, Nicely? I should turn myself in. I know that, but I don't know what to say. What man or woman is going to understand? Only a dwarf would.'

'You should do nothing,' I said emphatically. 'Not until I go check your apartment.'

She started to protest, but I reassured her. 'You don't have to go back with me. I've left my car around the corner. You get to sit and wait in there. Now, let's finish our coffees and get out of here.'

We drank up and left, smiling, my arm around Diamond – just two happy lovers now made up again. As if.

3

Clean-Up Work

My Dragonette '57 was looking particularly desirable in the mid-morning sunshine. The racing green paintwork gleamed, and the air-trimming just cried out to cut some breeze.

'We can have ourselves a mighty fine day today,' my Dragonette shouted. 'Let's head for the coast with the rag-top down, or maybe visit the hills of Tall Trees and go annoy a few elves. Yes, plenty of fun things to do, with a cute girl at your side, laughing as she lets her crowning glory loose in the slipstream.'

Or, you could go and clear up her dead boyfriend's body, and wonder how this was going to go down with the boyfriend's incredibly well-connected father, while she sobbed her dark brown eyes out all over your wagon's soft leather interior.

I left her in said wagon with a reminder not to move and went to find the lovers' cosy nest. It was in a block that had been so tastefully converted it hurt. I guessed it had once been something mundane like a small industrial unit – perhaps a tannery, if the sign on the wall bearing the legend 'The Old Tannery' was anything to go by. It's powers of observation that make a master detective, you know.

Dwarf Girls Don't Dance

There was no lingering odour of hide or lime in the empty entrance lobby, only the much more reassuring and discreet smell of wealth. Six sets of rooms and something more extensive built in the eaves. I guessed Roli would have bought the top floor and guessed correctly. The door lock was indeed a piece of work, and more importantly, showed no signs of being forced or opened with anything other than the key I now held in my hand. I took a breath and entered. Behind that was another door and that too had a very fancy lock. Two door entrances – everybody has them this year, didn't you know?

The rooms were nice, very nice: knocked through, light, but with many 'original features'. They didn't have too much of anything in them, but what was there was perfectly proportioned and placed just right. I walked through to the bedroom, which supplied more of the same. It was all immaculate: clean, tidy and completely devoid of anything as vulgar as a dead body – even that of the son of the Seneschal of the Citadel. Handkerchief in hand, I opened a few trunks and closets – nothing – not a single stitch of clothing or a personal, or even impersonal, belonging. I checked the kitchen, no food in the icebox, no tins on the shelves. The drinks cabinet was also empty, the glasses all clean and sparkling and placed upside down, except for two tumblers which stood on their rounded bottoms.

The bathroom was in a similar state to the main room and kitchen – not so much as an errant toothpick – a thoroughly professional job. But just how 'professional' was another matter entirely.

I took off my jacket, carefully placing it where it shouldn't shed any of the little fibres so beloved of the Guard section that deals with that sort of thing; the 'nit pickers' as they are lovingly called.

Next: a 'U-bend' is a smart piece of plumbing – and the detective's friend. I placed my handkerchief underneath it and grasped the locking ring. Of course, plumbers have tools to move such obstinate fittings, but they don't have dwarf fingers and thumbs. Well, apart from dwarf plumbers that is. The locking ring gave eventually, as did its companion ring. I didn't spill a drop as I carried the pipework through to the kitchen and spread the contents in a tray I found there. Dark, long, thick, dwarf hair and finer blond locks – but only the blond locks were still infused with Seneschalson blood. Professional, but not professional enough.

I scraped the solids up carefully into my kerchief and washed the rest down the kitchen sink, leaving the water running long enough to make sure that I – for one – left no evidence. I then put the soiled kerchief into a rubber glove I habitually carry to cope with the less pleasant aspects of my profession, dried the tray, and replaced it exactly where I'd found it. I tightened the 'U-bend' back into place in the bathroom, carefully running copious amounts of water through – it's the attention to detail that makes the difference.

I looked around again, getting onto my knees to check under the bed and other furniture, while mentally calculating the timeline of today's activities. Diamond said she woke up late after her Rage. Say an hour, two at the most, before she had called me. Half an hour for me to find the bar, half an hour chat, half an hour to get here. It was now Mid-watch, as a local horn blast helpfully reminded me. I felt a shiver run down my spine in big hob-nailed boots – I must have missed them by minutes. They could even have seen me. I got up quickly and put my jacket on.

Dwarf Girls Don't Dance

The entrance hall was still empty and still redolent of accumulated riches. I slipped out quieter than the whistle of a lipless ghoul. By the time I got back to my wagon, Diamond was gone.

The Happy Hobgoblin hadn't changed much in the months since I'd last been there. Except it was now called *The Dancing Dragon* and again – in case you were in any doubt – there was a sketch by the entrance: look it's a dragon and he's dancing and you will too!

The afternoon sunshine did the rest of the establishment no favours as it made its unaccustomed way in through the door held open by my foot. I shouted a 'hello' and was answered by 'The Curmudgeonly Cleaner': look, I've got a terrible job. I hate it, and you'll hate me too!

'Nobody here!' The cleaner pushed a mop around the floor as if he was still waiting to be given the instruction booklet.

I stepped in, and the sunlight departed gratefully as the door closed, sure now it wasn't missing out on anything that took place here after it had clocked off for the day. My eyes very quickly got used to the gloom – dwarves are good at that sort of thing. On closer inspection of the cleaner, I wished I hadn't made a closer inspection.

As folk go, I am pretty forbearing and take the different races as they come, except elves of course, but they deserve it for having had life far too easy for far too long. As dwarves go, I am remarkably broad-minded, because, truth be told, we are not the most tolerant of folk. We are suspicious of anybody who doesn't fulfil a set of requirements that are best defined as dwarvish, dwarf-like and dwarf. Plus dwarves have made 'grudge harbouring' into an art form and not only believe that no slight should go unpunished, but also that it should not go unrecorded.

This is why each dwarf family has a 'Retribution Book' that charts all successful reprisals carried out against transgressors. This is a much-prized possession and is handed down from father to son, and mother to daughter (everything in duplicate), with great love. Long winter nights (and they did get very long in the tunnels of New Iron Town) were always enlivened by readings of bloody family chastisements. We really did make our entertainment in those days.

So my open-mindedness is something of a wonder to my kith and kin, but even I have trouble with Will o' the Wisps. I know that they are just a type of gnome who live, or mostly lived, in the swampy ground of the Great River floodplains. I also know that there is no truth in the scurrilous rumour that they used to lure travellers to their deaths with the small lanterns that give them their common name of 'Jack Lanterns'. It's just that when they left – or rather were forced out of – their homelands, as the river was progressively improved for navigation, I wish they could have left the stink of the swamps behind.

Hence, Will o' the Wisps don't have much of a reputation for cleanliness. To employ one as a cleaner reeked of pure perversity.

'Afternoon, Jack,' I said, in friendly tones. 'I'm new in town, looking for my sister, Diamond. Heard she worked here.'

'Then you heard wrong,' the Jack replied, moving puddles of foul-looking water around the dance floor.

'Is that a fact? 'Cos I got it on good authority.'

'Never been impressed by no authorities – not since they kicked us out of our homes.' He rested on his mop and looking at me for the first time, spat in a puddle. 'You don't look much like her.'

I grabbed a chair and turned it around to rest my arms on the wooden back. 'A lot of folk say that, but our Ma, she reckons you could hardly tell us apart as children – apart from my beard, of course.'

'And what happened to that?'

'Soon learnt that here, Citadel women prefer something else to tickle them.' This won me a wheezing, half-choked laugh and earned the floor another ball of spittle, which the Jack slowly worked into the woodwork. 'Diamond use to work here. Don't no more.'

'That's a shame – it's kind of urgent.' I tapped my pocket in the time-honoured manner that spoke of financial compensation.

'Master Kingley, he don't like people coming round asking questions.'

I flicked a gold crown in his direction, and it was plucked out of the air with a speed that rather embarrassed the pace of his mopping. 'Now, I'd say Master Kingley doesn't need to be bothered, does he?'

The Jack gave me a slow shake of his head.

'Heard she was shacked up with her boyfriend, proper top-of-the-tree type.'

'Oh yes, that would be this Roli Seneschalson. She mentioned him.'

The Jack nodded.

'Yes, don't know where, mind, but you can guess it won't be in the Little Hundred. Didn't please Master Kingley that news, her leaving – good draw was Diamond. Her dancing was something else. No offence,' he added quickly.

'None taken. Any other dancers she might have mixed with? Members of the band maybe?'

The Jack shook his head.

'She kept herself to herself; not snotty like, more self-contained. Yes, that was her, self-contained. Shall I let her know you're looking for her?' he added, his eyes firmly fixed on my purse.

I nodded. 'There'd be some more corn in it for you as well. She'll know where to find me.' I left the Jack at his labours and happily departed *The Dancing Dragon*. The steam choked Citadel air had never tasted better.

I had obtained the information I was really after without even asking. So 'Master' Kingley owned the *Dancing Dragon*, did he? 'Master' Kingley also owned any number of the gambling dens, many of which Roli Seneschalson was rumoured to frequent – and where, it was also rumoured, he was fond of leaving his promissory notes.

You heard a lot of strange stories about Master Reepold Kingley around the Citadel; I had no idea if they were true. There was talk of Dark Crime Lords and sinister underworld orchestrations. I wondered how he was taking the loss of his star attraction. Maybe I had better go ask him.

Before I paid Master Kingley a visit, it would be useful to have an update from my 'society high life and low life' consultant, otherwise known as my tailor and hat maker, Gaspar Halftoken. I made my way speedily to the rooms where he did his cloth-cutting magic.

Gaspar, bless his curly gnome head and impeccably pointed boots, could see that I was worried and in no mood for our normal banter, so he drew me a map of Master Kingley with the minimum of fuss. Many people, apparently, found Kingley 'enchanting' and terrific company. Other people just found Kingley waiting for them when they came home at night and desperately hoped to be rid of him while they still had their limbs intact. I don't think I have ever found anybody, who wasn't of the female persuasion, 'enchanting.' If I did, I'd visit an

Dwarf Girls Don't Dance

infirmary, as I would surely be going down with something serious.

Master Kingley did like to spread his largess around and 'show people a good time', as it was commonly called. It seemed he was doing some of that spreading this very afternoon. At least that's what I was told by Gaspar. However, the purpose of this generosity was somewhat in doubt, at least according to the same source.

'He likes to think he's the elf lord's ring,' Gaspar said, 'but the word is that he's a bit of a goblin's outhole. Not that anybody would say that to his face, of course. Not if they wanted to keep hold of their own face.'

'So, could he really be some sort of Dark Crime Lord, Gaspar?'

'You're talking to the wrong gnome, Nicely!' Gaspar waved his tape measure around energetically. 'You want one of your friends at the Citadel Guard. All I can tell you is that the rumour is that he buys his clothes off the peg!'

'Axes and blood, Gaspar! How low could the fiend stoop?'

'You may laugh, Nicely Strongoak! But that may not be because he doesn't want to spread the corn around; it could be that he just doesn't want anybody getting too close.'

'Now Gaspar, that sounds just a little creepy.'

'Indeed. Let us just say that you won't spot many of the White and Wise at his events; so be careful.'

Gaspar thrust a new hatbox under my arm at the last moment to 'keep my pecker up'. Nothing like a new summer hat to do wonders for a dwarf's pecker – that and a party to go to – even if it is a Dark Crime Lord's.

It transpired that although the Kingliness of 'Master' Kingley might be very much in doubt, there was little doubt that he had pretensions to living like one. Or at least to how they had once lived. This meant that he needed a proper palatial pile of stones to rattle around in. He also needed to be near his many Citadel investments. This limited exactly how far away he could live from The Hill, as we locals affectionately call this ancient Citadel stronghold, built on a little lost mountain overlooking the Bay Area and the Big Sea beyond.

Tall Trees, the elven enclave way to the south, was out of the question, and the men and women of the ultra-exclusive Cliff Tops area did not welcome Kingley's 'sort' either. This was mostly because the current inhabitants' ancestors had made their fortunes from extortion and corruption generations ago, when such things went by different names, like conquest and subjugation. This qualified them as 'old gold'. It's a well-known fact that such men and women tend to look down on people who continue to do what their forefathers had once been so good at.

The answer, as worked out by Kingley and 'his sort', was to buy up a hilly area next to Cliff Tops, flatten any existing habitation – and hills – and build their own palaces. They renamed the area Cliff Top Village. The aspect wasn't quite as good as Cliff Tops, but they had the advantage of looking down on all the 'Old Gold', which must have pleased the villains and the similarly associated 'businessmen' that lived in 'The Village'.

Considering that this was the home of the cream of the Citadel's underworld, the security in Cliff Top Village was laughable. Or perhaps it would be better described as being 'designed with the criminal in mind', which considering it was all arranged by criminals, isn't so surprising. So every pocket palace was fitted out with all the latest alarms and tripwires, and there were grunts and runts strutting like their lives depended on it. What they hadn't done, was to consider the mindset of

Dwarf Girls Don't Dance

somebody who did not have nefarious intentions. Well, nothing worse than gatecrashing a party.

I found it remarkably easy to pretty much march straight up to the front door. Of course, I didn't exactly march. I drove through the pair of big black wrought iron gates with the rag top down, a crate of beazer-teaser in the passenger seat, and most importantly, the Silvestral sisters sitting snugly on the back shelf, dressed – or mostly undressed – for the outdoor dining season. The guards had more interesting things to look at than my credentials.

The Silvestral sisters are kind of noticeable – both over six foot, one blonde-haired, one red, with the kind of figures that would make an actuary burn his balance sheets and take up playing the lotto. The Silvestral sisters are also both enchantresses, and they are good at their job – their job being Vice. Vice – the prevention of it that is – on behalf of the Cits. Specifically the Citadel Guard Vice Section; the Filth Fellowship as they are affectionately known. That's where I first met them, and they took a shine to me, for obvious reasons. They help out if ever I need stunning women with the ability to stun from thirty-foot using a variety of non-lethal weapons. They are good with the lethal kind as well.

Now a lot of rubbish gets spoken about your average enchantress; she's not like a sorceress for a start. She doesn't cast spells, and she can't lure you into doing things directly contrary to your will. You can't use an enchantress as mitigating evidence in a legal trial – it's been tried, and usually folk go down for twenty years. What the average enchantress does have is glamour by the bucket load. The 'can't take my eyes off you as I light the log pit – oh look now my foot's on fire', sort of glamour. An enchantress shares this ability with the elves – in fact, if you could imagine an elf with humility, normal ears and a great sense of humour, you would get something like an enchantress.

Bit of a stretch, I know.

4

Kingley

Kingley's house was mock-fortress style. I say mock, because it had thicker walls and more battlements than the real thing. They also don't tend to come this big any more.

I parked the Dragonette in a car park that was probably in a different time zone to the main house. We then strolled down to where my cloth-charming social spy had informed me a pool party would be taking place this very afternoon. The screams and splashes kind of reinforced this.

The Silvestral sisters both had their hair up, dwarf style, held in place by two ebony sticks. It made them look even taller, and that, plus those enchantress vibrations, meant nobody was paying any attention to little old me. Now normally, as I was wearing a Gaspar Halftoken cream double-breasted, sea silk suit with the new solido-style straw hat, I would have been highly offended. But just for today, this was ideal.

I had me a look around. Something about the place gave me the shivers, but I wasn't sure what it was. It sort of felt familiar, reminding me of something from a long, long time ago. Something I had almost forgotten – if I had ever properly known it to begin with. I wasn't sure where this was all coming from, so I kept looking.

The pool wasn't bigger than many lakes, and I have seen bigger cows than the one that was turning on the spit next to it. Why, that other cow turning on the spit by the bar was bigger for a start. I hoped everybody was hungry. A few slim, gorgeous sun-browned bodies slipped in and out of the water. They probably just nibbled a lettuce leaf every full moon. I had lettuce once, it was inside a rabbit, but that's another story.

Further down the slope, there was a real lake with a two-storey boathouse that could have accommodated one of those tall ships downstairs; the sort that used to sail the trade routes, before steamboats came along. As if to highlight the difference, Kingley had a steamboat, a'paddling across his lake. The huge paddle-wheels looked like he'd left a couple of industrial mills short of a whole lot of power. I just hope the boat didn't get lost on all that lake. The occasional toot on its horn was probably just a fun way to reassure us everything was all right and they were still within sight of land.

The band wasn't quite a full orchestra, on account of there being no conductor. I suspected that Kingley wasn't the sort to put up with anybody running even a lemon-squeeze stall in his presence.

I recognised some of the faces chuckling away in their best summer finery. There were actors with dodgy reputations and aldermen with reputations as dodgy actors; criminals pretending they were legitimate businessmen, and legitimate businessmen liking to think they were as hard as the criminals – they weren't, not yet anyway. Not exactly top-of-the-tree material: men, women and some tidied-up runt goblins mostly, plus grunt security and plenty of gnomes serving. No elves or dwarves present that I could see, which was only partly good news.

Master Kingley was holding court in a summer pavilion that shimmered slightly in the sun. The result of the yards of gold sewn into the fabric, I surmised brilliantly. Kingley himself was very thin and very white. His hair was white, and his skin was paler than whey. He wore a white suit with white shoes made of leather so white and fine his feet might as well have been painted with two coats of gloss. Sunshades hid his eyes, but I had a horrible feeling that behind them, there would just be two white orbs, staring blankly with the all-seeing blind gaze of a marble statue. I had no idea what Master Kingley was, apart from very scary – certainly not enchanting, so far.

What I found singularly unpleasant was that Kingley had a look-alike personal assistant; a slightly creepy body at his beck and call who seemed to act as an intermediary between him and the world. He lacked Kingley's shades, but considering his eyes were the chilling blue colour commonly known as "murderer's eyes" this was really no improvement.

I'd heard of this sort of thing before, rich folk who kept fawning flunkey replicas to amuse themselves in all the wrong ways. His name, so 'Red' Silvestral had told me on the drive over, was Autumn, and he had a reputation for being as nasty a mouthpiece as you were ever likely to come across. Red and Blondie had done their homework. They are nothing if not professional. They had also been digging in the Citadel files for me. There was a big one with Kingley's name on it, but nothing close to an arrest.

Of Diamond, there was no sign, but that would have been too easy. The Silvestral sisters mingled and soon attracted a crowd of admirers. I took a drink from a gnome waiter who almost fainted when I said 'thank you'.

He looked a likely lad, all done up in traditional green three-quarter trousers and red waistcoat, with a winning smile and a knowledgeable expression. I aimed a buckskin in his direction, and this made it into his waistcoat pocket, almost without his hand intervening.

'I'm looking for some kin,' I asked casually.

He scratched his curly head while he gave this notion some thought. 'Would this be male or female kin, Master?' His accent was pure Little Hundred.

'Both.'

'Not today, Master – no dwarves here – yourself excluded, of course.'

'Any usually make it to these events?'

'Not as a rule, occasionally we have an important greybeard or two from the Citadel, even some from Skragsrealm and New Iron Town – but they never bring wives.'

'What about entertainers?'

'Diamond you mean, Master?'

'Might do,' I admitted. Sharp lad.

'Very nice lady dwarf, Diamond. Beautiful manners, even when they insist she dances.'

Well, I hadn't noticed the manners, but I was willing to run with that description. 'Nobody picking up on her absence today?'

'Not that I've heard – or on the Seneschalson's. He is normally here too, you see – escorting her.

I folded another buckskin around a card, and that made its way into his waistcoat in as speedy fashion as the first.

'Thanks?' I left a gap for his name.

Dwarf Girls Don't Dance

'Torito,' he filled the gap.

'If you hear anything about Diamond, I'd be grateful Torito.'

Torito nodded and moved on before we began to look like we were dating. However, all eyes were still on the Silvestral sisters. Well, nearly all eyes.

'Kingley, it's the dwarf snooper!'

The 'dwarf snooper' turned his head to see a familiar goblin form limp in his direction. Roli Seneschalson's goblin bodyguard, Cluff.

Autumn turned in my direction too, blinking unpleasantly. I also felt the attention of Kingley's stare, even from behind his sunshades. He raised a hand, and everybody went silent as if on cue – even the band. Neat trick.

'Easy, everybody!' shouted look-alike Autumn in a surprisingly gruff tone. 'We don't want no trouble!'

'Certainly not,' I replied, carefully eyeing the goblin guards, hands poised, reaching for their shooters.

'Well, well, well,' said Kingley, in a voice so devoid of warmth that I was surprised the pool didn't freeze over. 'The Master Detective Dwarf.'

I felt, rather than saw, the Silvestral sisters take positions protectively at my side. This produced a noise from Kingley's throat that I presumed was a cousin, once removed, to a laugh. 'Now those two I might well have invited,' he said. 'But not one of the elder races – not without good cause.' There was a quality to his voice that put me in mind of a glacier moving relentlessly to the sea.

'Security,' said Kingley's mouthpiece.

The security grunts took a step forward to join Cluff, and the Silvestral sisters went into their party piece.

'Now, you don't want to do that,' said Silvestral blonde.

'That's not a good idea at all,' Silvestral red emphasised.

'We think everybody should just calm down,' they added in unison.

The guards all agreed. Big smiles came over their faces and sad eyes filled with longing. Hands that had been reaching for shooters now reached out pleadingly for a touch, a stroke, or anything.

Not a soul seemed untouched, apart from Kingley that is.

'Enchantresses! My, my – you don't really think your charms would work on me?' His rasp of a chuckle broke the spell, and with a shake of bewildered heads, coarse hands groped again for their ironmongery.

That wasn't in my master plan – time for the not quite so masterful backup-plan.

'Ladies, if you would be so kind?'

Swiftly, the Silvestral sisters reached up, removed their adornments and let their hair tumble free, so that each was now standing, crouched ready for action, ebony sticks at hand.

'No wands! No wands!' shouted Autumn, throwing himself down between his master, and us, nearly knocking Kingley out of his wicker chair.

I smiled and walked forward, flanked by the Silvestral sisters.

'No, I'm sure we don't need any hex work, Master Kingley, do we? Lovely social event like this! I was just after some burnt cow, a glass of bubbles and an answer or two to a couple of legitimate questions.'

Kingley was flinching – obviously no fan of magic. Autumn was almost curled up into a ball.

'They could just be sticks, Kingley,' said Cluff, edging slowly my way. 'You know, just sticks for the hair.'

'Oh yes, Limpy – they could be sticks,' I said. 'I could have walked into a small fortress with two enchantresses armed only with two sticks each. Guess you've just got to ask yourself, Kingley; do I feel a lucky Pixie today?'

Kingley thought about this – it didn't take him long. I don't think he had ever relied on luck. In his gambling dens, the dice had seven sides, and the house never lost.

'Step down, Autumn' he said to his look-alike – interestingly almost sounding more like he was asking a question than giving an order. Autumn picked himself up and dusted himself down before confirming.

'Yes, step down, everybody.'

Kingley then smiled a smile so white, tooth soap manufacturers would have given their eye-teeth to know his flossing secrets.

'Hey, it's a party, everybody get back to having fun!' he said in his skin-grating rasp. And fun all the guests started to have again – by order.

'And you,' Kingley continued, with ice in his voice, looking pointedly in Cluff's direction. 'Remember, it's Master Kingley. Now give me some more sunshine.'

'Yes, boss – of course, Master Kingley.'

Cluff lowered his head and shuffled off out of Kingley's sight, still leaning heavily on his cane. I obviously didn't know my own strength – ha.

'And Autumn?' Kingley addressed his man again.

'Yes.'

'Some chairs for Master Strongoak and his friends, please.' Autumn signalled for the furniture.

'So, Master Strongoak – come tell me what can I do for you and your delightful friends?'

Another smile flashed those too-white teeth in my direction.

Kingley beckoned us under his canvas to the chairs hastily sourced by his gnome helpers. I sat, and the Silvestral sisters stayed standing – wands readily to hand – to Kingley's continued discomfort. Autumn took a position slightly behind Kingley; the blue eyes never left me for a moment.

'I wish you'd instruct your friends to put the wands down, Detective,' the mouthpiece said. 'Those things are notorious for going off at the wrong moment. I'd hate to see an accident of a thaumaturgical nature taking place.'

'Yes,' Kingley agreed. 'Certainly not before you tell me what in Fince's Nine Hills you are doing here.'

'I'm looking for Diamond,' I said, answering his question and ignoring his suggestion – all the time watching his reactions.

'The peeler?' laughed Autumn, gruffly.

They both seemed genuinely surprised, or as surprised as you could imagine two ice-cubes ever getting.

'Diamond?' said Kingley, with a short laugh. 'Diamond is a friend's best girl.'

I had to give him a small silent clap for that one; even the Silvestral sisters were impressed, and they don't impress easy.

'And any sign of the girl – or the friend for that matter, Master Kingley?'

Kingley shifted in his seat, in a manner I interpreted either as displeasure or very bad bum grapes.

'And your interest would be what, Master Detective?'

I didn't see any reason to be too cagey about this.

'I'm acting on behalf of Diamond, and my client has gone missing.'

Dwarf Girls Don't Dance

'I don't think it's the business of an employee if their employer decides to make themselves unavailable for a few days,' Autumn said, with an unpleasant air.

'Quite so,' Kingley agreed.

'It is, if part of the employee's job is to be concerned for the employer's welfare.'

Kingley couldn't argue with that and didn't try. He simply put his hands together and rested his chin on the very white steeple thus formed.

'So Master Kingley,' I repeated, at the risk of getting tedious, 'have you seen or heard anything from Diamond or Roli Seneschalson – please?' Hey, good manners cost nothing and a fist in the mouth often offends.

'Sorry, Strongoak. Last time I met the Seneschalson… must have been at one of my Gaming Houses, weeks ago. Diamond I haven't seen since she hung up her dancing shoes.'

'And that wasn't a problem for you?'

'I won't pretend the club didn't suffer, but what can I say? Young love and all that?'

I somehow didn't see Kingley as the romantic sort.

'How about you, Master Autumn? You haven't come across Diamond in your travels have you?'

The assistant gave me a look that could have cut glass, but I've been stared at by better than him and survived. Still, I could feel the hackles on the back of my neck rising in anticipation of fight of flight. I know which one I favoured.

'No', Autumn replied flatly, which seemed his preferred manner of speech.

'My manciple seldom goes anywhere I don't,' Kingley replied.

And that was pretty much that.

There didn't seem any more to learn from Kingley, so we said our goodbyes and left, safe in the knowledge that we wouldn't be missed. No way could I top having a 'manciple' anyway.

I drove thoughtfully back to the Citadel. I wasn't sure what we had achieved exactly, but we still had our crate of beazer teaser, so all wasn't lost.

'One of these days, Nicely,' said Red, putting her hair back up, 'that bluff is going to be called.'

'Yes,' her sister added. 'How about you splash out and get us some real magic wands?'

'Come on, ladies! You know there are no such things as magic wands!'

'Try telling that to Kingley!' Red added. 'Or that creepy Autumn body.'

It was a good point. They both sure were worried about the possibility of magic getting splashed about, Autumn even more than his boss. Personally, I've always found wands rather laughable – a wizard's staff has the distinct advantage of being available for cracking open a head or two. But wands, I ask you? Rub two together, and you could probably get a good fire going.

'What did you make of Kingley?' I asked the sisters. 'Where does somebody like that come from?'

Red lent forward, as if she was worried about being overheard, which considering we were topping 90 was hardly likely. 'There have been rumours that have reached our ears. One reason we were so keen to come along with you today and see for ourselves.'

'In addition to the sheer joy of your company of course, Nicely,' Blondie added, leaning forward to kiss my ear, trying to save my feelings. Hey, I'm a sensitive sort – headbutt me, do I not bruise? And nut you back harder.

'So, how about you let me in on these rumours now and why not mention something before, eh?'

'What? That our Master Kingley just might be a Snow King?' Red said, sitting back.

'Snow King!' I said, with some frustration. 'I'm a humble dwarf from New Iron Town. I've never even heard of a Snow King, give me a break! A Snow King sounds like a frozen creamed ice!'

'Not much point in having told you before then,' said Blondie, sitting back with her sister as she scored the point.

'You've heard of Snow Queens?' Red explained, sensing my frustration.

'Well, sure.'

'Then who do you think Snow Queens snuggle up to at night?'

'Oh, right!'

Snow Queens were bad news. They took enchantment to a whole new level. Generally, enchanters can't make you do anything against your will, but they say Snow Queens can convince you to chew off both your own feet and then get you to go out dancing afterwards.

I realised something else too.

'Is that why Kingley could shrug off the enchantment of you fine ladies?'

'Certainly looks that way,' Red concluded. 'Unless he was just hot for your own hunky body instead, Nicely.'

'Which he couldn't be blamed for,' Blondie added sweetly.

'That aside,' I agreed, 'how come I didn't feel an irresistible urge to throw myself into the pool or something similar when we had our little showdown? If he's an enchanter, he's strictly second rate.'

'He was wearing sunshades, Nicely. Remember that. If he ever takes them off in your presence, be on your guard,' Blondie warned.

'It's an eyes thing, as well as voice, with enchanters of a Snow King's pay grade,' Red added.

'Enchantment is similar to magic, Nicely, but it's not identical. There are no spells to learn, no incantations to be chanted. It's more natural, more instinctive and fun. Like us!' said Blondie, laughing. I had to laugh along. They don't come more natural than the Silvestral sisters, I'm delighted to say.

'Just be careful if Kingley whips his shades off,' Red continued, 'as you might learn more about his abilities than you would like to know!'

'But we could sense it on him.' Blondie looked to her sister for confirmation.

'Oh yes,' Red agreed. 'That place was stinking so strongly of enchantment I could barely smell the mutton.'

'Did you notice anything?' Blondie asked me.

There was a feeling I had picked up on. Not so much that somebody had walked over my grave, more that they had tiptoed. I told them as much.

'You're pretty sensitive to that sort of magic,' Red added.

I chewed this over instead of the spit-roast meat I'd missed out on.

'So, could he get me to bite my feet off?' I had to ask.

'It's hard to say,' said Red.

'I mean, we can't even get you to cut your toenails.'

'Ladies, please!'

'We don't know, Nicely!' Blondie continued. 'We're probably not in his league. But one thing is for sure with all enchantment;

it's a whole lot easier to convince you to do something you would quite like to do anyway!

'To exploit a weakness, to build on a fault over time, that way, you can really get a grip on someone,' Red added.

'That way you can get somebody to do something and they might not even know they'd done it!' Blondie finished triumphantly.

Widergard could sure still throw up surprises. Legends have a nasty habit of remaining not quite as legendary as they should do. And, of course, the bad guys of old are generally pretty well equipped to become the bad guys of the present too. Experience of raiding and looting, for example, being very good practise for not-so-organised crime. Naturally, not everybody who once would have become a Witch King, sorcerer or necromancer could now become a Dark Crime Lord – many went into politics.

I dropped the Silvestral sisters off at Guard Central, where they were due at work, and went to my office to check with my answering service for any messages from Diamond. There were none. There were no messages at all, and I kind of regretted the Silvestral sisters' evening shift. They certainly were a lot of fun.

5

The Wizard's Clinic

It was too late to undertake the next visit on my list, but it's never too late to find a wizard. It's often too early, but never too late. My uncle, Lately Kneesplitter, had a saying about wizards: never mess in the affairs of wizards, they charge by the hour. 'The Wizards Clinic' did exactly that, but time was very much of the essence to me as well.

The 'Wizards Clinic' is one of those walk-in, one-stop, consultation places where you can turn up and pretty much be guaranteed to get any magic-related query answered in sixty-one minutes – that way they can charge you for two hours. Of course, magic being a somewhat elusive element in the Citadel, and a wizard's grasp of it being somewhat slippery as well, you never knew exactly what you were going to get – or who for that matter. The only people you could rely on for magic in the Citadel, and Widergard in general, were pixies. And this is probably why they had one on reception, perched behind a miniature desk just perfect for her twelve-inch frame.

'How can I help you, Master Dwarf?' she said, in an attractive high-pitched and slightly mischievous voice that went very well with her colourful powder blue and yellow two-piece suit. Perched on her head was a jaunty white cap with the finest of red feathers sticking out of it. She looked like 'Miss Autumn' from a calendar for *Pixie Mechanic*. Her presence in 'The Wizards Clinic' came as a surprise of rather epic proportions, as I hadn't been sure about the clinic's credibility at all. I'd only spotted their sign on Elf Gate Avenue the previous week, and then only because the traffic was snarled up after another street-train had overheated, steam blowing everywhere. With nothing else to do, I read their sign a few times over, wondering whatever had happened to apostrophe use. The 'Wizards Clinic': was this a clinic for wizards, a particular clinic run by a singular wizard or a clinic chock-a-block full of wizards? 'Apostrophe misuse is the first step towards anarchy', as Uncle Kneesplitter was also fond of saying.

I did mean to ask the receptionist what the score was with regard to punctuation and the clinic, but the pixie looked too cute to act that shabby.

'I need to see a wizard, winsome one – somebody who knows something about potions.'

She did that pixie laugh that's so endearing, and I expected to see her fly off, but instead, she picked up a speech horn hardly bigger than a baby sea shell and spoke a few words into it that were far too fast for me to catch.

'Please take a seat, Master Dwarf,' she said, replacing the little horn. 'A wizard will be with you soon... and don't worry, consultation doesn't start until you are in the surgery.'

Smart girl, she had obviously dealt with dwarves before.

I sat down in the small waiting room and picked up a glossy scroll put there to distract anxious clients from whatever it was that had brought them in to consult their local hexpert.

I'm not sure that *Wizardry Today* did the job, as it didn't seem designed to instil confidence – not if articles on 'How to Beat a Boggle', 'Reliable Wart Removal' and 'First Steps in Fire Magic and Burn Alleviation' were anything to go by. I hadn't got much further than finding out why you should want to beat a boggle in the first place, before a red light came on over one of the doors that led off the reception.

'The wizard will see you now,' said the Pixie. 'You may enter.'

I got up and entered.

'Potions,' I exclaimed to the Wizard sitting behind the aged oak desk in the impressively gloomy and book-lined study that awaited me behind the door. He took a draw on his long stem, rosewood pipe and blew a smoke square; an impressive trick if you know how.

The Wizard pointed me to a seat before answering in a friendly enough sort of way.

'Nothing illegal, I hope, which includes most love drafts now, I should add – since Citadel Ordnance 62 dot something or other, published in whenever it was. Which is a bit of a shame as they were always a reliable source of income, the love potions. Even more so than poisons, which should fill me with more optimism than it does.'

The certificate on the wall behind the desk informed me that I was talking to 'Ratchett the Generally Reliable'. And that the Citadel Licensing Authority had found him "fit for the dispensing of services connected with the art, practice, or spells of magic, by which occult forces or spirits are harnessed in order to produce preternatural effects in the world". In clear text at the bottom, there was a disclaimer to remind customers that: "YOUR BODY MAY BE REPOSSESSED IF YOU DO NOT KEEP UP PAYMENTS ON SPELLS INVOLVING NECROMANCY".

Dwarf Girls Don't Dance

The wizard had a crumpled, but serviceable pointy hat, perched over a serviceable, but crumpled, sort of face. He sported a full beard, wire glasses and all the right robes and looked like he had cast a spell or two in his time. I sat and gave him my best, "love drafts, what me?" kind of smile; before adding, 'I'm looking for something that might have been slipped to somebody in a less than legal manner. A person of the dwarf persuasion.'

'Interesting, and what might have been the effect of the aforementioned potion?' he continued in his friendly tone.

'To maybe mimic, or perhaps bring on the Rage?'

'Ah, the Rage!' Ratchett stood up and, muttering quietly to himself, walked to the tome-lined bookshelves. He peered short-sightedly at one volume, and went to claim it, only to reveal that it was one of a number of false spines designed to pack the shelves with appropriate-looking fillers.

'Fetch and blast it! I asked them to let me bring my own reference material down here, but they said my books didn't convey the right image! Too many egg and coffee stains on them and not enough impressive chemical burns.' Ratchett then strode angrily across to the window, pulling at the drapes. 'Hate these curtains too. Why they think we have to work in total darkness, I just don't know!' He yanked back the curtains to reveal some very modern window frames.

'That's better; I can at least see you now, Master…?'

'Strongoak,' I said, warming to the winningly crotchety old wizard. 'I take it you aren't in charge here then?'

'Good gracious, no! I couldn't afford the rent on this smart an address, as close to the Elf Gate as it is. Sadly only the wrong sort of people can these days. Bit judgmental, aren't I?'

He puffed away, not at all put off by his own boss-directed haranguing.

'But you're working for them?'

He nodded glumly. 'I call it damage limitation. If I don't work for them, somebody else is bound to, and they are likely to do much more damage than I am capable of. This way, I can keep an eye on the owners and their worse excesses and hopefully earn my supper at the same time. Very good gnome eatery just around the corner, but you probably knew that.'

I smiled, 'I have been known to pop in there for the odd nibble.'

'Oh, yes.' He smacked his lips at the thought. 'And they do have some very odd nibbles – who would have thought a whole piglet could have fitted in a bun?'

'If the bun's large enough, why not?'

He puffed away contentedly at his smoke and then his mind snapped back into focus. 'We'd better be getting on; the deceitful sprite at the desk will have the stopwatch out.'

He put his pipe down on the desk and concentrated in what I can only describe as a wizard-like fashion – as if consulting his own personal mental library that existed somewhere just behind my left shoulder. 'A potion for the Rage, you say. Well, I have heard of such a thing. Indeed I have.'

This was interesting.

'Where?' I asked.

'Yes, that is the question.' He hit his head impatiently with the palm of his hand. 'Damn and blast it! Do not get old, Master Dwarf!'

'Well, I prefer it to the option generally offered to people in my profession, the not-getting-one-minute-older alternative offered to many Detectives.'

'Quite so, quite so! However, consider this: you are a wizard holding the unimaginably powerful forces underlying the nature of reality in your hands, and at a crucial stage you can't remember if you need to be evocating or invocating or just giving the phial a really good shake?'

'Sounds, err, embarrassing?'

'Well, if destroying a couple of levels of the Citadel could be considered embarrassing, I suppose so.'

'And you could do that?'

I hated sounding so sceptical, but I've not been sure about a lot of so-called magic, as I may have mentioned before. It looks a lot like cheap stunts and some head trickery to me, apart from the pixies of course, but everything is different with them. Bless their little red feathers and cute kisses.

'Oh, yes! I could do that once!' Ratchett continued. 'At least I think so – blasted hard to remember some times.' He looked sadly down at the desk, and I felt a wave of sympathy come over me for the ageing wizard.

Then suddenly, his warm brown eyes sparkled again.

'Of course – Mercenaries Dark Brew 52!'

'Sorry?'

Ratchett, the Generally Reliable, got up and paced excitedly. 'In days when such things were more common, swords-for-hire might be slipped a little something from their masters to liven them up for a particularly bloody encounter. It was said to bring on something akin to a dwarf Rage – turned them into uncaring war machines!'

'That pretty much describes a dwarf battle Rage.'

'Exactly, and that is what they tried to achieve for everyone, irrespective of race.'

'And what if it was given to a dwarf?'

'Well, as so many of your kinsmen live permanently on the cusp of apoplexy, Brew 52 would cause a transient immense

Rage, followed by a blowing of all the fuses and goodnight New Iron Town.'

I pondered on this for a moment before asking: 'But it can be given to a normal man, you say?'

The wizard stroked his beard in the regulation manner.

'Well, that rather depends on what you mean by normal. A fit warrior or barbarian brawler and no problem, anybody more "delicate" than that, well, it would probably kill them. No, make that "definitely" kill them.' He sat down again, looking sombre. 'I sincerely hope that nobody has been adding this into the ale of anyone of your acquaintance.'

'I'm not sure, would it be easy to disguise?'

'No, the stronger the drink, the better – perhaps one of those sweet spirits your race are so fond of?'

I had a think, and then I got up and held out my hand.

'Wizard Ratchett, it's been an education.' We shook.

'Only too pleased to have helped.' And indeed he did seem genuinely pleased, in a slightly forgetful way.

'One last thing,' Ratchett said, as I made for the door. 'I don't know if it's my place to say this, but you do know that you are under a spell, don't you?'

This took me by surprise.

'A generally beneficial spell,' he continued, 'but I've not really seen it's like before, and it may have ramifications of which I am not aware – at first sight that is.'

I thought about this for a moment. 'I was once kissed by a wild pixie,' I said by way of explanation.

'Ah yes,' he replied, smiling. 'That would explain it. A very fortunate thing – to have been kissed by a pixie. Good evening then, Master Detective.'

Dwarf Girls Don't Dance

The receptionist was waiting for me, also smiling, bill in hand, as I left Wizard Ratchett's room.

'Your bill, Master Dwarf.'

I approached the desk and bent over to examine the damage, and in doing so, took hold of one of the receptionist's wings and tugged gently.

'Hey careful wid dat!' she shouted.

'Sure, Mistress Spriggan!' I replied.

'Tose tings don't come cheap!' The little creature had changed her tune and accent, not to mention her total look – no cute pixie now. As Ratchett had let on, she was indeed a spriggan, a sprite.

Spriggan's are the less attractive, more thieving, less flying, cousins to pixies. Their magic is confined to a certain personal form of glamour that makes for a perfect disguise, plus an ability to relieve your purse of gold at a rate even a wagon mechanic would envy.

'Why don't yoos pick on somebody your own size?' the now recognisably less attractive sprite spluttered, her lank locks barely concealed by a scarf that had seen better days – probably spent straining whelks.

'I'm not aware if impersonating a pixie is actually an offence, but I'm sure there are by-laws covering such a misrepresentation on business premises.'

'And what makes you such an expert?' she said, readjusting the false wings that completed her disguise.

I flipped my badge.

'Yeah? A goose guard, so what?' she responded, unimpressed; 'goose guards' being a popular name in the underworld for those of us in the private sector who were thought to be employed to just run around making a lot of noise. Obviously, they had never met a goose with a mean disposition and a very good aim.

'So, I shouldn't maybe get my old comrades from the Cits to come down and check your paperwork?'

The grumpy spriggan was replaced by the image of the smiling pixie again.

'And how will the Master Dwarf be paying this evening?'

'Reluctantly,' I said. 'Reluctantly.'

The wizard had provided me with plenty of food for thought. I was still hungry for the real thing though, so I partook of supper in the gnome eatery Ratchett had mentioned: *The Digwell Inn*.

The food was rather splendid, and their 'pig-in-a-bun' had never tasted better. Ratchett never came in, which was something of a shame, as a long chat to put the world to rights with a wizard of his ilk would have been very welcomed. The next time I had occasion to try the Clinic, he no longer worked there. I kind of regretted this, as I like to think we would have got on well.

6

The Seneschal

The next day dawned, bright and cloudless. I got up early and was in the office before the early bird had been caught, worm in mouth, by the even earlier raptor. I made a couple of calls, then put the office speech horn back down and checked the news scroll for the criminal weather report. Yes, from what I could see, it was indeed the perfect day for some misrepresentation, deceit, and obtaining entry under false pretences. I just love those kinds of days.

The Seneschal's House is an unassuming place. Well, as unassuming as you can get if you happen to live in just about the choicest spot in the highest of the five levels that make up the wall-ringed fortress that is the Citadel.

When the local 'Royals' were all persuaded as to the merits of the democratic system and not-getting-your-head-cut-offness, and then provided with alternative accommodation, the Seneschals stepped in to keep things going as the Citadel's political system was clarified. This was not the work of minutes. The Seneschals did a pretty good job and managed to not make enemies. This, in the Citadel, is an accomplishment. Then, after the new

Councillors and Aldermen were invested, everybody forgot about the Seneschals for a while, until they realised how very convenient it was to have a family around with some knowledge of how the whole being-in-charge-without-shouting business worked. The rest of the elected officials not having that much of a clue as to the difference between 'ordering' and 'requesting'. The Seneschals prospered, in an unassuming style, and the role became the last officially sanctioned inheritable post in the Citadel. Naturally, it was a completely unpaid advisory role only.

Sometimes, of course, free advice is the most expensive kind there is.

Getting to see a notorious underworld figure like Reepold Kingley was a doddle in comparison to finding time to spend with the Citadel Seneschal. I wasted a tedious couple of hours in my office at the *Two Fingers* speaking with no joy to a succession of flunkeys. The Seneschal wasn't taking appointments no matter what ruse I tried.

Fortunately, I had a hand-written and signed apology note from his son that, when folded in an appropriate fashion, gave no clue as to what it might contain, only who the author had been. I mean, waved under the right noses, with the right spin it might even lead someone to think it was a promissory note that needed immediate attention. This worked like magic, or at least how magic is supposed to work. In my experience, the real thing is unreliable and over-rated, whereas bribery and corruption are as dependable as the ice on a Mountain Troll's jolly-sack.

The Seneschal's study didn't have a desk in it. It had a lot of books, though. Desks are for people who do official business and have official jobs. Books are for people who have time on their hands. It seems that the 'purely advisory' amongst us don't need desks, only books. This puts them at a disadvantage when trying to appear intimidating. The Seneschal, instead, employed the 'I'm so important not only do I not need a desk, I don't even need to work' approach. This can be intimidating too. Not many people don't need to work.

The Seneschal stood in his book-lined study, his mane of fine silver hair falling slightly over one eye, back straight and his knees bent just right. He was practising his putting.

'Before you say anything, Master Dwarf,' he started, without preamble, 'I am not responsible for my son's debts, or his mistakes, or indeed very much else he does these days.'

The Seneschal holed his putt from twelve feet, straight into an upturned ale mug, probably bought for the purpose – the Seneschal's First Level House didn't look like the 'ale mug' kind of residence.

'So before you begin your undoubtedly well-prepared hard-luck speech, I suggest you save your breath and leave through the same door you came in by.'

I cut the preamble too. 'My name is Nicely Strongoak, Seneschal, and I'm a Master Detective, accredited by the Citadel Law Department. I'm currently acting on behalf of the popular entertainer known as Diamond.'

The Seneschal was momentarily thrown off his stroke – literally. He missed the next put by two feet. He regained his poise quickly – fast enough for the almost inevitable denial. 'Never heard of her, I'm afraid.'

'That's a shame. My client is missing, you see, and as your son is currently the companion of my client, and is not replying to my calls, I'm talking to you as a courtesy to see if you can shed any light on the matter before my interview with the Citadel Guards.' I checked my watch. 'Which will be in less than two hours.'

The Seneschal recovered from this even quicker.

'Well, I'm sorry, Master Detective. I can't assist you either with that or the whereabouts of your dwarvish dancer friend.'

'I never mentioned she was a dwarf, Seneschal?'

'I just assumed…'

'Or that she was a dancer. I just said she was an entertainer.'

'Well, again…'

'You assumed she was a dancer? That's very strange. You may have heard the expression "Dwarf girls don't dance"? Yes, a strange assumption that Seneschal – but duly noted.'

The Seneschal looked around; I got the impression he was wishing he had a nice big desk to hide behind.

'Well,' he admitted finally, 'I may have heard a rumour that my son had found… someone… who was his…'

'Be very careful there, Seneschal!' I interrupted, looking with interest at some of the beautifully bound books on his shelves. These weren't bought by the yard. Then, lacking anything to sit on, I went to stand next to a fireplace that was big enough even for roasting one of Kingley's oxen. 'The Citadel has strict laws concerning racially defamatory language.'

The old man was certainly piqued now. 'I am perfectly aware of that, Master Dwarf. I was just trying to refer to my son's condition in a manner that didn't seem unsympathetic coming from a father.'

'I wouldn't worry too much about that. He doesn't seem to. So, could you tell me where he is, please? I'd like to talk to him before the Guards get their go.'

The Seneschal put on his best 'I'm not a politician but…' smile, and I knew I wasn't going to like what came next. 'We seem to have got off on the wrong foot here, Master Detective.

Dwarf Girls Don't Dance

Of course, I have heard about my son's dalliance, but I can assure you that is all it was.'

'Not what he told me, Seneschal. From what he said I gather it was wedding bells all the way.'

'That is not true!' the old man said, losing his smile.

'The sort of gem my client was wearing on her finger when I last saw her didn't look like it was there just in case she forgot her own name.'

'That is not the case! My son would have always recognised the proper formalities. There are ways to do things in the Citadel.'

'Uh-huh, well, why don't we ask him? If you could tell me where he is, please?'

The Seneschal picked up his golf ball. 'I haven't seen him since the evening before last. He attended a White Gown Charity event for me in the evening.'

'He left early.'

'I don't think he did.'

'I'm telling you differently.'

For the first time, something like real worry lit across the Seneschal's face, and he began to show his age.

'Look, detective – probably your client has just moved on – you know what entertainers are like. And my son is probably nursing a very bad hangover in one of the disreputable clubs he frequents, and he will turn up in a day or two, a little older and no wiser.'

So, I had the official line at last. It was something like I suspected it would be, but like a hobgoblin's loincloth – it just wasn't going to wash.

Job done, time to move on. Well, almost done. 'Thank you, Seneschal. I think I've taken up enough of your time. I'll see myself out.'

The Seneschal couldn't believe his luck.

'Oh... what about the Citadel Guards?'

'I'll cancel the appointment. I guess I might have to chalk this one up to experience and take the loss.' The Seneschal seemed to believe this too. Boy, did he not know dwarves.

'When I hear from him, I'll let him know of your inquiry, Master Strongoak.'

'Yes, thank you, Seneschal. As you say, he's probably just nursing a sore head and a broken heart somewhere. I'm sure you'll hear from him in a day or two.'

Except you were never going to hear anything from him again, Seneschal, not ever again. His kind of dead don't say nothing.

I left quickly, leaving the door just ajar. Through the conveniently sized crack, I heard the one sentence I wanted to hear as he picked up his speech-horn, dialled, and spoke: 'I need to speak to Kingley, and I need to speak to him now!'

That was enough; I was out of there faster than a selkie down a water slide.

I made plans, and I made them quickly.

I met Torito and his chums just outside of Cliff Top Village, as arranged. He was in a large catering wagon as he had previously explained: 'We'll be picking up some of the heavier equipment from the party, Master Strongoak; the outdoor braziers and the like.'

He handed me some company overalls. I looked at them doubtfully.

'They were the largest size we have', he added.

Dwarf Girls Don't Dance

No way was I going to fit into them, so in the end I decided to hide under a pile of dustsheets and hope security was lax.

I parked the Dragonette under some trees where it wasn't too obvious, climbed in the back of the wagon and then we made our way swiftly up to the Village and the residence of the (maybe) Snow King Kingley.

Torito had called me earlier that morning – up with the lark, like all hardworking gnomes. His task to start the day was washing out the empties from Kingley's party, ready for return to the recycling plant. In amongst the dead men he had found one empty bottle of Dark Star; an acquired taste, and really only us dwarves acquired it. Torito could confirm that nobody at the party had been drinking the treat. He thought I should know. He was right. Smart lad. Now, following my little entertainment with the Seneschal, my suspicions were really aroused. Especially after I'd read the titles of the half dozen books concerned with 'Potions and Powders' that had been sitting on his bookshelves.

Kingley's little pile sat smugly at the top of Cliff Top Village, not caring a dragon's scat what anybody thought of it or its owner. Torito dropped me off out of sight of the guard hut, while he drove around to the kitchen entrance. I snuck into the main house by a side door that opened into the boot room. I knew it was the boot room because there were an unfeasibly large number of boots in it. Boots for every occasion and task in fact. Plus all the polishes and conditioning sprays required to keep these resilient boots in tip-top condition. No 'body-dumping boots' there for me to find sadly, but I didn't let that put me off.

It was very quiet in the house. Very quiet and very white – woe betide anybody that hadn't taken their boots off in the boot room! White ceilings and white walls and luxurious white rugs thrown over wooden floorboards of a wood so bleached that it looked more like marble. The real marble was reserved for a white staircase that wound up, and up, to a first floor so far away, it should have been lost in little white clouds.

I wasn't surprised that Kingley wore sunshades.

I could hear a few sounds percolating up from the kitchens now. Torito and his boys doing the gnome work and what sounded like a cook and helpers. I'd expected a few more servants around to avoid, but help seemed thin on the ground; maybe that's why Kingley hired in caterers? Kingley probably had plenty he wished to keep hidden – a collection of little clay shepherdess figurines finished in pastel shades perhaps?

There was still going to be muscle around, unless they were all out on a job. I imagine Kingley had plenty of jobs for his help. The nature of such employment it didn't pay for me to dwell on; they wouldn't be out buying more shepherdess figurines, of that I was sure. Goblins just can't be trusted with fine porcelain purchases.

It didn't take me long, especially considering the house's size, to come to the conclusion that nobody was at home. 'S'no Kingley', I muttered to myself. I bit my lip a little at my matchless wit and departed through the boot room, not even stopping for a shine, but doing a little thieving to keep in practice.

I headed for the cover of Kingley's extensive shrubbery and then made my way stealthily down to the waterside and the conveniently isolated boathouse. The paddle steamer was anchored in the centre of the lake; a smaller steamboat attached to the unpointy bit. I couldn't see if that had a steam-coracle attached to it! Fortunately, the greenery was sufficiently dense to hide me from any inquisitive eyes on the lake, or in the houses.

Dwarf Girls Don't Dance

There was a small jetty next to the boathouse. A number of little boats, skiffs and what-have-you were tied up there. I had a quick nosy around the different watercraft and then entered the boathouse by the tall, open lake doors. As these were fixed in position over the lake, this involved a certain amount of precarious dangling over the water and associated trepidation. I was wearing a perfectly good suit for sard's sake!

As befits what I take to basically be a garage for boats, the central portion of the downstairs boathouse had an inlet where I assumed the smaller steamboat was parked when not in use. There were a variety of long, thin competitive rowboats hanging on the walls and paddles aplenty. At the back of the room, I found a larger, upturned rowboat.

I downturned it.

The inside had recently been well cleaned and oiled, judging by the smell, but I could still see a trace of something that I suspected wasn't red wine on the woodwork around the gates that hold the oars. I don't think rowing normally gets that hard.

There was a door at the rear that I surmised led up to the house proper. It was locked, but not for long. Behind the now opened door, there was a flight of wooden stairs. Boy, sometimes I even amaze myself with my deductive powers.

I made my way up the steps while a whole lot of music made its way down. The stairs creaked like they were auditioning for a role in a haunted-house, rolling picture. Fortunately, the music was even louder. To my surprise, and then concern, I recognised it: Diamond's dance music from *The Happy Hobgoblin*. I upped my pace.

There was another door at the top of the stairs. It had a very convenient keyhole. I pressed my eye close. The room on the other side had curtains or blinds closed against the morning sun.

There were three seated goblins that I could see in the surprisingly spacious main room, and they were having themselves a party. The grunt I could take, but the two smaller runts might be tricky on account of the fact that they favour shooters and shoot well. I just hoped there was no more muscle lurking out of sight.

They had started their fun and games early, and a couple of large spirit bottles stood half-empty on the table in front of them while others, I judged, had already been consigned to the Great Glass Graveyard. More soldiers stood waiting at attention on a nearby chest of drawers.

At the moment the goblins weren't drinking though. All their attention was fixed on the dwarfess in front of them. This was because she was dancing, and they shaved on a regular basis. If her dance at *The Happy Hobgoblin* had been calculated to make any red-blooded male chew off a knuckle or two, that was only for starters; this was the full no-holds-barred, adults-only, hand-devouring version.

Diamond was down to what, in some quarters, are described, with a ridiculous lack of imagination, as undergarments – a one-piece, wasp-waisted girdle and matching hose. I knew what she was doing; the goblins didn't.

'I'm having her first!' declared the grunt, cracking his knuckles in anticipation and not taking his eyes off Diamond for a second.

'We said we'd draw straws,' complained Runt One – the grubbier of the runt pair – outfitted in stained shirt and kecks.

'Seniority we said,' insisted his better-dressed, besuited, associate.

'You said! 'Cos you is senior!' Runt One replied, making what he obviously considered to be a sound point.

'Seniority always goes first!'

Dwarf Girls Don't Dance

'You can take your seniority and stuff it where you keep your brains – using both hands,' Grunt interrupted. This was a lot of what passed for wit amongst his kind.

'You'd better watch your mouth,' warned Senior Runt. 'The Snow King'll have your guts for garters, and he'll make you take them out first too!'

'You think he's going to be pleased if we start mishandling his prize doorstop?' Runt One pointed out.

'Snow King's going to have to top her today, anyway – we just need to keep her juiced up until then. No one will know anything.' The grunt wiped his mouth on his sleeve, but it didn't help much; he was in full seepage mode – drool dripping from the corners of his fang-filled mouth.

I loosened my hand axe and quietly opened the door. Fortunately, all their attention was still on Diamond, whirling faster and faster to the music, her pupils becoming larger and larger as the whites seemed to disappear.

The wasp-waisted girdle now came off in a single promise-filled movement.

'I got to have her!' the grunt shouted and jumped up.

That seemed to be the signal for mayhem.

Diamond, now fully taken by the Rage, whirled around again, but this time there appeared in her hands, as if by magic, two large bottles. The first was let loose and found the nose of the large grunt, breaking it with a satisfying crack and sending him sprawling. The second bottle had her full weight behind it and connected with Junior Runt's jolly-sack in a manner that wasn't likely to raise a smile. The other better-dressed runt went for the shooter I'd guessed was abiding snug under his jacket.

He would have made it too, as Diamond was still unbalanced and bottle-less.

However, my hand-axe had already found the runt's shoulder. The finger of the hand holding the shooter got the wrong kind of signal and fired the gun straight into his own guts. His screams didn't last long as the welling blood in his throat soon choked the last life out of him. He fell, in sections, like a puppet with its strings cut.

Diamond, by now, had jumped onto the neck of the floored grunt and was beating a rhythm with his skull against the floorboards. I let her get on with that while I picked up groaning Junior and gave him a New Iron Town nod. They say there are harder things than a dwarf's skull, but they are usually mined from under the ground. The runt went west for a *long* while.

It had finally dawned on Diamond that the grunt was no longer playing with her and she looked around for another playmate. The Rage had fully taken her now, and she didn't recognise me – or that's what I like to think. She leapt at me like one of those stripy cats they have down south, but I am not a stranger to dwarf courtship rituals, and I landed one straight on her jaw. This took her to a better place for a shorter while than the one the grunt now occupied.

The music on the melody maker had come to a halt, and the room suddenly seemed as quiet as the main house – less white and more red in the current interior decoration.

I suddenly became aware of the chugging of a small steamboat, getting closer. I drew the curtain back a peep from the main window and saw Kingley and Cluff in the small steamer, making waves away from the paddleboat. So that was where he hung out, smart lad – nice and easy to defend and even easier to see anybody coming. They should have stowed Diamond there and cancelled the goblin party; too late now. A shooter had shot, and Kingley now had to find out the 'why and how'.

Dwarf Girls Don't Dance

Kingley looked to be about as cross as a person wearing his style of wrap-around sunshades could be seen to be. Quite right too – in his position, I'd be looking like a dragon with mumps, but I wasn't in his position. I was in the position generally known as 'having the upper hand', and if I wanted to maintain that position, I needed to do some imaginative personnel rearrangement.

By the time I had finished, I had constructed a nice story, all played out in simple images like a picture book for Kingley to read. Well oiled up, the two runts had obviously fallen into an argument with the grunt over Diamond. A shooter had been drawn, and one runt had got it in the gut and the grunt had been hit in the face, but not before the second runt was knocked out. Diamond had been an innocent bystander, injured by a wayward bullet. It wouldn't hold up to more than a moment's inspection, but it didn't have to.

Kingley was already shouting as he came up the stairs. The Snow King had lost his cool. What he was wishing upon his goblin guards was enough to shock my sensitive soul, especially as he was insisting that he was going to make each of them do it to the others. The sight that greeted him as he came through the door stopped him in his tracks, as planned.

'I think that's far enough, Master Kingley,' I said, from the comfort of the armchair I had placed in position to cover both entrances.

Kingley turned slowly, something halfway between a smile and a rictus coming across his face. 'Well, if it isn't the nosy dwarf. I think this is the second time you've arrived on my estate without an invitation; this really won't do, you know?' He reached for his sunshades, taking them off just like the Sylvester sisters had mentioned he would.

I sprayed him full in the face with the leather conditioner I had removed from the boot room. It must have really stung, judging by the noise he made. I don't think he was going to enchant anybody, clawing at his eyes like that. Certainly not the Citadel Judge when he got placed before her.

Cluff wasn't far behind him. He'd been sent around to the boathouse's main entrance to stop anybody from running out. I shot him in the other knee, the good one, just because I'm an equal opportunity hobbler. He fell just as quick as when I'd kicked him, and was now making even more noise than Kingley. Can't have that, there could be more of his sort around. I introduced him to the back of the shooter, and he shut up good.

I waited to see if any more company was on the way. Autumn and a whole lot of the hired-help were unaccounted for after all. It seemed I was in luck. Maybe they were getting the shopping.

Kingley, meanwhile, was trying to find some water for his weeping eyes, but really shouldn't have taken those narrow steps in that condition. Halfway down, he missed his footing and bounced a bit before making a very satisfactory thud. He was still breathing when I found him, a state of affairs I thought about remedying, and then decided to leave it to the justice system. Nobody goes around removing the Seneschal's son, not even accidentally, not in the Citadel.

I found a good length of rope in the boathouse and showed the world that I hadn't forgotten any of the knot-tying skills learnt in the New Iron Town Junior Rangers (Head-Lopper Troop; motto: 'Keep Your Bonce On'). I trussed up those that needed trussing and put sheets over those that didn't. I then sat down and waited for Diamond to come around with a stinking Rage hangover. It took a while. I guess the kiss on the jaw hadn't helped.

Dwarf Girls Don't Dance

When her eyes flickered open they didn't register very much at first or give much away; except perhaps for an unfocused stare that asked, shall I kill you, or further consider whether you are worthy to father my children? After a moment or three, she managed to finally focus on me, registered her bound hands and immediately expressed her gratitude: 'Dwarf! I'm going to suck your eyes out.'

I sighed. 'Eat your pancakes, Diamond.'

She saw the stack of battered goodies I had made in the boathouse's small kitchen and then soused with syrup. She set upon them with a will and considerable aplomb, considering her hands were still tied. Eventually, she managed to land back on Widergard and said: 'Took you long enough to find me, Master Detective.'

I sighed again. 'Yes, sorry about that. Next time you're kidnapped from my car, maybe leave me a note detailing exactly where you're being taken. Then I won't have to wear out those famous detective skills.'

'I will, when a goblin isn't pointing a shooter at my head. Oh, by the way, you can untie me now. I was never into this kind of thing.'

Checking that her eyes had indeed returned to normal, I obliged.

'By the black pits of Oria, I'm still hungry' she said, rubbing her freed wrists and heading to the small kitchen. She found a further selection of victuals, piled them onto the one plate and started eating – this time with her hands. After she'd refuelled, she took a breath and looked up.

'You've never doubted me, have you, Nicely? You never thought I did for Roli?'

'Your nails were immaculate, Diamond. You don't keep a manicure like that if you've been knocking somebody about. Just look now.'

She checked where the rough and tumble with the grunt and runts had done its damage to her manicure. 'Huh, just got them how I liked them too!'

'And in your drinks cabinet there were two glasses put away the wrong way up. The wrong way up if you've been brought up in a place where ceilings shed grit into your grog. The obvious answer was that you had been drugged with something to make you think you'd killed Roli, while in a Rage.'

'But why kill poor Roli?'

'It wasn't intentional, Diamond. Well, I don't think so. Not that it's any consolation. The plan, as I read it, was to get you out of the way and let a heartbroken Roli think you had run off. The drug they used to kick-start you was, sadly, too much for Roli.'

Diamond struggled to hold back the tears. 'So, that's what actually killed him?

'I think so. But Cluff here, I'm guessing, tried to put you in the frame.'

'But who was behind it?'

'The Seneschal, probably. He wanted the two of you split up.'

'He's dead.'

'That could be… tricky.'

'No, a man's head comes off as easy as a dwarf's you know,' Diamond said, with total conviction.

'It does, but I think the plan was put into action by Kingley, the Snow King, in exchange for payment of Roli's debts and perhaps some veneer of respectability.'

Dwarf Girls Don't Dance

'That's his head too. And he's a lot easier to get at!' She looked across to where I had dragged Kingley's body.'

'Quit with the decapitation please, Diamond! This is not Rage work!'

Diamond pointed with a hand full of dead bird to the prone grunt. 'Cluff worked for him too. Roli met him at the Happy Hobgoblin before his dad brought him in to babysit.'

'Yes, they just didn't know that Roli was going to cut out early from his charity work, or that the Brew 52 potion would do more than knock him out.'

'So why didn't the frame work? How come I woke up next to Roli, instead of the Citadel's finest?'

'There was a guard wagon or two on the way to your place. I checked with some friends in the Cits. They all got involved in a little goblin-on-goblin street activity that delayed them. I saw the end of that little war.

After you walked out, Cluff must have gone for fresh orders from the boss here and then removed Roli's body and cleaned the place up. They probably put a tail on you and would not have been at all happy when they saw us talking, so they lifted you.'

'What I don't understand, if the plan was to knock me out with this Brew 52 drug, kidnap me, and then make Roli think I had run off, they should have known that as soon as I was free, I'd go tell Roli the truth. I was never going to be bought off! And I'd be back even if I had to crawl all the way from the Rust Hills.'

'I know, Diamond, but I'm thinking that maybe they weren't ever going to take the chance and let you go.'

She gave this some thought too.

'You think the Seneschal of the Citadel, would really have ordered this?'

'I think the Seneschal would probably have believed whatever the Snow King said and not thought too much about it. Kingley has a habit of persuading people. I do also think he expected his son would come to his senses after his girlfriend "ran off".'

'Roli wasn't like that.'

'No, I don't think he was. I'm also concerned about Kingley's mouthpiece, Autumn.'

Diamond shivered, 'that is one very scary individual. Sometimes I wasn't sure if he was the tail or the dog.'

'Really?'

'Oh, yes. Very, very unpleasant individual. Kingley could be quite a charmer when he wanted to be. Autumn was just cold.'

'I'm going to look out for this Autumn.'

'Then be careful, Nicely.'

Diamond was still considering her options too.

What do you think the Seneschal knows?'

'I'm not sure what Kingley has told him. I'd like to think he believes his son is sulking and you are safely back in the Rust Hills, and this is why the Seneschal is continuing to walk and breathe unaided for the moment.'

'For the moment?' she asked.

'For the moment,' I replied.

'So, Master Detective,' she said, with a weary smile. 'What now for me?'

I looked around at the prone bodies of the goblin kidnappers.

'Up to you, but personally, I wouldn't really want to hang around answering a lot of questions from the City Guards about my personal life.'

Her face brightened.

Dwarf Girls Don't Dance

'Really?'

I shrugged.

'Diamond, you are the client. Whatever you say goes – beheadings aside. I think Master Kingley is going to have enough explaining to do when the Guards drag the bottom of the lake and find the body of Roli Seneschalson.'

Diamond took the news like a veteran.

'Is that where you think he is?'

'I'm afraid so. After your kidnapping went so spectacularly wrong, like I say, they were forced to improvise.'

'The Seneschal's going to take that badly.'

'I'd like to think so. As to how clean he can keep his hands, I don't know. Kingley is going to have the whole mine down on his head and go away for a long, long time, that's for sure. I don't think anybody will miss him.'

'So, I just go?'

'At least for the moment. You've been through a lot, and I think a trip to somewhere warm might be in order. Sell the ring; I don't think Roli will mind too much.'

She looked at the rock on her ring finger.

'No, I think I'll keep this. I was never afraid of a little hard work.'

'No, I guess not, and don't forget to hang on to my card.'

She gave a sort of half-smile, and collected her clothes. This was something of a relief. There is only so much half-naked feminine a dwarf can take.

Torito and the caterers gave Diamond a lift back down from the Village, Kingley's other house help having vanished like the dew on a summer's morning. I sat down, poured myself a drink, lit a pipe and put on the music; remembering Diamond dancing back at the *Happy Hobgoblin*. So very much alive and so totally in control. I hoped very much she would stay that way, but like they say, dwarf girls don't dance... they Rage!

I finished my drink and poured another. Only then did I call the Cits. I sat in the fading afternoon sunlight and smiled to myself; they can't arrest you for that – well not yet, anyway.

7

Kellisgrund

I wiped condensation off the carriage window and looked out. A dark line that marked the beginning of the flat, dull greyness of the sea terminated the flat, dull greyness of the landscape. The threatening sky loomed over both of them as if to provide a lesson in proper heavy, flat grey dullness.

The concealed sun had reached as high as it was going to get and was now giving up on the whole daylight illumination business as a bad job. What light there was struggled to barge its way through the heavy curtain of sleeting rain. A windfall of pathetic farm animals dotted the landscape of Kellisgrund, looking bruised and neglected. A few looked up as we steamed on past, wearing wearied expressions that hinted at a desire for dining-based amelioration.

The powerful locomotive ate up the miles on a trackway as straight as a pithogue's plumb line on bath night. I could only just make out the engine's powerful main lamp cutting through the gathering gloom ahead of us, and it wasn't even mid-afternoon – my how I loved being back in dwarf country.

Kellisgrund was technically once only a gateway territory to the old dwarf kingdom of Skragsrealm, which lay some distance ahead across the choppy water of the Eskrag Strait. Lacking any significant mineral wealth, with numerous islands and inlets and a nasty habit of becoming flooded if enough folk all sweated at the same time, the dwarves of Skragsrealm were only too happy to cede the Peninsula of Kellisgrund to local men. In return, these men would then provide a resilient buffer zone against marauding goblins or over-officious elves. It seemed a good deal for everybody, well, excepting the men and women of Kellisgrund. How little everybody knew then.

Thanks to its northern location, Kellisgrund suffers from long, cold winters where the sun is as rare as an Elf's modesty. So the men and women of the newly forged Nation of Kellisgrund huddled in their new country in low homesteads throughout the long, uninterrupted nights, unable to dig in the frozen soil and hoping that the livestock would see them through to the cold, wet spring. During the cool summers they mostly just tried to keep their feet dry, and the midges out of their hair – although 24 hours of daylight does have some compensations if you're really into late-night reading and worrying about power bills.

It is the dark winter nights that are most said to influence a nation's vital force. The men of Kellisgrund have acquired a reputation for being patient and methodical, but also depressive and forbidding, given to extended bouts of drinking. During these so-called 'jolly ups' they can fly into a fury at a moment's notice and set upon anybody they consider to be a threat, an interloper, or have the wrong colour eyes.

The women of Kellisgrund have acquired a reputation for being able to put up with the men of Kellisgrund, without killing them – well, without killing too many of them. They are even more patient than their menfolk, and many will wait decades for the opportunity to kill an errant husband.

The dwarves of Skragsrealm do not altogether approve of the men and women of Kellisgrund as they consider them flippant, over-cheerful and amicable. That tells you everything you need to know about the dwarves of Skragsrealm.

Dwarf Girls Don't Dance

The men and women of Kellisgrund have fair hair and grey eyes that have taken in too much sea and sky. They are deceptively tall, but tend to stoop – possibly a product of having to spend so much time with their dwarf neighbours. They are very resilient and, despite all the odds stacked against them, very successful. This is what has surprised everybody.

Lacking good farming land, historically, the Kellisgrundians became good fishermen. With large fleets of boats, they then became very good at trading too. Their dourness was interpreted as a form of honesty, as if only virtue and probity could result in such a gloomy outlook. They are actually very honest folk, so maybe there is something in it after all.

To become successful, they simply needed goods to trade in. Fortunately, they had a whole dwarf Kingdom to the north, populated by creative and productive dwarves who, unfortunately, were not blessed with the best personalities for getting on with other races. It was the perfect arrangement and everybody gained, which didn't stop the dwarves from harbouring resentments – nothing can stop a dwarf doing that, well nothing apart from an early tomb.

I had been travelling for some ten hours across the bleak Kellisgrund landscape since changing trains at the border town of Secklefeld. During that time men and women had embarked and disembarked at a number of small stations located, apparently at random, in the unchanging landscape, but gradually the carriage began to fill to capacity. And just as slowly the line of the northern horizon grew thicker as the mountains of the distant Old Dwarf Kingdom, Skragsrealm, came into view.

One very old woman, carrying a very well-behaved pig, and carting a large bag, had been with me for some five hours. She'd stared straight ahead, unseeing, for all that time. No scrolls or books to distract her from her gazing duty, perhaps replaying the eventful highlights of her life of pig-rearing over and over in her mind. The pig, by comparison, was interested in everything going on around him; watching people come and go and looking hopefully at their packed meals. I felt sorely tempted to pull a face at the pig, but us dwarves tend to disapprove of social interactions with supper.

I guessed both pig and pig owner were heading for Kellishaldt, as was I. Kellishaldt is the second city of Kellisgrund, a seaport, and it was there, in the new and pristine Kellishaldt Keep, that Diamond was now imprisoned awaiting trial for murder. Kellisgrund still enforces the death penalty for murder, but – in this case – not if I had anything to do with it.

I had arranged for a wagon to be waiting for me at Kellishaldt's Central Station, which was located some way out of the port itself (did I mention the Kellisgrundian sense of humour?). The wagon was a big old Heslington 650, built like a train with a boiler that could burn anything combustible and produce enough steam pressure to permit snow to be ploughed. It was waiting just as I had arranged. I hadn't arranged for the driver.

'I have instructions from Arbiter Skunglard to deliver you to his office,' the uniformed man said obstinately when I refused to play passenger.

I didn't want to be unpleasant, but the last thing I needed, on what I suspected was going to be a difficult case, was a babysitter, and I told him as much: 'So, if you don't mind, I'll just take the keys and be on my way.'

The driver was lined and gnarled, like something that had been pulled out of one of the famous Kellisgrund peat bogs. He wore a ridiculous jaunty driver's cap proudly on a head where the salt had long achieved prominence over the pepper in the follicular cruet set.

'So?' I asked again.

Dwarf Girls Don't Dance

'I am just waiting for you to tell the wagon where it should be going to,' the driver replied, unwavering. 'It will be… interesting.'

Eventually, I got in the wagon's passenger seat and waited as he got in the driver's side.

'Don't think I'm sitting in the back,' I told him. He nodded, as concerned as chalk.

'So, what do I call you, driver?'

'I am known as Lippy.'

'And why is that?' I said, regretting the question almost before I had finished asking it.

'When I was a child, I once said to a teacher "thank you" and not just "thanks",' he explained.

I was going to just love Kellisgrund.

Up close, I could see that Lippy was probably younger than I'd first imagined. Late midlife for a man, his looks more the product of outdoor living in a climate designed for indoor living. As he turned the wheel, found the gears and pumped some steam, I could see there was some strength in those limbs too – Lippy looked handy.

All the people from the train were now walking away from the station towards the town. Somebody could have laid on a steam bus or two, but that was not the Kellisgrund way.

"We have legs, so we can walk."

As we pulled out of the parking circle, I spotted the old woman holding her pig and pulling a large case. I asked the driver to stop, which he did.

'Can we give you a lift somewhere?' I asked her.

'Am I looking ill?' she replied, scowling, somewhat put out. I didn't have an answer to that, and so we drove off again.

'She must really love that pig,' I observed.

'It will be a meal for the family,' the driver replied.

'Celebration or commemoration?' I wondered.

'A celebration,' he said confidently. I shot him a sceptical look. 'It is my mother,' he said by way of explanation as we drove on past the old lady. 'It is her birthday.'

'Of course,' I observed, with a sigh, and leaned back appreciatively into the surprisingly warm and comfortable seat.

'Wulsk hair,' said Lippy, noticing my reaction. 'Very soft, very good insulation – very dangerous animal. Good for car seats. If you ever see a wulsk, run very fast away from it.'

'Will that do the trick?'

'No – it will not be fast enough. But you might as well die trying.'

Ah, a Kellisgrundian joker!

Kellishaldt was a muddy-looking bright blur through the rain that had now transformed into something like a very wet sea mist. Kellishaldt was very well lit – it had to be, as the darkness of the late afternoon here had a quality that made it almost a living entity. Shadow and gloom seemed to crawl over the countryside, pouring into every hollow, as the sun departed to warmer climes where it felt much more at home and appreciated. The inky pockets pooled their resources, the perfect cover for unseen things to begin their clandestine machinations, and Kellishaldt formed an illuminated island surrounded by an ocean of blackness patiently waiting for the lights to go out. We arrived at our destination, and this wagon's passenger, at least, was grateful to get indoors and give his over-active imagination a rest.

Arbiter Skunglard was every inch a legal man, and he amounted to a lot of inches as well, which is far too much law for my liking. His bird-like eyes only accentuated the beakiness of a long bent nose positioned above a mouth that looked like he was currently sucking bitterfruit with his outhole. Dressed in arbiter black with ridiculous short trews and long socks, he really did grasp his robes as if he was continually about to address a peer bench.

Dwarf Girls Don't Dance

Arbiter Skunglard's office looked like every other such office I had ever seen, the law books, the scrolls, the same old certificates on the walls that might as well admit to his interest in necromancy for all they got read. It lacked the two things I most value in an office: a dartboard and coffee. That's the problem with his end of the law business, no appreciation of what justice is really about.

Skunglard took a seat behind his desk, and I sat on the other side without being invited, pulling up my trousers a few inches to stop any irritating knee indentations in the bottom half of my new all-weather, insulated, double-breasted, back-belted suit. He asked for my credentials. I gave him the letter that I had received from this very office.

'No,' he said, sounding a little irked. 'I require your professional credentials – your Citadel Registration, your license, membership of any professional bodies and such like.'

'Now why would you be needing that?' I felt obliged to ask. 'You sent me the letter on behalf of Diamond, so presumably, you felt reasonably sure of who I was and what I did, but in case you're mistaking me for some other dwarf detective called Strongoak, here's my badge.'

I flashed him the gold button, but didn't feel obliged to let him paw it in the manner he seemed to want.

'Master Strongoak,' he chided in his best courtroom fashion. 'I am not sure what your normal working routine and procedures may be, but I will require respectful attention. Daily reports, to be on my desk no later than 7.30 a.m. the next day, and full receipts for any expenses with nothing over 50 crowns to be paid without prior approval. I am not feeling confident with regard to your ability to carry this out.'

'Well, that's all fine, Master Arbiter. I require a decent cup of coffee and a warm bath, but in lieu of them I'll settle for seeing Diamond – as soon as possible.'

'Master Dwarf, I don't like your manners!' Skunglard stormed. 'I don't like the way you look, the way you sit and I don't even like what you are wearing!'

'Look, Skunglard, you can insult my haircut, my dwarvish bearing and take umbrage at my lack of refinement – you won't be the first or last to do that I'm sure. However, I won't sit here and take fashion tips from a Kellisgrund rook when I am wearing one of tailor Gasper Halftoken's finest creations.'

Skunglard looked like he was about to have some form of brain grume – he was certainly spluttering and going a very unhealthy shade of purple. I continued before he found his tongue again.

'Furthermore Arbiter, you seem to be under the misapprehension that I am working for you, which I can assure you I am not!'

'Of course, you are working for me!' Skunglard finally spat out. 'Are you so ignorant of the law that you believe that a remandee can hire himself or herself a private detective?'

'No, I am not,' I replied, as relaxed as milk. 'But there is nothing in the law to stop a private detective who has already been hired from continuing to do his job.' I took out Diamond's contract, signed in Gallgot's Coffee Lodge a lifetime ago, from my inside jacket pocket. I flattened it out and placed it carefully in front of him. 'You'll find this is all in order.'

He put on a pair of wireframes and looked over the scroll. 'This is two years old,' he said at first glance.

'And suddenly there's terms of limitation on an employment contract?'

He read quickly, and looked it over twice, but finally had to grudgingly admit: 'This all seems in order.'

'Good,' I said, picking up the scroll and replacing it carefully in my pocket. 'Now, perhaps you would be so kind as to bring me up to full speed and then arrange for me to see our client.'

Dwarf Girls Don't Dance

Skunglard scowled like an expert, but did as I requested, summarising the salients like the arbiter he was. He then picked up the desk speech horn and asked to be connected to Kellishaldt Keep. He got through and said a few words in the consonant-rich local tongue that they only use when outsiders they want to annoy are present.

'I have made you an appointment for two after midwatch,' he said, putting the horn down carefully. 'If that will be satisfactory?'

I nodded, ignoring his tone of voice, which was in that particular form of sarcasm that men and women of the law use when they believe nobody can take a swing at them. If he kept that up, he was going to learn different.

'I will need your detective licence, as you will have to be registered with the court authorities to be granted a temporary license to proceed with your enquiries. And I will need updating if I am to be effective on our client's behalf.'

I nodded again and passed my credentials over the table.

'I'll pick the badge up tomorrow. I feel kind of naked without it. You know, like going out without a hand axe in the lining of your coat.'

I showed him my hand axe, and he blanched a little.

'There are laws here about carrying a concealed weapon.'

'It's not concealed Skunglard; I'm just keeping it warm.'

Lippy was waiting in the outer office, along with an impressive young clerk. She was tall, with very dark hair and looked like she could tackle a wulsk singled-handed and then give it a hair cut. Lippy was obviously impressed. Everybody in the office had overheard the conversation that had just taken place. Half of them were amused, and half were shocked, and both halves were trying not to show it. I went along with the amused half and picked up my half-cape coat and the Hat from the office stand.

'Come on, Lippy, we've a call to make.'

'Good woman – tall and strong,' he said as we walked out. 'This is very good. Hopefully, we will come here again. I like to see tall and strong women. They are very agreeable.'

For a man who was getting on, Lippy obviously still had a spring in his step.

We got back to the Heslington without being blown away and only suffering minor frostbite damage, and Lippy pumped the wagon a couple of times to get some steam up. 'We have an hour or two to lose first. I need to drop off my trunk at the *Skragshelder Inn*, do you know it?'

Lippy nodded. 'Of course, cheap but comfortable,' he said approvingly.

'Which is music to my ears, but more importantly, is there anywhere in this berg where you can get a decent cup of coffee?'

'Yes' said Lippy, 'just a short distance from *Skragshelder Inn.*' He swung the wheel and we headed off. The fog had now turned to some sort of sleet, and I felt glad for my hat and cape even in the warmth of the wagon.

We drove quickly through the busy Kellishaldt streets, which seemed to be arranged in a nice tidy block formation. That famous Kellisgrund design sense. I checked in quickly at the *Skragshelder* and the front desk arranged for my trunk to be taken up to my room.

Lippy and I then headed out again. There were plenty of folk around, despite the weather. The tall grey men and women of Kellisgrund dressed well for protection against the elements, plenty of Skragsrealm dwarves, dressed well for protection against anything or anybody, and more goblins than I would have expected. There were also flashes of some very blond heads that at first, I assumed to be elves.

'No, Huldre,' Lippy explained after I asked. 'Nomadic uskhal herders.' Seeing my lack of comprehension, he mimed a set of big antlers. 'Uskhal, yes? Live in the far snowy lands north of Skragsrealm and pulls the carts of the Huldre?'

'Oh, yes – the animals with the ringing bells.'

'Those are the ones,' Lippy said, taking the large wagon down a street designed for something much smaller.

'I thought they were called usk?'

'That is correct also, but we call them uskhal. The Huldre, they were once very uncommon to see in Kellisgrund, even in Skragsrealm I believe. Now they come much further to the south – even to Kellishaldt.'

'So these Huldre,' I asked, as we drove past another small group of bundled up blond heads, 'are they men or elves?'

Yes,' Lippy replied. 'That is the very good question.'

The coffee room was in the entry hall of a large lodge called the 'Wisklehald', which was built some years ago, in the style that is generally known as 'in-your-kisser', when you could not put too much marble inside a building. A revolving door, not much smaller than a water mill wheel, opened onto a chequered marble floor that led to a magnificent marble staircase, with a polished marble handrail, while marble columns supported marble ceiling panels that looked far too heavy to be put to this use. I just hoped that the local woodworm hadn't been methodically eating their way through the support timbers, especially awaiting my visit.

Lippy declined the pleasure of my company as he was 'on duty' and so he sat in the wagon while I went to see how the locals murdered the magic bean. The trick it seemed was to boil it, until it disintegrated, in some form of preserved milk that was guaranteed to last the winter without going 'off', presumably because it has never been 'on' to begin with. You then infused it with twig scrapings to give it that 'just retched' flavour and served it with enough sugar as could reasonably dissolve without leaving more than an inch of sludge. The whole drink was called 'coughee' with the emphasis on the phlegm. Fortunately, as we were in what passed for a major city on these parts, they also did a coffee for outsider trade, and that was reasonably drinkable as long as you didn't smell the 'coughee'. With typical restraint the local name for this brew for outsiders, as Lippy had told me, translated as 'wrong coffee'. I took my 'wrong coffee', found a window seat next to a radiator and went over what the arbiter had told me, comparing it with the notes I had made previously.

A man by the name of Danwright Dollund the Second, ageing scion of the Dollund dynasty, one half of the mighty 'Dollund and Halfaxen' trading empire, had been found dead by staff in his study in Dollund Hall early on a midweek morning, a fourteen-night previously. He was also, famously, or infamously – depending on your point of view and race – the owner of the Heartstone, the most precious of Dwarf gems. Dollund had been beaten to death, his toughened steel coffer was open, and of the Heartstone, there was no sign.

The Heartstone is a jewel without parallel. The stories written about it are so many, and the legends so convoluted, that it is impossible now to discover exactly where and when the dwarves actually found and cut it. The Heartstone is the largest, and hence the most famous diamond ever found, nobody doubts that. It dropped out of the public eye decades back and then around twenty years ago it had turned up on the bosom of Danwright Dollund the Second's goodwife at a charity event and the whole of Widergard went 'Heartstone mad'. Dollund would say nothing about how he had acquired it, and nobody came forward to complain, and so it now became the Dollund Heartstone and dwarves everywhere wept.

The evening before his death and the Heartstone's (presumed) robbery, Danwright Dollund had entertained one 'Sanctity Sureseam', a dwarfess of his acquaintance, believed by staff to be his mistress. She had been there when the staff had gone to bed and had, they presumed, let herself out – as she had certainly done many times before. Later, on arriving at Sanctity's rooms, officers of the Kellishaldt Keep had found her in the bath, scrubbed up better than a wizard's whistle, with her previous night's clothes in the wash machine. This didn't sit well with them.

Nothing else in Dollund's study had apparently been touched, other than the coffer where, it was said, the Heartstone was kept. The door to that was swinging on its sturdy dwarf-made hinges. Whether theft had always been the motive, and Dollund wouldn't co-operate, or the beating had been the result of a lover's tiff, driven by dwarf aggression, the Keep officers were not speculating. Everybody else was. The Keep officers were able to ascertain that 'Sanctity Sureseam' had once worked as an exotic dancer called 'Diamond' and she was rapidly charged with causing Danwright Dollund's departure from this realm. Of the Heartstone there was no sign.

8

Diamond

In Kellisgrund, you are guilty until proven innocent, and sometimes even after that. Maybe it is the climate and those dark winter nights, but guilt is something almost palpable here that goes along with the clean lines of the furniture and the faint smell of fish. The police were not pursuing any other lines of enquiry for Dollund's murder. It did not look good for Diamond.

Diamond, however, was looking very good, considering she'd had over two weeks in Kellishaldt Keep and the best part of two years in Kellisgrund itself. Her hair was piled high and in good fettle and if the Keep uniform didn't do as much for her as an evening dress, at least you could still tell which side she buttoned her blouse on.

'Arbiter Skunglard has to go!' I said, sitting down on the efficiently designed seat that came with the functional table placed in the middle of the clean and practical interview room where I found Diamond waiting for me.

'I see,' she answered levelly.

'Why in the whole of Widergard did you pick him?'

'I didn't,' she explained. 'All arbiters are assigned by a type of lottery system – as long as they have experience in the law as it applies to your case.'

Dwarf Girls Don't Dance

'So, Skunglard has experience at least?'

'Oh yes, but usually as a prosecutor.'

'Well, let's hope he remembers whose side he's on!'

'All arbiters work for truth and justice, not for individuals,' she said, smiling.

'Now I just bet that's been written up somewhere big and proud!'

'Above the door to the Law Courts.'

I had to laugh; you've got to love a country that believes in truth and justice. I believe in them too. I just wouldn't want to be arrested in one.

Diamond put her hand across the table and quickly gripped mine.

'Thanks for coming, Nicely.'

'Hey, it was a quiet week, and Kellisgrund is lovely at this time of year – or will be if it ever stops raining.'

'Generally – at this time of the year, it only stops raining to snow.'

'Now, I just knew you were going to say that!' I sighed and started business, as I knew I had to eventually.

'So why not give me the full shiny, and then we can both think about going somewhere better to work on our tans.'

'The first thing you need to know, Nicely, is that I wasn't Danwright Dollund's mistress.'

'Glad we've got that one cleared up! And you've told the Keep detectives this?'

'I've been keeping pretty quiet about everything until you got here. I thought it's what you'd most probably advise.'

'You good little murder suspect you!' I said, with just the right patronising tone to have earned me a slap anywhere else and at any other time. I scratched my chin. I needed a shave and wanted a bath, preferably with enough hot water to melt an ice cap, but there were other priorities.

'So what did you do for him, Diamond? You don't mind me still calling you Diamond, do you? I think I'd choke if I tried to say "Sanctity" with a straight face.'

She smiled properly for the first time. 'I think I'd strangle you first!' She leaned back in her chair and looked me straight in the eye.

'What do you think I did for him, Nicely?'

I thought for a moment, and then it was obvious.

'You danced for him.'

'Give the dwarf a pickle! Yes, I danced for him. I gave an old man some pleasure. It's how we first met.' She drummed her fingers on the table as if undecided about something. I didn't prompt her.

'When I left the Citadel I didn't really have anywhere particular in mind to go, Nicely. I just wanted to get away from Kingley as quickly as possible, before he had a chance to get to me!'

'You needn't have worried on that score, Diamond. Kingley went quite meekly in the end, like the heart had gone out of him.'

She did not look convinced. 'Don't be fooled by his act; I've never trusted him or that creepy Autumn guy he kept around.' She shivered. 'There was always something particularly unpleasant about him.'

I had to agree.

'Did they finally get him too?'

I shook my head. 'Autumn got away. Seems he was still on the steamboat in the middle of the lake when we had our run-in with Kingley and his grunts, and he somehow slipped away before the Cits could pick him up.'

'That won't help me sleep nights, Nicely.'

'Don't worry – he's probably slunk back to whatever stone it was that Kingley found him under.'

Dwarf Girls Don't Dance

'I hope so, Nicely. Like I always said, Autumn could give me bigger shivers than his boss. Anyway, I didn't want to head back to the Rust Hills. I admit that New Iron Town had some appeal—'

She let that one hang as she smiled at me.

'But then I considered Skragsrealm. It seemed a reasonable option. I tried living in Skragslanding, but wasn't convinced that I was getting anywhere. One day I was looking across the Eskrag Strait at Kellisgrund and thought, why not?'

She glanced around, taking it all in. 'As strange as it may seem, Kellishaldt has proven ideal.'

'Really? A place where they murder the magic bean so brutally?'

'There are more important things in life than coffee, Nicely.'

'We have got to get you out of here, Diamond! This place is raddling your mind.'

'Seriously, Kellishaldt made very good sense. A good-sized town, lots of passing traffic and enough dwarves around for me to not stand out, but not too many to take too much of an interest, if you know what I mean?'

'I do, actually.'

'I tried various casual jobs, but nothing really paid the bills, so I sort-of drifted back into dancing, which is how Danwright met me.'

She gave me the hard stare before continuing: 'You believe me about him, don't you?'

'I have no reason to doubt you, Diamond.'

'Thanks, Nicely – that means a lot. So, I was not the old man's mistress, however, he did ask me to marry him.'

'Whoa! Now, that's news from the old bird!' I leaned back, took my hat off and scratched my head, mulling over the implications of this little dragon blast.

'Did anybody else know of this – anyone, like the rest of the family?'

She shrugged. 'I can't say for sure. It's not like he wanted to advertise, especially after I turned him down – but you only need check the Heartstone.'

'How so?'

'He had my name engraved on the casement.'

'Now that is – interesting.'

'*For Sanctity* – wedding gift, if I was so inclined, which as I say, I wasn't.'

'So you turned him down why?'

Diamond looked at me, her forehead furrowing into a frown. 'Dust and dirt Nicely, do you really have to ask?'

'Yes, because the local detectives will too, Mistress Sanctity. What exactly put you off accepting the proposal from the fantastically powerful and very well-insulated Danwright Dollund?

'He was an old man, Nicely. A very sweet and now rather unhappy old man, who had lived an active and adventurous life but was still looking for some magic in his old age; a final adventure. He thought it was me, but it wasn't.' She blanched slightly. 'Not that there was anything nasty about him – just; I mean, I could have killed him! As I'm sure you're aware – especially after Roli.'

I nodded. I knew. We both knew.

'So that's the crazy thing – they all think I've killed him and stolen the Heartstone. Why would I have done that? I could have had everything! The gem included!'

'That is a very good point for our team, Diamond.'

I could see her relax a little. Jail is never fun, even a nice new one like The Kellishaldt Keep; especially with the shadow of the goblin's necktie hanging over you.

'Tell me, Diamond, did you get to meet the family much?'

She nodded. 'Sure I met them. I wasn't a dirty secret that he kept hidden away. I was often a guest here and at other houses he owned.'

Dwarf Girls Don't Dance

'So what were your impressions? Moreover, what did old man Dollund think of them all? And might any of them have suspected something with regard to his true intentions towards you?'

She gave a sort of half-shrug.

'It's hard to say. I think Passaloll might have. She's technically still the current Mistress Dollund – a truly frightful woman. Danwright freely admitted to me that he married her in error; devastated after the death of his first wife Emilis, who, incidentally, he was properly devoted to. Passaloll is poisonous – a redhead who unfortunately bears a strong resemblance to the young Emilis.

'She loathes me with a passion, and I have to say I reciprocate the feeling completely. It would be wood ants and honey and no regrets! But Danwright is, was, very good to her and their daughter, Semeline, and maintained this even after her infidelity.'

'Bedroll hopper?'

Diamond shrugged. 'I don't know the full story, but it seems there was some blond charmer involved – a couple of years back – younger and probably on the make. Fullerall I think the name was. Passaloll has a place out near the Kellismarsh. Bit of a comedown after Dollund House. Danwright never did officially divorce her, for the daughter's sake. They were what they call here "sundered" – not together, but not fully apart. Danwright made sure they were both well looked after.'

'But he would have made this sundering official if you'd married?'

'Oh, yes! No doubt. Maybe even apply for custody of Semeline too. She's nice enough, but she could just turn into her mother without the proper child management.'

'That's some motive for Passaloll,' I felt obliged to mention.

'Maybe, but I can't imagine her having the gumption. Anyway, Danwright also has three children from his first marriage to

Emilis,' Diamond continued. 'The youngest, Hassally, who is a sweetie, but not the sharpest arrow in the quiver. Pallis, who fancies herself as royalty and who has married somebody so dull that he could make moat water look interesting. And then there is the son and heir: Danwright Dollundson.'

'And what of him?' I asked quickly

'About as much fun as a goblin's tea party. No, that's unfair. It's hard to know what to make of him. He's very serious, and there's something sad about him, but sometimes you can sense there's something else going on underneath. A very different Danwright Dollundson maybe – a little looser – but, hey, he has always been nice to me!'

'Good. I'll get straight on to them tomorrow.'

'And Nicely, I also have something of another favour to ask of you. Not directly related to all this, but sort of important.'

'Just ask, Diamond. I didn't come all this way to take in the scenery – of which there is none anyway.'

'I'm sure that the Keep officers have been all over my rooms with a fine-toothed comb…'

'The finest, I'd say. You could probably pick out all the nits of a pixie's kitten with it.'

She leant forward and spoke conspiratorially: 'I kept a bag at work, packed in case I needed to scarper speedily. That's all not much use now I know, but I also had a few keepsakes in there, including some bits from Roli – nothing valuable – well only sentimentally so, you know?'

'Of course, Diamond. I'll pick it up. Will I have any trouble collecting it?'

'No, Rosie the hat-check knows all about you!'

'Only good things I hope.'

Diamond laughed in that infectious way of hers, throwing her head back. 'Don't flatter yourself, Strongoak!'

Dwarf Girls Don't Dance

I felt a certain tightness about the chest as I thought what the hangman's rope would do to that lovely smile of hers, not to mention that lovely neck. It was my turn to put a hand across the table.

'Don't worry, Diamond, I'll get you out of this place.'

'I know you will, Nicely,' she said tersely. 'But that's not all you're here for.'

'It's not?' I said, a little taken aback by her sudden intensity.

'No, Nicely. We're going to find the low life that beat up that lovely old man. And I want him to swing for it!'

'That sounds like a reasonable course of action, Diamond. He will get what's coming to him, one way or another.'

'Or another?'

'I promise,'

'Good. The Seneschal never did.'

I sighed; the whole matter of the death of Roli Seneschalson was still a very sore point for me too. 'His involvement in the death of his son was never proven, Diamond.'

'But we knew!'

'We didn't, Diamond. Kingley was far too difficult a figure to pin down. I began to believe he had the Seneschal totally under his thrall.'

'Really?'

'Yes. The Seneschal just went to pieces too quickly. He was a broken man.'

'Good,' said Diamond. She didn't say it with any particular malice. It was just a statement of fact. It was a good thing that the Seneschal was broken, and his office that had lasted generations was now over.

'So, what about this nightspot, Diamond?' I said to bring us back to the here and now. 'What's it called for a start?'

She laughed again.

'You will not believe this, Detective Strongoak.'

9

The Hat-Check Girl

The *Happy Hobgoblin* (Kellishaldt) was located in a so-so part of town. It had a bright new light proudly flashing its identity out into the sleet-swept night, and I bet the owners were really proud of the great new name they had thought up.

Well done them!

Or maybe one of them had once been on the trip of a lifetime and after visiting the fleshpots of the Citadel had decided that this was what Kellishaldt really needed – a *Happy Hobgoblin*.

I'd learnt from Lippy that this was considered to be the 'racy' quarter of the town. I'm not sure what sort of races they were used to, but these sprinters wouldn't have got out of the blocks in the Citadel.

Still, at least the nightspot promised to be warm, the locals know how to insulate in Kellisgrund. I'm not sure if this is down to their inherent miserliness, which is well known, or good building regulations, either way, I was grateful. My Citadel acclimatised frame was having trouble with the weather, which once upon a time I would have called 'a mild start to winter'.

I was now on foot, having sent Lippy (and the Heslington 650) home for the night for his mother's celebratory party, presumably to tuck into my other fellow passenger – the one with the trotters. Forced to use the poor man's pony, I needed every inch of tread on my boots as the pavements, although flaunting a good coat of salt, were still as slippery as a politician's morals.

There was no doorman at *The Happy Hobgoblin*, probably far too subservient a role for the egalitarian folk of Kellisgrund. I paid my fee in the local coinage at a small booth, which looked as welcoming as the entrance hall to a sexual health sick bay, but at least the entrance price didn't empty the purse. I then went to check the Hat and half-cape, walking down a corridor and staircase whose gloom was only alleviated by some small black and white glossies of ladies in various stages of undress. Even they couldn't add much to the surroundings.

The girl at the counter was thinner than a goblin's tuskpick and paler than moonlight on a snowdrop. Strangely attractive in a slightly elvish fashion, this could not be Rose, surely? It wasn't; this was Sithery. Sithery was perfectly happy to point me in the right direction for Rose, in the nightspot proper, where Rose was apparently now busy serving drinks. I handed across half-cape and the Hat, which Sithery treated with the respect it deserved and, after walking through a double set of doors, was pleasantly surprised by what I found. A strong but not unpleasant colour scheme, unobtrusive but more than adequate lighting and an aroma, not of the quiet male desperation I had envisaged, but what my educated nose judged to be some form of sausage. Well done, *The Happy Hobgoblin,* Kellishaldt – you've just got your first Strongoak 'Crown of Approval', and I've been to bigger towns which didn't warrant a hint of the regal headwear. Now, for two crowns, they just needed something to provide something decent to drink while I visited.

'What is your pleasure, Master Dwarf?' asked the attractive barkeep who, with dark hair and ruby-painted lips, didn't look local, but did look much more Rosie.

'Do you have anything to keep a night's chill out?'

'I surely do have, but what would you like to drink first?'

'How about something like a dark winter warmer then?'

'I do have the very thing for you. Our dwarf customers are rather partial to it at this time of year.' She pulled a small dark bottle from beneath the bar, took its cap off, and poured, with the proper respect a decent ale deserves, into a tulip glass designed for the very purpose.

'There's always sediment, so you have to be very careful.' She placed the glass in front of me with a flourish. 'There you are. Master Dwarf – it's called *Hammer Head*, which is something by way of a warning.'

I lifted the glass; the beer had already cleared to leave a nut-coloured brew with a beautiful creamy head. I took a sip – 'Two Crowns' to *The Happy Hobgoblin*.

'Thanks, Rosie. It is Rosie, isn't it? Diamond mentioned I'd find you here.'

'Ah,' she said evenly, 'Nicely Strongoak, I'm guessing. Well, well, well – you're taller than I expected.'

'New boots,' I said, supping the ale. 'Just wait two weeks, and I'll have worn the soles right back down to normal dwarf size.'

'Is that so?'

'Oh yes – make that one week if I have to keep walking around after you, asking you out for dinner.'

'Oh yes, Diamond was right about you, I can see that!'

I raised an eyebrow.

'Especially about you not being as funny as you think you are.'

'Ouch! No need to worry about the shoe leather, I think I've just been cut down so low I'm going to need help now to hang my hat up.'

Rosie wiped a cloth across the bar top, moving my beer with care.

'I didn't say not funny, just not as funny.'

I raised my glass to her in thanks. 'This is very, very nice. I'm tempted to have five or six and then roll over and see if anyone wants to tickle my tummy. However…'

'Don't worry – I know why you're here, Nicely. And the staff all appreciate the help; nobody believes that Diamond did what they've got her locked up for!'

'I'm sure she'll be happy for the support.'

Rosie grabbed some pots and started drying them.

'I can't talk seriously now – I have to do the conviviality act for the management.'

'And there I thought it was my baby blue eyes!'

'They're nice eyes and the right number too!' She looked around quickly. 'Just for now, take in the first two acts like you're here for the duration.'

'Can do – it seems a reasonable sort of dive. Certainly better than the outside promised.'

'It is,' Rosie nodded. 'There's a local saying, "In Kellishaldt we hang our curtains with the best side facing in".'

'I can understand that,' I agreed.

'Really? Because they also say that in Skragsrealm the dwarves hang their curtains with the best side facing out.'

I took another sup of beer. 'There could be truth in that too.'

Rosie raised a perfectly plucked eyebrow. 'You're like Diamond – she's not a dwarf diehard either!'

'There's good and bad in everybody. It's mostly just the elves that forget this.'

She did the eyebrow trick again.

'Mostly,' I admitted.

'I have a break after the second act,' Rosie continued, 'and then I'm back for a stint in the cloakroom – come and catch me there, but don't make it too obvious. Oh ho, management alert!'

I smiled and ordered another beer, as Rosie slipped back into work mode. I paid and left her a large tip. Rosie smiled cheerily, and I got up and found myself a seat nearer to the small stage. The *Happy Hobgoblin* was reasonably well attended for the time of night – which, of course, might have been wickedly late for the notoriously hard-working locals. The audience was mostly men, with a scattering of gnomes, and a table of dwarves in one corner. They who eyed me with regard, but were more interested in their beer than me.

The first performer went by the name of Elska, and she played an instrument that resembled a packing crate set up for slicing an unfeasibly large number of eggs; it had more strings attached than a 'best-buy' deal at the second-hand wagon mart. She was either suffering from a digestive problem, bum grapes, or a broken heart. For some reason, as she struck the last chord, she took off her top and then, proudly sporting an excellent full set, bowed to the audience and departed. The audience clapped politely – even the dwarf table who would normally be rather more boisterous – so I clapped along with them, not quite sure about what I had just experienced.

Next up was a set from a Kellisgrund comedian called Lardon and, for future reference, I made a mental note not to put myself through such a thing again. Comedy, I have concluded, does not travel well in Greater Widergard. He lacked the aggressive acerbic quality you find in Citadel comedians or the finesse and charm (and piss-filled balloon and fart canon) that comes with a dwarf comedian. Somehow I sat through his self-depreciating observations on the monotony of Kellisgrund weather, and Kellisgrund social life and just Kellisgrund in general, without putting him out of our misery. At least he kept his clothes on.

Rosie was at the hatcheck with a suit that shouted 'management' lurking nearby. I smiled politely and handed over my ticket stub.

'Kellisgrund humour is sometimes an acquired taste for the visitor I am told,' Rosie said, conversationally.

'So are breakwind fruits, but I never really saw the point of trying to acquire the taste, to be honest.' I took the Hat, and my half-cape and the bag tucked underneath it.

'Well, I hope you will try us again another night,' Rosie said brightly. 'The acts change nightly.'

'I'm sure I will – comedian aside, it's a nice little place you have here, and the beer really is a treat.'

'Why, thank you very much, Master Dwarf. And next time you must try the usk sausage, it's a local delicacy.'

'I'll remember that.' I smiled at Rosie, and she smiled back. I smiled at the management too, and he smiled and wished me a good night. We were living in Smileshaldt, in Smilesgrund, of that there was no doubt.

Still smiling, I stepped out into the cold evening air, and somebody put a hood over my head, punched me in the stomach, and half-a-dozen of Kellishaldt's finest lifted me into a meat wagon.

I am guessing that the officers of the Kellishaldt Keep do not get much excitement in this town. Fights and thievery and such like, but not an actual juicy murder to be solved – and of a prominent resident too. This got the boys all a little overexcited; that and too much protein in the diet. They apparently eat a lot of seafood in Kellisgrund and quite a lot of it pickled. Pickled seafood to break your fast, pickled seafood for lunch and some nice seafood, pickled maybe, for supper. It can't be good for the digestion all that pickled seafood – it's bound to make you crabby.

They put me in one of those nice clean interview rooms, identical to the one where I'd spoken to Diamond. That was their first mistake. They should have sorted out somewhere with blood still on the walls and a nice line in damp and unidentifiable odours. Nobody is going to be intimidated sitting in a room that looks like a nice new, well-scrubbed, Healer's House.

They really did shine a light in my face too. I thought they were being ironic, especially as it was one of those table lamps with the nice clean lines that they are so good at designing hereabouts. But it turns out they were serious. And they had a good guard and a bad guard. Some folk watch far too many rolling pictures.

Good Guard and Bad Guard took it in turns to ask the questions:

'Where was the Heartstone?'
'How long had I been conspiring with Diamond?'
'Was I the muscle?'
'Had I actually beaten up on Old Man Dollund?'

And when they didn't like my answers, they took it in turns to hit me. That was their biggest mistake. If they thought that physical violence was the answer, they didn't know their dwarves, certainly not this one anyway. And that is indefensible, what with there being a whole kingdom of them right across the strait.

Dwarf Girls Don't Dance

The Bad Guard had what he seemed to think was a winning sense of humour. What was it about comedians in Kellishaldt?

'So dwarf,' the funny guy said from behind the light. 'When you do the business at home with the dancer, do you stand on her shoulders to turn the lights off or does she stand on yours?'

'No, jack-for-brains, we keep the light on – presumably your goodwife turns the light off, so she doesn't have to look at you.'

That earned me a slap – maybe it was too close to the truth.

'Then tell us again, where did you meet Diamond?' said another flatter, more disembodied Kellisgrund voice from behind the light.

'I can't tell you "again", because I didn't tell you the first time.'

'Oh yes, because you are some big-noise from the Citadel?' chipped in Officer Overexcited. 'Some big noise "Master Detective"?'

'That's right, the Master Detective who is not obliged to answer your questions.'

'Then where is your fancy badge Master Detective?'

'I told you, go ask Arbiter Skunglard! He's processing the temporary license.'

'Oh, yes – so you can solve the crime that the slow and stupid Kellisgrund Keep can't solve. Is that it?'

'You said it, brother!'

That earned me another slap from Officer Overexcited. 'I am not your brother!'

'Hey!' I had to complain, 'this is getting tedious! Just go see Arbiter Kungslard!'

'We are not in the habit of waking our law-abiding arbiters in the middle of the night on the word of some door-stop.'

I stared hard into the light. 'Oh now you've gone and done it. A few slaps between colleagues is one thing, but name-calling? That's fighting talk! What's the matter, your good wife been getting some dwarf action?'

There was some real feeling behind the next slap. It sent the chair tumbling, and me with it. That did hurt.

'Enough, Krole!' said Officer Flatvoice.

'Give me half an hour alone with him,' his overexcited colleague shouted, unpleasantly spraying spittle into the cone of light.

'This is not getting us anywhere, Krole.'

I had to agree with them. Somebody picked me up and found a new room with a new chair for me to sit on. The room also had a bed in it, so I decided to lie on that and try to get some sleep, which was the work of moments.

10

Grundrund

High Captain Gobblod, in a country full of tall grey-eyed men with greying hair, was taller and greyer than most. He had my badge sitting on the desk in front of him, freshly delivered by Arbiter Skunglard that morning, but if there was any apology pudding around he wasn't eating it today.

'My men seem to have been a little bit over-zealous,' he did admit.

'Oh yes, it's that sort of "over-zealous" that gives law-enforcement such a good name.'

Gobblod coughed discreetly. 'You have to be aware, Detective Strongoak, that Danwright Dollund was a well respected and highly valued member of the community and that his death has been felt by everybody, including my officers.'

'My client isn't exactly happy about it either.'

'She is still our main suspect. And as the Heartstone has not been found, suspecting an accomplice, my men have had her place of work on watch for the last two weeks.' He played with my badge as if advanced tinkering might just make it disappear.

'Obviously when they saw you coming out…'

'They just jumped to the wrong conclusion!'

'They were perhaps… precipitous.'

'Not to mention ironhanded and unprofessional.'

'The man in question has had some… personal issues recently and has been put on compassionate leave.'

'Great! I get the bruises, and he has time to tidy the garden!'

'Master Strongoak…'

'Master Detective Strongoak,' I reminded him.

'Yes, Master Detective Strongoak – it was… unfortunate.'

'No, missing a train is unfortunate. Getting hit by a train is very unfortunate. Being held down while a train hits you is just nasty.'

'And so, in the spirit of co-operation…' Captain Gobblod grunted in a rather unconvincing manner before continuing, 'it has been decided that you may accompany one of my officers who is now assigned full time to this important case to assess Mistress Diamond's culpability. You will be there, strictly as an observer, mind. It is my officer who will be in command at all times, and it is beholden on you to follow their instructions to the letter. Do you understand?'

I nodded.

'Do you understand, Master Detective?' he repeated more emphatically.

'Yes, I understand,' I said finally – but wouldn't you know it? I only had my fingers crossed behind my back! Naughty Nicely!

Gobblod pressed a button on the desk horn.

'Please ask Detective Analyst Grundrund to step in, Myla.'

And in Detective Analyst Grundrund did step, and a mighty big step it was. She was very tall and had masses of blonde hair swept-back like wheat in a summer storm. She was wearing leather trousers the colour of ox blood, so tight that you could hear trapped air particles squeaking when she moved. A long split-back burnt umber leather coat flapped like dragon's wings behind her as she strode in through the doorway. She was as impressive a figure as ever carried a Guard or Keep officer's badge. Detective Grundrund was also a goblin.

'Master Detective Strongoak, this is Detective Analyst Grundrund, one of my best people. She will be your liaison with my force.'

'I see,' I said, getting the picture straight off. Some help this would be, unless goblins had achieved a remarkable degree of emancipation in Kellisgrund!

'Detective Strongoak,' the goblin said, acknowledging me with a nod, her pronunciation perfect despite the slight lisp caused by the impressive fangs that overhung her bottom lip.

'Detective Grundrund.' I replied, in similar fashion – well, without the speech impediment.

'Please remember, Strongoak, that you are only here in an advisory role as a courtesy, following our little misunderstanding and to assist in your client's defence. Am I understood?

'Of course, Sir, and I'm sure that we both appreciate the effort you are going to.'

I stood and offered my hand. He took it, and we shook, both candidly acknowledging that we each had a job to do and sometimes that meant having to spend more time polishing the unicorn's horn than we were altogether happy with.

Grundrund turned first and strode out of her superior's room without another word. We walked down the stairs to the vault where the guard kept their wagons. I tried not to break into a run.

'We will take the unmarked vehicle,' she said, pointing. 'Remain inconspicuous.' I didn't recognise the make, but the wagon had a boiler big enough to power a street train and sufficient iron plating to protect it against anybody lurking with intent to wield a battering ram. There were chains on the wheels to help with the snow and chains on the doors for reasons that probably didn't bear thinking about.

'Ah, yes,' I said, 'the "unmarked" vehicle. No one will suspect a thing.'

'Gaddergast 4-0-2, good wagon. Sturdy.'

Grundrund took out a key that might have doubled as an anchor for a small sailboat. She opened the driver's door and leant over to open mine. I had just about had my fill of being driven around, but I thought I'd find another time, and person, to argue the toss with.

'I am a goblin,' Grundrund said, sitting, her hands relaxed on the wheel. 'Will that be a problem?

'No,' I said. 'And I am a dwarf. Will that be a problem?'

'We shall see,' she replied, with no trace of humour.

Pumping some steam, she drove from the Keep's lower level and out into the traffic with the confidence that comes from manoeuvring around in what is essentially an armoured siege vehicle.

We drove through the city centre on the main thoroughfare for some fifteen minutes before she spoke again.

'From Citadel, yes?'

'New Iron Town, then the Citadel guards – before I went private.'

'I did not ask for your life story,' she remarked, now turning off the High Street and onto the road leading to the seafront. In common with other coast towns I am familiar with, that road then led to the fancy estates dotted along the beach, like architectural pearls on a road tar string. All of them with prime views overlooking the Eskrag Strait.

Dwarf Girls Don't Dance

The wind now whipped straight across that stretch of water, and it carried hail that pinged against the plating like so much shrapnel. We continued to drive some distance out of town, and then we drove some more, and then some more for good measure. This was very desirable residential dirt indeed. The sort of places where the houses had landing stages that threatened to stretch right across the Eskrag Strait, all the way to Skragsrealm. And you could tie a small armada up on them too. In between estates, there were patches of boggy, unproductive looking land, which did not seem to deserve the name pasture, but animals were grazing out there. The largest deer I had ever seen, each equipped with a chime around their neck.

'Usk,' said Grundrund. 'Make good sausage.'

'They would certainly make a lot of sausage.' Of that, there was no doubt.

'I dislike the countryside.' Grundrund turned her nose up with distaste as she looked out the Gaddergast's windows at the flat land and fat deer.

'What, with all this good fresh air, warm sunshine and green pastures?'

'In Kellisgrund the air usually smells either of animal leavings or fish, the sun seldom gets warm and what you might think to be a green pasture would most often turn out to be a swamp and would suck you down.'

'Why not try for a transfer elsewhere?'

'Why would I do that? I like Kellisgrund – it is just countryside I hate.'

Eventually, we pulled up in front of a surprisingly modern set of gates. With the amount of metal involved in their construction, age wasn't going to add much more in the way of security anyway. The very large brick walls on either side were topped with lethal-looking barbed wraithwire, which was even more discouraging to the casual nocturnal visitor.

'Dollund House,' said Detective Analyst Grundrund, rather unnecessarily – I didn't think we had stopped for iced creams in this weather – besides you don't need that many bedrooms when you're dishing up desserts; not unless you offered extras other than berries and sprinkles.

The gates opened automatically, smoother than freshly-oiled wyrm skin. The Gaddergast 4-0-2 took us, purring like a large cat, down a drive long enough to warrant its own service station, and up to an entrance porch that could have sheltered a small hamlet from inclement weather.

'The rest of the Dollund family at home?' I asked the goblin, as she sprang out of the wagon, impressively agile.

'Family all have own homes,' Grundrund replied, in that clipped Kellisgrund manner that was getting just a tad annoying.

'How soon until I interview them?'

'After the funeral.'

'They're putting old man Dollund under the ground before the trial?'

Grundrund gave me a nod that managed to be clipped as well – barely a tilt of the head in my direction.

'What if my investigation throws up something that requires a further examination of the body?'

'There will be no need for further examination of the body.'

'And if I should happen to discover a pressing need to speak with the family before the funeral?'

'Repeating the question is not going to make it any more likely that I will change the answer to what you want to hear,' said Grundrund.

Dwarf Girls Don't Dance

So there I had it! I'd hate to see Detective Analyst Grundrund when she was not being co-operative.

'We do not miss things,' she added by way of explanation as she rung a bell that could have been heard in Skragsrealm and even made the usk look up from their nibbling.

The door was open by a housekeeper called Dorisk, who looked like she had been crying non-stop for the last two weeks. One person at least was missing old man Dollund as much as Diamond. Dorisk led us down a hallway, which, by itself, could probably have explained the paucity of trees in Kellisgrund. The wood-lined corridor led to a wood-lined office that was currently occupied by Dollund's gnome scribe Pentiant Ore. Pentiant had been mentioned in the documents I had finally managed to extract from Diamond's Arbiter.

Pentiant was of special interest to me, as apart from Diamond and the unidentified killer, he was the last individual to see Danwright Dollund alive. According to his testimony, he'd left Dollund Hall at around midwatch, to drive back to his rooms in Kellishaldt proper; a journey of some half an hour. He'd seen Diamond, still with Danwright, in his study before he left. In fact, he had said goodnight to her, none of which Diamond denied.

A distraught Dorisk had called Pentiant at first light after she'd noticed lights still burning in Dollund's locked study. Pentiant had immediately informed the Kellishaldt Keep and jumped straight into his wagon, arriving back at Dollund Hall scant minutes before the officers. Pentiant had found Danwright sitting in his favourite seat by the last embers of a fire, severely beaten around the head. His hands were tied, and he had choked on his own blood. No wonder Dorisk was still distraught.

All of this Pentiant repeated to me in a matter-of-fact manner that didn't seem to indicate a lack of feeling, but rather the sense that if he didn't deliver it so impersonally, he might start screaming and frothing at the mouth. With a side option of floor rolling on the cards as well.

Pentiant was rather a strange model of a gnome. No bright colour combinations or embroidered waistcoats he, instead, a rather sombre tailored coat and kecks combination, with a spread collar shirt sporting a fishbone knotted tie in a blue so blue you wanted to lie under it looking out for the occasional cloud. His boots were elegant rather than functional, with a neat three-buckle fastening that made me think about asking for the name of his cordwainer. On his curly head he wore a smoking cap in darker blue velvet. I suspected he lived with his mother.

Pentiant was civil, clear and precise in his replies and was in every way the perfect witness. As the late Danwright Dollund's scribe he was vital in keeping the administrative side of the business ticking over until the provisions of the will were read out. I got the impression that after that important event, he might take himself off and have a quiet and respectful nervous breakdown.

'What time did you leave, on the night before Master Dollund died please, Pentiant?' I took out a little notebook bought specially for the occasion. It helps give the right impression for some witnesses. I generally lose them almost immediately.

'We have asked all these questions,' Grundrund said.

'And now I will ask them again.'

'An hour before midwatch,' Pentiant replied.

'And was this your normal time for knocking off? Seems a little late?'

Dwarf Girls Don't Dance

'Master Dollund is not, was not, a morning person. It was not uncommon for me to be here that late. It works out well for me as I have an aged mother who needs a lot of assistance in the mornings.'

I nodded. A fastidiously dressed, gnome boot-fancier who lives with his mother – that filled in a few pertinent details about Pentiant.

'And how do you let yourself out?'

'There's a button on the drive that opens the gates and closes them automatically after you.'

'How about getting in at night?'

'Not after dusk, not without calling ahead and making an appointment.'

'And the rest of the staff leave before you?'

'Yes, all part from Dorisk, of course. She has rooms in the staff wing.'

'Doesn't seem an excessive amount of security, Pentiant?'

'This is very law-abiding country,' Grundrund chipped in.

'Not so law-abiding that old men don't get beaten to death in their own houses it seems? Which might indicate a requirement for a higher level of self-protection.'

'Unless the assailant was known and already here, of course,' Grundrund added, obviously not in a hurry to make any friends of the dwarf persuasion.

'Which I am ruling out, of course.'

Pentiant gave Grundrund a quick, questioning look that I was certainly going to explore later.

'And you were the first to see the body?'

Pentiant blanched slightly at the mention of the murder itself. I was sorry for his sensitivities, but his boss didn't expire through too much seafood.

He nodded.

'How come Dorisk didn't find the deceased?'

'The study door was locked. She doesn't have a key. I do.'

'And was your master's key found?'

'No key has been found,' Grundrund added.

'I was asking the scribe,' I reminded her. The scribe shook his head.

'And can you tell me, please, Pentiant, has Torfull Halfaxen been to visit?' I referred to the head of the dwarf side of the mighty Dollund and Halfaxen empire.

He shook his head again. 'I understand that Master Halfaxen has not been well, of late – he is, after all, no youngster, even by venerable dwarf standards. I am told that the whole episode has upset him greatly. The two families are, after all, very close.'

'How close?' I asked.

Pentiant coloured slightly before speaking. 'I have been told that there was some falling out between the first Danwright Dollund and Torfull Halfaxen, long before my time of course. However, relationship between Danwright Dollund the Second and Torfull have always been good, even given Torfull's ah…'

'Come on, Pentiant, spit it out! You won't hurt my feelings. I'm a big enough dwarf to take it.'

'Well, Master Strongoak – Torfull Halfaxen can be difficult; he tends to get rather… obsessive about things. He can brood on matters for months, years even. Something can happen, and you've forgotten all about it, but he comes back to you as if it happened last week.'

'My, my,' I said, eyeing the goblin. 'An obsessive ruminating dwarf! Who would have believed such a thing possible?'

'It is hard to credit,' Grundrund agreed.

'What of the son?'

'Heldwide Halfaxen has been to pay his respects to the family and ask if there was anything that he could do to help.'

'And was there?'

'You would have to ask the family.'

'Thank you, Pentiant,' I said, having learnt enough for now.

'If we could see the crime scene now, please?' Officer Grundrund obligingly asked.

The gnome took a set of keys from the drawer of his immaculately organised desk and led us back down the corridor to the master study.

We passed some impressive brushwork hanging off the planking, mostly depicting the history of 'Dollund and Halfaxen' and an interesting history it was. The Halfaxens were renowned as a family of jewellers and craft-dwarves, with a history as purveyors of the finest of Skragsrealm luxury goods. The Dollunds were upstart Kellisgrund traders, with a growing fleet of ships, but desperately in need of some class.

It was the murdered man's father Danwright Dollund the First who first approached Torfull Halfaxen about an alliance between the two families. The alliance became a merger, and the company became a major purveyor of luxury goods, with a high-end reputation. Dwarf skill and man's vitality combined, or so the story goes. Of course, such is the difference in longevity between the two races that the first Danwright Dollund has long gone to his reward, while the dwarf co-founder of the company is still very much with us. And now the son of one founder is gone, and Heldwide Halfaxen looks set to step in for his father, but who would be taking Danwright Dollund's place?

'Not too many goblins,' was Grundrund's terse observation as she passed the succession of paintings depicting the rise of 'Dollund and Halfaxen'. It was true, but hardly unique in that respect. At least they weren't being slaughtered, as you would have seen in many similar dwarf wall ornamentations.

The scene-of-crime was still roped off. The fire hadn't been lit again, so the room was chilly with the faintest spoor of death still in the air. The study wasn't huge, by the standards of the wealthy – on a clear day, you could see the far wall with no trouble if you squinted. There were a couple of comfy seats pulled up close to the cold fireplace, and lounging daybeds near enough in case activities required them. The desk wasn't so big that a dragon could land on it, but in some parts of Widergard, you would need to be careful about gnome squatters moving in underneath. The chair by the desk had carving so ornate that you might have supposed it had been spun by a wood-pulp spider. On the wall behind the desk was a painting. It had been hiding a large coffer, but was now hinged back to display the open coffer. I didn't need to get any closer to see that the coffer did not currently contain a fabulously brilliant diamond that the Keep Officers had somehow overlooked.

I moved around the desk to have a look at the subject of the painting – a portrait of a beautiful woman in the prime of life with the trace of a smile on lips that were made for smiling. The artist had caught a loveliness that went far beyond her luxuriant auburn curls, clear skin and piercing green eyes. Her mixed-race was also evident, but what her ancestry might have been was not immediately apparent. She had her hand raised to touch her silk gown right over her heart, as if she was about to present the watcher with something so precious that she cherished it beyond words – her love maybe? Hey, Strongoak – you're getting soft!

'That is Talensia Dollund, the wife of the elder Danwright Dollund and mother of the deceased. It is said he never, ever, recovered from her death.'

'So I've heard.'

'She was very much the matriarch of the family for many years and had considerable influence on her children and grandchildren.'

'It sounds like you approve?'

'Of course. If the example is a good one, and it is known that Talensia Dollund was in every way to be admired. She did good work.'

Thumb font powder was all over the place, but the arbiter had told me that nothing unexpected had turned up. I took in the position of the desk, facing the fire, but not the door and the opened wall coffer above it. Then I checked the coffer itself – a reputable dwarf make, of course. A Guklon 450, a coffer that I knew vaguely: key and combination job. The key could have been found, but presumably, the combination would have had to be beaten out of the man.

I had a little walk around, giving my dwarf senses and sensibility full rein. There was a pleasant spring to the patterned floorboards, which were in a beautiful selection of different woods. An intricate inlaid bursting sun design formed a centrepiece made from the most exotic timbers – good work, craftsmen who knew a thing or two about timbers had been employed here.

I had a quick look around the rest of the room. The windows were unforced, and the chimney had a grill of the type used to stop smaller miscreants. There was nothing in the furthest corners but frosty air.

'Any new light you can shed on matters, Master Detective Strongoak?'

'A little early to say, Detective Analyst Grundrund – but hardly the cut and dried case I was anticipating.'

'And that's your expert opinion?'

'It is my opinion.'

'And what would you suggest then?'

'I need to do a little thinking and maybe catch up on my sleep. It was a busy night – last night, I mean.'

'Yes, so I hear. I was not on duty.'

Which was as close as I got to an apology from anybody that day.

Officer Grundrund dropped me back at the *Skragshelder Inn* and brusquely wished me a good night's sleep. There was a message from Lippy at the front desk, dryly referring to his presence here all day today and my absence for the same period. The note accompanied a spare set of wagon keys. This was particularly useful, as the last thing I was considering at that moment was a good night's sleep.

I made my way to my room, which as Lippy had promised was functional but comfortable. The design was faultless, although perhaps a little soulless. I didn't imagine I would be spending too much time there, though. At least the windows had a good set of thick curtains – blinds leave too many gaps for inquisitive eyes. I closed the curtains against the night chill and put on a sidelight.

My trunk was where the inn runner had left it in the centre of the room, and I soon sorted out what I was looking for – which wasn't my sleep nightwear but clothes for a very different evening's activity. They came in black and had a matching hood and mask.

I made sure I had plenty of layers under them too, as that's always recommended for heat retention and I might be hanging around for a while. I put a top coat on over my more functional eveningwear and took the inn backstairs to their wagon park.

The Heslington 650's engine was still warm, and the wagon was fully fuelled and required little pumping. Thank you for putting in the extra hours, Lippy. Priming gave me just enough time to consider my options. I didn't know the town well enough to try anything tricky with regard to covering my tracks. Might I have a new shadow pinned on me? I kept my wits about me, and as far as I could tell, by the wagon's two rear mirrors, I wasn't being followed.

It seemed to take forever to get back to Dollund House. The Eskrag Strait was breaking up choppy, and enough spray was reaching the road, and me, to warrant giving the screen wipers some heavy exercise. They chased each other across the glass in the growing dark like two underfed bats. Outside the rain had changed to nasty big slushy flakes of snow.

I drove past the entrance gates to the house without slowing and looked for a place to pull up. I found a small grove that afforded some cover, but before I parked, I jumped out and quickly flashed my dwarf light around. After all, if I had found this to be a suitable hiding place, then there was no guessing who else might have used it before? Sadly the bad weather had destroyed any useful signs that might once have been there, and so I tucked the Heslington 650 quietly away and lit myself a pipe. I didn't open the windows. There are plenty of things around that rely on the nose more than the eyes. I did not want any unnecessary attention tonight.

I couldn't afford to wait too long, just in case Pentiant decided to knock off early. Reluctantly I left the Heslington's cosy interior, doffed some work gloves and shook off my coat. Now dressed in a figure-flattered, water-repellent, dark charcoal, I made my way back to the house gates. Of course, when I had packed my burglar outfit, I hadn't quite considered the fact that the ground might now be dusted with an inch or two of snow.

So, doing my best impression of a flitting shadow, and hugging what cover I could find, made my way to the gates.

There was a bush nearby. It was a thorn bush – naturally. The thorns were good at their job, properly pointy and penetrating. If only everything in life did their job as well as thorns, how much more orderly existence would be. My, but the life of a detective is just full of non-stop glamour. I shone my dwarf night light around again, but not even my eyes could see anything that looked like a clue amongst the spines and shafts. I climbed further in, got as comfortable as possible, and waited. I do good waiting. I'd win medals for waiting, if only they handed them out. They will one day – well, I'm still waiting for one.

I was just wondering if they were going to dig out deep-frozen dwarf here come the spring when I saw wagon lights coming down the well-laid drive. I attempted to rub some life back into my limbs; I might not have that much time to do what I needed to do. In the end, I needn't have worried. The massive iron gates swung open, and Pentiant's wagon drove majestically out, leaving behind a small fart of smelly steam and I had plenty enough time to slip through before the gates automatically came back together.

It was that easy.

I slipped back into the shadows, but Pentiant hadn't even slowed down to check behind him, because that's what folk do when they want to get home. Burglaries happen to other people, just like murders.

It was a reasonable dogtrot up to the house, but at least it warmed me up. Breaking into the house itself was more challenging. I had previously checked that the windows to the study were unforced and they certainly seemed intact, so I needed another point of entry. I found it in the coal chute.

Dwarf Girls Don't Dance

A lot of older houses have abandoned the 'black stuff' for their heating and gone over to more modern fuel alternatives. For the average burglar, this is a huge bonus, because householders seem to think residual coal dust is going to dissuade illicit night-time activities – far from it. The coal chute is an easy access point and, surprisingly, rarely considered worthy of being fitted with an alarm. The internal bolts that held the chute's cover in place would probably have been fitted when the chute was built. Although all the screws may have remained rust-free, the chances were that the masonry around the strike plate might well have aged.

I'd wondered if I'd find the coal cover broken, but it wasn't. The Kellishaldt Keep officers hadn't been that negligent in their search. Now I just needed to see if the internal masonry had remained strong enough to keep the strike plates of the bolts in place.

It hadn't.

Interestingly, when I got the chute cover open – the work of minutes with dwarf muscle – I noticed that the bolts themselves had recently been worked to and fro. Detective Analyst Grundrund investigating or something very different going on? The coal chute was a tight fit, but dwarves have flexibility as well as strength, just another reason why it's great to be a dwarf.

I shone my nightlight around the cellar, looking for footprints, but the floor was surprisingly dust-free. Somebody took housework very seriously. I then looked around for a coal-lift to the different floors. A house this size wouldn't run with staff walking up and down the stairs with full scuttles. The lift was where I expected, but it didn't seem to be in operation. There was precisely nothing else of interest in the cellar.

A small wooden staircase led to a locked door that was very soon to become an unlocked door. Now the fun could begin.

11

The Night Shift

I walked back into the late Danwright Dollund's study some half dozen hours after I last vacated it. I swung my nightlight around the room. Nothing had changed, although the heavy curtains had been drawn and the temperature had fallen. It seemed to have dropped a good ten degrees, but most of that was probably in my imagination.

It took a while to find what I was looking for; the house builders had been clever. The 'bouncy' inlaid floorboards in the sunburst design had to be pressed in exactly the right order. This I worked out by counting around clockwise first using Danwright Dollund's date of birth, then his wife's date of birth and then finally, and successfully, his eldest son's.

Folk are so predictable.

The last one was the capper, after that, the inlaid woods of the centre of the sun opened up like a flower to reveal the pleasingly round door of the real coffer set securely into the concrete floor.

I looked at it thoughtfully for some moments before I spoke: 'You're light on your feet for a large lady, Officer Grundrund, but you've got to work on the shallow breathing. They could hear you all the way back in Kellishaldt.' There was no response at first, then, finally, she stepped out from behind the curtains.

'And your dwarf lamp is as bright as day to me. Goblin night-vision is even better than a dwarf's.'

'It must be, because I certainly never saw you tailing me. Full marks for that.'

'Save your marks, Detective Strongoak – I did not tail you. I never left Dollund House.'

This surprised me, and I let it show.

'You knew I'd be back?'

'Oh yes, you left far too easily and too quickly, dwarf – and I do not think you are the sort of dwarf who requires many early nights'.

'I have my moments,' I insisted.

She looked at me levelly before speaking: 'Oh yes, levity with implied sexual content. I understand this.'

'Detective Grundrund, you sure know how to kill a good line.'

'Good,' she said with conviction. 'I do not have time for humour.'

'In that case, why don't we just turn on the main lights and make ourselves more miserable.' I walked over to the wall mounting, and flicked the switch on, turning to find Grundrund pointing a shooter the size of a small cannon in my direction.'

'Please!' I said, 'Shooters?! Officer Grundrund, now you're hurting my feelings! After we were starting to get on so well.'

She looked at her weapon, shrugged, and then holstered it carefully before coming to check the floor coffer. 'I looked everywhere, but could not find another coffer. What made you suspect this was here?'

'The coffer behind the painting, it's an elf's smile.'

'And what is an elf's smile?'

'It's a phoney – a deceit, meant to throw you off the track.'

'That comment could be considered now by many as offensive,' she examined the new coffer with the care of a dragon-slayer checking the fire-retardant properties of their new armour.

'Generally only elves,' I added. 'Why, have you suddenly got a dose of pointy-ear passion?'

'As an officer of the law, I treat all races with equal impartiality.'

'Of course, Officer Grundrund – I would expect nothing different. And, joking aside, my opinion exactly – but…'

'But what, Detective Strongoak?' she asked, straightening up.

'How many elves does it take to change a light fitting?'

'I do not know, Detective Strongoak, how many elves does it take to change a light fitting?'

'Only one, but they have to be able to speak goblin or gnome to get someone to do it.'

She grunted again loudly, at which point I realised that this was actually an appreciation of the comedy. 'A good joke, Strongoak and not without some truth, of course.'

She walked across to the previously opened wall coffer.

'I checked the manufacturer of this though. It is a good dwarvish make.'

'Sure, not too much wrong with the coffer.'

'Then, why were you suspicious?'

'You just wouldn't put it into a wall.'

'Why not?'

'Walls can be stolen.'

The goblin contemplated this idea.

'A good point. I will remember that.'

She returned to her previous position, looking down at the opened sunburst. 'And how did you realise this one's location?'

'The spring in the floorboards was missing over this area; there was certainly something more solid here.'

'I trod too heavily,' she rebuked herself, then squatted down and examined the new coffer door carefully. 'This is a better coffer, yes?'

'A Guklon 608 – top of the range – as good as they can get, and built solidly into a concrete base that is still going to be here when Widergard has been worn down flatter than an elf maid's tits.'

Grundrund nodded again, stood up, and then pointed to the floor strongbox. 'And what do you suppose might be in this Guklon 608?'

'I'm willing to put gold on you finding the Heartstone – all bright and shiny – and untouched by my client.'

'I thought you might say that. Did your client know the other coffer was here?'

I shook my head. 'Not as far as I know. Although she has seen the Heartstone – and recently. Dollund offered it to her, by way of a wedding gift.'

'Ah,' she exclaimed, 'that is interesting.'

'Isn't it just?'

'Can you open this – this Guklon 608?'

I looked down at the coffer's front door. 'This is a belt-and-braces job; you need the key and the combination and the right order to use them both.'

I sucked my teeth in the best goblin mechanic's fashion. 'You'd probably be better off trying to blast the door off with black powder. Of course, then they'd be no Dollund House left either.'

Grundrund took this all in her stride.

'So what do you think happened here? That the would-be thief beat up on the Elder Dollund to get the combination to the wall coffer, and then what? Lost his temper completely perhaps and killed the old man when the "elf smile" was found to be empty?'

'Not my job to figure that out, Detective Analyst Grundrund. My job is to get my client free from Kellishaldt Keep and from where I'm standing there doesn't look like much evidence pointing in her direction saying that she needs to be kept in there.'

The large goblin grunted again and stood up. 'No, not much evidence...' she said thoughtfully.

An uneasy feeling began to creep over me. 'Now, why do I feel that you're about to take my best shiny chain mail and trample it all into the mud?'

She grunted again before speaking. 'Do you drink, Master Detective?'

'It has been known,' I replied cautiously.

'Good, then we will go and drink beer.'

'Well, if you insist – but you should know, I rarely go all the way on a first date.'

'Ah yes, levity with implied sexual content again – do you not find it tiresome?'

'Not at all.'

'I see. It must just be me then.'

Which, I had to admit was a pretty good line, especially coming from a six-foot-plus, leather-clad, muscle-bound, blue-eyed, blonde-maned goblin.

We took her wagon. I wasn't given much of a choice in the matter. She assured me mine would be returned to my hotel –

maybe the local pixies would drive it? Then again this didn't really look like pixie country, too cold and blowy. A pixie wouldn't get fifty feet without needing to stop and refuel on high-grade nectar, which was in very limited supply. Hobyahs though, this looked a good place for hobyahs, crouching in hollows ready to jump on wayward strangers or naughty children. Oh yes, watch out there's a hobyah about.

Grundrund did at least let me pick up my topcoat, which saved me from looking too much like I was carrying a big sign advertising 'houses to be robbed wanted'. We drove back towards Kellishaldt, but took a turning off the main road inland and watched the house prices drop as we drove alongside a river that I'd barely noticed before.

'This is Kellismarsh,' Grundrund said, noticing my interest. 'And that is the Kellis.'

So, this was the mighty River Kellis, after which a port and a whole country was named and what a stinking ditch of an excuse for an inland waterway it was as well. As for the Kellismarsh, it was hard to decide where the land ended, and the water began, if water it was: as dark as a tax comptroller's soul, barely noticeable in the moonlight. I imagined fish inventing legs simply to get out of there.

A variety of ship hulks littered the ill-defined banks, all in various degrees of decay and looking like beached leviathans from the scary bits of the old maps. Most were actually reminders of the days of old, when men and dwarves of valour struck out to find exotic new lands, only to find that elves had got there first and were charging landing fees.

'It is best for strangers not to use this road,' Grundrund added.

'And why might that be?' I just had to ask.

'Because it is underwater at high tide,' she explained.

I looked out over Kellismarsh. What a midden it was. I could just see a distant line of lights which seemed to mark the position of another main road, but otherwise, I guessed it all looked pretty much the same as when us dwarves had moved out and left Kellisgrund to our new neighbours.

Our destination was built on stilts on a small island that barely warranted the descriptor 'landmark'. There was a large inn sign bravely blowing in the wind and on that was written: the *Mud Dragon*. Along with the legend, there was an interesting picture of a large ooze-impacted reptile – all unbelievably sized jaws, too large limbs and stunted wings – that I took to be the mud dragon in question.

'A mud dragon – I mean, really?' I said.

'Really,' Grundrund replied.

'Please! Are you telling me – an honest to goodness *mud* dragon?'

'Yes. And please do not ask me to repeat it again.'

And that seemed to be that.

There were only a half-dozen or so other wagons pulled up outside the inn, but when we did the short dash to the finely carved door and got inside, I was surprised to find it heaving. Maybe they ran a wagon-share pool.

We found a small table in the quieter end of the room, and Grundrund quickly ordered us two beers by the simple method of raising a single pierced eyebrow. She raised it with minimum effort, despite the amount of mug metal she had drilled into it – this was an eyebrow that expected to get its own way.

It was only safely seated, with a beer in front of me, that I realised the majority of folk in the room were goblins. Large grunts like Grundrund, clothed for action and featuring every type of body jewellery and needle paint, and plenty of smaller runts in the chalk-stripe suits they favour so much.

'Company satisfactory, Master Detective?' Grundrund said, attacking her beer with relish.

'Yes. Why, is there a reason it shouldn't be?'

'I know some of your brothers and sisters from Skragsrealm are smidge twitchy around goblin-kind.'

'Us New Iron Town dwarves are a lot more sophisticated. Some of us have even taken to using forks, as well as knives – at least for suppertime.'

'Good!' She took a larger slug from her beer, emptying her pot and then ordered us another two.

'Thirsty work hiding behind a curtain?'

She didn't answer. I needed to cut back on the small talk.

I downed my beer as well. It wasn't half bad. 'Thirsty work, creeping around in the dark.'

The barkeep brought more beers, and I lit a pipe while Grundrund puffed on one of those leafsticks that they prefer.

'So why don't you tell me why you've brought me here, safely away from any prying eyes and inquisitive busybodies, Detective Analyst Grundrund?'

'Evidence,' she said.

'Oh, yes?'

'I fear the Captain has not been completely… open…with you.'

'Oh yes?' I repeated, pitching the directness of my tone up a notch or two.

'There might be some… evidence… that has not been brought to your or your client's attention.'

'And what about our arbiter's attention?'

She shook her mass of blonde hair. 'I am not sure about that. But… he could possibly know.'

'Oh!' I sipped my second beer. 'That doesn't seem to be very sporting now, does it? He's supposed to be on our side for a start, plus your captain told me to my face that he was going to offer every assistance he could, and I kind of think the law requires that too.'

'Not until after this evidence has been processed.'

'I see. And might this hypothetical evidence be taking a very long time to process?'

'Oh yes, a very long time. They like to be thorough.'

'Perhaps since the day of the actual murder.'

She nodded.

'Well, that does seem to be a long time, doesn't it? And you're telling me this why?'

Grundrund had another long drink and looked around the room. 'Did you know, Master Detective, there are ten times as many goblins in jails as all the other races put together?'

'I didn't – but I'm not surprised, to be honest.'

'No, me neither,' she admitted. 'And all because the goblins will not learn the laws or learn to obey them.'

'And why do goblins not do that?' I asked, genuinely interested in her answer.

'Yes, it's a good question,' she said, her voice taking on a note of irritation. 'Because assuredly so many never do!'

'That sounds like personal experience coming out there.'

'I do not mind admitting that my father headed up a particularly notorious gang involved in smuggling, and worse, concentrated around the Kellishaldt dockside.'

'An activity that didn't appeal to you?'

Dwarf Girls Don't Dance

'No. He was stupid. I am not stupid. The laws are not difficult, and it is actually much easier to operate within them.'

'Why do you think goblins don't – mostly?'

'Because the elves made them,' she said without hesitation.

'I can see how that might do it,' I had to admit.

'It is stupid and we are not a stupid race. Sometimes I despair of goblin-kind!'

'But you believe in the law, personally, I mean?' I asked.

'I do!' she banged down her pot, causing a couple of glances to be shot in our direction. 'I do believe in Law. Very much so.'

'Because it applies to everybody the same?' I hazarded a guess.

'Exactly, Master Detective! I thought you would understand. Even agree.'

'Perhaps I do at that.'

'In the eyes of Law, goblins are everybody's equal!'

'And there is a law that says that evidence should be shared with the defendant?'

'There is! So, if – for example – a glove was found at the scene of the crime, then the defence should be aware of this.'

'I couldn't argue with that,' I admitted. 'What sort of glove, exactly?'

'The sort of glove a dwarf woman wears.'

I felt a very cold sensation in the pit of my stomach that had nothing to do with the beer. 'Why a dwarf woman?'

'The long kind of glove that many now wear to protect their nail designs that are so popular.'

'Nails designs?' I had to ask for some clarification, a little confused.

'You do not date much do you, Master Dwarf? Or is it that you don't date your own kind much?'

She had me there – but dwarf women are not exactly thick on the ground in the Citadel. Which, perhaps, partly helps explain what I was doing here.

I grunted.

'Elaborate nail designs are very much fashion for dwarf women,' she explained. 'With different coloured enamels, engravings and even inset stone. Many of your women have therefore taken to wearing of gloves to protect these investments in body decoration.'

'Okay, and one was found at the murder scene then?'

'Oh yes, and covered in blood on the knuckles. It is being tested now – a very long procedure it seems; explaining why there has been no obligation to tell either you or your client.'

I chewed a nail, as if by reflex. Diamond wore gloves; she took them off too. I'd never thought through the possible ramifications.

'So Skunglard – does he know?'

'They say that the assignment of arbiters to cases is completely random, Master Strongoak. It would be terrible to believe it could be otherwise. That some form of corruption could take place, do you not agree?'

'Without the faintest wraith's breath of a doubt.'

'The law is there for everybody, Master Strongoak – goblins and dwarves.'

'It surely is,' I agreed.

'And it should be respected.'

'Especially by its Officers.'

'Especially.'

I wouldn't go as far as to say we were bonding, but I liked this law-abiding goblin and so proceeded to reciprocate on the free exchange of information. 'Danwright Dollund asked Diamond

Dwarf Girls Don't Dance

to marry him, that's why she'd seen the Heartstone – it was offered as a betrothal gift.'

Grundrund took this in her stride and then gave it some serious thought. 'And there is proof of this?'

'If we find the Heartstone, there should be.'

'Who knows of this proposal?'

'Officially?'

'Yes.'

'Just you, Officer Grundrund, a goodwill gesture from my client.'

'Which probably should be confirmed I think before it is reported to my superiors.'

'Oh, most certainly I'd say.'

'And to do that we need to open the Guklon in the floor?'

'It would seem the easiest way.'

'Have you any idea how we might do that, Master Detective?'

I smiled my best smile. 'Funny you should mention that, Officer Grundrund, but I do. I don't think it's going to contravene any funeral formalities if we pay Torfull Halfaxen a visit is it?'

'Torfull Halfaxen?' she exclaimed, raising both eyebrows. 'Why Torfull Halfaxen?'

'Apart from wanting to know how he has taken the death of his partner – the Halfaxen Company bought Guklon Coffers way back when Torfull was a nipper.'

'I see. I see. Making Torfull the most likely source for a top range Guklon coffer?'

'The nail right on the head is banged.'

'It would mean going to Skragsrealm.'

'It would indeed,' I agreed. 'They do say that you have to travel to know more about where you came from.'

The large goblin looked at me strangely.

'They also say that nothing beats travelling for reinforcing your prejudices.'

'Very good! I've not heard that one before!'

The detective stroked her chin, reflectively.

'We hear that there is quite a lot of activity of wrong sort in Skragsrealm and Skragslanding these days.'

'Oh really?'

'They have put a tough new Captain in charge to sort things out.'

'Think it'll work?'

'It might,' she said with a laugh. 'It is a woman! Sadly, not a goblin.'

'No, I don't think that would get the dwarf vote.'

'More fool them. I am just wondering if, under pressure, they might now be exporting their crime.'

'That, my dear detective Grundrund is what I would call a thought. Now, drink up, we need another beer.'

We had another beer and then another – it was good beer, and I was warming to the company. I caught the big goblin glancing at the chunky watch on her wrist, so rugged that it would undoubtedly be able to operate at the bottom of the sea, and probably at the bottom of a volcano too. Something that might have been second cousin to a frown hurried across her brow.

'I hope I'm not keeping you, Officer Grundrund?'

'It is no matter,' she replied. 'I was just hoping to have sex this evening.'

As conversation stoppers go that one takes a lot of beating.

We drank up.

I made a call of nature on the way out. It's always an education to see what is scrawled up in the local boghouse – but apart from a few choice words about the sexual availability of certain members of the local community, and the national leaders, the goblins of Kellishaldt seemed a fairly content bunch. That was probably a good sign, at least as far as Kellisgrund was concerned. The future of government is written on the boghouse wall.

Grundrund was out on a jetty built over the sluggish dark mass that was the Kellis. I joined her. She stared on impassively out over the water.

'Do you think you could swim to the other side of the Kellis, Strongoak?'

'Why, considering throwing me in?'

'It was a serious question.'

'Maybe – yes, probably.'

'Seriously?'

'Well, I wouldn't actually be doing it with a smile on my face.' Grundrund gave me a very solemn look. I continued, 'but, unlike many dwarves, I don't have an absolute distrust of water. I save that for elves.'

She made a small grunting noise. 'How about swimming the distance under the water, Strongoak?'

'I'll pass on that.'

'A trained man can hold his breath for just over eight minutes when under the water. A gnome for seven minutes. Did you know that?'

I shook my head.

She looked at me questioningly, 'I have heard that dwarves can hold their breath for twelve minutes?'

I nodded then in affirmation. 'But not when swimming.'

'Ah, I see! Well a goblin,' she continued, 'a goblin, this goblin can hold her breath for over twenty minutes. A goblin could make that swim.'

I looked impressed. I was impressed. We walked away from the jetty.

'And how long can elves hold their breaths then?' I just had to ask.

'Not known, nobody has ever tried to drown an elf to find out,' she replied.

'Now that I do find hard to believe.'

Grundrund repeated that small noise that I now knew was as close to a chuckle as you were likely to get from her. We walked back off the pier to find her wagon. A group of goblins were messing about near the Gaddergast 4-0-2, walking on some narrow planks across what looked to be a particularly nasty stretch of boggy ground.

'Suck-mud, you'd disappear in a moment,' Grundrund explained before haranguing the hotheads in no uncertain terms.

One, obviously the wannabe leader gave her some lip back.

'What business is it of yours, gazzloxk?'

I had no idea what a gazzloxk might be. Grundrund did. She lifted the young goblin from the ground, one-handed, and proceeded to give him what might under other circumstances be called 'a clip around the ear'. This clip nearly took his ear off. She then threw him to the ground. He didn't want to get up.

'Why risk your life being stupid? Suck-mud can take you down in minutes. That's if the mud dragons do not get you first.'

Grundrund let his friends collect the prone goblin, and the group staggered off together.

'Fools!' Grundrund swore, getting into the wagon. 'Young male goblins, sometimes they refuse to use the brains their mothers gave them! Most would rather sit on a street train going to the wrong place than ask for directions.'

'Young males of any race surely?'

Dwarf Girls Don't Dance

'Goblins are worst! I teach my children not to be so stupid – not to disadvantage themselves because of ridiculous notions they are told concerning how they should be.'

'You have children?' I asked, suddenly feeling rather light-headed.

'Of course,' she said firmly. 'It is sensible to have your children when you are young, when you have the energy required for their upbringing.'

'I see.' And so then I just had to ask the obvious: 'And is there a husband and father at home?'

'Oh, no. That is not a requirement for successful upbringing of children.'

'Right!' I breathed a sigh of something strangely like relief.

'And is there a Mistress Strongoak and little Strongoaks?'

'No,' I conceded.

'Then you must hurry up. You are not getting any younger.' Grundrund looked at her big chunky watch before then asking: 'So, have we done enough bonding now to form an effective team?'

'Oh, plenty,' I replied quickly!

'Good,' she said, pumping the wagon. 'This has exhausted my supply of small talk.'

Grundrund drove me back to the *Skragshelder Inn* for some much-needed sleep. I lay down on the inn bed, but my mind wouldn't stop racing. Concern for Diamond was already forging some strange connections in my thoughts and questions were flashing up like fireflies in a spring sky.

Diamond didn't kill Danwright, so who did, and how and why?

Was the Heartstone actually even in the coffer?

They were all good questions, but they felt like the wrong questions. So how could any answers help? Maybe tomorrow would yield some results, or maybe just more questions. Hopefully, the right ones at least.

Grundrund and I set out early to avoid the rush. There was a lot of daily traffic, especially of men and women going to work in Skragsrealm, where wages are higher, but accommodation is at more of a premium. We took the Skragsrealm-Kellisgrund Unity Tunnel.

The idea of joining Kellisgrund and Skragsrealm across the ten-mile Eskrag Strait, and hence linking the two lands, had first been mooted many, many years ago. Dwarves and men threw the idea backwards and forwards like an iceball for a few decades, discussing designs, locations, and most importantly, who would pay for a bridge or tunnel. In the end, it was agreed to build a bridge. A design of profound beauty was decided upon, which, even as a model, was praised for its elegance and splendour, with cable-stays thicker than dragon legs and mighty support towers like the fortresses of old.

The dwarves of Skragsrealm went ahead and built a tunnel.

Dwarves prefer tunnels, they're better at tunnels, and you don't get so much weather in a tunnel. What's more, the tollbooths are on the dwarf side of this particular tunnel. It was named the Skragsrealm-Kellisgrund Unity Tunnel, but everybody still calls it 'the Bridge'.

We plunged into the enormous mouth of 'the Bridge' without slowing – not that we had exactly been speeding. Traffic in Kellishaldt didn't speed.

The journey gave me more than enough time to be impressed by the dwarf construction work. Beautiful masonry joints showed not a trace of moisture, and there were even some impressive decorative features – well impressive to dwarf aesthetics anyway. Reinforced buttresses and elegant struts and stays with just the right amount of carvings.

In hardly any time at all we were through and rising rapidly back onto more reassuring fully dry land. I enjoy a tunnel as much as the next dwarf, but when they run under large amounts of water, you can't help but get a little queasy. Enormous fans pull out the stale air and fumes, but you still wouldn't want to linger in the Bridge, so we didn't.

I wound down the window as we approached daylight at the end of the tunnel and slowed for the tollgate. I was immediately hit by the smell of dockyards full of exotic goods and spices, dried fish and the sea. Kellishaldt was very much a river port, but Skragslanding definitely faced the sea. Its fragrance was a heady cocktail once sampled, never forgotten. And, like a sea mist disappearing on a mid-summer's morning, I felt twenty years roll back in the blink of an eye.

I was in Skragslanding for the very first time, a younger and more optimistic dwarf.

BOOK TWO

12

Skragsrealm

I had only been in Skragsrealm for a fourteen-night, and I was already beginning to think the move from New Iron Town might have been a bad idea for this wannabe private operative. I was even wondering if my whole desire for a career in law enforcement was a ridiculous fancy. I'd enjoyed my probationary years in the Iron Watch well enough, and getting my detective badge had been a breeze. But by then, the tribulations of the civic establishment were feeling a little too commonplace and parochial. Even the offences were getting too familiar: the Rage-fuelled homicides, the blood-disputes and the lust-crimes; dwarves can be a predictable bunch sometimes. Yes, it was good to do my best for the common good and help lubricate the workings of the fine municipality, but I'd just about had my fill of stupid axings and greedy gropings. And so I decided to go private and try my hand in that capacity elsewhere, in the port of Skragslanding in the Old Dwarf Kingdom of Skragsrealm.

Skragslanding seemed like a good choice of location to set up business. Skragslanding was one of the main towns of Skragsrealm, and there would be plenty of dwarf trade to provide me with breakbread-and-butter work and, as a main port as well, there was sure to be some more exotic employment to keep me fully entertained. I'd briefly considered the very multi-racial Citadel as an option, but rejected it as being too uncertain a location for building up regular clients. I knew that Skragslanding was home to many races other than dwarves: men, gnomes, tree-friends, even trolls and goblins now made a living in the built-up area that flourished around one of the safest harbours in the Northern World. Not too many elves, from what I had heard.

Shame!

Still, with this volatile mix, there was sure to be plenty of employment for a keen up-and-coming young detective and Shield-for-Hire. Or so I was hoping at least.

The reality was that Skragslanding smelt. It smelt mostly of fish. Not that dwarves are particularly great fisherman, but having such a marvellous natural anchorage means that you can make a decent living by charging other folk for the pleasure of landing their fish.

That is a very dwarf thing. We can put up with a pong for that!

Skragslanding also had the stink of corruption and vice that goes hand-in-hand with a major port and the flow-through of large amounts of gold.

Don't get me wrong – I'm not saying there is anything particularly more corrupt about my fellow dwarves than other races, in fact, I would say we rank higher on the virtue scale for courage and honesty and modesty than many. I didn't mention elves directly there, did I?

The halls and chambers and palaces and galleries of the Old Kingdom of Skragsrealm are some of the most safe, law-abiding and decent places to be found in Widergard; which is why so much of the other stuff has been shovelled down to Skragslanding. I had anticipated this. This was why I'd assumed that there would be a need for my services after all. I just didn't realise there would be quite so much waywardness! So much villainy and debauchery, in fact, that it seemed almost redundant for anyone to try to amend or address any particularly criminal act that seemed likely to go unpunished or even acknowledged. Old goblin gangs flourished, and regularly added to the fun and games of an evening by beating each other up. Of course, there are nice parts, there are nice parts anywhere if you have the gold, but down in the docks life was often brutal and short – and smelly. I did mention the pong didn't I?

I was brooding on this very thought in a quayside inn with the jolly name of *The Blind Cow* when I became aware of some noisy activity in the end room. Lacking any other entertainment, I picked up my pot of ale and went to have a look.

There were a couple of dice tables in the room and at one of them a young man, with curly auburn hair and an engaging smile – probably the younger son of a local big-wig – was playing skulls and bones. He was winning, and he was winning big.

It's a simple enough game played with five normal six-sided dice that each have three sides with grinning skulls and three with crossed bones. The trick is to get a full set of either, and the skill is to bet on how many throws, after the initial roll, it will take you to achieve this. The rest of the table bet against you. Hit it right, and you clear up, get it wrong, and you pay out in accordance with how under, or over, your target you were. It's a good game for losing a lot of money quickly and just occasionally for winning a packet too. This young man had enough corn in front of him to start a chicken farm.

I looked carefully around, searching for the likely lads. There are always likely lads hanging around when somebody is winning big. I spotted three of them, seated together at a corner table, one sporting goblin fangs. He was a good bit shorter than a normal grunt and wider than most runts – a nasty looking piece of work judging by his scars. The other was beat up worse than a bat in a blender and weaselly in the way that gives weasels a bad name. The last lad was a well-built Easterner. He didn't have any scars, but he did have the sort of self-satisfied smile that made you want to give him a few. They all had a touch of the sea about them – too many ports, too much cheap drink and too few aspirations. They were ignoring the gambler in exactly the same way everybody else wasn't.

That was their first mistake.

Their second was drinking in the same inn as me when I was looking to make some money.

Their third mistake was passing their wine bottle anti-clockwise; don't you just hate that sort of breach of manners?

The chicken farmer was drunkenly collecting his spoils, buying the inn a round of drinks in the process, which always goes down well. I didn't stay to get my beer topped up as the short grunt and the weasel had already moved out ahead of the victorious dice player. I waited until the Easterner followed Curly to the door.

The ploy was simple. The flush young merry-maker would be staggering around looking for his wagon, key in hand. The Easterner would then approach him, usually to ask for a light or directions. Next, the other two would jump out from where they were hiding, and together they would roll the victim for his purse and whatever else he had about his person. If he was lucky, they wouldn't cut his throat.

Dwarf Girls Don't Dance

In The Iron Watch Instruction Scrolls, the way of dealing with such a situation is very clear. Officers are to approach the assailants, after it is clear that an offence is about to take place, make their identity known, give two verbal warnings and only then, if unsuccessful, apprehend using minimum violence. The problem was, I wasn't in New Iron Town, I wasn't an officer any more, and I don't think these likely lads were going to be put off by the force of my personality. More importantly, there is a very thin line between 'offence about to take place' and 'bleeding with life-threatening wounds'.

Therefore I did what the action the instruction scrolls don't suggest, but you soon pick up after a few months of Guard Patrol. I pre-empted the situation. You can pre-empt the situation either by removing the potential victim from the hazardous situation, which usually means having some transport, or option two: you wrap a boardball stick around the knees of the stalker while throwing flammable cleaning fluid into the faces of the other two assailants. The boardball stick, of course, doesn't wrap well, but the crack of breaking knee is very satisfying.

"They can't run without their knees," as my old Physical Activities teacher was oft fond of saying.

The cleaning fluid, removed from behind the bar, satisfactorily distracted the other aggressors – they really do mean it when they write 'Keep Away From Eyes' on the bottle. More importantly, this then enables you to throw a lighted match at the more dangerous of the pair, while attending to the other with two solid boardballs swung in the sock that you had slipped off under the table.

The whole exercise need only take a couple of minutes. Then you can be away with the unhurt, grateful, not-victim, driving away in the wagon that they had nearby, which – if he looks well-insulated enough – would have auto-prime.

Unfortunately, the swinging sock only gave the weasel a glancing blow, and he was back up on his feet in seconds. The grunt in the meantime had found a horse-trough to put his burning hair out and was not well pleased.

I mean, honestly, a horse trough!

Only in Skragsrealm would they keep a horse trough about the burgh! The crippled Easterner was urging his friends on with what I can only describe as intemperate language, but wasn't inclined to get to his feet any time soon – if ever.

The weasel had a knife; weasels like that always have knives. I didn't even see it magic into his hand. The knife looked sharp enough to split leather without taking it off the cow. His eyes, fortunately, still weren't working well. Little grunt was by now roaring towards me, and things were getting out of hand.

Fortunately, the designated 'soon-to-be' victim hadn't read the script, or at least objected to his role in the play unfolding. He applied a reassuringly chunky bottle of spirit, which had previously been nestled comfortably in his coat pocket, to the weasel's knife arm.

Ouch!

The bottle didn't actually break or even make much of a noise, but must have hit something sensitive because the weasel dropped his knife with a loud curse. He turned angrily to Curly, which was a mistake, as Curly still had the bottle in his hand. Curly swung the aforementioned chunky bottle with the considerable strength of the totally bladdered and this time the glass receptacle did make a noise when it connected. A very satisfying, but hard to describe crack, which might just have been the sound of a jaw breaking. I'm guessing that this was the case because Weaselly was now clutching his face in agony.

The grunt by then was close enough to run his groin right into my boot, so he did exactly that –with my assistance. It was all far too much fun, but we needed a hasty departure before our luck ran out, or reinforcements arrived.

'Where's your wagon?' I asked with some urgency, very conscious of our assailants, even if two out of three of them weren't properly conscious at all.

He looked at me with a pair of the greenest eyes I had ever seen and pointed vaguely with his remarkably still intact bottle of spirit. 'It's a Red Dragonette '32 – wonderful bodywork don't you know?'

'Certainly do,' I said, grabbing his arm and leading him urgently in the direction he had indicated. 'A very beautiful piece of work, the Dragonette.'

'Should be hereabouts,' he waved the bottle again. 'Wonderful wheels – my favourite ride and I've got six– or is it seven? You know I really can't remember?'

'In which case, how about loaning me one?'

'Certainly, my dear dwarf friend – no problem at all! Let me know what colour you fancy and it's yours.'

I looked at him to see if he was serious – I really couldn't tell. Perhaps he didn't know either.

'Oh, look! There she is now!' Curly pointed to a Dragonette parked nearby; it was indeed a lovely set of wheels and redder than a ruddock's breastplate.

Curly approached with the caution of the crocked, and I watched him fumble for his keys before, coughing discreetly, I suggested: 'How about I drive?'

'Splendid idea! Absolutely splendid!' He threw the keys in my direction, and I picked them out of the air with no trouble.

'Jolly good reactions, wouldn't do to give my ride to a drunkard after all.'

'But you were happy to get behind the wheel yourself?' I asked, opening the driver's door and getting in. I reached over and flicked the passenger latch up – Curly fell in.

'Ah, but that's different,' he replied. 'I knew I was drunk!'

I couldn't argue with that logic, so I pumped minimal steam – blessings on auto-prime – and let the Dragonette tick over for a minute before asking the obvious, 'So where to then?'

'Well, home, of course!' he answered.

'And where might that be?'

He blinked a couple of times, before replying: 'Don't you know who I am?'

'I don't know you from the Rat Catcher's recorder teacher, on account of you not having introduced yourself.'

'Splendid, absolutely splendid!' He laughed again, although I couldn't see the joke. 'You can call me Duffy – absolutely everybody does! Assuming they're not slower than moatwater that is, and whom might you be my noble rescuer?'

I handed him one of my nice new cards, which he just managed to focus on. Carefully he read the legend aloud: "Nicely Strongoak, Detective and Shield-for-Hire." Marv'lous! And what exactly does a Shield-for-Hire do?'

'Takes care of folk.'

'Like you took care of me?'

I gave my best impression of a modest shrug. Then added, by way of an explanation, 'they were watching you win at dice. You might be advised to keep your good fortune a little quieter in the future?'

Dwarf Girls Don't Dance

'Now where's the fun in that, eh?'

'There may not be someone around to help next time.'

'A good point!' He considered this for a while, a variety of expressions chasing themselves all around his easy good looks. 'In which case, I think I would be well advised to hire myself a shield.'

He put his hand into a coat pocket, pulled out a fist of crumpled notes and waved them in my general direction.

'No thanks,' I said. 'The first time is always free.'

'Ah, just like moondust!' He snuggled into his seat and closed his eyes before murmuring quietly: 'Carry straight along beach road until you come to a small palace. Got more scary water-spouts than a busy night at the sexual disease dispensary – that's Laskgard Lodge. Can't miss it. Ring twice, somebody will come fetch me. Bring the wagon back next time. G'night, Detective Strongoak.'

And with that, he fell fast asleep, and I had found my inaugural position as a private operative in Skragslanding and new wheels to boot.

I followed Duffy's directions. This was my first time driving in Skragslanding, and I got a whole new perspective on the place. The berg really was an interesting mix: solid stone dwarf buildings interspersed with higher wooden affairs probably built by men, some exotic (to my eyes) elfin creations and even blocks of crowded gnome burrows. Not a spot of flat land was wasted, not a spot was without its own history, and not a spot was where you wanted to be hanging around on a wet winter's night.

Duffy was right; you certainly couldn't miss Laskgard Lodge. It was a fair heap of stone, put together with equal measures of creativity and eccentricity in a style I would call mock Dwarf Hall. Basically, the effect is to make the building look like it has been carved out of solid rock when actually there isn't any mountain present. I rather liked it.

The night had turned grim and the waterspouts were, by then, working overtime. Hideous contorted faces leched and leered and sent the water streaming well away from the valuable masonry. And what a lot of masonry there was.

Two rings at the lodge doorbell brought me the attention of a doorman who had seen it all before and engraved it on a series of runestones as well. He was tall and grey with the demeanour that I had already learnt was typical of the men of nearby Kellisgrund – and he was drier than a desert pisspot. He took one of my brand new cards and sighed professionally.

'I found him in a dockside inn,' I explained to the doorman, as together we hauled the unconscious man from the Dragonette's beautifully tooled, passenger seat.

'Yes,' he replied. 'It is surprising what one can find in those places. I blame the lack of fibre in the diet. When I was younger, we ate a lot of lichen, very little trouble then. Yes, more lichen in the diet is the answer.'

'He said I should hang onto the wagon,' I explained. 'On account of the likelihood of him needing my professional services as a Shield-for-Hire in the future,' I added, as we attempted to support the now bone-less man by putting his arms across both our shoulders. Our height difference made such an operation pretty much a non-starter. Duffy wasn't tall, but there certainly was a considerable height difference between the doorman and me.

'A very good idea,' the doorman said, as we manoeuvred Duffy back onto the car seat to attempt his transportation in some other manner. 'It undoubtedly makes sense to consolidate such supervisory activities into the one role, leaving me to wipe his outhole when he is at home.'

I took Duffy's feet, trying not to laugh, while the doorman picked up the thinking end. 'Do I take it that you are not enamoured of Master Duffy's evening perambulations?' I was obliged to ask.

'Master Dwarf,' the old man said, fixing me with a stare that had taken in far too many grey northern winters. 'I would happily lay my life down for Master Duffy, and I love him more than ever a father ever loved a son because I do not have to worry about seeing my own worse characteristics displayed in him. But occasionally, especially on nights like this, I could happily hang him from an iceball hoop and use him for target practice.'

By then, we were in an entrance lobby that was not only larger than my current set of rooms; it was probably larger than the house that contained them.

'Now Master Dwarf, if you could help me carry him through to the library, there is a good fire in the grate. I know from experience that he won't do anything ridiculous, like trying to educate himself.'

I did as requested, and we settled Duffy safely on his side, covered with a rug obviously already there for that very purpose.

'Thank you, Master Strongoak,' he said. 'The family lawyers of 'Murko and Murko' will be in touch tomorrow, just to formalise the understanding. They will provide you with a contract and contact details for me, if necessary.'

'And what do I call you?'

'Why, I am Jeskyn, Master Strongoak.'

'Thank you then, Jeskyn.'

'My pleasure. Now I must wish you a good night, and I hope that this will be a satisfactory arrangement for all parties concerned.'

Jeskyn gave me a short bow and then showed me out. At the door he offered one parting shot: 'And the best of luck, Master Strongoak – which I sincerely hope you won't need.'

I drove home in a red '32 Dragonette with auto-prime and silver trim and was feeling pretty pleased with myself. It lasted all the next day as well.

13

The Nine Idlers

'Master Dwarf, I hope I find you well?'

Duffy had an attractive voice, just right for the speech horn. He could have sold fright masks to a goblin, not that he needed to sell anybody anything – not personally anyway; people did that for him.

I had spent the previous day doing a little research on my present employer. It transpired that I was pretty much right about Duffy, except he was the eldest son, not youngest. The heir to some company based in nearby Kellisgrund that was so famous for selling expensive things that I'd never heard of them – not being a particularly well-travelled young dwarf, or that well insulated either. I presumed the family elders had packed him off to Skragsrealm because he was less likely to cause serious trouble here in the years required to exercise the youth out of his system.

The local social scrolls were certainly full of him, and I also learnt a lot about who in Skragslanding has been seen with whom, and where, but not why I should care a pixie's fart about any of it. His wagon I could get to care about. It was the drive of a lifetime.

'Good day, Duffy. How may I be of service?'

'Just wondering if you would swing by the lodge around first watch tonight. We'll be having cocktails and then heading on out with my crowd to a jolly-sounding event in aid of – one moment, please.'

I could picture him with his hand over the speech horn while he asked the ever-attentive Jeskyn exactly what charity he was 'aiding' this evening.

'Of course,' he said, back on the line, 'the event is in aid of "disadvantaged dwarves" without their own transport – or so Jeskyn says. Though I do believe he may be making a joke at your expense.'

'As you're paying for both his time and mine, it's probably at your expense.'

'Good point. Jeskyn you're fired!' There was a pause at the other end while Jeskyn responded and then Duffy came back on.'

'Apparently, he can't be fired as I'm going out this evening and won't be able to find my own footwear, let alone wipe my own outhole. Very colourful vocabulary, our Jeskyn.'

'He does have a particular way with words. And will we be taking the Dragonette? Only we might just be able to squeeze the Lady Willow in the back seat, but nobody else.'

'The Lady Willow? Very good.' He did actually sound impressed. 'You've been doing your homework.'

'I wouldn't be much of a shield if I couldn't tell your friends from your enemies.'

'Then that is a skill you must teach me!' he said, with a laugh that sounded just a little forced.

'Sometimes,' I said carefully, 'a little distance is all that is required.'

Dwarf Girls Don't Dance

'Indeed! Well, don't worry, it's all friends tonight – time for you to meet the "Nine Idlers"!'

'Right.' I said, letting not a trace of hesitation creep into my voice. 'The "Nine Idlers", that will require a larger wagon.'

Duffy laughed enthusiastically. 'It most certainly will! We'll take the Fallingsturger, and you can pick the Dragonette up later.'

I was about to ask exactly what a Fallingsturger was when Duffy hurriedly wound the conversation up: 'Thank you for this, Nicely – must rush now. Jeskyn is going to need to organise some bog-leaves.'

He put up the horn before I had got my Fallingsturger inquiry out or was able to ask about dress codes. The last one was awkward. I didn't want to put on my party frock if I was going as the hired help and would end up sitting in the kitchen. In the end, I didn't really have much choice. I hadn't pitched up from New Iron Town with a full wardrobe, and a guard's wages don't stretch to made-to-measure anyway.

I do have a decent eye for a well-cut piece of cloth, even lacking the proper budget, which means I tend to spend the odd half-day looking in tailor stores for 'no-shows'. Most good tailors in major towns, invariably run by successive generations of gnomes, have a back room filled with suits at various stages of completion that customers have never come back for. Maybe the wedding fell through, or maybe they were knocked on the bonce and dragged off to a slave mine in the Farthest South. These things happen, I'm told.

I'm not the only dwarf to know this of course, but I am very tall for a dwarf, and that means they can usually find me something of quality that might have been cut for a stocky, short man. And I don't have to cough up the whole hoard for it either.

Happy ending.

So as soon as I was able, after first arriving in Skragslanding, I had a good look around and found the *Gumbersolo Brothers*. A wonderful place, the *Gumbersolo Brothers*, not just multi-generational, but multibrothered too: a thriving and enthralling hive of gnomic industry. And in their back room, they found me just about the most enthralling garment ever: a double-breasted, silent check, three-piece, bum-freezer, with six pleats and narrow turnups on the kecks. It was weather-proofed and fully insulated to withstand more degrees of frost than you could ever conceivably expect to experience, while wearing a three-piece suit, that is. I had no idea who might have ordered it, and it's poor form to ask, but it was perfect for the tail-end of a Skragsrealm winter that was refusing to let go of the weather and allow spring to bring some relief to the hard-pressed locals.

So in my Gumbersolo Brothers special, I took the Dragonette out for a steam to Laskgard Lodge to meet the Nine Idlers. I wasn't paying for the fuel, and the road had been ploughed and gritted, so I decided to open her up and see what she could do.

She could do a lot.

I soon found myself at the impressive gates of Laskgard Lodge. I don't know how I had failed to take in their fabulousness the previous night. I mean, copulating dragons captured in wrought iron – not something you see every day, not even in Skragsrealm.

The wagon circle at the end of the Laskgard Lodge drive was blocked by something that looked like a cross between a siege wagon and a mobile home. This I surmised was the Fallingsturger. Either that or the Midwatch Express from the Rust Hills had been seriously derailed and was currently parked out front. I don't know why they just didn't hold the party right here inside the Fallingsturger. There was certainly enough space and what it, perhaps, lacked in charm, it certainly made up for in durability.

I arrived early and was immediately told I was late. I didn't argue, as it's bad form while the rent is due. Jeskyn wasn't really chiding anyway, just giving me the heads up on Duffy's organisational skills.

I left the Dragonette and hopped into the Fallingsturger's driving seat. While I was adjusting the seat and mirrors, and wondering about little things like turning circles, a bejewelled rabble of men, elves and gnomes seemed to explode through the Lodge's front door and spill into the vehicle that I was currently trying to get to grips with. The Nine Idlers had obviously already started doing their bit for charity, if the charity was actually the 'Brewers and Distillers Benevolent Fund'. They had all donated heavily and, judging by the bottles and flasks carried on, would continue to do so for the rest of the evening. Well prepared against the bar running short, you have to admire that kind of thinking.

'Off we go, Master Strongoak!' shouted Duffy.

I started the Fallingsturger. It made a noise I can only describe as throaty. I carefully manoeuvred it down the drive and got it out onto the main road without destroying the gates. I would hate to sard the sarding dragons. Despite Duffy's protests the Idlers all refused to remain seated and that, in conjunction with my desire to keep us safely on the road, prevented me from taking stock of who exactly the Nine Idlers were. Names were thrown around, including one 'Princess', which I took to be a pet name – but who knows?

I concentrated on the road, which was rising gradually to a large ridge that over-looked Skragslanding and hence boasted some splendid views right across to Kellisgrund. Just right for those that didn't require easy access to the beach or quayside. Our destination certainly had a view and a tower for every day of the week, in order to do the viewing.

It wasn't until after I had safely deposited the revellers at the event (which, somewhat improbably, had something to do with supporting the orphaned children of kelp farmers), and parked the Fallingsturger, that Duffy was able to give me the full low down on his friends. As I had sort of suspected, I was not in the kitchen with the hired help.

We sat at a 'reserved' table, in a prime position, of course. Duffy sat back, pulling on a tapered, oval-shanked Ranger, sending a fine smoke-ring ceilingwards and then, smiling, considered his friends out on the floor. They were dancing in a style that might best be described as 'larking about'. All except for a silk-robed woman, of indeterminate age, with long fine hair, who stood by the edge of the dance floor clapping delightedly along at the antics of her friends.

'So, let me tell you about the Nine Idlers, Nicely.'

'It's not in the contract,' I replied.

'No – bear with me. You'll see why. First off – and this in no particular order – is my gnome friend Bergerollo, or Berger for short.' He pointed to where the gnome in question was currently trying to slow dance a statuesque leather-dressed warrior woman in a manner that was not at all right considering their height difference or the fact that the band was playing an up-tempo number.

'He seems to have his hands full,' I casually observed, trying not to sound too coarse.

'It may not be obvious, but in my humble opinion, Berger there is the greatest artist of his generation and possibly the most important of the Age.'

Dwarf Girls Don't Dance

Duffy must have noticed my eyebrow leap up like a homecoming salmon. 'I kid you not, Nicely – he might even be redefining exactly what it means to be an artist.'

'Now, that's something you don't hear every day.'

'Indeed not.'

I looked on with new interest at the small gnome currently recovering from a playful slap from the raven-haired warrior-type that had sent him flying, much too everybody's obvious amusement. Duffy shook his head in mock despair.

'He does keep trying – who knows, maybe one day he might succeed.'

'Maybe.'

'Do you like art, Master Strongoak?'

I took a bite of my fruit cocktail. I take the job seriously.

'When I have stains on the wall that need covering,' I admitted, 'but I would say my taste is pretty traditional: scenic landscapes, small children with big eyes and blood-soaked battle scenes featuring triumphant dwarf armies slaughtering thousands of the enemy – you know, popular art.'

Duffy laughed. 'I think perhaps, Master Detective, that you like to put on something of an act, yes? To play the part of the barbarian, while hiding the true, more thoughtful, dwarf inside.'

'Unless the act is getting people to believe that the outer barbarian hides something else other than an inner barbarian.'

Duffy laughed again, expelling more smoke.

'Either way, Duffy, collecting art has not been top of my list of priorities I have to admit.'

'Well, Master Cynic – you must get Berger to show you his studio. Also, I have several pieces of his at Laskgard Lodge. You might want to consider an investment.'

'So what about his dancing partner?' I asked, anxious to move the subject on before Duffy attempted to improve me further – I was beginning to think I preferred the drunk gambler.

'The warrior princess?'

'That's the one.'

You really had to admire this tall, muscular woman with a mane of dark hair that just demanded to be called 'raven'. She wore large, heavy bracelets and the obligatory leathers that tend to go with raven hair; in this case, tanned a blue so dark it almost qualified as raven too. Fortunately, her eyes were of a lighter shade of blue that looked exactly like the sea off the coast of Skragslanding never would. These were the colours of seas much further south than I had yet to venture.

There was a lot more scrap metal distributed over the rest of her body that might have provided some sort of protective function, but most likely was just there to look really intimidating.

'She's a Warrior Princess,' said Duffy.

'Uh, didn't we get rid of all the royals?' I ventured. 'Put them into a hole in the ground somewhere in the Desolate Wastes?'

'So they say – but I don't think the word ever reached the Princess's part of the world, which is so far to the east that you've probably started coming back around again.'

'A long way from home then?'

'Oh, yes. Skragsgrund was about as far as her family could send her, after the unfortunate incident with the over-amorous Prince and his half-dozen bodyguards.'

'The real thing then,' I said, rather amused and also slightly awed. 'Warrior Princesses really do exist?'

'Oh, yes, Master Dwarf.'

'Suddenly Widergard seems a whole lot better place.'

'I agree.'

Dwarf Girls Don't Dance

We both considered the other options and found them wanting.

'Apparently, the Warrior Princesses would be sent into battle first, along with their all-women company, as a goad to the enemy – a way of saying 'we think so little of you we can't even be bothered to send out our men to defeat you'. The enemy would fall into the mistake of trying to crush them with an under-manned troop and find most of their best soldiers wiped out.'

'As a way of toughening up the girls in the family, it probably beats embroidery.' I observed. 'And you just call her what?'

'Princess.'

'Really?'

'Yes, really we do, it's what she prefers – and who are we to argue?'

An admirably well-groomed and well-dressed figure waved casually at us as he led a flaxen-haired woman around the floor in an energetic caper that managed to combine maximum effect and minimum effort.

'What's the story with handsome there?' I asked.

'That is Luce,' said Duffy in a tone that spoke of admiration and something else I couldn't identify. 'Luce the Balladeer.'

'Really? And is he good at his job too?'

'The best I have ever heard. And he can fill a room without any boosting of sound as if he's just singing to you alone; bring the audience to tears or make them smile like babes, and he seems to do it without even raising his heart rate.'

'Well, I'll look forward to hearing him then. Does he know the one about the dragon hunter's daughter?'

'I'm sure he does.'

'All 56 verses?'

'He probably wrote 54 of them – a wicked and rather coarse sense of humour, our Luce.'

'Excellent!'

'The only problem with Luce is actually getting him to sing these days. He's always finding some excuse or other to not take to the stage.'

'There's something almost, without wishing to be insulting, elfish about him? A bit too pretty?'

'That would be Bardic blood,' he replied, explaining exactly nothing to me.

'And that means?'

'The Bards were said to once be as powerful, as important, as wizards are – or were – at least.'

'Really? I find that hard to believe. Minstrels?'

'It's true, Nicely. In fact, it is suspected that bards share a common ancestry and could draw on a similar source to wizards for their abilities.'

'Well, doesn't that just pin the tail on the dragon!'

'It is said that once upon a time, the power of a bard's voice could level mountains.'

'A nice analogy, Duffy.'

'Or maybe more. Is the power of a spell in the words or the voice that says them?'

'I'll let you know when I see one that works!'

Duffy laughed. 'Well, they say that when the dark powers first grew, one of the first things they tried to do was kill all the storytellers, as they feared their skills nearly as much as magic. Many, many bards were slaughtered, and some say the bloodline ran thin and so the stories concerning the power of the bard's died out too.'

Dwarf Girls Don't Dance

'Certainly never made the dwarf histories – at least not the ones I got taught.'

'No? Well, every folk has their own storytellers, of course, but to those who heard them, the bards it seems were…' He hesitated.

'Something of a race apart?'

'Exactly and Luce, in my bones I do believe, will one day be a talent worthy of a story or two himself.'

'And how about his attractive dancing partner?'

'That is Mansel.'

'She seems to be very happy there, basking in his glow.'

'She does, doesn't she?' Duffy took a drink. 'The thing is this – Mansel is a treasure – and a treasure trove heiress.'

'Lucky Luce?'

'You'd hope so. However, Luce's gold is all in his voice and fingers. That is a fortune beyond measure, but Mansel's parents don't understand that sort of currency.'

'Oh dear, what does Luce think about that?'

'It's hard to say what Luce thinks about anything.'

'A problem?'

'Not really, it's just that our Luce is not a straightforward character and there are additional complications.'

'Such as?'

Duffy coloured somewhat – to his credit. 'Mansel's parents and my parents – they have been friends for many, many, years and when we were both born – well, it was hoped, perhaps more than hoped…'

'Yes,' I said innocently.

'Please, Master Detective! Do not make me spell it out! Mansel and I are good friends, like brother and sister, but nothing more than that. Never can be!'

'Which brings us to the Lady Willow.' I looked at the slim blonde elfin figure as it effortlessly made its way around the dance floor accompanied by a rather less elegant sober-looking man Duffy identified as Osk. 'Not really sister material is she, Lady Willow?'

Duffy's colour went up a notch or two more before he spoke. 'Not, mine anyway.'

'Then what's the problem?'

Willow sent a dazzling smile in our direction, sadly not for my benefit.

'She obviously doesn't exactly hate the sight of you, Duffy.'

'Her parents – Willow's a full blood and an only child. They are very protective.'

'And they're here, are they?'

'The Citadel.'

'That's a long way away.'

'Yes, but she was sent here to keep her away from temptation – not engage with it.'

'I see, well relationship counselling isn't exactly part of the job, but if you ever need an outsiders view…'

'Thank you, Nicely.'

'And how about Osk?' I looked at the sturdy figure, still concentrating his way around the dance floor.

'My best friend from childhood.'

'Any romantic entanglements? Brilliant talents? Under a sorcerer's spell maybe?'

Duffy laughed good-naturedly. 'None of the above. Osk is over here in Skragsrealm completing his studies – some day he'll be running my father's estates in Kellisgrund.'

'You mean your estates?'

Duffy looked at me strangely, 'not the way I'd put it, but yes, I suppose so.'

'Perhaps not from the same sort of background as the rest of you?'

'Luce's family aren't rich or powerful,' Duffy explained, 'if that's what you are insinuating. Nor are Berger's for that matter. We're not that sort of group!'

'Hey! Just an observation – no criticism intended. My occupation depends on a surplus in the economy that allows folk to indulge in interests other than survival.'

'You're forgiven then.'

'And the tall, elegant woman I saw earlier, with the long straight brown hair?'

'That is Sansire,' said Duffy – his voice tinged with respect.

'So, what's Sansire's story?

'Yes, what is Sansire's story?' said a low, quiet, feminine and faintly amused voice from about two inches behind my left ear.

'What does she bring to the party?' I said, not missing a beat.

'She is a seer,' replied the quiet yet attractive voice.

'Well, there is a thing! A genuine far-spy, eh? Not many of the genuine article around these days,' I added.

'We prefer the name seer, and yes I am the real thing, Master Shield-for-Hire who did not seem to hear me walk up right behind him.' Sansire didn't sound impressed.

'Now, if that was the case, Mistress Seer – I wouldn't be holding this shooter in my right hand under my left armpit, would I? It's a small weapon – called, rather crassly, a "one-shot", but it's no less deadly because of that. And it is pointed directly at your heart, which would be a shame, as it would ruin a perfectly good jacket. But you knew all that didn't you, Sansire, you being a genuine far-spy and all.'

Duffy choked on his drink.

'I told you he was good, Sansire!'

'And for your information, Mistress – it wasn't your footfall that gave you away. It was your otherwise rather lovely and distinctive perfume, and that's the main reason we are not currently trying to plug the flow of your blood with this otherwise perfectly functional tablecloth.'

Sansire came around to join us, not at all at a loss. She looked at me evenly. Up close, I could see that she was probably a lot younger than I had first assumed, perhaps the youngest of the group. There was something about her looks and manner that made her exact age hard to place. One second, she looked like a young child, the next like the oldest sage. Yes, I realised – she was certainly the real thing – or as close as you were going to find in this Modern Age.

'And would you have shot me, Master Dwarf?' she asked, her voice like her looks, in possession of an elusive ageless quality.

'It wouldn't have made me happy,' was all I gave by way of an answer.

14

The Foreshadowing

'Moving on then,' said Duffy, pouring some more drinks for the seer and himself, while I sipped my fruit juice.

'Moving on,' I echoed. 'I'm wondering why the 'Nine Idlers' – who don't actually seem that idle by the way – are only eight in number? And not a dwarf in the mix, which seems strange considering we are in Skragsrealm.'

'Very well worked out, detective,' said Duffy, uncomfortably. 'We did, do, have another friend, a very good friend. A dwarf in fact, by the name of 'Buns', but we don't see him anymore.'

'So, what happened?' I pocketed my one-shot very deliberately. 'If it's any of my business, which I feel it probably is.'

'What happened,' said Sansire, 'was that I had a foreshadowing.'

I was heading into deep water here, and I didn't have my inflatable sprite wings with me. 'So,' I said finally. 'I'm guessing that it isn't looking like pastries and posies for everybody in the future?'

'One of us is going to die, Nicely,' Duffy said, coughing back a small catch in his throat. 'And I have a nasty suspicion it could be me, which I would rather didn't happen – and I'd like you to do something about that, if it's all the same to you.'

'That sounds eminently reasonable – all part of the service. Perhaps a few more details might help, mind.'

'Of course,' said Duffy, exchanging a glance with Sansire.

The band, unfortunately, decided that now was a good time to take a break. The elated dancers came back to the table, and the conversation was curtailed at Duffy's request. More drinks were ordered, but I'd had enough fruit for one evening – us Dwarves can make everything we need naturally without the requirement for oranges or limes or even sunshine. Clever us, eh? We do usually require a regular intake of ale, but I was taking this job seriously, and it sounded like I needed to as well.

'Oh, my dear fellow,' said Berger as he sat, noting the lack of the brown stuff in front of me. 'I can see from your expression that you are a dwarf after my own heart and that the restraint on your ale consumption is most trying. However, look on the bright side!'

'Which is, Master Berger?' I asked.

'More ale for me!' he said, jumping up and running off again to freshen up his tankard.

'I don't know where he puts it,' the Princess said ruefully.

'Hollow legs,' said Duffy.

'Hollower head,' Luce observed.

The chatter flowed freely like that all the evening. If the company intimidated Osk, he certainly didn't show it. He was fully a member of the fellowship. They were a likeable crew as well, young with enough gold kicking around not to have to worry about little things like the drink's tally.

It was rather disconcerting to have been told that one of them had an appointment to walk with the wraiths. I didn't know how the mechanics of far-sight worked, but if this result could be avoided so much the better. I'd do my best, that was for sure.

Dwarf Girls Don't Dance

The next dance, when the band got back from their pipes, was a slow number, and Duffy took Willow's arm, while Mansel and Osk had another spin after Luce did not take Mansel's hint. Berger meanwhile was turning a cloth into art with various items from the finger-bar, to everybody's amusement.

I took the moment to ask Sansire to dance. She was surprised, but said yes – generating much amusement from those left behind.

'You are light on your feet, Master Dwarf,' she observed after we had completed our first circuit.

'Please do call me Nicely, otherwise I'm going to feel like I should still be wearing the driver's cap.'

'I'm sure you'd look very smart in it.'

'Oh yes,' I replied. 'I wear hats well, but putting matters millinery aside, how about you give me some more details about this foreshadowing of yours?'

She sighed heavily. 'I really wish I could, but it's obscured.'

'How so?'

'I think, but I'm not sure – magic is involved.'

'Magic? Involved in the murder?'

'Yes. I'm sure. It's put something like a curtain over the whole episode. It's so frustrating – I can't tell who is killed or who the attacker is. I just know that the nine of us are together and Buns is right in the centre of everything. Dressed strangely, I can see that, but I see him quite clearly – and there is the undeniable taste of death. Then the screaming starts, followed by the crying.'

'And why, Duffy?'

'Because I am with him when the fear starts. It's horrible.'

'I'm sure it must be,' I said sincerely.

'It's why Buns went off – he figured that without him there was no chance of the whole terrible affair ever happening. No 'Nine Idlers' present, you see? And he would never take a chance on any of us getting hurt, especially not Willow – yes, especially not Willow.

'I'm sorry,' I interrupted. 'Do you really keep saying "Buns"?'

Sansire coloured rather prettily, 'it was a pet name – you know how unwieldy some of these dwarf names can be?'

'But "Buns"!'

'As I pointed out, he has very nice buns.'

'Dwarf's do.' As if to emphasise my point, I exercised a rather nice turn at the end of the dance floor using my buns to maximum effect before I continued.

'I still don't see why Duffy is so convinced that he is the victim?'

'Maybe it's because he's at the centre of our little group and… because I don't feel his presence afterwards.'

'Axes and blood! So he is killed?'

'No – it's not that easy. He could be there, but different.'

'Sorry – you'll have to explain that.'

'Something big that changes somebody, it makes it hard to pick up their "signal" – to use a modern expression.' She looked down at me. 'It isn't all bad; marriage will do that to a person too.'

'I see – dead or married – good stuff this farseeing.'

'It's only because of the magic,' she said rather crossly. 'It's all over the vision, like the smell of blood – old magic, bad magic. I've never felt anything like this before and, Master Dwarf, it scares me!'

'My apologies, Sansire. I can see that it does indeed worry you. It worries me too. I'm just wondering what we can do to prevent it happening.'

'Me too, Nicely. Me too.'

Dwarf Girls Don't Dance

We finished our dance, which as dances go was not at all a bad thing. Of course with that particular pixie now out of its cage, everybody wanted a dance with Nimble-footed Strongoak. The Princess was first. Fortunately, it was a formal number, called the Wizard's Three-Step hereabouts, but known to both of us by different names. It meant that we could make with the footwork without any embarrassing incidents. I didn't fancy the sort of slap Berger had shrugged off.

As if she was reading my mind, the Princess spoke, 'I don't bite Master Detective!'

'Oh, I don't know about that, Princess! Berger seemed well-bitten.'

Princess found this very amusing. 'He is a bad boy, that Berger! He likes the large women, and he sees me as a challenge, I think.' Her accent was what I can only describe as 'cute'. Quite a contrast to the metal and leather!'

'And he enjoys "seafood" as well,' she added. 'Does that translation work?'

'Yes, Princess – I get your drift.'

'Now, I think I have made the mistake!'

'Not at all,' I replied hurriedly, trying to get my mind away from the physical presence of the six-foot, well-muscled, but remarkably well-shaped, royal warrior in front of me.

'What do you think about Sansire's vision, Princess?'

She shrugged without missing a beat. 'I think it does not matter.'

'And why's that?'

'Because if anybody tries to kill my friends, I will kill them first.' She unintentionally gripped my hand, and it knew that it had been gripped.

'Apologies to the hand, Master Dwarf.'

'Nicely, please call me Nicely.'

'Good, I will call you that then. It is a nice name. Better than Buns.'

'And how well did you know, Buns?'

She took a moment to consider. 'Not very well. We only made Big Sleep together once. Is that also correct?'

'Princess, you said it!'

'It was fine, but I think he really had cow eyes for the Lady Willow – he would get very hot in his parts in her presence.'

'Boy, Princess – your language teacher must have been working overtime with you.'

'Oh yes, we worked a lot of overtime!'

I decided at that point that I really needed to question the Princess under different, less intimate circumstances. The Princess passed me on to Mansel, and the band moved on to a number that was, apparently, based on a Kellisgrund folk song. It was up-tempo and jolly. I don't really dance up-tempo and jolly, and neither did Mansel. I also had the feeling that the Kellisgrund folk could not really write up-temp and jolly either, but by the second verse, we had trod on each other's feet enough times to relax and begin to enjoy the idiocy of it all.

'You're not like Buns at all,' said Mansel, slapping her right foot with her left hand in what seemed to be the required fashion, before hastily adding, 'Sorry that made it sound like I think all dwarves are alike; which I don't, of course! Not really. No reason they should be is there?'

I raised an eyebrow at this.

'Oh, dear! Look, can you help me out here please, Nicely? Before I dig myself a trap so deep a troll couldn't climb out.'

'How would you describe Buns then, Mansel?'

'Very serious, very determined – even about having a good time'. We both stopped and slapped our left feet with our right hands. 'I remember him saying once, "tonight I will get very drunk", and he did – just as he'd planned.'

'And a man wouldn't do that?'

'Get drunk? Oh yes! Of course, a man would, but I think it would always be more spontaneous, just to let it creep up on them, as and when the need took them.'

'I've known dwarves like that. Probably too many.'

'Who would plan for like a military manoeuvre?'

'Yes. Like Duffy has done in the past too?'

We both, on cue, executed a strange posterior wiggle that was probably as unattractive as anything you will ever see on a dance floor, this side of a ghouls' masked ball, but when done on mass is strangely endearing.

'I'm sure I don't know what you mean, Master Strongoak.' Mansel said finally, dropping the temperature a few degrees.

'Well, he hasn't employed me for the odd occasion he might have supped a stoop or two too many. Sometimes when Duffy goes out for a drink he doesn't intend to come back without a beard, does he? And I'm not interfering here, but he's employed me to look after him, and I intend to do that to the best of my ability. Plus he seems a likeable sort who doesn't deserve to be carrying the weight of the world on his shoulders.'

Mansel thawed rapidly and stopped dancing. 'Oh, foodally! I've had enough of this stupid tune!' She held out her arm. 'Let us partake of the night air, Master Dwarf – before we rejoin the others.' I led her out to find a quieter spot.

The air we partook of was of the regulation Skragsrealm vintage, complete with the lingering twang of the sea and the things that swim and crawl in it. We were out on a terrace that provided a rather spectacular view over Skragslanding. For the first time, I began to appreciate what attracted folk to the town and, moreover, what made them stay. Twinkling below us, Skragslanding looked exciting and adventurous and full of possibilities. What more could a young dwarf in search of a new vocation want?

Mansel had rescued us a couple of drinks on the way out: beazer teasers with something a little red and sticky in them that bubbled up in a pleasing fashion.

'They're called "Fire Mountains", Mansel explained. 'The red is blood-fruit spirit.'

I had a small taste – lovely. I could see I was going to have to get used to a different class of drinks in this company. I'm adaptable.

'Wonderful,' I said, carefully putting the glass back down. 'However, I am driving and shielding Duffy.'

'Of course.' Mansel looked off into the distance. 'He wasn't always like that. Duffy, I mean. With the drinking, it's only since he met Willow.'

'I see, and how does that make you feel?'

'Me?' she sounded genuinely surprised. 'I'd like to see Duffy happy, of course. He's like a brother.'

I looked more closely at the young woman. Her curly blond hair gave her an air of frivolity that she didn't seem to fight to contradict. Her rosy cheeks gave her an almost indecent appearance of good health. She seemed to be exactly what she was, a fun-loving young woman with no responsibilities or wealth problems.

'I know I'm not deep,' she said, as if reading my mind. 'But I'm not stupid either.'

'I didn't think you were, Mansel.'

Dwarf Girls Don't Dance

'I worry that Luce does. He's so talented, so insightful.'

'Mansel, I think deepness is kind of over-rated. I'm not deep either, but I'm pretty wide, and I'll take width over depth any day.'

She laughed, in her natural, unaffected manner. 'I like that, may I use it someday?'

I bowed. 'Of course.'

'Thank you, Nicely.'

'Could you just tell me, didn't your parents have hopes of an alliance, a romantic alliance between Duffy and your own family?'

She gave another small laugh, 'That was never going to happen, was it? Duffy always saw me as something of a little sister. He never got on with his own, you see. No, that was a non-starter.'

She finished her drink and looked seriously at me. 'And I'm afraid you had better speak to Willow about why Duffy disappears off for days to dockside inns.'

'I will.'

'Don't leave it too long. I think those two could do with some impartial advice.' She laughed again in her unselfconscious way.

'Oh, listen to me, won't you? Don't I sound just the very pith of sagacity? Whereas everybody knows I'm just a poor little rich girl with less brains than a boobel.'

I really wanted to know what a boobel might be, but Mansel was up and away. We went back in, and the band broke out into something with a bit more rhythm, and the gnomes on the cans started laying down some slippy beats. I approached the last skirt wearer of the group.

Willow, of course, danced like a dream. She was not that tall for an elf, and every step was a positive joy. She was as light in my arms as pixie dust on a snowflake. I hadn't much experience of elves, there weren't that many in New Iron Town, and they certainly didn't get into trouble or cause it. Most of my impressions were ill-informed by the old stories and gripes, and they are pretty one-sided affairs I have to admit. But I always try to leave any prejudices aside when dealing with any race other than my own and have got on well with men, gnomes, goblins and even the occasional troll. Willow didn't make it hard for me to seriously reconsider any personal negative elf policy. After the fleet-footed escapade, we stayed on the floor for a slower number.

'Duffy told me you were from the Citadel, Lady Willow. Is that right?'

'Close by, anyhow. It's better that way. Living on the Hill can get rather stressful at times.'

'The Hill?'

'It's what they, I mean we, call The Citadel — on account of it being built on a mountain. The name tells you something about the attitude and humour of the inhabitants, I think.'

'Sounds like my kind of place, my lady.'

She gave me an appraising look. 'Yes, I think you might like it very well, Master Detective.'

'Nicely, please.'

'And you must call me Willow. Yes, I think you would fit in there, Nicely. The Hill is very gregarious, sophisticated in the true sense — and above all it's fun!'

'So why are you here then, Lady Willow? If you don't mind me asking?'

'My parents think it's too gregarious, sophisticated and fun! So they sent me here! Which they considered to be the very opposite.'

Dwarf Girls Don't Dance

'To do what exactly, or are you really one of the 'Nine Idlers'?'

'Why no, they sent me here to write! I'm a poet, Master Dwarf – did my fame not precede me?'

I didn't even pretend to be scolded. 'Lady, unless it has five lines and involved the daughter of a local tradesman I'm not likely to know any of your poetry.'

She laughed in a way that should come with health restrictions, certainly if you're driving afterwards and need to watch the road. 'Ah, such tales of the offspring of merchants and retailers have sadly past me by, but there really is no need to feel dull – this is elf poetry and is considered fairly impenetrable even by many elves.'

'Are you any good then?'

'Oh, straight to the point there!' she pondered, as I spun her around and back into my arms. 'Am I any good? Well, some folk think so – or that I show promise, which is as close to good as you are allowed to be at my age. And so to develop that promise and to keep me away from the distractions of the Big Bad Citadel my parents sent me here.' She looked across at our table, where Duffy was cracking open another bottle of bubbles.

'The irony being that it is here that I met Duffy. Exactly the sort of "distraction" my parents were most concerned about.'

'Which feels like the real thing, I take it? The full "moon and June" those poets write about?' I said, trying not to let a hint of envy enter my voice.

'Yes, as you say, the full "moon and June" that those poets carry on about, Nicely. You have hit the distraction nail bang square on the obsessive head. The poet in me is very happy about that, but the rest of me is very sad.'

'People marry out all the time, Willow.'

'Not in my family, Nicely. Not in my family, they don't.'

The band finished with a flourish and announced a break for supper, which sounded good to me. The 'Nine Idlers' were all for going on to a new nightspot that had just opened – the *Tipsy Troll* or some such rhubarb. While they were making up their minds, I grabbed a few of the local sausages and put them in some breakbread to soak up all that fruit juice I'd been imbibing. In the obligatory absence of ale, a sausage wrap was exactly what the inner dwarf required. That went down so well; I added another half dozen to the sausage patrol.

A dwarf cannot have too many sausages, and I had a feeling it was going to be a very long night. I wasn't wrong: the Nine Idlers knew how to party, and they liked to practice. We got a lot of practice during that long winter and sudden spring.

15

The Eagles

'The Eagles are coming, the Eagles are coming', came the cry, with the sound of stamping feet and the smacking of shieldwork – audible evidence of the massed battle happening in front of me. Thousands of voices then raised together in unison: 'The Eagles are coming!' And they were, and they did, to great effect.

The 'Skragslanding Eagles' iceball team wasn't messing about! A rapid series of passes, some deft skating and the iceball was through the hoop and the bell rung! The cheer was not just enough to raise the dead, it could have sent them out to complain to the Noise Abatement Fraternity about the racket disturbing their rest.

Iceball is principally a Kellisgrund sport, but with so many men living in Skragslanding it wasn't surprising that they had a local team: the Skragslanding Eagles. So when the Kellishaldt Wolves come across the Bridge to play against them, the competition is beyond fierce. For the Nine Idlers, the rivalry was equally intense, as the favours were evenly split. Duffy, Osk, Willow and Mansel were for the 'Wolves', while The Princess, Luce, Berger and Sansire favoured the home team.

The match had attracted a large and diverse crowd – men, goblins, gnomes and the occasional troll. There was even a smattering of blond-heads that I assumed belonged to elves – Willow aside, I didn't know elves were sports fans. And, shouting loudest, a whole bunch of dwarves – all Eagles fans of course. They were cheering most enthusiastically for one particular dwarf out on the ice: Skragslanding Eagles' lead-skater Delvefar 'The Axe' Deepmine. Although the shortest figure skating, what he lacked in height, he more than made up for in stability. It seemed, despite some serious attempts, nobody could overturn Delvefar – and boy could he jump! When he was flying through the air to make a catch you did not want to get in his way, or you would certainly learn why he was called 'The Axe'.

Iceball had never made it to New Iron Town, where the dwarves favoured more traditional sports such as competitive spear throwing and wolf hunting – usually at the same time. To me, the whole iceball thing seemed to be an excuse for exercising the lungs and elbows. A very good excuse – indeed, I might add, I quickly began to see the attraction. Most of the Idler's activities up until then had revolved around nightlife, but they all took the afternoon's iceball very seriously.

Iceball is played on a long-frozen stretch of water with two posts at either end. The goal is simple: to throw the iceball (originally actually that) through a hoop to ring the bell behind it. Five skaters per team and each player can only hold the ball for five seconds before passing, a period usually counted off by the more-than-willing spectators – all pretty straightforward and simple.

How do you get the ball from the opposition?

There's the fun.

Dwarf Girls Don't Dance

And the answer is: pretty much any way you want short of actual bodily injury – no, including actual bodily injury. That's why you have a lot of reserves. Of course, even if a skater is rolling in agony on the floor, or bleeding profusely, he still has only five seconds to pass the ball or let it go. It's not a game for the feint-hearted or fragile, which of course is not the reason why elves don't play it – of course not.

The iceball is very hard, so the skaters all wear large heavy catcher's gloves. They also wear sensible padded helmets, and shin and chest guards, but that still leaves a lot of body to get in the way of an iceball. Not that anybody would seek to do that deliberately; it is against the rules and considered bad form. A good body hit does always get the audience into the spirit of things, or so I'm reliably informed.

'Did you see that, Master Dwarf? Now, that was a throw!' cried the Princess, who was sitting next to me. 'And such distance too. Three-two to the Eagles!'

She leant forward.

'Tonight Duffy,' she said, poking the man in front. 'Tonight your team will be eating numble fries!'

'My dear Princess,' said Duffy, turning around and missing some exciting action that saw the Eagles' right-wing skater splash spectacularly into the shieldwork and netting that protected the crowd. 'The expression is numble *pie*.'

'Incorrect, the numbles – the heart, liver and guts – they are much better fried, no? A little salted flour is all that is needed.'

She looked at me for cooking confirmation.

'I'm a steak kind of dwarf, Princess,' I admitted. 'Charcoal on the outside and still bleeding in the middle – preferably.'

'Master Strongoak, to miss out of the numbles is to miss out on the essence of the animal! It gives you its strength – the rage of the bull, the agility of the goat, the majesty of the stag!'

'The smell of the sheep?' I ventured.

'We do not eat the sheep,' she snorted with derision.

'Because?' I asked with genuine interest – being something of a fan of hogget.

'When the Banished One returned, he did so in the form of the sheep,' the Warrior Princess explained patiently. 'And when consumed, he entered into the being of the people and thereby was able to corrupt them and cause their downfall.'

'Ah right,' I acknowledged. 'There would be that – I suppose.'

'Look, the winger is bleeding on the ice!' shouted Osk. 'Bad form! Bad form!'

'I don't think he has much choice, Osk,' I mentioned to the man seated on my other side.

'He should have been taken off and bandaged, Nicely. That's the team guide's job – to look for these things.'

'Know the game well then?'

'Oh yes,' he said, and his face broke into a rare grin. 'I played for years at the top level.'

'For the Wolves?' I said, impressed.

'Oh, yes, the first team. I was practically born on skates.'

'Do you still play?'

'Sadly not.' He held up his hand, and I noticed, for the first time, that his right hand was seriously damaged – a deep stitched cut across the palm splitting the webbing between thumb and point finger.

'Ouch,' I said with conviction.

Dwarf Girls Don't Dance

'I lost a glove while playing and encountered a skate at the wrong moment and in the wrong place. A game arbiter got me off in time – probably saved my hand.'

'I sense a "but"?'

'Oh, it's not too bad, but it has robbed all the strength from my throwing hand.' He moved his thumb to demonstrate the obvious lack of mobility.

'It would do that,' I agreed. 'You're lucky you still have a thumb!'

Osk grinned again.

'I can still give the other Idlers the run-around, or skate around perhaps I should say – well, all except Buns. He is a canny iceball player. How about you, do you play?'

'No – and the chances of me ever taking it up have just decreased considerably! I like both my thumbs. In fact, I'm very attached to both of them and intend for it to stay that way.'

'You should try – it's fun!'

Some of that fun had just broken out into a full brawl in the ice that was threatening to include the spectators. Berger and Mansel were already engaged in a mock sword fight that involved two of the rather splendid 'wizard staff' sausages that they sold here at Skragslanding.

'Yield, Eagle-supporting scum,' shouted Mansel, 'before I run you through with my savoury snack.'

'Never!' cried the gnome, countering well against Mansel's height advantage. 'No Wolf shall claim victory here while I still have processed meat to defend myself and the good name of the Skragslanding Eagles! Have at you!'

Despite some impressive staff-work by Berger, he was finally brought lower by a sausage thrust that left him with red sauce leaking down his front.

'Oh, ship-peas Mansell!' said Berger, looking down crossly. 'That was my third best top as well – I'll never shift that stain!'

'Let that be a lesson to all Eagles who would worry our gates!' the woman responded, gleefully shortening the sausage considerably with one large bite.

Meanwhile, out on the ice, 'The Axe' was at the centre of the ongoing bust-up, in typical dwarf fashion, and one of the two-game arbiters had decided he needed to go cool off before the ice melted.

'Ah!' exclaimed Osk in disgust. 'The game is getting soft! It was just an exchange of opinions!'

Duffy laughed at his friend. 'His "opinion" appears to have put our left wing into traction, Osk! Look!' He pointed to where a 'Wolf' was being helped off the ice. 'Any more discussion like that and we're going to run out of reserves!'

This exchange of opinions had upped the tempo of the game even further. The Wolves were desperate to seek justice for their injured skater and even the score. The loss of Delvedeep had momentarily robbed the Eagles of some of their shape, and with a swift series of well-judged passes, the Kellishaldt Wolves had rung another bell to even the score.

'Three apiece! Now Princess,' shouted a laughing Duffy, 'we shall see who will be eating numble fries!'

The Princess glowered at her friend – which on her was not a bad look.

'Who is your gold on, Sansire?' I asked the seer, when the din had quietened enough for us to be heard.

'Sadly, the gift does not work like that, Nicely!' she shouted back. 'Otherwise, all seers would reside in mansions as rich as dwarves!'

I laughed along with her, but then thought again on what she and Duffy had told me about the death premonition and Buns' voluntary departure from the fellowship. Without any degree of control, Seerdom really didn't seem to have a lot going for it.

A huge roar greeted 'The Axe's' return to the ice. The Eagles were not going to be outdone on their home ice, and they put everything they had into all-out attack as the clock rapidly ticked through the last quarter.

Delvedeep was immediately targeted, which proved to be the Wolves undoing. He wasn't given an inch of ice to work in. Then, on a mazey skate from deep in his own half, Delvedeep shot towards the Wolves hoop and made a tremendous leap, screaming for the iceball. Three Wolves, nearly flying as high as their rival's namesake, immediately brought him down. It was all a diversion, though, and the iceball instead went to another skater who had clear ice all the way to the hoop. He let fly and DONG, the bell rang out!

The Eagles were up 4-3 and time had run out.

Delvedeep scrambled out from beneath the disappointed Wolf skaters, unbroken if not completely unscathed. Not that he let that worry him. A victory lap of the ice by the whole team had the locals roaring their approval.

Duffy didn't take it too bad – he bought everybody at the after-match party a drink, of course. This was a fun affair too, which, because this encounter traditionally marked the end of iceball season, went on longer than most after-match parties and spilt out onto the ice as well. The Nine Idlers had all found skates and were speeding along in a line. This would eventually, when the leader put the brakes on, result in the tail skater being whipped around at great speed and flung into oblivion. Luce was bringing up the rear, and he did indeed hit the safety mesh in a bone-jarring fashion.

'It's alright!' Luce shouted reassuringly. 'I am horrendously drunk and didn't feel a thing.' Yes, the man did have style.

I, quite sensibly, was watching from the stands – like a good shield should do. To my surprise, I was joined by Deepseam 'the Axe' Delvedeep.

'So you're the replacement, are you?' he said, sitting down without any preamble.

'Not that I'm aware of,' I answered cautiously.

'For Buns.'

'Not sure I'm following you.'

'A fruit juice drinker too,' he added with some disgust. A fruit juice drinker isn't a compliment as far as dwarves are concerned.

'I really don't see that this is any business of yours.'

'I'd heard that Duffy Boy had hooked up with another dwarf – from Iron Town too, I'm guessing. Just wanted a look at him.' He looked and didn't seem impressed. 'Tall as well, must be all that fruit juice.' Tall isn't a compliment either in dwarf circles.

'Look Master Delvedeep, I don't know about your source of intelligence, or why it should concern you, but I'm "Master Duffy Boy's" driver, and that is why I'm drinking fruit juice – although I will drink fruit juice whenever the fancy takes me. Understood?'

Deepseam grunted and got up. 'Think you're tough, do you Iron Town dwarf? Well in Skragslanding we have two of you for dinner. So you'd better watch yourself – especially around Skavernslager.' And with that, he went to leave, but I wasn't letting him have the last word.

Dwarf Girls Don't Dance

'Master Delvedeep, I enjoyed your antics on the ice this evening. Very entertaining, thank you.' He looked at me unsure how to take this, but headed off anyway.

'And it's New Iron Town!' I shouted to his departing back, before sitting down again with a thud.

'And what was that all about?' I said to myself. 'And where is Skavernslager anyway?'

The answer to the first question was not immediately available but the other question was finally solved when the short Skragsrealm summer eventually rolled around. Duffy, by that time seemed to be coping quite well, with his excessive drinking that is, although I was now well used to a regular monthly call from Jeskyn. It had thrown me the first time, mind – when the night frost was still painting the town silver.

'Master Strongoak, this is Jeskyn. I hate to bother you at this time of night, but I wonder if you would mind collecting Master Duffy?'

'No problem, Jeskyn. Any ideas where I might find him?'

'I do believe he is still in the country.'

'Excellent, that narrows it right down.'

I found Duffy down by the docks, carrying a bottle of something I suspect is usually applied for removing barnacles from boats.

'Sorry, Nicely, old chap! Do excuse; it's that time of the month,' he explained, waving the bottle in a worrying manner.

'And what time would that be, Duffy?'

'Why, the time of the month I ask Willow to marry me, of course.'

'I see, and the time of the month she turns you down I take it?'

'Willow's parents. Very high up the Tree. They are not keen on the idea of her marrying out.'

'Not keen?'

'Yes,' Duffy gave me a slightly sickly grin. 'In the same way that starving villagers are not keen on the idea of a dragon coming to inspect their crops or ask about their young unsullied daughters.'

'That keen, eh?'

'Oh yes,' he replied, managing to stagger and drink at the same time. 'Do excuse my manners – I clean forgot to offer you any of this very fine drop of "bed-wetter"; guaranteed to induce an oblivion so complete that you're advised not to sleep on your best mattress.'

'Time to get you home I think, Duffy. While there is still some "bed-wetter" left to remove the barnacles.'

'Surely not! The night is still young!'

'No, it's the morning that is young. Everything else is getting old.'

'Oh yes,' he managed finally, after a good look around. 'That would explain the light.'

'It would too,' I agreed. But Duffy's lights were out by then. I caught him as he fell. I was always there to catch him at that time.

16

Skavernslager

Some folk think dwarves don't like the summer, that we shun the light and prefer to hide away in our tall halls far from the warmth of the sun. In which case, why would we fill those aforementioned halls with brilliant light and channel every available sunbeam to illuminate the farthest corners of our deep palaces?

We love the summer – we go crazy for it!

There is a word in old Dwarvish that translates as something like 'incision frenzy', which describes how, after a long hard winter, a dwarf enjoys nothing more than to be cut out of his underwear and greet the sun.

Okay – some things have improved since Old Dwarf days, but the sentiment remains the same.

Naturally, when your race has evolved in harsh northern climes, where a smaller and attractively stockier stature is a great advantage, it is harder to cope with the temperatures and humidity found further south. But never believe we don't welcome the summer!

We survive the winter and come alive for summer.

The Nine Idlers welcomed summer too, but they had better taste in undergarments than dwarves used to run around in.

So, Idler life got even more exciting: for starters, Berger had an exhibition, which was greeted with general adulation by most of

Skragslanding. I went along of course, but had to admit that I didn't really understand what was on offer.

'The problem, my dear fellow,' Berger explained at the opening, 'is that dwarves are very literal folk. They tend to deal in matters where feet and yards are important – no, vital, otherwise, mines might collapse, bridges fall down, and lives be lost. I don't think this equips them for the abstract. Whereas the gnome…'

'Smokes too much pipeweed?' I finished for him, looking at the vibrant, swirling colours on his latest canvas.

'You might well be right, dear fellow! You might well be right.' He laughed and went to glad-hand some more potential clients.

Of course, my mystification did not prevent me spending some hard-earned gold on a couple of Berger's colourful compositions with an appealing design. I may not know what I like, but I can appreciate a solid investment a league or two off. And these pictures had real gold leaf in them too – can't argue with real gold leaf.

Next up was a rather special birthday for Mansel. She was quite a bit younger than I had realised, given Duffy's remarks about parental collective hopes. Mansel was a very sweet thing, funny and apparently unaffected by her family's impressive fortune. A positive advertisement for vast wealth and an expensive, if rather neglected, education. She hired a ship for her party. It wasn't a big ship; I've been on bigger mountains, but not that much bigger.

Osk then passed some examinations that seemed to matter, and I had to drive the Idlers to the only restaurant in Skragsrealm where they did his favourite dish exactly as he liked it. I think it would have been quicker to take the ferry back to his native Kellisgrund. That would certainly soon be the easy option, if the proposed bridge across the estuary goes ahead.

Dwarf Girls Don't Dance

And finally, as summer proper settled in for its short northern stay, Luce actually did a public recital. This recital was no small matter, and for the first time, I saw the urbane, unflappable Luce, properly nervous. Luce had taken to confiding in me, because – or so he insisted – I was the only one who had never heard him orate before, therefore I was less likely to be disappointed.

'It's not the actual speaking, Nicely,' Luce said one afternoon, as I collected him to join the others for early drinks, which was a regular fixture in the Idler's social diary. A diary that also included pre-drinks, drinks, late drinks and last drinks.

'It's the anticipation that does for me.' He finished with some consternation. 'What if I'm not as good as they remember?'

He wasn't as good, of course. He was better. Everyone agreed.

The hall chosen for the event was a very old, stone-clad, timber-framed building with sloping sides, known as the Last Fear. It was not built by either dwarves or men, which I found intriguing. There were hints of elvishness about it, but somehow more primitive, or 'closer to the earth'; elves can be annoyingly flamboyant at times. I asked Mansel about the Last Fear as we settled into our seats – especially about this strange name. She admitted her ignorance but went on to explain: 'The scholars' best guess is that the old nomads originally built it, or fisherfolk who occupied this land when the dwarves were still spreading through the mountains and men hadn't come to Kellisgrund. As for the name,' she shrugged. 'Most people think it meant a refuge from fear, a stout defence against marauding trolls perhaps?'

'And where did these nomads go to?'

'They moved on, I suppose.' Mansel smiled, a rather winning smile I had to admit. 'Isn't that what nomads do?'

'I have heard rumours about these people,' Willow said, joining in our conversation. She was looking particularly stunning that evening. Dressed up for the occasion in an off-the-shoulder, one-piece green dress that fitted snugly with no visible means of support; remarkable in more ways than one. As if it wasn't hard enough to keep your eyes off her, she was also wearing a necklace of emeralds so exquisite that my dwarf senses were almost overwhelmed. I had never seen emeralds of such depth of colour and vibrancy, but I had heard about them: Greenwood emeralds, the most valued of their kind. She was wearing a King's ransom of sparklers – as they use to say when we still had that kind of body in charge.

'Apparently,' Willow continued, 'the nomads live mostly in Skragsrealm proper now and even further north than that. I really must find out more about them while I am here.'

I nodded, trying not to stare too hard at the Greenwood emeralds and the chest below them, which was also worthy of note. You can take the dwarf out of New Iron Town, but it's hard to take New Iron Town out of the dwarf. I was glad when the recital began, as it provided me with some distraction.

Whoever had built the building, they certainly knew a thing or two about acoustics. As we all hushed and Luce walked out, from the very first words, his speech filled the hall, but at no point did he seem to raise his voice. There is tremendous power in a voice like that. Maybe the mountains had better look out.

The Bardic style was more than simple poetry or storytelling, Luce accompanied himself on a small lap harp for a start, but it wasn't exactly singing either. It was its own beast. Whatever, it was totally enthralling, spoken magic that could fill you with such longing – longing for a time or place you might never have encountered before, but missed dreadfully. I didn't have a word

Dwarf Girls Don't Dance

for the feeling – the elves probably do, they have a word for everything; even humility. Or so I've been told, but I've never had any personal experience.

The Idlers loved the show. The audience loved the show, and I loved the show. The man had talent, many talents, as he then proceeded to show by drinking his own weight in ale. That is a highly enviable talent, but even I have to say that his 'bardery' probably tops this.

All of these activities were mere warm-ups for the main event of the summer: the trip to the 'Cottage' for Mid-summer's Eve and the Longest Day. This cottage, I was intrigued to find out, was called Skavernslager.

Duffy and the Nine Idlers all loved Skavernslager Cottage. I think it had been built as a wedding present for Duffy's father or grandfather – he was rather vague about that, as he was about most things concerned with his family. Apparently, the Nine Idlers had been going there for years to celebrate the Kellisgrund Mid-summer's Eve holiday.

Mid-summer is a very big thing in Kellisgrund, as it is in many other places. Even us dwarves have been known to go a little wild and drink the odd barrel or two of something sticky on this special day. The Kellisgrund Mid-summer's Eve as with most things connected with this gloomy-sounding place, had more than a hint of the melancholy about it – witness their full name for the event: 'The Sun's Death Festival'.

For Duffy and Willow and the rest, it was a fourteen-night of drinking and partying that culminated in an all-night bash, with a huge fire lit at midnight watch that signified that now the days were getting shorter and soon winter would be with us again. Like I said, cheerful bunch in Kellisgrund it seems. Remind self to never go there.

There are other traditions too naturally: Drinking the Dying Sun, the election of the Long Sun King and the subsequent burning of the Long Sun King (hopefully in effigy) and eating the Moon and Sun Cake. This is a dairy-filled treat that apparently can clot a heart-vessel at a hundred paces. Yes, it all sounded very jolly, but I wasn't too sure what my role was to be – apart from driver, which was no hardship in this interesting part of the world.

We had driven steadily uphill for most of the morning, due north from Skragslanding into the mountains proper, my stunted little dwarf spirit soaring with each mile. And what a sight opened up before us: Dwarf Castles, Halls, and Keeps grew almost organically from every prominence, spur and ridge. Of course, these were only the stony outcrops of the deeper tunnelled homes that I knew would be riddling the hills and mountains to produce a honeycomb realm of amazing complexity.

They say you can travel from the East Coast of Skragsgrund to the West Coast without once needing to see daylight – but then again us dwarves are a bit like that sometimes. The truth is that a lot of the larger dwarf families rather value their isolation and would prefer you to use the front door. However, an entire realm underpinned by a labyrinth of unmarked passages does rather explain why the dwarf postal service never really took off.

Mind you, it might have also been the pack of wolves that they say can still be found in this part of Skragsrealm.

We drove on.

The town of Skavernslager itself was small, as dwarf towns tend to be, unless, like New Iron Town, they are industrial. A dwarf's idea of communal living is a large family hall – very big on family are dwarves, not so hot on neighbours. 'A neighbour is a stranger that hasn't robbed you yet', as the expression goes. But dwarves need public organisation too, and so they tolerate a few villages and towns with stores and such like, mostly run by gnomes it should be said.

We turned off the Skavernslager main road before reaching the town proper and headed down a steep valley besides the river Skavern. At the end of the gorge, settled comfortably on the centre of a medium-sized island in the middle of Lake Skavernslager, surrounded by a small wood, was a building that looked like it belonged on the wide grasslands of the Far South. Its large timber frame, wide windows and thatched roof as out of place as a wart on the nose of an elf princess.

Skavernslager Cottage was actually built on a rise on the island. This made it look quite a bit larger than it was – not that it was exactly small. It did have a score of bedrooms and more bathrooms than you could reasonably expect to visit in one lifetime. It only had the one kitchen, but that was the size of a smallish barn in itself – some 'cottage'. From the outside it was actually a rather modest-looking building, especially with regard to decoration, which was enough to tell you it was not dwarf made. This was strange, because this is prime dwarf territory after all; witness the number of dwarf halls with the requisite pillars and battlements perched high up on the hillside of the river valley overlooking the lake.

I parked up the Fallingsturger, packed full of laughing folk and their luggage, by a small wharf at the lakeside and everybody tumbled out. There was a large rowboat tied up to a wharf, but it could hardly accommodate all the folk, let alone the trunks and cases and hatboxes and hampers – lots of hampers I was pleased to see. In the end, it took three trips. I was on the last trip, doing my best to look as if I was completely at home on the water.

Truth is, I am not as bad a sailor as many dwarves, but neither am I exactly web-footed.

There was a surprisingly long wharf on the island. I commented on this, and two iceball hoops in the shallows were pointed out to me. Apparently, the lakeside had been dredged and filled near the island to provide an artificially shallow area that froze quickly in the winter to produce an iceball rink. Duffy and his friends and family sometimes over-wintered here and what sort of cottage would it be these days that didn't have its own iceball rink?

You needed a large wharf then to have some place to tie up your boat and not get your tootsies too wet during the summer. There was a boathouse on the island next to the wharf. It contained a smaller pleasure skiff and all the iceball bits and pieces, including a big chest of balls and catchers' gloves and padding. I knew this because a lot of our food hampers were later piled in the cool of the boathouse until required.

We unloaded the trunks and boxes in stages, and then everybody helped carry them up to the cottage. I mostly did the heavy lifting from the boat, but there was an awkward barrel of Summer's Ale that needed to get to the cottage. I rolled it along the wharf, hefted it onto my shoulders and then stepped onto the island proper for the first time. I felt a peculiar rush, and for a second, I was light-headed. Fearing for the beer, I had to put the barrel down and get my breath for a moment. I looked around but had no idea what I was expecting to see – apart from something strange. I was not the sort of dwarf to be subject to attacks of the vapours! The feeling finally passed, and I picked up the barrel again and headed for the cottage.

Most strange.

Dwarf Girls Don't Dance

There was a lovely stretch of lawn sloping up from the lakeside to the terrace, and from there a splendid set of double doors opened into an entry room with a fantastically ornate wooden floor laid out in a sunburst design. A ridiculously long staircase, just right for dancing down, led to the bedroom floor. Spirits were high and elf, gnome, men and women were soon pounding up and down these stairs, throwing windows wide open and picking their favourite bedrooms.

Everybody seemed to know where he or she was going, which left me feeling just a little uncomfortable as I stood on the cottage threshold. I felt like I required an invitation, just to ensure that the cottage did not take umbrage at my presence. I wasn't sure where to go.

The Idlers had always been exceptionally pleasant to me, and they were a good crowd, but I was still being paid to be here. As if sensing my problem, Duffy took me to one side while the others were still in excited constant motion. We went into the main room. A rather wonderful room it had to be said. Solid ironwood pillars supported a vaulted ceiling, and there was another marvellously inlaid floor of beautifully polished different woods. There was a fine portrait of an attractive woman, with more than a passing resemblance to Duffy, staring down at us. Almost regal, I'm not sure if she approved of this dwarf in her house or not.

'Nicely, I am deeply grateful for all your help.'

I started to say something, but Duffy put his hand up, requesting me to stop.

'Please, let me finish. Your presence has not just been a reassurance, but I have valued your insight and advice too. Your friendship even.'

I tried again, but again the hand was raised.

'So for this week, I would like you to consider yourself my guest – not a Shield-for-Hire. I have picked out a room for you that I hope will fulfil your needs and I want you to consider yourself one of us!'

'Thank you, Duffy. That's very considerate, but really...'

'No buts, Nicely... it's an order! You are ordered to enjoy yourself! And that means joining in I'm afraid! Completely! You might just wish you had stayed back in Skragslanding.'

Luce came running downstairs and breathlessly interrupted us: 'Duffy, you dirty dog! There's a new lute in my bedroom. I suppose you expect me to be doing all the entertaining again?'

'Sorry, Luce. You've wandered into Nicely's room.'

Luce blinked a couple of times, fully taken in.

Duff laughed and put an arm around me companionably. 'Can we prevail upon you to give us a dwarf song or two, Nicely?'

'Better tune that lute, Luce – your fingers are going to be bleeding.'

Luce laughed again and beat Duffy around the head with an embroidered cushion that had probably once supported a Dwarf King's lower cheeks.

I headed off with the barrel to check the pantry – a guest's privilege. I was not disappointed.

17

The Day of the Long Sun

The Day of the Long Sun started with a bang – quite literally. A four-finger maroon exploded at some ridiculously early hour, tumbling everybody out of bed with a mixture of giggles and groans as the whole cottage shook in the aftermath of the powerful explosive. This was another tradition that the rest all knew about. I, on the other hand, was found at the top of the stairs holding a shooter in one hand and a half-axe in the other, dressed in not much more than my embarrassment and improvised nightwear.

'Nice shorts,' said the Warrior Princess, casually passing me on the landing to go downstairs to where the fun and games were about to start. 'Very snug.'

'Somebody could have told me,' I muttered.

'Now where's the fun in that, Big Boy?' said the Princess.

I went back to my room, put my weapons away and threw on a tunic before joining the others for the First Drink. Another tradition new to me, but I liked the sound of this one.

This may have been the first drink of the day, but was several hangovers away from being the first drink of the week. The last seven days had been pretty much non-stop partying – albeit in a very civilised style. Of course, there had been time in between for taking in the sun, rowing (for those inclined) and swimming (for those capable). I had applied my talents to mastering the tricky demands of that most onerous of labours: fishing. Or, in my case, as the Idlers dubbed it: taking a worm for a swim. They had a point, I had to admit, and so after a day or two, I cut the worms out of the operation and simply watched the float bob up and down in a very relaxing fashion.

Then I caught a fish. It was a large fish as well. Presumably one with a suicidal impulse.

Berger was quite taken by the same activity as well, but he never really got the point of it, and would insist on pulling fish out of the lake on a regular basis! Although I felt this was against the spirit of the endeavour, I still did my bit helping with the eating of the former lake inhabitants. Well, it would have been rude to do otherwise. My own catch I let go, partly because I didn't feel I had earnt it and mostly because Berger said sludge-skippers were bad eating.

But finally, after all the messing around, the big day (literally) was upon us.

'The maroon should have been lit at first light,' Osk complained, looking down at the hole in the lawn that was all that remained of the explosive wake-up call.

'Then you should have got up and done it, Osk!' replied Duffy loudly, although I doubt that anybody but Duffy would have been allowed that pleasure.

'Stop complaining, you boys!' Willow chided. 'It is time to toast the Long Sun. Here comes Luce and Mansel now.' And down the lawn they both came, looking very fetching in His and

Hers matching tabards and little else. They were long enough – but only just.

The two of them were manhandling a hot urn strung between two poles. A small folding table appeared as if from nowhere, and the urn was placed on it. The contents smelled like coffee, which was all right with me. I had become very partial to this drink – which had never really conquered New Iron Town – since cutting down on the beer. It just might become a habit. It sure beat fruit juice.

Beakers were found, filled, and passed around, just in time as the sun – which had never really left the stage, just dipping behind the hills – was now back for the main event. Without a cloud in the sky, it promised to be a perfect summer's day.

Yes, just perfect. The sort of day to remember all your life.

'The Long Sun!' went up the cry; mine as well – just marginally behind. Beakers were raised, and the First Drink drunk, or almost not in my case. I was expecting coffee, but not the added spirit that gave it a punch like a kick from a grumpy glaistig's goat hoof.

'That'll set you up for the day my dear fellow,' laughed Berger, slapping my back as I spluttered.

'What's in this?' I asked.

'That would be the Water of Life,' Berger confided. 'Strong stuff, the Water of Life!'

'The Water of Life,' toasted a laughing Luce. We drained our beakers, and Duffy topped them up again. 'One more duty at present,' he said, serious now. 'The King or Queen of the Long Sun must be anointed. And who will reign over us this day?'

This promised to be fun, and I looked around to see who the lucky fellow was going to be – Duffy presumably. It was only then I became aware that everybody else was looking at me.

'Oh, no! 'I said, attempting to hold up my hands, while not spilling too much of my First Drink. 'No, thank you very much! Really, I don't think it's a good idea!'

'However,' said Duffy, 'the custom is that whoever spills the First Drink, must make amends by taking on the onerous duties of the Long Day's Monarch.'

'Unfair,' I shouted, but to deaf ears.

The Idlers were not hearing a word of an excuse, and now all eyed me very seriously. A chant started as they closed in: 'Long live the King. Long live the King. Long live the King.' Which was kind of ironic as the King of the Long Sun, it turned out, was scheduled to die at Midnight later that same day.

Well, ain't that a sap sucker, as we say in New Iron Town.

In the meantime, I had to admit, I was being treated pretty well – as befits a king. I was handed a rather special linen suit that incorporated summer flowers and greenery that fitted suspiciously well. So much for 'who shall be picked to reign over us this day?' I had been stitched up in more ways than one, but as Willow, Mansel, Sansire and the Warrior Princess had carried out the needlework, I didn't struggle too much.

There was a mighty fine headpiece to go with my outfit as well. Ornate doesn't even begin to describe it. The frame was simple, but it was covered with masses of gold foil in a design inspired by the summer Long Sun, with sunbeams trailing behind me like a big cat's mane. I could have lived without the yellow face paint mind. Suitably attired I then went about my kingly duties, which basically involved ensuring that nobody flagged.

A large trestle table was erected on the lawn, and this was the setting for the day's different meals. I say meals, but essentially there was just the one long continuous meal – the Long Sun

Dwarf Girls Don't Dance

Meal on the longest day. A light breakfast of fruit, including some particularly juicy clingstones, followed by smoked fish—prepared from our own lake of course—and freshly boiled eggs; all just to stimulate the taste buds for the accompanying chilled, vintage, beazer teaser.

Lunch was a simple affair, consisting mostly of meats. I think I counted around thirty different types, reflecting every different branch of domesticated animal and a lot of wild ones, presented as cold cuts, sausages, pastes, pasties and pies. Oh, and lots of green leaves and cherry apples for those that like that kind of thing.

This was simply the warm-up for the main event; a hogget that was spit-roasted from late afternoon for about six hours. This was trimmed as it browned and consumed in a type of breakbread made with herbs and slathered in a sauce hotter than a dragon's tonsils. The hogget was followed by the ceremonial delight of the Moon and Sun cake. This was an enormous affair of beaten egg spume, to represent the moon, with a butter and lemon curd cake below, to represent the sun – and a mountain of clotted cream in the middle – just because everybody loves it!

And in between the meals, there were of course games – a lot of games! Hiddle-piggle, jump-the-dragon, find-the-ring, bump-the-barrel, hide-the-wand, just for starters. Oh but the Idlers like their games. As the King of the Long Sun, I was expected to not only oversee the events; I was supposed to know the rules too! I soon gave up on pretending to follow whatever was going on, and just entered into the spirit of the occasion by handing out fines to transgressors. And if a lot of these fines did involve being nice to a yellow-faced dwarf with a shiny hat on – well, it's not every day that you get to be king.

Was there a lake of wine?

I'm not sure because I quickly moved on to beer, given how moderate I'd been in my consumption since meeting Duffy. And there was a lot of beer, but I endeavoured to do my best to remedy that situation. There were four different varieties on offer. First the light, fruity, hoppy summer ale, perfect for daytime drinking, next a refreshing bitter ideal to refresh the mouth in the afternoon, then a malty, biscuity, pale ale with a deceptive punch that complemented the hogget perfectly. Finally, a stupendous, very serious, strong, ghoul-kicking Dark Ale to finish.

Yes, I remember the beer well. It's funny what sticks in your mind.

You certainly had to pay attention to the Dark Ale. This was a work of beauty – with a colour was like the oldest dragon hide, not be rushed and best approached with care. The Warrior Princess was drinking it out of a two-pint flagon. You have to admire that in a woman, of any race.

I was still enjoying the malty pale when the Idlers all disappeared back into the cottage. I was briefly alone, adding last branches and twigs to the waiting bonfire while they were all upstairs changing. Another tradition of the Festival of the Dying Sun was that the celebrants all dressed up as somebody else for the evening – became somebody else for one night only. Fancy dressing with a point you might say. As the King of the Long Sun, I was already ahead of the game.

Berger was first down. I thought he had changed his mind about fancy dressing at first. He was outfitted in a well-tailored, two-piece suit in a light summer material, with a contrasting snap-brimmed hat. His boots were not of the normal gnome style, but a much more elegant design incorporating braided inlays and piping. It was only when he waved a hand axe in my direction that the bird fell off its perch.

'You've come as me, Berger! You disrespectful gnome!'

'Disrespectful?' he said, talking out of the side of his mouth in a very strange fashion. 'Better be careful friend, I know people that could cut you down so low that I could use you as an elbow rest.'

I had to laugh. He did 'do' me rather well, I suppose. Not that I talk out the side of my mouth – not at all, do I?

After Berger came the Warrior Princess, dressed very simply in the sort of rough cloth skirt and loose top a serving wench would wear in the type of historic epic that also features tin armour and swords that kill without drawing blood. The reason for this became clear as she approached me and executed a genuine curtsey, while bowing her head.

'Your majesty,' said the Warrior Princess, 'may a simple serving girl get you something that your heart desires?'

My mouth had suddenly gone very dry, and I managed to croak a request: 'More pale ale would be most welcome, royal wench.'

'Yes, your majesty,' she replied, and went to top up my pot.

My attention was then distracted as, with a flash of light and a large puff of smoke, Luce appeared in Wizard's garb. He looked very impressive in a robe with a full beard. It didn't exactly suit him – it just looked very familiar. I had a strange feeling of something that might have been akin to the foreshadowing that Sansire had spoken about and a chill did a sprint up my spine. I hoped this wasn't far-sight, as I did not think it boded well for the usually immaculately clean-shaven and well-groomed Luce. Too much beer, or not enough, Nicely?

Willow came next, but she was just wearing the green dress she had worn for Luce's recital. I say 'just' because nothing Willow ever wore could ever be a 'just' with or with the string of

Greenwood emeralds at her throat. She smiled at me, and I did a double take. It wasn't Willow; it was Mansel! She had lightened and straightened her hair, and worn long, you couldn't see her give-away round ears. But there was something else about her too, something much more grown-up and elfin even.

I bowed deeply as she made her way elegantly towards the bonfire.

'My Lady,' I said.

'Your Majesty,' she replied, the merest tilt of her head acknowledging the respect between equals.

'Not deep, but wide,' she whispered, as she walked past.

Duffy and Osk had kept it simple by just exchanging outfits. Some say clothes maketh the man or dwarf. I say they are wrong, but Osk certainly seemed to have more of a spring in his step wearing one of Duffy's rich, tailored creations.

Next down was Sansire and didn't she look a sight! The habitually soberly dressed seer was totally unrecognisable. She was attired like one a Skragslanding's finest ladies of buyable virtue, made up, rouged up and dressed up from top to tail in silks and other fabrics I had no names for. She even carried a fan! I had to give her a round of applause; it seemed fitting.

Which only left the real Willow to appear.

'So where's Willow?' I had to ask finally.

'Why, your majesty. I am here, as I have always been here.'

The voice made me jump, and I turned around, but I still couldn't see her. The others were obviously in on the jest as they were all laughing.

'Where are you, Willow?

'Everywhere!' her laughing voice rang out again, but I still couldn't see her.

'Who are you then?'

Dwarf Girls Don't Dance

'Why your majesty. I am the spirit of Summer Never Ending, of course.'

And with that Willow appeared, as if from nowhere. Except next minute she was gone again – or so it seemed. Looking closer I realised that she hadn't disappeared at all – she was there, but painted head to foot in a summer palette of paints that seemed to mix and undulate and reform as you tried to watch, before she blended, dancing, back into the scenery again.

'Elf magic?' I wondered aloud.

'Earth magic,' Willow replied. 'Older, darker.'

We lit the bonfire when the strange midsummer magic twilight fell upon us – not dark enough to call night, but not bright enough to still be day. The flames didn't mind. They took to the sky with an impressive enthusiasm that spoke of the dragons of old. And then it was time for me to die. The fire was hungry for that too.

Before I was burnt, in effigy I am pleased to relate—and not a bad one at that, although the smile was scary—I had a last duty to perform. I had to toast the Dying Sun. This is an important task as it beholden upon the toastmaster to give thanks to the Dying Sun, which now having reached its peak was henceforth therefore in decline. Get it wrong, and the Dying Sun might not put in a good word for you with the New Sun that arrived after the shortest day. I am pleased to say that there was a special drink to go with this toast too: the Last Drink – very literal, the folk of Kellisgrund.

Duffy carried the Last Drink out in a gold ewer on a gold tray with nine gold wine cups. They were not much larger than a pixie's footbath. He presented the tray to me with due ceremony and backing away as I took it from his hands. The ewer was an exquisite piece of workmanship. I filled the gold cups with a clear, slightly oily amber liquid, with what I hoped was the appropriate degree of reverence.

I walked around and offered each of the Idlers a gold cup from the tray. They each took one and waited solemnly for my toast. I looked for inspiration in the clear liquid, which was now moving slightly disconcertingly at the bottom of the cup.

'Dear Sun,' I began, without a clear idea in my head, however as I looked into the bonfire-lit faces of the folk standing excitedly around me, the words suddenly came easily. 'We give thanks to you, in the certain knowledge that your warmth, like the warmth of true fellowship and love, shall never be forgotten or taken for granted.' I lifted my glass high and exercised my impressive dwarf lungs: 'To the Dying Sun!'

'To the Dying Sun!' the Idlers shouted back and we all finished our drinks in one swallow and then went totally and utterly, completely, out of our noggins.

Very out of our noggins.

There was lots of wild dancing around the bonfire accompanied by Luce's miraculous lute playing. There was song, and there was laughter and more dancing, and I think wild pixies may have joined us at some point with a host of instruments made from summer flowers. Certainly, I would insist that the animals of the small woodland joined in, gambolling and prancing and skipping in their own fashion.

Later the sky was lit up by Northern Lights made out of elf silk, and Willow flew up to collect them and dressed us all in the greens and blues and violets. These shimmered and glistened, as did we, as we danced as if the sun would never die and neither would we.

How could we? We were the summer.

Dwarf Girls Don't Dance

Quite a few other clothes were discarded as the evening went on and people disappeared in pairs, and at some point, the Warrior Princess whispered in my ear: 'I think it's time we cut you out of your kingly attire.'

'And then what will I wear?' I said rather foolishly.

'Why nothing, your Majesty!' she said, giggling. 'Nothing at all!'

She took my hand and led me away from where the bonfire still crackled and spat, the body of the King of the Long Sun still smiling scarily as the flames engulfed him. Long into the non-night, the fire burned until finally, the day of the Long Sun was finally over.

I woke with a start. Something was wrong. It was as wrong as a wraith in a dinner jacket. I looked across the bolster to where the Princess slept quietly; her hair spread out in a jet-black tide. That wasn't wrong, that was quite the opposite, but something else was very amiss.

I jumped out of bed and found some kecks. Catching a glimpse in the mirror, I realised I was still wearing the make-up of the King of the Long Sun. It looked faintly sinister in the morning light, but now wasn't the time to fix it.

I didn't wait for boots; every sense was working on overtime and willing me out of there. I briefly kissed the Princess as I shook her awake. She stirred and smiled.

'Well hello, Master Strongoak – who's a clever detective then?'

'No time for that now, honey. Grab a wrap and wake the others – something bad is going down.'

I flung the door open and ran along the corridor to Duffy's bedroom. The hair I habitually put across the bottom of his door was still in place, so nobody had been in and out that way since I'd seen them disappear much earlier.

Another door opened further down the corridor, and I looked up at the face of a very worried Sansire. On seeing me, her expression turned to one of shock, as colour drained from her face.

'It wasn't Buns,' she stammered. 'It was you; it was always you!'

'Get a grip, Sansire! What are you talking about?'

'My foreshadowing – it was you I saw, not Buns. That means… oh, no!' She wilted against the door and was caught by a bleary-eyed Osk.

'What's going on, Sansire?' He looked across at me. 'Nicely?'

'Wake Duffy and Willow, Osk. They should be okay. Then join me downstairs.'

The Princess stumbled out of my room, gathering her wits and holding a very useful looking chair leg.

'Princess, try the other bedrooms, please?'

I ran to the stairs and took them two at a time. Bursting into the main living room, I was relieved to find Luce and Berger both asleep under blankets on loungers, which only left.

'Mansel!' I shouted at the top of my voice.

The two sluggards came around slowly. The room looked little different from last night, except now the large double doors onto the terrace were wide open.

'Oh, no! Mansel!' I shouted again, running out through the open doors. My eye was drawn to the rowboat, bobbing on the water some way from the wharf. I ran towards it.

I saw her green dress first, and then her dyed dark hair spreading out in the water as she floated – face very much down. I waded through the water, which wasn't deep at this point, because of the iceball dredging, and turned her over. Her eyes stared the million-mile stare, and I didn't need the large, dark, angry bruises around her neck to tell me that it had been broken. The Greenwood emeralds were gone, and so was Mansel.

I went into automatic mode, my Watch training kicking in. The Princess, true to her warrior nature, carried the body back to the cottage. Sansire had followed me down the stairs and had collapsed on the lawn when the seriousness of events had become clear. Willow, in shock herself, was trying to comfort her. The men were looking as if they thought it was some terrible dream – Luce, in particular, seemed unable to function properly. Duffy just stood, like he had been carved from alabaster.

Only Osk seemed to be fully awake and present, and he understandably was very worried about the prone Sansire.

'Osk,' I said, firmly but not unkindly. 'Sansire will recover – it's shock. We have another problem. Mansel is still warm. The rowboat is still here. Whoever did this could still be on the island. I need you to grab something intimidating and come with me.'

Osk nodded and headed into the house.

'Duffy!' No reaction. 'Duffy!' I tried again, before resorting to shaking the stunned man back into some semblance of normality.

'Why, Nicely?' he managed to croak. 'This wasn't supposed to happen.'

'I know, but it has, and we have to deal with it. Keep everybody together out here. Do you have a shooter?'

He shook his head.

'In that case, let's hope he hasn't either.'

'He?' Duffy looked at me again.

'Folk don't strangle themselves Duffy, or steal jewellery.'

Osk returned with a large poker from the fireplace and looked more than capable of using it with prejudice.

'Let us go,' he said determinedly. 'He could be getting away.'

The two of us covered the island in under an hour, but there wasn't a sign of any intruders and no indication that any other boats had been pulled up. The skip was still in the boathouse as well. We checked the house carefully, watching each other's backs. Luce's, Berger's and Mansel's beds were unslept in, the rest of the upstairs rooms still not touched. There was no basement, and the loft ladder was still in place, making it impossible for anybody to be hiding up there as it didn't pull up.

I checked anyway.

The loft was full of interesting flotsam and jetsam collected over the years, including a powerful-looking spyglass. There was a door from the loft onto an area of flat roof. I took the spyglass out there and opened it. It afforded me a great view of the lake, all around the island, but the water was as undisturbed as an elf maid's mirror. There was nothing floating and no conveniently placed boats on the far shoreline that could have pointed to an easy means of escape.

'Anything to help us, Nicely?' shouted Osk, calling from a million miles away, from a land where everything was still sunny, and people could have a mid-summer party without one of their number getting their neck broken. It was a land that didn't exist anymore. I wondered if it ever had done.

'Not a thing,' I called back, closing the spyglass and then returning to the others still sitting shocked on the lawn.

'We need to make this official now,' I told Duffy.

He nodded dully, the nod of a man who has lost more than a friend.

18

Dunkiln Delvedeep

The local law enforcement went by the name of Chief Reeve Dunkiln Delvedeep. He oversaw the Skavernslager region, which was actually a lot larger than I had first assumed. Delvedeep was full-bearded, nearly as wide as he was tall, had a slow way of talking and looked like a comedy dwarf from the rolling pictures. On the wall of his office, there was the head of a wolf that I later found out he had killed single-handed, armed only with a fruit knife. The wolf looked surprised. I imagine Chief Reeve Dunkiln Delvedeep had surprised a lot of folk during his time in charge.

Osk had rowed me across to where I had parked the Fallingsturger a lifetime ago. From there, I drove to Skavernslager, found the Reeve and kicked the investigation machine into action. He organised his team of deputies and put out a general alert for any strangers found or seen in the vicinity of the Lake. Two deputies jumped into an old Etchingham that had been converted for heavy weather and pumped up the steam. Delvedeep himself got in the Fallingsturger passenger seat, but seemed to be more interested in me than the details of the attack.

'Iron Watch, eh?' he rumbled, as he pulled on his pipe. 'Old Snaggletooth still giving the new recruits a roasting?'

'He's retired now.'

'Is that so?'

'Well, he was old – especially for a dog!'

Delvedeep chuckled and then continued: 'And these are friends of yours out on the lake?'

'Officially, I am the hired help, but yes. I like them well enough. All of them.'

'You're taking it in your stride then, if you don't mind me kind of saying so.'

I looked over at Delvedeep.

'Is that what you think? In that case, the Watch trained me well, because inside this "taking it well" exterior there is one very ticked-off dwarf who is likely to tear to pieces, limb-by-limb, whoever is responsible for this abominable act when he finds them. However, letting the Rage out now is not going to help my friends or find the murderer, is it? So I'll keep it bottled until the appropriate time comes around, and then woe betide anybody who gets in my way, because that's what us dwarves do, isn't it?'

The old lawman took a satisfied pull on his pipe. 'Yes, son. I reckon that's what we do. For good or ill, it's what we do.' He smoked in silence for the rest of the drive back to the lake, his deputies' old Etchingham chugging along behind us.

'Large hands, very large hands,' said Chief Delvedeep, squatting down and examining the bruises on poor Mansel's neck.

'So it would seem,' I replied noncommittally.

'Not a woman's hands.'

'Apparently not.'

'Well – not a normal woman's hands.' Delvedeep scratched his chin absent-mindedly. 'A Warrior Princess, that's a different matter, I'd imagine.'

'I told you, she was with me.'

'Yes, so you did. And how was that?'

'My winning personality, I suppose,' I said edgily.

Delvedeep made a noise remarkably like a harumph as he straightened up. 'Very nice defences for all of you. The owner in bed with his elf lady, his servant man spooning with this seer woman and you with the warrior princess. The other three passed out in the front room after the festivities had come to an end.'

'That's about it, although I don't think either Duffy or Osk would care for the description "servant man".'

'That's as maybe – as I see it, one's the master and the other is the servant. Perhaps not a situation he was happy about?'

'And so he decides to kill a perfectly innocent and lovely girl for no apparent reason?'

'Who is dressed up as the elf lady?'

'Which is the tradition on Midsummer Eve. To dress as somebody else.'

'Not our tradition, is it, Master Strongoak?'

'No – not our tradition!'

'And there is you all dressed up as the Long Sun King as well. Also, not our tradition.'

My edginess was rapidly becoming something a little more hostile, and I knew I shouldn't have been allowing him to wind me up, but I was not at my best. I seldom am after friends have been sent to the Utmost West.

'Excellent, Chief Delvedeep! I'm sure an in-depth comparative cultural analysis is going to yield results here! Could I just perhaps also bring to your attention that a priceless emerald necklace has been stolen as well! Perhaps that might have a bearing on the case?'

He appeared to give this some thought. 'So, perhaps it was a wandering troll who just happened by and, after noiselessly rowing to the island on the off-chance there were some valuable gems lying around, then cunningly enticed the Lady Mansel out onto the water where he robbed and strangled her? Before disappearing like a pix in the sunshine!'

'I don't know, Chief Delvedeep. I'm only sure it wasn't one of us that did it!'

'Us?' the old dwarf repeated.

I stormed out to find something to kick.

One of Delvedeep's deputies had brought a trunk of crime scene gear along with him. Snaps were being taken and thumb fonts recorded from the rest of the Nine Idlers crew – all of the necessary routine that accompanies a suspiciously premature death. The Princess wasn't there. I found her sitting down by the shore, staring over the water. I joined her, too cross and angry at the world to speak. Finally, it was her that broke the silence: 'We failed them, Nicely.'

'That's hardly fair...' I began, but I knew what she meant and sighed. 'Yes, we failed them, Princess.'

'Not because we were in any way responsible, Nicely, but we are the kind of folk whose job it is to take care of the others who do not see what we see, who do not think as we think and who will not act as we will act. These things we do, we do so that they can go on being like that and behave as they do; to be happy. We let our guard down.'

'And caught ourselves some of that happiness for a while. We were on an island in the middle of the lake!'

'Yes, but we were wrong, weren't we?'

'We were,' I admitted.

'It won't happen again.' The Princess walked off to join the others, still being interviewed on the lawns.

I walked back to the house – there was something about this house that didn't feel quite right. Or rather it did feel right, or at least as right as it ever had been since we had first arrived on the island and I had my taste of seer stuff. None of which made much sense. I wasn't happy and needed to have a nose around. Unfortunately, one of Delvedeep's deputies grabbed me and decided that I was officially still on the suspect list and thus not free to roam as I wanted.

We were rowed back to the shore side where a fleet of wagons was organised to drive us all separately back to Skragslanding. Although it remained Delvedeep's case, for now, the Chief Expiration Investigator, who would establish the cause of death, was located in Skragslanding. I had used my time wisely before finding the Reeve to contact Jeskyn to give him the briefest outline of what had occurred. Ever the dependable manservant, he hadn't wasted time on pointless questions, just took the details and said that arbiters and families would be contacted. I wasn't surprised then when we were met at Skragslanding's Keep by a whole mob of folk demanding attention and waving credentials. Mansel's folks had not yet got there, which was something at least.

Chief Delvedeep looked them over sourly, before turning to me.

'I suppose I have you to thank for this reception?'

'Just protecting my client's interests.'

'Your client is it now then?' he said.

'Always was.'

He harumphed again.

'Chief Delvedeep – wouldn't happen to have a relative in the iceball game, would you?'

'My youngest, Deepseam. Why?'

'No reason,' I replied, 'no reason at all.'

Chief Reeve Delvedeep clamped his pipe firmly between his teeth and ushered us all through the uproar and into the keep. Once in the keep, we were put in separate holding cells. They were sparse, but not uncomfortable and so, lacking anything else to do, I went to sleep. It's a knack I have, and it's one I have always tried to cultivate through the years. Nothing ever got solved with a weary mind.

It was some hours before they got around to questioning me. Delvedeep didn't waste time on preambles.

'I'd like to know more about this far-seeing,' he said, pushing my pipe and leaf back to me across the table that separated me from him and a long thin man who I took to be a local law enforcement officer.

I filled my pipe before speaking: 'You've spoken with Sansire, of course.'

'I'd like to hear your version.'

'Well,' I said, lighting up. 'As I understood it, she had this vision —a foreshadowing of a death—of one of their group. For various reasons she thought it would be Duffy, it wasn't that clear a premonition! I gather that not many are. The only friend she could see clearly was a dwarf that goes by the name of "Buns" – you'll have to check out his proper name.'

'I will. Carry on,' said the old dwarf.

'She must have convinced Buns that the vision had some veracity, because he kept himself well away from the group after that, the idea being, if he wasn't there, it wasn't going to happen.

Dwarf Girls Don't Dance

Unfortunately, it seems it wasn't Buns that Sansire saw in her vision – it was me wearing the Lord of the Long Sun's make-up.'

'A very cloudy vision, wouldn't you say?'

'Yes,' I agreed. 'And that I find interesting, because Sansire was very clear that the reason for her "vision" being so poor was that magic was involved. Apparently it interferes with the clarity.' I lit my pipe and looked across at the officers.

'And what do you think?' said Delvedeep.

'I'm no expert on magic, in fact, I'm not really sure if I give the whole subject much credence. There didn't doesn't seem to be much magic involved with a theft and a nasty strangulation. More goblin mischief rather than sorcerer territory I would have thought.'

'A reasonable point,' Delvedeep added noncommittally.

'So I don't understand where the magic comes in.'

'Tell me about this Last Drink you all partook of, a potent tipple it seems?'

'The perfect drink for turning your head inside out.'

'Magic?'

'I don't know. Perhaps more mushrooms than magic.'

'So, Master Detective – anything else to add?'

I had been thinking about this while waiting and drew on my pipe before speaking: 'You have to remember that whoever did this didn't have much time. I don't think Mansel had been dead for more than a few minutes, not before I was awake and then downstairs and making a commotion. Although it's summer, the lake is still cool, and she could not have stayed warm for very long. I've timed the row across to the island. It takes the best part of half an hour to get there or back. I was up into the loft with that spyglass in not much longer than that, yet I didn't see a thing out on the water. The timing is getting very critical.'

'But still, you say none of your friends could have been responsible?'

'No way! Haven't you been listening? Everybody else was otherwise preoccupied. Unless you're considering that either Osk or Sansire, or Duffy and Willow, or all of them, conspired together to kill Mansel. Plus they managed to do it without waking Luce or Berger! And you can rule out Duffy and Willow because of the hair I put across the door!'

'A strange way to behave towards your employer, surely?'

'Not at all, Chief Reeve. I am, was, his Shield and that meant tracking his activity, so I could anticipate any difficult situation he might place himself in. And you can rule out Osk and Sansire too because I saw her coming out of her room and there was no way either of them could have got back up the stairs past my room without me hearing them.

Deepseam took a long pull on his pipe. 'So tell me, Master Strongoak,' he blew smoke out appreciatively, 'what exactly was it that woke you, anyway?'

He had arrived at the one question I had no answer for. 'I don't know,' I finally admitted. 'Honestly, I have no idea at all. I just woke up and knew there was something wrong – something very wrong.'

'More magic?' the old dwarf inquired levelly. 'Are you perhaps a far-seer or wizard as well as a detective? Do you have hidden powers, Master Strongoak?'

'No,' I said, gritting my teeth. 'I'm just a dwarf from the Iron Watch who came to Skragslanding to try their hand in the private sector and now wishes that perhaps he was still at home locking up drunks on pay-day.'

'Yet after a day of drinking and a glass of something that could "turn your head inside out", wake you did?'

Dwarf Girls Don't Dance

I sighed the sigh of the perplexed. 'Maybe Mansel did cry out, or there was something else that a dwarf would notice that nobody else could? I was the only dwarf there after all.'

'And that's it, is it?'

I thought about some of the strange feelings I had on reaching and leaving the island. I'm sure that wasn't anything to do with magic either. Magic was bigger, more lights and explosions, wasn't it? This was something else, and included a more familiar sensation – one that I couldn't quite put my finger on.

'Yes,' I said. 'That's it!'

We were not all released from the keep at the same time. I'm not sure if this was strategic, but it had the effect of making this one dwarf, at least, feel very isolated – as if I had just woken up from a very long sleep, where I had been dreaming a dream that turned out to be a nightmare. I was back to real life and, amongst other things, I needed to make a living. I didn't think I could bother Duffy for my normal corn.

Mansel was buried back home in Kellisgrund.

I did not receive an invitation, and I didn't feel like barging in. The Idlers seemed to have relocated en masse to the capital of Kellishaldt, on sureties of course, while awaiting news of whatever the keep detectives might turn up. I wasn't holding my breath.

I was also focussing my efforts on discovering more about Mansel's death. Not that these efforts were getting me anywhere either. Trying to infiltrate the underworld of a strange country is not exactly an easy undertaking. I grew myself a rough beard and hung around some cheap dock inns, but if anybody was trying to sell a string of very expensive emeralds, nobody was breathing a word about it.

A gnome stoker on a sea-going steamship explained it to me thus: 'Nobody, lessen they're off their curly top on moondust, is going to be trying to sell those sparklers in these parts. Any sense they're going to jump a boat to someplace, like the Citadel, and trade them there and get a good stake on a new life in the sun.'

I couldn't help but think he was right. That didn't stop me looking, though.

I guess I was kind of hard to get hold of, not that I imagined anybody was trying, but, to my surprise, Berger did eventually track me down, in the *Blind Cow* of all places.

'This was Duffy's favourite dive,' he said, getting up onto the stool next to mine and putting down his glass of the yellow beer the men make in these parts.

'You know, I do believe you are right,' I replied, looking around, 'although one rat-infested drinking hole looks pretty much like another in Skragslanding.'

'And have you been doing a lot of looking?'

'Oh yes – as I'm looking for a particularly large rat.'

'Isn't that for the keep to do?'

'I get the impression they are looking elsewhere. Mostly up there own outholes.'

Berger looked at his drink, rather morosely before replying: 'I think the investigation is getting bogged down in administrative detail. The Skragslanding Watch assumed authority, but Kellishaldt Keep is very keen to be in there, seeing as how so many of its folk are involved.'

'Save us from the petty officials.' I downed my drink and slammed the glass onto the woodwork, beckoning for the barkeep. 'How is everybody?'

Berger looked sad. 'I suppose we are all grieving in our own way.'

Dwarf Girls Don't Dance

I ordered another drink for us both. Grieving? There would be time for grieving when I saw the murderer swing and maybe pulled on his boots.

'You're going to keep looking, aren't you?' Berger said, sipping on his yellow beer.

'I'm going to keep on looking.'

'Good. I hoped you would. If you need anything, let me know.'

'I will Berger. Thanks.'

'What for?'

'Coming to find me.'

We shared a few more drinks and then Berger headed off to leave me growing my beard. Just before he left he handed me a full-looking envelope.

'This might help. Take care. Stay in touch.'

I saluted a goodbye and waited until he had left the inn before checking out the contents. I expected some relevant correspondence or perhaps useful addresses. What I got was a whole lot of the folding money the men in these parts of the world are so fond of.

Berger is good folk.

The inquest into Mansel's death was a non-event. I was the only one of us there, the others had all sent representatives. After the expiration investigator delivered his 'Unlawful Killing by Unknown Assailant' verdict on Mansel, I didn't feel much like talking to any of the remaining Idlers anyway, which was good, as I supposed they weren't keen on talking to me either. I thought I might hear from the Princess, but there you go. 'Isn't life a kick in the jewels,' as Great Uncle Egregious Bodyblow always used to say.

The next time, the drive to the cottage took an age, accompanied as I was by no expectations and certainly no laughter. The Skragsrealm days were shortening, the leaves were browning prematurely, and the air even had the promise of an early snow in it. Hopefully not tonight. Some of these roads were bad enough as it was, although the Dragonette still handled like a dream. I really had to get me one of these some day. Duffy hadn't asked for his wagon back, but there was only so long I could hang on to it before I felt cheap.

The rowboat was still tied up at the wharf, just as if nothing had changed. It had of course; everything had changed.

I didn't get in the rowboat. I just sat on the Dragonette's hood and waited. It wasn't long before I heard the wagon approach. It was the reassuring chug of Chief Reeve's Etchingham, in no hurry – after all, the only way out was past him.

He stepped from the wagon, stretched a bit and relit his pipe before wandering, with his distinctive rolling gate, over to me.

'I thought I'd be seeing you again, son.'

'That's why I waited for you, Chief Reeve.'

'Something on your mind?'

'Why don't we take ourselves a little trip?'

Delvedeep looked at the water with an obvious dislike.

'You'll be doing the rowing.'

It was getting dark by the time we reached Skavernslager Cottage, but the chief had brought a torch. We soon found candles and lit a few lamps too. The cottage looked sad by the flickering lights, evidence of the investigation everywhere; font dust still marked prize items and the blankets that Luce, Berger and poor Mansel had slept under were folded up and back on the day beds.

'So?' said Delvedeep finally.

'There was something about the place that didn't make sense. Not that last time we were here.'

'Such as?'

'I'm not sure…' I looked around.

'No rush, son,' said the old dwarf, making himself comfortable on a footstool.

I paced around the ground floor and then wandered up to the bedrooms. Although my own belongings had been returned to me, the bedroom I had used was otherwise just as I had left it – as we had left it. I tried not to let that cloud my thinking.

I went downstairs again.

'It's different,' I told Delvedeep. 'Whatever it was, it's different now.'

'Is that so?'

'Yes. Your people should have let me back in. It's too late now.'

'Maybe I should, but the law's the law, and you were a suspect.'

'I was?' I laughed incredulously. 'What, I saw Mansel out on the water and ran downstairs, strangled her and hid the necklace all in the minute or two that it took for the others to join me?'

'It was one theory.'

'Axes and blood! That's it!'

'What is?'

'The necklace – it was still here! After Mansel was killed, the necklace was still on the island! Here, but hidden.'

'You've got a good nose for a gem, Strongoak.'

'I have.'

'I see.'

'You felt it too, didn't you?' I looked at the old dwarf smoking contentedly in the candlelight, his expression giving nothing away.

'I wasn't sure, to be honest. But I could feel something. I worked the mines as a young dwarf, and my gem sense had become quite attuned to locating precious stones.'

'You never lose the knack.'

'If the emeralds had been taken, what was making me twitch? There weren't any other stones of that quality here. So, I put a watch on the road just to be sure.'

He scratched his head with some vigour. 'And no unaccounted traffic has been and gone from this island since.'

'Yet, it's gone now hasn't it, the necklace? We're too late!'

The old dwarf nodded.

'It feels that way to me as well. I don't think the necklace was taken on the night of the Lady Mansel's murder. I think it was hidden here, somewhere we've not been able to find.'

'I am telling you, none of the Idlers did it! They didn't have the opportunity, not to mention that they all also lacked a motive. Plus, how about the means? Those bruises were not caused by hands as small as a woman's, or Berger's for that matter.'

'The Warrior Princess?'

'Was with me!' I insisted. 'Plus Luce keeps his nails long for harp playing, and they would have left cuts.'

'Glad you mentioned that.'

'Also Osk's right hand is damaged from an iceball accident. He can barely grip a fork properly.'

Delvedeep got up and walked to the window. 'But what makes you think I'm talking about the Idlers. We might both have been thinking too much like dwarves.'

'How do you mean?' I joined him at the window. He pointed with his pipe at the shoreline.

Dwarf Girls Don't Dance

'A man could swim that distance with no trouble – slip in and out. Hide the gems 'till later, just in case. We have always been thinking in terms of a boat.'

'It's true,' I agreed.

'Just because no dwarf would attempt it.'

'And trolls?'

'Better swimmers than you'd imagine, some trolls,' Delvedeep said sagely. 'Not fast, but persistent.'

'An elf could probably get there and back in half the time.'

'Yes. Very handy swimmers the elves, or so I'm told.'

'I think this is one misfortune we can't hang on the elves, Chief Reeve.'

Delvedeep's face broke into a rare, genuine, smile. I don't know,' he said. 'I'm willing to give it a go if you are.'

We blew out the candles and made our way back to the lakeside. We parted company with a promise to keep each other informed if we came up with anything new.

A week later, I received a message from an apologetic Duffy to say that he was off for a break with Osk. The Lady Willow's family had finally arrived, and she was going away with them. The Warrior Princess had been called back home as soon as news of the murder has broken. Berger was now in Kellisgrund, painting, and Luce was nowhere to be found. Duffy gave me the Dragonette as a gift. Driving it didn't feel right now and I gave Jeskyn a toot on the horn and asked if I could drop it back. He said he would come and collect it. When he arrived, Jeskyn was his unchanged phlegmatic self.

'Thank you very much, Master Strongoak, for your assistance during this time. I'm afraid young Master Duffy is not at his best at the moment.'

'I'm afraid, Jeskyn, my assistance was not as much help as it should have been.'

'I do believe that you did your best, Master Strongoak. And, as is always said, that is all that can be asked of anybody.'

I'm sure it was kindly meant, but it felt worse than many admonishments I have received. I handed him the envelope to give back to Berger. I hadn't deserved that either.

My next Dragonette I would earn.

Six weeks later—all avenues of investigation exhausted—I was sailing out of Skragslanding and looking back at the rapidly vanishing port and the far off distant mountains of Skragsrealm. The breeze whipped up smoke from the ship's steam engines, and smuts must have got in my eyes, because I suddenly found them uncharacteristically damp.

Three weeks after that and I was in the Citadel and signing up with the Citadel Guard.

BOOK THREE

19

Torfull Halfaxen

I looked around at Grundrund, suddenly aware that her piercingly blue eyes had been on me for some time. We were well into the Skragslanding hinterland, still climbing steadily.

'You have been a long way away,' she observed.

'A very long way, or a very long time at least,' I said, bearing in mind where we were now driving.

'Was journey worthwhile?'

'That, Detective Analyst Grundrund, is often a difficult thing to decide on.'

She pumped the steam, and we continued to climb to our destination. I admired the view. There were some hair-raising drops available. It was a fine winter's day; you could see right to the bottom of the ravines and the rocks that would be more than willing to bash your brains out. Finally, we passed through a suitably modest gatehouse the size of small palace and approached our destination: Halfaxen Deep.

We arrived at a parking circle outside of a frontage that could have graced a major Citadel monument. Two mighty pillars, carved into the shape of cowering dragons, and a lintel on which a wise dwarf stood leaning on a large battle-axe; just in case you had forgotten your destination.

Like all such dwarf halls, Halfaxen Deep was built into the rock face. Enough clearance had been carried out to allow a number of formal gardens to be built out front. Water cascaded down the hillside to fill the various pools and water features. There were even some plants, but only really big impressive ones.

I got out of the wagon and looked down from the heights of Halfaxen Deep. Far below, I could see a dark blue pool glinting like a huge sapphire in the setting of the valley end – a jewel with one small flaw in the middle.

'Lake Skavernslager,' Grundrund said, by way of explanation.

'I never knew we were that close,' I replied, half to myself.

'Oh, yes. You know of it?'

'Something like that,' I replied.

'All this land hereabouts, it is owned by the Halfaxens. They have done well.'

'Haven't they just.' I slammed the wagon door shut, following Grundrund up to the massive wooden entrance doors.

The knocker was in the shape of a large, snarling wolf's head. I lifted and dropped it once. The BOOM threatened to bring the hillside down.

Grundrund looked at me with a tired expression best read as, 'is that really necessary?'

I looked at her with what I hoped was an expression that showed my disdain for any race that might contemplate the use of a doorbell when a heavy iron wolf's head was available.

She looked back at the vast expanses of oak door and sighed.

'What?!' I exclaimed, feeling a need to defend my kinsmen.

'Did not say a thing,' said Grundrund.

Dwarf Girls Don't Dance

Eventually, the door was answered by a dwarf that knew how to do 'dwarf' properly. He had the beard to the waist; he had the family knots in his hair, he had the leather jerkin fastened with a belt so wide it acted as a girdle, and he had an honest-to-goodness soft floppy felt hat. On anybody else, I might have laughed. I was not about to laugh at him – not until I had a weapon in my hand.

'Yes?' he said bluntly, looking straight at me and illustrating the legendary dwarf affability that has made us so many friends amongst other races.

'Here for Torfull Halfaxen; we called ahead.'

He considered this for a while before staring at me again.

'Hmm. You can come in but not the goblin.'

'The goblin, as you so sweetly put it, is a senior law enforcement officer from Kellisgrund.'

'This is not Kellisgrund,' the doorman observed correctly.

'No, but I would hate to see an avoidable "incident" cause unnecessary friction between Skragsrealm and Kellisgrund.'

'I do not think refused entry would constitute the sort of incident of which you speak,' he said dryly.

'I wasn't referring to a refused entry. I was talking about the ruckus caused by a dwarf having to be taken to see a physic to get his own foot removed from his outhole.'

The dwarf in the felt cap considered this for a while and then turned, beckoning: 'This way.'

We walked through the doors into a chamber that could have contained more statues, but only if they had been stacked one on top of the other – which would kind of ruin the effect, admittedly.

Instead of carrying on into the Hall proper we took a side door to a steep spiral staircase that led up into a room located some way above the entrance and overlooking the lake. This arrangement is common in larger dwarf halls, and the room is known, rather sweetly, as the sunroom.

Torfull Halfaxen was sat in a comfortable seat, with his feet up on a stool, looking out over his domain, spectacles on nose, and reading a scroll by the low winter sunlight. The room was comfortably decorated, in a restrained style, old comfortable armchairs, a few hard seats, with a large fire in one corner. Portraits covered all the walls, except over the fire, which was empty of decoration. Torfull was dressed in the style that best suited an ageing dwarf who had made his packet and now didn't give a pixie's fart. He looked like he had just strolled out of a cast-off-clothes sale.

'Your guests, Master Torfull,' said the dwarf in the felt cap.

'Thank you, Fastspade,' Master Torfull replied.

'I tried to stop the goblin,' Fastspade mentioned, casual as you like.

'Yes, dwarves often have done,' Torfull replied. 'Fortunately, generally, with more success.'

This gave them both something to laugh about.

'No, it's no problem, thank you. We both had a drink first thing this morning,' I interrupted the chuckle-fest to remind the famous Torfull of his obligations as a host.

'Oh yes, the Citadel dwarf,' said Torfull, looking at me as he might something unpleasant he found in his beard one evening and couldn't for the life of him think how it got there. He gestured something to his toadeater, who went off on his errand.

'I went to the Citadel once,' Torfull continued. 'I didn't care much for it, far too many different races, far too many elves, not to mention... other... races.'

Dwarf Girls Don't Dance

'Yes, isn't the modern world a trial?' I sighed. 'But moving on from your holiday stories, we have driven a long way to ask you for some assistance.' I sat on the nearest hard seat; not having been offered anything better. Grundrund continued to stand and glower.

'Then you have a strange way of going about asking for it, young dwarf,' Torfull said, now fully bristled up.

'Master Torfull, please excuse my colleagues manners,' Grundrund interrupted, the very voice of reason. 'However, we have indeed driven a long way here today. We are investigating the murder of the son of your partner of many years, Danwright Dollund, and we are sure that you will wish to assist us in our duties.'

'Oh yes, of course, of course,' said the wrong-footed Torfull. He wasn't expecting Good Goblin, Bad Dwarf!

'Good. In the course of our investigation, we have found a second coffer in the deceased's study, in addition to the one that was broken into.'

'Oh, you found that did you?' said Torfull, slightly surprised.

'Of course,' said Grundrund, admirably straight-faced. 'We are the Kellishaldt Keep, after all, we are not local reeves. However, we are now keen to get access to the contents – without damaging the coffer.'

Fastspade came back, carrying a silver tray containing two glasses of water—the minimum requirement of any host—giving Torfull some thinking time. Fastspade put the tray down on a small table next to me. I took a glass of tepid water, another insult, and waited until the old dwarf had left before continuing.

'It's a Guklon 608, Halfaxen,' I added. 'We know that you installed it for Dollund senior and we're pretty sure what's in it. So, come on and save us some time.'

'That is the Dollund family's business,' said Torfull, every ounce the stubborn dwarf again.

'They didn't even know there was another coffer,' said Grundrund. 'I have checked.'

'Danwright's arbiter then?'

'The bequest is not for several days, Master Halfaxen. We are losing time, and my client is in jail facing the death penalty,' I added.

'It's not my business – even if I knew what the coffer contained.'

'Oh, you know!' I insisted.

'If I knew, I repeat, it is not my business and even should I feel inclined to help you, it is the client that sets the combination, and he is the only holder of a key!'

'Thanks for the water then,' I said, slamming down my glass and walking out.

'Do you not think that your attitude might have been, just touch, abrasive?' Grundrund enquired as we got back into her wagon.

'Not at all,' I insisted.

'Not at all?' she queried.

'Well, I didn't hit him, did I? And I can tell you, that took some doing. Anyway, I knew it was the only way he was going to give you the time of day – if I irritated him even more.'

'I see,' said Grundrund, nodding her head slowly. 'Is that dwarf mind thinking?'

'Probably – or just my genuinely winning personality.'

Grundrund pumped some steam. 'However, we did not learn much.'

'Apart from the fact that he's hiding something.'

'The missing painting over the fire?' observed Grundrund.

'Well spotted, detective.'

'And?'

'Who was it of? The person that he didn't want us to see?'

'Exactly.'

'Plus, he knows what's in that coffer,' I considered, 'and doesn't want to confirm it for some reason. Which makes me wonder exactly how Danwright Dollund got the Heartstone in the first place?'

'That has never been established?' asked Grundrund.

'No. It has always been something of a mystery. But I think it's kind of important.'

'Then let us see what we can discover.' Grundrund pulled out and we started the long drive back to Kellisgrund.

'We should try that approach again, Grundrund: "Bad Dwarf, Good Goblin".' I mentioned. 'I think it rather throws them off track.'

'I am always the good goblin,' said Grundrund.

'Well, aren't you the teacher's little darling?'

'It is a long walk back, Master Strongoak,' she mentioned casually.

I laughed, and looked out the window as Skavernslager Lake disappeared from view behind the hillside. Soon, at last, Danwright Dollund would be put to rest, and I could finally get to talk to the rest of the family. That would be fun.

20

The Vigil

The vigil for Danwright Dollund the Second was a solemn affair. There was no attempt at pretending this was some sort of celebration of a life well lived. It's not really going to happen when that life has been so cruelly terminated; even at Danwright's advanced years it could hardly be seen as the sort of departure he would have hoped for. His end was brutal, and it was messy. No way could that be glossed over with an extra coat of 'non-drip'.

A Kellisgrund vigil lasts three days. Detective Analyst Grundrund had echoed High Captain Gobblod's desire for me to not interfere with any stage of the proceedings, so I generally lurked unseen at a distance. I lurk quite well and didn't draw any attention that I was aware of. Score one hoop for the Citadel Lurkers.

Day One of The Vigil is called the 'confirmation'. This is an open casket affair where the local population can stroll past the deceased in order to confirm, to their own satisfaction, the identity of the dead man and confirm he actually is dead as well. This apparently has given rise to the colourful local expression 'pinching the dead flesh', meaning to establish the authenticity of somebody deceased. Cute eh?

I didn't exactly pinch it, but I certainly did check the flesh as I snuck through behind another group of respectful dwarves, obviously away on business and paying their respects as they passed through. The flesh looked quite good; the local painter of the departed had done a good job. If you didn't know the scale of the injury that had been visited upon him, you probably wouldn't have guessed exactly what had occurred. I'd seen the pictures, and it hadn't been pretty. That was the result of anger, or perhaps even Rage.

I followed the dwarves out and thought I saw a face I recognised, busy organising things, but I didn't like to stare – or be stared back at. He was a tall, broad man with a full thick beard a dwarf patrician would not have been ashamed off. He was losing it on top too, not a worry I had, fortunately. He had moved on before I could place the face.

Day Two of the Vigil is called the 'affirmation', where the recently departed is put to rest in a manner that precludes unplanned-for returns. Danwright Dollund's burial was a quiet, dignified and respectful affair, without the pomp and extravagance you might see elsewhere. Dwarf interments, for example, can involve expenditure that might cripple some small nation-states, but who wouldn't want a million Golden Emperor butterflies released over your procession, accompanied by the wailing of a hundred professional Wailing Mothers? As the saying goes: 'you can't take it with you, so why not ruin the children?'

Some of the White and Wise said a few nice words about Danwright Dollund Snr, before he was weighed down and taken off to be thrown in a peat bog in that peculiar Kellisgrund fashion. It would be the family peat bog, but you couldn't get away from the peaty and boggy nature of the ground in which he was to take his final sleep. That's the problem with living in a country where the ground doesn't always respect the essential difference between the solid and liquid states.

Six of the largest horses I have ever seen pulled the funeral carriage across the soggy turf. Each animal had hoofs ideally suited for redistributing its weight over a large area, or for squashing dwarf feet. The horses plodded on across the grey landscape, not exactly sluggard, but not in any obvious hurry to reach their destination. Danwright Dollund Snr., presumably, wasn't bothered either. The faces of mourners were hooded and veiled in respect, which did not aid suspect identification. I caught a glimpse of red hair poking out from the hat of an expensively-dressed woman who was holding tightly onto a similarly dressed young girl. This is I took to be Passaloll, judging by the way the other chief mourners were avoiding her.

The rain started in earnest as the procession reached the appointed place. Lippy, who was doing the driving duties in the Heslington 650, while I lurked in the back, looked up as the cloud cover dropped to ensure not a single blade of the mossy-grass, or grieving mourner, remained unsoaked.

'A good day for a burial,' Lippy remarked.

'Really?' I queried, wondering if this was more of that famous Kellisgrund humour.

'Oh, yes! The body will sink quickly now.'

And it did. Kellisgrund welcomed back its native son with a noise pitched somewhere between a defective boiler and drain clearance. As the mourners trudged back to their wagons, the rain turned to sleet, and then snow, as the temperature

Dwarf Girls Don't Dance

plummeted. This was another good sign because apparently: 'It keeps the body from wandering.'

Lippy drove us back to town with a whistle on his lips, encouraged by the auspicious nature of the weather.

Day Three is called the 'appreciation'. This is the normal mix of praise singing and mud-slinging with which folk all over Widergard commemorate the termination of a life. In Kellisgrund the wake is actually before the reading of the bequest, and, according to local tradition, both are open affairs. And today both were causing a lot of interest, especially the bequest – not that anything unusual was anticipated. In Kellisgrund they just like to know where the money is going. Who doesn't?

This ordering of events would never happen in dwarf circles as it is not a good idea to get drink inside a dwarf prior to their learning that they have been disowned, or hard done by, and dwarves are always hard-done-by, if not disowned. Bad enough them drinking afterwards.

Day Three of the Vigil was happening in the Kellishaldt Hallow Hall, a great gilded and bejewelled barn of a place that didn't so much inspire awe as insist upon it. The problem with this form of architectural design is that you have to go for it 'no holds barred'. You couldn't help but feel that the natural Kellisgrund inclination towards frugality, as well as innate good taste, meant that they hadn't invested in as many hundreds of lengths of gold cloth and stained glass as they should have done. The stonework probably needed even more intricacy in the carving to ensure the masons would go properly blind, and there must have been a tree or two still standing in Kellisgrund that could have been chopped down to fashion even more ornate seating. Sad to admit, but not everybody has a dwarf's sense of profligate extravagance. On Day Three, it wasn't sleeting, raining, or snowing, so that, in local parlance, made it a fine day. There was even the occasional outbreak of sunshine that attempted to give the occasion some cheer. Good luck there.

I had stood myself at the back of the hall. Detective Analyst Grundrund joined me.

'I have had no joy on finding out the provenance of the Heartstone,' she informed me. 'Dwarf record keeping is very poor.'

'No,' I told her. 'Dwarf record keeping is brilliant. However, most of it involves keeping it away from people like yourself. That is why we call it record keeping. We keep them.'

Grundrund gave her best goblin grunt.

On the platform Senior Officer Gobblod, and some other wonderfully uniformed Kellishaldt Keep top people, paid their respects to the family. They then spoke to the assembled about how every effort was being made to ensure that the perpetrator of this heinous act speedily got their just desserts. Gobblod must have missed me as he spoke because he never waved back when I waved at him.

The dynamics in the hall were interesting. I got my first good look at Passaloll and daughter Semeline. She was haughty, tall and striking, with her mane of red hair barely restrained enough for custom and good taste. Put her next to Red Sylvester, and she would look like a candle next to a blowtorch. Passaloll's daughter Semeline looked younger than I had anticipated. Lest it be forgotten, this was a young girl who had lost her Daddy. I hoped they were taking care of her. Judging by the way that Passaloll was hogging attention playing the grieving widow, I feared not.

Passaloll had menials in plenty surrounding her, but no obvious family apart from her daughter. They formed a tight-knit group on one side of the room, while on the other side there was the obviously 'rival' faction.

'That is Hassally and Pallis,' Grundrund explained quietly. 'The youngest son and Dollund's only daughter. The thin line of chalk next to her is not the eldest son, that is Cannly Boscomere, Pallis's husband, who is something big in gravel.'

I looked at her with one eyebrow raised.

'Kellisgrund is a very wet country, Detective Strongoak.' she explained. 'Gravel is big business.'

A little while later when the funeral meats were being cut, Grundrund, dressed soberly in grey funeral leathers, with her mane of hair tied in a topknot held in place by a jewelled caul, led me to meet the family group. Officer Grundrund coughed as politely as enlarged canines will allow and addressed the back of the son and heir, Danwright Dollundson—soon to officially be Danwright Dollund the Third—who had now joined his brother and sister.

'Excuse me Master Dollundson,' she said, 'may I introduce my colleague Master Detective Strongoak.' The man's face, as he turned, underwent a multitude of emotions, before settling on something midway between shock and surprise, his mouth half-open in a most unbecoming and uncharacteristic fashion.

'Hello Duffy,' I said.

The years had not treated Duffy badly, but neither had the birthday pixie turned up with magic dust every year. He looked like what he was – a successful middle-aged businessman; one who spent too much time running his business and not enough time running.

His hand came out, and we shook, because that's what friends do, even after twenty years.

'You're looking well, Nicely,' he said finally. 'Some new scars I see.'

'And plenty more you can't see, Duffy.'

'That's the drawback of being a Shield, I suppose?'

'Not too much call for that service these days Duffy, but the detective work has its own rewards as well.'

'I'd heard Arbiter Skunglard had a dwarf detective working for him – I never thought for a moment it might be you.'

'It isn't. My client is Sanctity Sureseam, who you might know as Diamond.'

'Ah, right. I see' said Duffy, the merest trace of his old ready smile dancing around his still full lips.

'Not sure that you probably do, but I hope I'll get the chance to explain.'

'Yes, please do, and don't leave it too long.'

'Of course not.'

We looked each other up and down, both unsure where we stood. We couldn't be friends, but we were hardly enemies either. Brother Hassally looked on with a faint air of embarrassment, but Pallis was taking everything in. Her husband looked like he would have preferred to be anywhere else, probably examining his collection of gravel.

Duffy broke the silence.

'I like Diamond, Nicely. I thought she made the old man happy.'

'Good —well —I'm not sure if condolences are quite the right thing to express, but I am very sorry about what was done to your father, and I will find who is responsible.'

'This time?'

'Exactly. This time it's my investigation.' Duffy nodded, perhaps appreciating the point I was making.

Dwarf Girls Don't Dance

The well-dressed dwarf I had seen earlier approached Duffy, a slightly quizzical expression on his face, interrupting without a trace of apology. 'Duffy, I think the company council are looking to speak with you – with both of us; before the reading.'

'Of course, thank you,' said Duffy, to my well-turned out kinsman. 'Nicely, you never met Buns, did you?' He seemed to catch himself for a moment before continuing the introductions. 'Apologies, I should, of course, say Master Heldwide Halfaxen.'

Never met the heir to the Halfaxen fortune and the final full-time member of the Nine Idlers? No, I certainly hadn't, which now struck me as somewhat strange.

'And, this is Master Detective Strongoak, Buns.' Duffy pointed me out like an exhibit at a Beast Garden.

'Please, call me Nicely.'

There was a polite cough from Pallis.

'My apologies, I am completely forgetting my manners,' said Duffy. 'This is my sister Pallis.'

'Delighted.' I executed a small bow to the slim and elegant woman – very much a female version of her older brother. In her face the winning smile had a very different effect.

'A pleasure, Master Detective,' she said, nodding back. 'A long way from the Citadel.' Somebody had been doing their homework. I had a feeling Pallis always did her homework.

'And her husband, Cannly Boscomere.'

I was offered a hand as loose as loam as he addressed me in a very smooth voice: 'Delighted also, I'm sure. I'm in gravel, you know.'

'I did hear, Cannly; it sounds fascinating.'

'Oh, you think so?' Cannly perked up. 'Then you must come along to our annual feast – it's quite soon.'

Pallis wilted slightly. 'Cannly, please! I'm sure Master Strongoak has other things to be getting on with.'

'No, thank you, Master Boscomere. I would be delighted!'

'Everybody should be there, "gravel and conglomerates" – the cream of Kellisgrund society.' He looked around for confirmation and was greeted by nods.

Duffy finally got to continue: 'And this is my younger brother, Hassally.'

'Of course,' said Hassally, anything but the runt of the family. 'Do call me Hass, everybody does.' He shook hands enthusiastically.

'And I prefer Heldwide to "Buns" these days actually,' he said. 'As Duffy is well aware.'

'Isn't he just the tease?'

Heldwide "Buns" Halfaxen nodded and smiled and then we finally shook hands too, both evaluating the other. I saw a prosperous, dwarf, elegantly attired in funeral grey just entering the prime of life. He was on the short side and, like myself, completely clean-shaven, which, while not exactly being a rarity, is still worthy of comment. His light brown hair was pulled back, but cut quite short, almost mannish, and there was no trace of the family knots. Fine features, an inquisitive expression and a high forehead suggested a keen intellect, but I saw something else in there that was harder to get a grip on. A yearning maybe, or something darker? I tried to look for it again, but it had gone – quicker than a politician's promise after Election Day.

What he saw in me is anybody's guess.

'I believe you have all spoken to Detective Grundrund, Heldwide?' I said, indicating the unmissable goblin at my side.

'Yes, briefly. Good day, Officer.' Heldwide executed a short, stiff bow, which Grundrund formally echoed.

'And now, Duffy,' Heldwide continued, 'if I could just steal you away. The Company Council, please?

'Certainly. If you will excuse me, officer. Nicely – well, we'll catch up after the formalities. A lot of catching up to do.'

'I'll look forward to it, Duffy.'

Grundrund and I watched as Duffy and 'Buns' walked off and joined a circle of snow-tops, and they all withdrew to another room, prior to the reading.

'You did not mention that you knew the younger Danwright Dollandson,' said Grundrund.

'No,' I admitted, 'I didn't.'

'There is history?'

'Isn't Widergard just full of it?'

'It might have been useful for us to have had that information.'

'Did I mention that I work for Sanctity Sureseam and not the Kellishaldt Keep, Detective Analyst Grundrund?'

'I do believe it has come up,' she said, with that strange goblin chuckle. 'On occasion.'

'That's all right then.'

'I, however, do work for the Kellishaldt Keep,' she continued as the Officers of Remembrance came out to read the Bequest.

'Yes,' I said, 'that has come up before as well.'

Grundrund chuckled again, before she was beckoned away by her senior officer, presumably to report on how I had behaved myself with the younger Danwright Dollundson, the establishment figurehead. Was he in for a surprise!

Not being constitutionally equipped to stand around when the finger bar is open, I went to see if I could find a sausage that needed a friend. I was pleased to see the tables were loaded and the chances of reacquainting myself with some of the local links were looking good.

'Hello, Nicely,' said a voice I recognised from right behind me, and twenty years fell away as if it was yesterday – again! 'Still a slave to the tubular meat product?'

'Sansire,' I replied warmly as I turned, 'it was never slavery, more an act of devotion. And you still move quieter than a pixie on tippy-toes, but I'd recognise your perfume anywhere.'

She hadn't changed one jot, still looking like a young girl one moment and a mature woman the next – perhaps with the balance more of the mature now. She held out her hands, and we kissed elf style on both cheeks. 'This is a surprise!'

'A surprise, what really, Mistress Seer?'

She gave me a sad look and bit her bottom lip – a mannerism she never used to have. 'I lost my gift, Nicely, after Mansel. I am a seer no more.'

For a moment, I was speechless. A death can have so many consequences.

'I'm so sorry, Sansire.' I meant it. I knew such gifts can be both a blessing and a burden, but when you grow up with something so special, it must be like losing a limb – or a friend. 'I didn't know,' I finished, rather lamely.

'You left us very quickly.'

'It seemed for the best, and I didn't exactly have client's beating a path to my door. Still needed to make a living.'

'I heard you went to the Citadel, yes?'

'Yes, I joined the local Guard for a spell and got the lie of the land before I went private again.'

'Do you like it there?'

'Very much so, it kind of suits me.'

'Yes, I imagine it would do.'

'That's what Willow once said. It's what brought the place to my mind first of all.'

Dwarf Girls Don't Dance

'Of course, Willow.' Sansire looked suddenly very tired and in danger of collapse.

'Do you – does Duffy – ever hear from her?'

Sansire shook her head. 'Not a word, after her parents took her away, it was as if she had stopped existing. Nothing Duffy could say, or do, made any difference. I don't think she could stop blaming herself; I don't think she ever will. I don't think any of us will.' The former seer suddenly looked her age.

'Here, let's find a seat, Sansire.'

'Why, thank you, Master Dwarf. You always were very gallant.'

She took my arm with a touch as light as a pixie's kiss.

We found a couple of seats in an alcove away from the main throng of people who were busy eating and drinking, ahead of the main event. I realised I was still clutching a plate full of sausages in my free hand and continued to take them on board while Sansire brought me up to date.

'The life of a seer is a difficult one. Too many people think the gift is something at your beckoning, rather than the other way around. What is told – to the White and Wise, or even the general population – is closely monitored. That's the job of Seer House.'

Sansire bit her bottom lip again. 'What I had told Duffy, what I told you was…' She paused to think. 'It was unsanctioned. That did not go down well with Seer House, and I was "reprimanded", although when my gift departed – they were very kind.'

'And now? For you, I mean. Are you all right?'

'Why Nicely,' she laughed, much more her old self. 'Of course, I am! I married Osk!'

'Osk!' I couldn't help but exclaim.

'Yes,' she smiled, her mind going back to that fateful night, as indeed was mine. 'You do not think I share my bed lightly, I hope?'

I coloured slightly. 'Such was never my belief, as you well know – even without your seer abilities.'

'Osk is a good man, Duffy's right hand. It allows me to help Duffy too. It's not been easy for him, or for Osk either. We are well-suited, Nicely – a good match.'

'I'm happy for you both. I admit I didn't get a chance to know Osk as well as I would have liked.'

'Well, there is still time for that. Here he comes now.'

I looked around and saw the broad, balding and bearded man that I had half-recognised on the first day of the vigil. Now I placed the face, of course.

'Nicely Strongoak! Well, I do declare!' he said, with much more geniality than I remembered, reaching to shake my hand. 'You are hardly changed!'

'Osk Everman,' I replied. 'The years it seems have been good to you too.' They had. This was a person who had grown into his skin, as we say in New Iron Town. He was warm and confident, but you knew that here was someone not to be taken lightly either. Sansire had chosen well, as you might expect of a seer.

'It is a real pleasure to see you again Nicely, but sadly the occasion is no better than those events that saw the parting of our ways.'

'On that subject, Osk – Sansire too – you should know I'm not here simply to pay my respects, sincere though they may be.'

'I know,' said Osk. 'One of my agents prepared a report on the strange dwarf spotted on the first day of the vigil. I have been lax in my reading, otherwise Duffy would have known too.'

'I'm actually working for Sanctity Sureseam. Is that a problem?'

Osk shook his head. 'Of course not. We all only seek the truth, as we have always done. But we can talk more on this later.' He turned to his wife.

'Sansire, my sweet, perhaps you will be kind enough to join us when you have finished your catch up with Nicely. Duffy would be grateful for your opinion.'

'Tell him I'll be there shortly.' Husband and wife embraced with real affection and Osk hurried off, politely requesting and organising as he went.

I realised Sansire was looking at me with some amusement.

'Do you find Osk much changed?'

'Only for the better – he looks much more dwarvish for a start and how could that be anything but a change for the better?'

Sansire laughed with some of the lightness of her old self.

'And how about you, Nicely? Is there a wife in the Citadel?'

'No.'

'I thought not, somehow.'

'Gee, thanks, Sansire.'

She laughed again. 'I never saw you as the marrying type. But has life treated you well?'

'Occasionally. The rest of the time, I think I must have insulted his mother.'

'Always ready with the quick return, but do I detect a lack… something missing in your life perhaps?'

'Too much insight can lose you friends, Sansire.'

'And Sanctity… this "Diamond"?'

'A client.'

'Nothing more?'

'Just a client, Sansire.'

'I believe you, Nicely. I'm not sure that most of Widergard would.'

'Well, thank you for that at least. Now how about the rest of the Idlers? I must ask about poor Luce first, of course. He seemed a broken man. Has he found some peace at least?'

Sansire looked uncomfortable. 'I don't think there will be any peace for Luce. He seemed to blame himself, though I don't know why. We tried to support him, but it was as if a darkness had entered his heart.'

'That doesn't sound good at all.'

'No. He shuns company, moves on frequently – as if not wanting to be found. He does not use his gift at all. The last time we met, I hardly recognised him, so great was the change.'

'One life lost, and many lives damaged. It always seems to be the way.' I sighed and put down a plate of sausages that had lost their appeal.

'Of Berger at least there is good news!' continued Sansire.

'Excellent! The gnome was a fine fellow!'

'And now a very rich fellow. He exhibits in the Citadel too, you know. I am surprised that you haven't caught up with him there.'

'I don't make too many exhibitions, unless folk I know take me along. I must admit, my appreciation of modern art hasn't improved much. Although I do still have the two canvases that I bought from him.'

'Two, you say?'

'Yes,' I confirmed, nibbling at my drink. 'From what I remember, he was calling it his "gold leaf" period.'

'And you have two? Then you, my friend, have done well!'

'How well?'

She named a figure that had me nearly choking on my drink. 'I'm glad I take home security seriously. It seems my walls are now worth more than the rest of the property.'

Sansire laughed at this. She was getting good at the laughing. I don't think she'd been laughing too much in recent years. Smiles but not laughs.

'How about our favourite Warrior Princess?' I had to ask.

'I thought you would be the one telling me, Nicely.'

I shifted rather uncomfortably. 'I didn't have a forwarding address, and she wasn't too sure about her plans, so…'

There was something of a hubbub in the main room as the goodfolk made their way in from the backrooms to the platform set up for the Bequest announcement.

'It looks like I am needed, Nicely. I had better leave the rest of my news about the Princess until another time.'

'But nothing bad?'

'No – nothing bad.' She looked at me in a manner that made me feel slightly uneasy. It must have showed on my face.

'I wouldn't lie to you, Nicely. All is indeed well with Zella, but you might be surprised.' She went off to join her husband and Duffy.

'Zella.' I rolled it around on my tongue, and it didn't sound too bad. 'She never even told me her name,' I said to absolutely nobody at all. They had no reply either.

The past is a nice place to visit, but I wouldn't want to buy a house there, let alone move in. I needed to be thinking about the here and now. Diamond didn't have time for reminiscences.

21

The Bequest

The hall had filled to bursting point. All seats were taken as the Chief Arbiter of Kellisgrund—a round, well-fed sort who looked more like a butcher than a legal body—brought the bequest to order. Disappointed attendants looked daggers at those they thought should vacate their choice positions.

I didn't mind standing.

I found a place next to Grundrund at the back where I had a good view across the throng: Passaloll and Semeline and acolytes seated to one side, Hass, Pallis and Canny to the other. On the platform, Duffy and Heldwide Halfaxen and a snow top, who was introduced to the assembled as the council leader of Dollund and Halfaxen, joined the Chief Arbiter. The presence of so many commerce folk, at what was usually a family affair, showed just how important this funeral announcement was.

The bequest went pretty much as everybody expected, to begin with. As the Arbiter now disclosed, Duffy inherited his father's share of the company, along with the main residence. This meant, given Torfull's retirement, that he would be running the business with Heldwide. Allowances were assigned for all the children, with an extra amount specifically allocated for Semeline's education, the details of which were outlined in a separate document. This raised a murmur or two; obviously, the mother was not going to get all her own way there.

I shot Passaloll a quick look. Her mouth was smiling meekly, but her eyes were as cold as cut glass in a deep freeze. She occasionally touched her nose and eyes with a small scrap of lace, so overcome was she with emotion.

The Chief Arbiter then announced that the widow herself was provided with accommodation and upkeep for life: in Laskgard Lodge in Skragslanding! This stopped Passaloll's rather forced snivelling and something very much nastier arrived on her face. I wondered if Jeskyn was still around to enjoy the prospect of her in residence. I don't think Dollund would have been that mean to him.

There was then the mention of various good causes, all of whom received generous gifts before the Chief Arbiter cleared his throat for the announcement of something that his tone, as he commenced, clearly indicated was likely to be controversial. He read the scroll very carefully, staring intently as if the words might change as he perused.

'Finally, to the matter of the Dollund Heartstone. I leave this to the Diamond who has brightened up my twilight years – Mistress Sanctity Sureseam.'

They often say, upon such occasions, that 'the place erupted'. I know what they mean now. Folk, including the now more angry than grieving widow, leapt to their feet.

'It's a lie,' she shouted. 'Some fabrication! The Heartstone is mine. It's mine!'

Other folk joined in, as if they all should have some say over what an old man could or couldn't do with the dispersal of his belongings. This, unfortunately, had the effect of completely blocking my view.

'Anything?' I asked the much taller goblin at my side.

'Genuine surprise is my reading.'

'The estranged widow seems the most annoyed.'

'Not happy at all,' Grundrund confirmed.

The Chief Arbiter called for some hush and eventually got it. 'Following on from that,' the Arbiter coughed dryly, 'and information we have received from the Kellishaldt Keep, it seems that the Dollund Heartstone cannot now be declared "missing". Danwright Dollund's bequest contains details for the opening of the coffer containing the gemstone, the location of which has been identified by a "consultant" advising the Keep officials.'

This caused another wave of murmurs through those here assembled.

'Hey,' I whispered, 'now I'm a consultant! Well, polish my shiny magic ring!'

'Be quiet dwarf, less your magic ring gets a very mundane boot up it.'

The Arbiter drew events to a conclusion: 'This second coffer will then be opened tomorrow, in the presence of the family, beneficiaries, myself and key officials. Thank you.'

There was a secondary eruption, perhaps more properly called an after-quake of activity, as folk left the platform.

'You had better put a double guard on Dollund's house tonight now that particular bird has sung!'

'Yes,' said Grundrund, still scanning the platform. 'A duty I will look forward to. You should know, Halfaxen's expression is interesting.'

I looked, but Buns was obscured as he accompanied Duffy off the stage as a whole tide of reporters and scribes bombarded him with questions concerning his reaction to his father's alleged murderer getting the family jewel.

'Probably just a typical dwarf reaction – they tend to think they have an automatic right to all precious stones.'

"Is it "they" now, Detective Strongoak?'

'Some of us have learnt that there are more precious things in Widergard than cut and polished minerals, Detective Grundrund.'

'I will make a note.'

In the middle of the fuss and bother, I spotted a red-faced High Captain Gobblod heading in our direction, his grey eyes flashing and his face set.

'It looks like your superior is after a conversation, Grundrund.'

'My boss, never my superior, Nicely.'

'My mistake. I wonder how long he thinks he can hold Diamond now? That blows her motive right out of the water.'

'We shall see. I believe it is about time that I lost you in the crush, don't you think?'

'Consider me lost.'

I snuck out of the hall amidst the over-excited crowd and then realised Grundrund was still behind me.

'I think we both must have got lost,' she said conversationally.

I smiled to myself. The dwarf and goblin were becoming quite a team. Who would have thought it?

To my surprise, Heldwide Halfaxen was outside the main hall in the cloakroom, waiting for us. He looked agitated and ill at ease.

'Detectives, I must apologise for my father's behaviour when you visited,' he said without preamble. 'I am afraid that as he has become older, he has got more… difficult.'

'It happens,' I said, diplomatically.

'Even goblins are not immune. Some become bad-tempered and prone to outbreaks of violence,' Grundrund added with a remarkably straight face.

Heldwide looked at Grundrund as if he wasn't sure whether she was being serious or not. I had no idea either. Angry goblins, whatever next? Conceited elves? Realistic men?

'In this case,' Heldwide ploughed on regardless, 'his attitude has unfortunately affected the merit of some business decisions. He has now been persuaded to retire. The result of a company vote, and that has not made him any more agreeable.'

'I guess it wouldn't,' I conceded.

'However, Master Halfaxen,' Grundrund said, all professional law-enforcement officer again. 'You should know that there are aspects of Danwright Dollund's murder that we believe your father can help us with. If we don't find any co-operation forthcoming soon, we will have to continue our questioning in Skragslanding – in the Keep.'

'Yes, of course, of course, Officer.' Heldwide shifted uncomfortably. 'We will make sure it doesn't come to that.'

'Good.'

Heldwide shifted uncomfortably. 'I wonder if I might have a private word with Master Strongoak? I assure you that it has no bearing on the case.'

Grundrund nodded politely, 'I'll see you in the wagon outside, Detective Strongoak.'

Heldwide waited until Grundrund was out of the front door before proceeding – he obviously knew all about a goblin's sense of hearing.

'Apologies, Nicely. If I may call you, Nicely?'

'Of course, Heldwide. It's the name my mother used to sew into my game wear.'

'Quite – only, it's probably worse with my father than you realise. There have been memory losses, and he's disappeared sometimes for days at a time.'

'Sorry to hear that, but presumably important business information is not just kept in his head?'

'Of course not, but it then becomes a case of acquiring the appropriate authorisation, for the company arbiters' benefit naturally.'

'I see.' I tried not to let my impatience show, but it must have because Heldwide hurried on.

'Anyway – that really isn't why I wanted to speak with you. To celebrate my father's retirement we have a party coming up – hardly great timing, but not cancellable now – and I'd be delighted if you could attend.'

'Me?' I said, taken aback.

'Yes. The remaining Idlers will all be there, and it will provide an opportunity for that catch up Duffy spoke about. And we never really had an opportunity to get to know each other… before. Please do come – I'm sorry I can't extend the invitation to your colleague. Some of my father's friends are what I do believe is now called "old-mine". They think racial integration went too far when elves were allowed to piss in the same pots as dwarves.'

The swearing coming from this very respectable modern dwarf made me laugh.

'Thank you, Heldwide. I'd be delighted, of course.' We shook hands, and I left to join Grundrund in the wagon.

'What was that all about?' she asked, pumping up some steam.

'Detective Grundrund, much to my surprise, it seems that there are still some sections of the dwarf community that would rather see a giant lob on their birthday cake than a goblin sitting at their dining table.'

'Hmm,' Grundrund grumbled to herself, pulling out and heading into the Skragslanding traffic. 'I think there are many goblins who would rather eat the lob than a dwarf's birthday cake.'

'All come a long way, haven't we? Do please drop me off at the Keep, driver. I have a client that I really should remind of my existence and continued interest in their well being. And perhaps you'd be so kind as to ask your colleagues to find her belongings that they appropriated outside the *Happy Hobgoblin*.

'Mud dragons eat dwarves,' Grundrund said, out of nowhere. 'Very tasty.'

22

Diamond Again

Diamond looked concerned, as well she might. Arbiter Skunglard had been leaving increasingly irate requests and then demands at the *Skragshelder Inn*—not a place I was spending too much time—for updates and meetings and all sorts of things that didn't really exist in this dwarf detective's word scrolls.

I put her bag, kindly provided by Grundrund, onto the table and then sat myself down before speaking: 'Hopefully, the good officers of Kellishaldt Keep have managed not to mangle everything in pursuit of their lawful duties.'

'It took you long enough,' she said, having a good rummage.

'You know me, Diamond, I go out for a quiet drink for an evening and come back six months later being chased by a barbarian horde.'

I sat patiently as she finished her rummage. 'I think it's all there,' she said.

'But no Heartstone, Diamond. And that was such a disappointment to the boys and girls of the Keep that they decided to bounce me around the room a few times.'

'Oh Nicely,' she said, putting her hand over mine. 'I do hope they haven't devalued your vital assets?'

'No, I cleverly put my face in front of anything that might have suffered serious harm.'

'Well done! And did they at least apologise afterwards?'

'What, for something which, not being in possession of an incriminating stolen gemstone, was obviously my own fault? No apology at all, but I was rewarded.'

'Oh, yes?'

'I got my very own goblin minder.'

'Oh – I'd hate to see what they do for punishment.'

'It's actually worked out quite well.' I leant forward, spoke low, and swapped to old dwarvish to give us some privacy. 'It seems that the aforementioned Detective Analyst Grundrund is rather a fan of Law and has therefore proved quite useful.'

'She?' Diamond said, raising a still perfectly clipped eyebrow. 'It seems that certain sections of Kellisgrund law enforcement could give the Citadel a run for their gold.'

'Indeed. Hopefully, I can update you on that after you are released.'

'Released?' she repeated eagerly.

'I don't want to raise your hopes too high, but old man Dollund's bequest has made it clear that the Heartstone has been left to you.'

'Isn't that a nod on the noggin!' Diamond sat back abruptly, taking that snippet of news in.

'Once they get this coffer open tomorrow and clock the inscription on the casing – well, I can't see anyway that they can keep you in here.'

Dwarf Girls Don't Dance

Diamond leaned forward and gripped my hand tightly, 'I can't tell you what a relief it will be to get out. My neck was getting very worried.'

'It's not alone there,' I admitted.

'So, what next?'

'According to the Chief Arbiter, you're going to be present at the coffer's opening.'

'Oh goody,' said Diamond, smiling, 'a day out. I think I could manage a change of scenery.'

In the end, it all got rather crowded in Danwright Dollund's study. Pentiant had shown us in. The young, elegantly dressed gnome, seemed very much on edge, as well he might be. Present about him were the key officials: the Chief Arbiter of Kellishaldt and High Captain Gobblod of the Kellishaldt Keep, plus Detective Analyst Grundrund and two scouts.

Family was represented by Danwright Dollund the Third, his brother Hassally, his sister Pallis and his stepmother Passaloll – mostly, I was guessing, because nobody had the nerve to turn her away. She had no immediate mouthpiece with her and looked rather nervous. The beneficiary of this bequest, Sanctity Sureseam, had been allowed out of keep clothes, but did have a bracelet attached to a large female goblin guard – who fitted the goblin stereotype a lot more closely than Grundrund. On her team were Arbiter Skunglard and a Master Dwarf Detective.

'I couldn't do anything about Skunglard,' Diamond whispered to me. 'It seems I am stuck with him.'

'That and your very own goblin,' I whispered back to her.

'Your one scrubs up better,' she tittered.

I looked over at Grundrund. I had become rather used to her over the last few days. Objectively, there was no doubt; she certainly cut an opposing figure. I wondered idly if the blonde hair was natural and then put that thought somewhere very, very far to the back of my mind.

Heldwide Halfaxen was also there. I wondered why at first, until the Chief Arbiter cleared his throat to ask for some quiet.

'I have asked Master Halfaxen here this afternoon, as the representative of the company who produced the deceased Danwright Dollund's personal coffer, to oversee this opening.'

The Arbiter opened a small locked purse and handed him a key and a piece of paper. Heldwide took it with due reverence.

'Tsk, tsk,' I muttered to Diamond. 'We're not launching a steamship here today, are we?'

Diamond giggled some more. It was good to hear. Hopefully, I'd be hearing it a lot more very soon.

Heldwide used the key first. This was the sort of little detail that was really helpful when opening a sophisticated coffer like the Guklon 608. Get the order wrong and you could try turning the key, or putting as many numbers in as you liked, but you'd still be trying when the ice giants returned and flattened everything. Heldwide also turned the key seven times; each turn rearranged the tumblers. He then turned it back one – tricky, tricky.

I sent Detective Grundrund a 'told you so' look, but she remained impassive. Heldwide then proceeded to dial in the numbers. This took some time. There were a lot of numbers.

Finally, Heldwide did something clever with the coffer handle, and the lid was open. He reached in, but Grundrund was quicker.

'If I might be allowed, please, Master Halfaxen.'

'Yes, of course. Just trying to help,' said the dapper dwarf, retiring quickly with what looked like embarrassment all over his cleanly-shaven face.

Dwarf Girls Don't Dance

Grundrund looked to Gobblod and got a nod. Strangely, at least to me, he did not seem to want to hog the limelight today.

Grundrund reached in with one large hand and brought out a clear crystal box. In the box was the Heartstone. Even in her huge grip, the gem was not diminished. There wasn't quite a 'sharp collective intake of breath', but it came close. My every dwarf sense responded to the presence of the gem – but my normal response was altered, changed in a way that was somehow familiar, but I could not quite place. Maybe it was the crystal of the box.

'The casing has an inscription,' Grundrund said, bringing my mind back into focus. She looked at Gobblod again, but he was impassive.

'Would you read it for us please, Officer?' said the Chief Arbiter.

Grundrund opened the box and read it out perfectly, and each word was a delight to hear.

'For Sanctity Diamond Sureseam, a diamond that is second only to her in beauty, in the hope that you will light my twilight years.'

'No!' screamed the former Mistress Dollund, 'it's mine!'

Passaloll seemed to undergo a remarkable transformation, becoming a thing of teeth and nails as she threw herself at Diamond. Fortunately, her goblin guard stopped the attack with one free hand. Unfortunately for Passaloll, this involved said hand holding her by the throat.

'Stepmother!' shouted Duffy, with as commanding a voice as any I have ever heard from him. 'That is quite enough. My father's wishes cannot be clearer. The Heartstone is Sanctity's.'

'Quite so,' added the Chief Arbiter.

'If you would put Mistress Dollund down please, guard,' said Gobblod. He at least was considering Passaloll's wellbeing.

'I think that is your cue, Arbiter Skunglard,' I said to the slightly shocked official hovering behind Diamond as if she might afford protection from the frenzied woman.

'What? What's that you say?'

'As Sanctity knew that she was being offered, not just the Heartstone, but Dollund's entire fortune if she became his wife…' I waited for Skunglard to take-over from me, but he still looked about as much use as a snowman in a firefight.

'A fact Officer Grundrund will confirm.'

The large goblin nodded her affirmative.

'Hence my client clearly has no motive to kill the deceased, in fact, Dollund's death works against her interest, and so you should ask for her immediate release.'

'Oh no!' said Skunglard.

'Oh yes!' I almost shouted back at him.

'No, that's not the way we do things in Kellisgrund. There must be a trial, oh yes! Justice must be seen to be done.'

'Nicely?' said a worried Diamond. 'Surely this isn't right?'

'Are you joking?' I really shouted now. I was now threatening to lose it myself. 'What sort of Arbiter are you? Whose side are you on?'

'The side of justice, of course,' the old fool said, readjusting his gowns.

Grundrund stepped forward to prevent me getting at Skunglard. 'Not the place,' she hissed quietly, but urgently.

'Please calm yourself, everybody!' said the Chief Arbiter. 'Arbiter Skunglard, of course, has the right to see his client's name cleared by trial. I will set the date tomorrow, when we are all more recovered.'

Dwarf Girls Don't Dance

'Right?' I steamed. 'My client has the right to be release from your keep!'

Grundrund now had my arm pinned behind my back. I shrugged, and she let me go, just in time to collide with Passaloll as she stormed out.

'You have not heard the last of this, you and your annoying little peeler!' she whispered poisonously in my ear.

She really was a lovely piece of work, but I would worry about her later. In the meantime, I had to watch Diamond's worried face pleading with me as her guard took her away – the threat of death still hanging over her head.

23

Retirement

The urgency of Diamond's predicament was preying on my mind. They wouldn't even let me stand surety for her. Apparently, it just wasn't done for murder suspects. Not even when their case was as good as dismissed. I wanted her out of there; certainly, before glove evidence came into the picture.

I was not in a party mood, and the weather had changed to match my furious state of mind. The first proper snowfalls of the winter were forecast, but hopefully not for another day or two.

The Heslington handled well, and the bridge made the first part of the journey easy enough. I was going against the flow of traffic, which helped, but Skragslanding was pretty snarled up when I surfaced again. Wagons were steaming in the rapidly cooling air, as their drivers steamed up inside. Hitting your horn always helps in these circumstances, and I was pleased to see that the folk of Skragsrealm were the same as folk everywhere when it came to indiscriminate horn use.

The roads cleared a bit, and I could make better time. It seemed much further in the inclement weather and a lot wilder too, far more of that 'nature' stuff that gets folk so excited. The hill climb wasn't easy, and this was not the weather to make driving errors. I could bring those nasty drops to mind far too easily.

After what seemed an age, Halfaxen Deep was finally in sight. The gardens had been cleverly covered to provide extra parking space, and it was needed. I put my coat on the backseat and handed the Heslington over to a gnome help. Then, holding tightly onto the Hat in the stiffening breeze, with the first snowflakes falling, went to enjoy the party. Yippee.

Fastspade was not in evidence, which was a good start. Heldwide was doing the host's duties in the entrance hall.

'Master Strongoak,' he said, shaking my hand warmly. 'So pleased you could make it!'

'Thank you for the invitation, Master Halfaxen,' I responded.

'That's the formalities over!' Heldwide replied, laughing. 'How were the roads?'

'Not bad, getting a little icy, but the wagon didn't seem bothered.'

'Very good road holding, the Heslington. Now please, leave your hat, and whatever else you wish to lose. No formalities this evening.'

I thanked Heldwide again and went through to Halfaxen Deep proper. Wonderful food and drink smells rode the wave of heat that hit me as the inner doors were opened. The food hall was a sight, with so many roaring open fires that you almost didn't need the artful coloured lights on display throwing fascinating red, blues and yellow shapes against the walls and ceiling as they did.

A, quite frankly, almost shameful amount of food was in evidence. You have to give it to us dwarves; when it comes to something like this, we know how to do it properly. If anybody goes home from a dwarf party still hungry, they probably had their jaws wired together beforehand. Either that or they are grass-munchers, in which case they are so very much at the wrong social function. Don't get me wrong, vegetables have their place – mostly under large slabs of burnt and bleeding meat.

In the food hall, I counted ten suckling pigs on spits, various assorted fowl – including a goose that needed two gnomes to lift it – a hogget over a huge fire-pit and a pike that probably would have eaten the goose given half a chance. Dwarves like pike, it makes a change from all that meat – in fact, some dwarves consider pike to be something like a vegetable.

There were actually vegetable dishes available, of course. Dwarves have a great appreciation of gnome cookery and are admirers of the various spicy bean dishes that they concoct. Their seven-bean spicy special is particularly popular after a busy working week. Preceded by seven or eight pints of good strong ale it is considered to be an excellent evening's diversion, being both cathartic and purgative.

I hadn't seen so many dwarves in the one room for a very long time. All dressed in their best finery, with gold chain chinking and rings flashing. I could hear the familiar hard consonants being spat out and it gave me a strange feeling, like I had suddenly been transported back to New Iron Town: 'and he woke up and realised it had all been a dream'.

However, it wasn't a dream, it never is, and everything wasn't right in the state of Skragsrealm, no matter how much the good dwarf folk ate and drank. There were also plenty of taller figures in evidence. Some I could place, many I couldn't. I spotted Sansire, looking elegant and talking to Duffy by a table of finger foods.

Dwarf Girls Don't Dance

The Main Hall was reserved for the serious business of drinking and dancing – two activities that dwarves enjoy immensely – frequently at the same time. I was very pleased to see a familiar gnome head bobbing up and down excitedly by a barrel of beer that was nearly as large as he was. I went over.

'I should have known you wouldn't be able to refuse an invitation to a free party,' I said, as the gnome sampled the ale.

'Nicely, my dear fellow! My, dear, dear fellow!' shouted Berger, turning and spilling his beer everywhere. 'They said you might be coming! Well met, oh yes, well met indeed!'

The hug I received was enough to warm the heart of even the most stonehearted of dwarves. Detectives are made of sterner stuff, of course.

'You've grown,' I did have to comment. 'Rich,' I added, after I saw his face drop. 'Or so I hear?'

'Yes, it appears I have,' Berger said, with a very forced sigh. 'I had hoped to die an unrecognised genius, starving in my garret. But alas,' he patted his round belly contentedly, 'it seems I will have to suffer the blight of wealth and success and just hope that my creative spirit can still flourish in the midst of plenty. It's a chance I know, but I'll just have to take it.'

'There is certainly plenty here, even for you.'

Berger nodded happily, but his eyes were somewhere else as he spoke: 'A very bad business this, Nicely. I tried to get back for the Vigil, but my paymasters in the Citadel consider it very bad form to not turn up for a meet-and-greet being held in your honour.'

'I don't think Dollund Senior would have held it against you.'

'No – but it's not for the dead, is it? Never for the dead.'

Berger fixed me with a concerned eye.

'This is your area of expertise, Nicely. Is it just me, or are things getting rapidly worse? Is wickedness becoming commonplace again? It's just that, after Mansel's murder and now poor Duffy's father, and all this talk of Dark Crime Lords. I can't help but think we're heading to a very grim place.'

'Seriously, Berger – I don't know.' To give myself a moment, I filled up a convenient flagon. Good beer can help bad thoughts.

'I would say,' I continued, 'that wickedness has always been with us, perhaps always will be. Yes, we gave it a good kicking for a while. We thought it had all gone away. Sadly it was down, but not out. It's found a new way of worming itself into the apple to spoil things.'

Berger nodded in agreement as I continued: 'It doesn't have to be all marauding dragons and necromancers. Evil's woken up to the modern world and it's finding new ways to exert its will. And what's worse, I think it's beginning to find much of what today has to offer very much to its liking.'

'Is that our fault, Nicely?'

'Only if we let wickedness get away with it.'

'Well said, Master Detective!' cried Berger, spilling more beer. 'Come let us drink to that, after all this is a day for celebration.' Berger lifted his flagon. 'Buns comes into his own!'

I toasted along with Berger. Buns comes into his own. I hadn't considered it that way, but I suppose that was indeed the case.

Yes, it was a day for celebrating, but celebrating was still the last thing on my mind. Not wishing to be churlish, we toasted Master Buns again and had a couple more drinks and caught up on the sort of things normal folk talk about.

Normal. I think I fooled Berger.

With the party in full swing, I saw the opportunity for a little quiet detecting. I was up the spiral staircase quicker than you

Dwarf Girls Don't Dance

could say, "Fleas, you fool! That's why I'm scratching" and was outside the door of the sunroom in a pixie twinkling.

The sunroom had a good dwarf-made lock. I am a good dwarf lock picker.

A full fire was dying down in the grate and lit the room well enough for my dwarf eyes. Above the mantel, there was now a rather prosaic picture of Halfaxen Deep by moonlight. It wasn't the kind of picture I would give pride of place to, and I don't think Torfull would either. Closer inspection of the wall around the edges showed that the frame didn't quite match where the sun had previously bleached the wall paint.

'So, what did you take down and why, Master Halfaxen?'

I looked around the rest of the room in case the answer was hidden behind a trunk or the daybed, but I wasn't that lucky.

In fact, my luck had just run out.

Thankfully Torfull was already well lubricated, and so he fumbled with his keys at the door. I dived down behind the daybed and held my breath.

Torfull was singing a merry little tune from his younger days, punctuated by swigs taken from a bottle of something sticky. Black Star, or my nose was mistaken.

I heard him sit down at his desk, and open a drawer. I smelt pipeweed, and then a little later there was a 'click' of a flint and the satisfied sigh of a dwarf enjoying his pipe. So, Torfull was having a little break for a smoke, hopefully prior to getting back to his guests before both he, and me, were missed.

'Oh my darling, if only you were here today,' murmured Torfull. 'You should see the hall, never has it looked so magnificent. You would have loved it – tra la la. A queen you would have been, if only, if only – tra la. But you're here with me now. I know it somehow – tra la la. Here in spirit if not in body.'

Oh my – it seems Torfull Halfaxen wasn't digging with a whole shovel. Or perhaps it was the Black Star talking.

'And soon your picture will be back in its rightful place, and we will be shot of that lanky New Iron Town fool!'

Now that wasn't nice, was it? I didn't mind the lanky. Never been called that before.

With a whole cartload more of 'tra las' Torfull finished his pipe and topped up with his favourite tipple. There was a knock at the door, and another dwarf entered.

'Torfull, your guests are looking for you,' said Fastspade.

'Oh, let them!' Torfull responded with the grace of a five-year-old.

'Heldwide is also asking.'

'Hang it all! Whose party is this?'

'His?'

Torfull went quiet. The arrow had hit home. I heard the sounds of tidying away and the grumbles of an old dwarf getting up.

'I'm coming Fastspade, I'm coming! Give me a moment.'

With Fastspade's help, Torfull was finally up and out of the room. They forgot to lock the door, which saved me a job. I had a last quick look around, but there was nothing else that resembled that most endangered of species: the clue. I would have given the keys to my Dragonette to know who his darling may have been. I had a suspicion it probably wasn't Buns' Mum.

I decided to get a quick breath of fresh air and use this as an excuse for my absence. I made it down the stairs unseen and walked out of the front door and almost straight into Torfull Halfaxen.

Dwarf Girls Don't Dance

'Look where you are going, young dwarf!' Torfull almost spat.

'My apologies, Master Halfaxen, I was just getting some air.'

'Oh, it's you!' he grumbled, recognising me. 'Typical New Iron Town! Can't see what's in front of you!'

'A splendid party,' I said, attempting some placation. 'I must thank you for the invitation.'

'Don't thank me, Strongoak! My son's idea.' He shook snow off his feet. It was now getting quite deep outside. 'I don't have a tendency to share my table with goblin lovers. No more than I share it with goblins.'

Torfull shook himself and walked past me and into his hall. He was very much 'old mine' and should probably be buried in one.

I put enough snow on my shoes to give myself an alibi and then came straight back in. Too cold out there for us lanky Citadel softies. I tried some of the other reception rooms and was pleased to find even more food and drink. I also found Duffy sitting by himself, in a foul mood, with a large bottle of beazer teaser for company.

'Hi Duffy,' I said casually, as if it was just another day in Skragslanding. 'No, Sansire? I thought I saw you two talking?'

'Sadly, Sansire is not feeling very well. She has gone to bed, and Osk is looking after her,' replied Duffy.

'Sorry to hear that.' I paused and took a drink from the bottle he had now placed on the table at his side. 'They seem very well matched – devoted even.'

'Yes, they are very happy. Sansire is also a tremendous help to my business. I would be lost without them. I would like to give her an official position, but she keeps refusing my offers. Anyway, she said that she would catch up with you in the morning.'

'Morning?' I queried.

'Well, yes. Nobody is going to be safe to drive. This storm seems to be coming in quicker than anticipated.'

'Axes and blood! I have no time to party a whole day away!' I replied, still rather cross from my chat with Torfull.

Duffy looked at me coldly before speaking: 'No, we all know how well that turned out for Mansel.'

I turned on my heel and stomped out, Duffy's apology following me out of the room.

'I'm sorry, Nicely. That was uncalled for! Nicely!'

I wasn't in the mood to listen to that either. I stomped out, not sure of my destination. Things were livening up in the main room, and I could hear Torfull Halfaxen getting into his paces – voice roaring above the hubbub. The polite 'fine dining' was well and truly over, and those that were meant to be impressed would be suitably impressed by now, or like me, not give a pixie's piss.

The rest of the night would be given over to the old songs, as Torfull and his cronies relived the glory days of their youths: the boardroom battles won, the take-overs beaten off and empires built; different language but the same age-old sentiments.

I'd had a bellyful of all of it – bloody dwarves! I stomped with a purpose now and nearly stomped right into Heldwide Halfaxen as he entered the hall from what I took to be a scullery.

I don't think he recognised me for a moment, but then his concentration seemed to click back into focus again. 'Ah, my dear Master Detective, how goes it with you? Come, you don't have a drink, let me get you something a little sticky?'

'No, thank you Heldwide.' I tried to remain polite – after all, he wasn't responsible for his father's continued bloody-mindedness. 'Got a dragon to slay and not a lot of time to do it. What with the snow and all.'

'Of course,' he smiled understandingly. 'I'll have your wagon brought around.'

'Please make my goodbyes.'

'Consider them made.'

A thought went quickly through my head. 'And apologise to your mother from me. I didn't even get a chance to pay my respects.'

'My mother lives at her family home in Old Iron,' Heldwide said, looking at me unblinking. 'She is very traditional and not particularly social, especially when it comes to the others who share Widergard with us. I think, perhaps, that you understand this sentiment?'

'Certainly,' I said, smiling. 'Only too well.'

We shook hands. I picked up the Hat from where I had carefully placed it and went to wait for the Heslington.

24

Huldre

I headed down the mountain in a rotten frame of mind. I was sick of obstinate, dunderheaded men and even sicker of obstinate, dunderheaded dwarves. I was also now even more conscious of how the days until Diamond's trial were ticking off alarmingly fast.

The wind and snowfall had picked up big time, but the Heslington wasn't really too bothered. It was made for this kind of weather. It would stay on the road as long as I could find it, which, admittedly, was getting harder to do. Thankfully there was some moonlight to help me out, as well as the twin beams of the Heslington's own impressive headlamps that cut through the blowing snow like an axe through elf – as the saying goes. Of course, the other thing required to stay on a treacherous road is good brakes and, picking up speed as I steamed down the hill. I suddenly realised I didn't have any – brakes that is.

Somebody had shred my fetters.

It was one of those moments when, if you believe the scrolls, everything goes into slow motion. A falling snowflake can take a week to settle, a blink of an eye is a phase of the moon and glaciers grow and retreat in the time a water drop falls. All the while, the true horror of the situation takes hold of your insides and then shows on your face.

That's so much unicorn widdle.

When the world is moving that fast, then it can only feel faster as you are caught up in the whirlwind as well. I was only conscious of one thing: my situation wasn't going to get any better. The slope was getting steeper, my speed was increasing, and memory reminded me that there was a serious set of curves coming up with some precipitous drops to the side. So I intentionally did what I was bound to do anyway at some point.

I drove off the road.

The smaller trees and branches were no competition for the flying Heslington, but then it came up against timber with more resilience. There goes the paint job. Eventually, it met the granddaddy of all pine trees, and that's when the fireworks show started.

My, but they were pretty! Brilliant flashes of light and dazzling colours bursting in my vision like a gnome carnival display. The bangs and detonations were impressive too, but at least there wasn't that one big explosion that would have heralded the demise of the wagon's boiler, and me along with it.

In the end, the display came to a halt, and the world returned to normal speed, but, by then, I was trapped in treacle. Don't you just hate it when you get trapped in treacle? Yeah, it's awful not being able to move your arms and legs without wading through all that thick mucky stuff – that always for some reason tastes of blood. But you have to do that hardest of actions and move, or otherwise, you never work out that it's just a seat harness and you can't get out of your seat because of the annoying fact that somebody invented seat harnesses.

Who is responsible?

Curse them for their brilliance – making it so hard to get out of a crashed wagon when all the seat harness has done is save your life! Some folk have no consideration for the needs of the bleeding and emotionally compromised.

Eventually, the wagon threw me up onto a pile of the white stuff. I found this funny and thought about just lying there and having a proper little giggle until nothing mattered very much. It seemed the easy answer. This was not an option, I remembered, as there was somebody else depending on me and she had a body that looked even softer than the big white pillow I was currently lying in.

I suddenly wanted to lie on that body and have her stroke my head until it was all good again. Besides, I was getting kind of cold now, and in the absence of a nice warm eiderdown cover, I needed to stay warm. I remembered that from somewhere.

So, I moved. Well done me.

Now, I have done moving before, and I knew from experience that it is not meant to hurt this much. Certainly not every littlest bit of me – even my eyelashes felt broken. Fortunately, no bones were – not that I could tell, anyway. Presumably, now just one huge bruise, I stumbled back to the wagon to get my fitted, expensive, beautifully warm overcoat from the back seat, only to find the garment gone.

Now, this really wasn't on. Cutting a fellow's brake cables was one thing, but stealing his Gaspar Halftoken original Greatcoat just isn't done! That made me angry, and anger brought me properly around and allowed me to take proper stock of the situation, which looked to be a proper mess of epic proportions.

Circumstances didn't look good at all.

Dwarf Girls Don't Dance

I seemed to be mostly intact, excellent news, but without adequate clothing, not even my dwarf constitution, was going to be able to cope with the long walk to the nearest habitation. I also had to trudge through the fresh fall of light, powdery snow, which would sap my strength further.

The snow had fortunately stopped for the moment, and the wind had also dropped. I checked my watch to see how long I had been out of it, only to find that it had broken at exactly a half-hour after midwatch. Just the sort of clue a detective likes at a crime scene, but no help at all when you *are* the crime scene.

My pipeweed and flint had been in my coat too; not that I was thinking of stopping for a smoke, but a fire might have been nice – for a short while at least. I was chilling down rapidly, and there was nothing in the wagon to help me.

Or was there?

I took out my pocketknife and set about the leather seats with some urgency. Wulsk hair was indeed soft and surprisingly springy. I just hoped the renowned insulation properties were all they were cracked up to be. I tucked my kecks into my socks—it was no time to be concerned about sartorial elegance—and then stuffed handfuls of wulsk hair down each of the legs. My kecks were pretty spacious, and I soon had to set about another seat. The contents of that then went inside my sark, with careful attention to the sleeves. I set about the backseat and quickly added an extra layer of hair under my jacket – can't have too many layers they say.

I reached for the Hat, which was still firmly in place. Gaspar Halftoken hats stay in place, bless them. It was only then that the full extent of the knock I'd taken came to me. The Hat had a large dent in it – a dragon's bone was broken! Now somebody was really going to have to pay for that damage!

More wulsk hair went into The Hat. I filled it with wulsk hair because some ridiculous amount of heat is lost through the top of the head, you know? And I was very keen on heat-retention at the moment. I even managed to get wulsk hair into my driving gloves, can't save too much body heat in sub-zero temperatures when you've crashed your wagon, as my old Mum never used to say.

My footwear left something to be desired as far as the terrain, and the amount of snow cover, was concerned. I addressed that problem by removing the headrests and slitting them open lengthways. I didn't actually need to remove much hair from them, just enough to slip a foot inside each one. I then improvised some fastenings with my laces, and I had, what I hoped, were a pair of fully insulated snowfloats. I stepped out from the wagon and tried them out.

They worked!

Not only were my feet now much warmer, but the headrests did indeed spread my weight over a larger area, and I didn't sink into the snow.

I was pretty much home and dry, just the matter of trudging an unknown number of miles to civilisation over deep snow in sub-zero conditions. And getting up a slope first of all, with wagon headrests on my feet. Fortunately, the wagon had ploughed a useful furrow for me to crawl up in a highly humiliating fashion – lucky me. The defunct Heslington had also smashed a small sapling on the way down, and this now provided a useful dwarf-sized staff.

Finally, I found the road, and I set off at a reasonable pace. The moon was still out, and I was feeling very pleased with my ingenuity and cunning, and was keeping the inner dwarf happy by thinking of suitable vengeances to be rained upon whoever

Dwarf Girls Don't Dance

had put me in this predicament. You can keep very warm that way. Us dwarves have done it through the long winter northern nights for generations. Whole families would sit together plotting retribution on their enemies and saving on heating bills. Oh yes, how those long winter nights must have flown by.

I got into a strange sort of rhythm, my breath sounding unfeasibly loud in the still night air. I looked around the pine-covered hillside, and jumped as a tree unloaded its burden of white stuff near by. In the distance, I could just hear the faint sounds of usk bells. They sounded rather jolly.

These are the sort of conditions that had forged the modern dwarf through uncounted Ages: hard, unforgiving, but democratic in their oppression. They made dwarves strong, resilient and the match for any race in Widergard. And there is something majestic about those unblunted northern mountain peaks, the unsullied outlook, the raw intensity of nature – and, quite frankly you can blow it all up a dragon's outhole as far as I'm concerned. Give me a sunset over a beach on the Gnada peninsula and nothing colder than the ice in my cocktail. But I wasn't going to let myself be beaten then, not by Skragsrealm or a malicious mechanic. I would get through this and somebody would pay.

And that's when the wolves started to howl.

The reintroduction of wolves into the inhabited parts of Skragsrealm had been a controversial affair; it had made the news scrolls as far away as the Citadel. A strange alliance of hunters and conservationists had decreed that it would be a 'good thing' that would benefit the countryside by re-establishing the wildlife 'balance' that the later were interested in and the economy that the former did so much too boost.

Nobody thought to ask the usk herders or the local livestock farmers. It was all going to be great – completely 'natural' it was said. Sadly the folk saying it were forgetting that these weren't natural conditions that the wolves were being reintroduced to and hadn't been that way for uncounted years. These were by and large managed lands that relied on said management to stay 'natural' – and that management didn't feature wolves. By the time that it was realised that Skragsrealm had something of a disaster on its hands – wolf numbers had shot up uncontrollably, thanks to the abundance of all that wildlife and the failings of those same hunters. Not that hunters had all suddenly become bad shots or anything, but these were not the wolves of old days. These were the survivors, the pups of those that had managed to endure the expansion of the various folk of Widergard and scrape a living in the most hostile northern parts of Skragsrealm and troll country. They were smarter, and more resourceful, and aware of the possibilities offered by the garbage heap and landfill; released into the comparatively lush southern lands, they were obviously going to thrive and once established they weren't going to be budged. It was a victory for the animal kingdom. They howled again.

Lucky me.

I needed to get a move on, and so I did. That's all pretty relative of course. My getting a move on wasn't a match for the getting on of the four-legged beasties that now obviously had my scent. The first howl was now joined by another cry of the blood-freezing variety, and pretty soon it was clear that I had an accompanying pack considering the option of dwarf for a late supper. I took stock of my weaponry. I still had my pocket-knife. That should do the job – I could just about cut my own throat rather than be eaten alive. I had my improvised staff as well, and

Dwarf Girls Don't Dance

I took precious moments to work on it with the knife. I now had a pointy stick – that should also put the fear into the wolves.

The howls were now generating a panicky cacophony of usk bells. I reached a brilliantly deductive conclusion – where there were usks, there should be usk herders. That was good for me, hopefully. Usk herders would have all sorts of ways to deal with wolves – bet they didn't rely on pointy sticks and pocket-knives. With added purpose, pocket-knife and pointy stick held protectively in front of me – because they're better than nothing, I attempted to track down the usky source of the usk bells.

It didn't take me long. I could see one or two large horned shapes in the moonlight, moving under the trees. I assumed they must be usk. The only problem was that they were in the valley down below me and I was on the road at the top of the valley looking down. No way was I going to be able to climb down there safely, not if I wanted to be sure of making it down in one piece. I had no idea what to do, but in the end, the decision was taken out of my hands.

I'm not sure what made me turn – some instinct from those dwarf ancestors I'm so keen to disparage probably, but turn I did, with pointy stick to the fore. That's what the wolf hit first, knocking me backwards and impaling itself further as it pushed the stick through the snow and onto the frozen ground below. I can still see its luminous yellow eyes if I close mine and I sometimes wake up at night with its rancid breath on my face and the sound of snapping jaws loud in my ears.

I don't get back to sleep easily on nights like that.

The wolf's remarkably advantageous self-injury would have been a lot more appreciated if, when knocking me backwards, he also hadn't succeeded in knocking me down the sides of the aforementioned snow-covered valley. Over and over I went, in a fashion that in comedyland usually results in some poor unfortunate ending up in the middle of a giant snowball. I didn't, although I certainly felt covered in enough snow to do a fair impersonation of a snowdwarf.

Plus, for the record, it was all much more painful than it looks in the funny pictures. Fortunately, dwarf bones don't break easily. The adventure does still hurt as much, of course.

I eventually found myself spluttering and disorientated, down at the bottom of the slope and facing the evaluating stares of a whole herd of the largest deer in Widergard. They are nearly twice my size at the shoulder, with antlers even wider. They were huddled together by a large boulder, near a small stand of pines, with the large males looking out and the smaller females and young completely encircled. Their heads moved from side to side nervously, bells ringing, but I was pretty sure it wasn't me they were worried about.

It wasn't.

I heard the sound of the wolves before I saw them. Slowly they came out of the shadow of the pine trees, not much more than shadows themselves. I'd lost my pointy stick in wolf, but improbably I still held on to my pocket-knife. I stuck it out in their direction, and because of some obvious miscommunication between my brain and feet, suddenly found myself advancing towards them. To my even greater surprise, I saw them begin to retreat. Score one for the bold dwarf!

'Best not to move,' said a soft, steady voice from just behind me.

'I think I've got them on the run,' I replied, in what I hoped was a similar tone.

'The wolves are not running from you!' he said, a little more insistent.

Dwarf Girls Don't Dance

It was then that I realised that the large boulder was moving.

'Wild wulsk, please be very careful!' said the voice from behind me again.

Clouds parted, and the true nature of the boulder became apparent. The wulsk made the usk look like they needed to shape up and eat their greens. Maybe twelve foot in length, with hugely muscled front and rear legs; his whole body was covered in masses of coarse hair, all growing over the soft, dense woolly under layer that was currently so soft and warm next to my skin. Not that you paid his potential insulation properties much notice when your eyes were fixed on the massive curved horn, the length of a broadsword, that protruded menacingly from the front of his skull. An encounter with that would ruin your day, and if one wasn't worrying enough, there was another smaller horn, just as sharp-looking, bang centre, at the top of that hefty skull.

The wulsk carried a spare.

You could see why the wolf pack had retreated; one absent-minded shake of the head from a wulsk could spear a wolf more effectively than any pointy stick could ever manage.

The huge animal was ambling along, chewing steadily, without a care in the world. Mind you if I had his thick fleece and armaments I wouldn't worry too much either – I might even be inclined to tell the taxman what he could do with his levy requests. My attention was brought back to the moment when I realised that the ambling was in my direction.

'Keep very still!' whispered my guardian angel, but it was largely unnecessary because, at that moment, I really didn't have either the energy or inclination to go anywhere.

On and on came the wulsk, until eventually, he paused directly in front of me, and smiled. Of course, he wasn't really smiling, he was pulling back his upper lip and opening his mouth to get a better smell of me. I hope he liked dwarf, but not in that way.

'You stink of wulsk,' whispered the tiny voice from behind.

Of course, I smelled of wulsk. I had wulsk hair stuffed almost everywhere wulsk hair could be stuffed. I hoped it wasn't anybody he knew. Wouldn't that be embarrassing? Your mother? What a coincidence! Do they shear wulsk or skin them? Please let them shear them! The wulsk continued to sniff… and chew. I continued to not move away. I was getting to be an expert at that. I could do it all night, by which time I would have frozen so stiff that 'not moving' would now be my only career option. Not that there is much of a career in 'not-moving' these days – certainly not one you would want to consider anyway.

And then the wulsk licked me.

It was a slow-motion lick: halfway between basting and flirting. The wulsk tongue stopped doing whatever it did when the beast was chewing and instead the unfeasibly long muscular mouthpart left the double-horned head and had a good taste of Strongoak. I hope he didn't like it, but neither did I want him to object violently to this dwarf/wulsk hybrid before him. I just wanted him to wander off and maybe, someday, in years to come he could tell all his, comparatively little, grand-baby wulsk about the night the wolf pack had run off, and he had met a dwarf/wulsk that came tumbling down the slopes of the valley.

'Gosh, Grandpappy,' all the little wulsks would say, 'and then what happened? Did everybody live happily ever after?'

Yes.

Especially the dwarf/wulsk I was hoping.

Finally, after what felt like an age, and empires and hem-lengths rose and fell, that is exactly what he did do – wander off

– although I am, quite frankly, guessing about the grand-baby wulsks.

'Good,' my kindly helper said. 'The wolf pack will not be back again tonight. They do not like to have a wulsk nearby. The usk will not wander either.'

'That's a relief.' I finally turned to face my benefactor.

As I had suspected, it was one of the blue-eyed, blond-haired men that Lippy had called Huldre, way back in Kellishaldt at a time when my heart used to beat without threatening to burst from my chest. He was dressed in what looked like a rather strange and almost humorous mixture of layers of different coloured felts and wools – said the dwarf with his suit and hat stuffed with wulsk hair.

'Very useful, the wulsk,' he nodded to me. 'Good to have around.'

'If they don't accidentally impale you first I suppose.'

He now shook his head, emphatically. 'Oh no, gentle are the wulsk. Only eat the plants and bark of trees – best not to scare them, mind. What he made of a dwarf who smells as you do, I do not know.'

Before I could add any comment regarding my current state of being, he had turned away, beckoning. 'Come, it is not a night to be playing around any longer.'

I didn't get a chance to comment on the amount of playing around I had been up to. He could move quickly through the snow, thanks to snowfloats which were considerably more efficient than two converted wagon headrests.

The usk herder held a pointy stick like I had wielded. It was a very fancy pointy stick, and it had a nice, metallic sharp end, but it was, in essence, a pointy stick. I almost laughed at the irony, until I saw the cut-down pelleter in his other hand. An indiscriminate provider of mayhem, whatever you load it with, a pelleter is the perfect answer to a pack of wolves. I felt better already, but not as good as I would have felt with the weapon tucked under my own arm.

'One moment,' my guide said. And to my surprise he took off the snowshoes and gave me the pelleter and with a leap he was running away on top of the fresh fall, barely leaving a dent as he went. He wasn't away long.

'That's a neat trick,' I had to admit, as he returned.

'It only works when you run,' he replied, tying back on his snowfloats. 'And sometimes it is best to not run, but to be more careful. But the good news, for now, I can tell you, it seems the wolf pack has gone.'

'That is good, on account of the fact that dwarves don't run too well with bits of wagon tied to their feet.'

'Smart thinking, dwarf.'

I would have blushed if I hadn't felt half-dead.

My guide then led me confidently past the usk, murmuring a few words of comfort to the large beasts – not that they particularly seemed to need it now. There were a lot of usk, but eventually, we came across a circle of small dwellings – part hut and part something less permanent. Each round building had a perimeter made from tree poles – almost all meeting at the top, but leaving a hole large enough to provide ventilation. Peat turfs had been laid up against the poles, presumably before the winter frosts had set in. These turfs were now almost totally covered with a layer of snow, and each final set-up looked invitingly snug, if a little vulnerable. It was only when I got up close that I could see the circle of huts was itself surrounded by some type of large spiky bush I was not familiar with, and didn't want to get any closer too, not judging by the size of the thorns. Large enough to put a wolf off certainly, but a wulsk probably wouldn't even have noticed as it trundled through.

Several more Huldre stood guard inside the thorn ring, pointy sticks and pelleters to the fore. A couple of them moved a section of the thorn aside, and we walked through and up to a larger round construct at the centre of the circle. A tight-fitting, peat-covered, door section was moved aside to expose an inviting glow, accompanied by a blast of warm, food-rich air.

All the joys of home.

25

The Snow Queen

The Huldre hut seemed remarkably spacious considering the number of people inside: men, women and a gaggle of children. They were all seated around a small, bright-eyed, cross-legged, elderly woman sat next to a stove with a chimney that reached to the apex of the hut. She was talking quietly but clearly, and her audience was totally enthralled. I didn't recognise the language, the cadences and intonation seemed almost elvish, but the words themselves were manish – goblin even!

My guide put a finger to his lips and pointed me to a free floor cushion on one of the numerous platforms that made up the floor. I sat down gratefully and was offered a brightly coloured blanket, which I snuggled into. I was cold – the sort of dangerous cold that freezes body fat like so much pig butter. A pot of something warm magically appeared in my hand. I tried it – it was tasty, meaty almost, but with a good slug of something intended to put hairs on your chest and then plait them. I began to relax as the full realisation of the narrowness of my escape sunk in.

Dwarf Girls Don't Dance

Somebody was going to be disappointed. Somebody was going to be very disappointed, and very locked in a small room for the rest of their life.

The Huldre drink was wonderful and was doing everything that needed doing and then some more. The woman's voice became more melodious, sing-song even, and without even being aware of it, I fell asleep.

I woke some time later, no idea where I was or what I was about. The smiling figure of my guide brought things into perspective. He had removed his hat, and his blond hair was revealed as a thick thatch that was very different from an elf's silken locks. To my surprise, I now found myself dressed in a similar style to my hosts. I don't think I had ever been so colourful.

'Sollon' he said, pointing at his chest.

'Thank you, Sollon,' I replied, very, very thankful. 'I am Nicely, Nicely Strongoak.'

Sollon nodded approvingly.

I looked about – most of the audience had now dispersed, and there was just that small stove with the long chimney where the storyteller had been sitting.

'Your hut…' I began.

'Toopuk,' he corrected.

'This toopuk is beautifully comfortable.'

'The largest we live in to protect us from the wolves. It is called…' he thought for a moment, 'The Last Fear. Yes, that is the name in your tongue.'

'I've heard that name before. In a different place.'

Sollon shrugged. 'We have been in many places. We do not always stay, but perhaps we leave a mark.'

'Well, thank you, Sollon. It is very warm and comfortable.'

Sollon picked up a handful of my wulsk hair and run it through his fingers. 'It is all about insulation.' He pronounced the word strangely, with far too much 's' for my ears. 'This was good thinking.'

'It was one of my better moments.'

'Did your steam wagon…' he searched for the right word. 'Did it break down – an accident?'

'No,' I admitted. I owed it to these people, to tell the truth. Just in case anybody was out there still looking for me. 'My wagon had an "on purpose".'

'Ah!'

'It was broken deliberately.'

'I see.' Sollon thought about this and the implications. 'Then wulsk saved your life, I think?'

'Along with you.'

'I was in the right place when you come tumbling down the hill, like a baby usk just been born.'

'Lucky then I landed on my feet – in one way at least.'

This took Sollon a while to process and then he shook his head delightedly. 'Yes, very good – to land on feet! Very funny, to land on feet.'

A slim, attractive, blue-eyed young girl came over and joined Sollon. I think he must have retold my joke, because she laughed too. I had the audience on my side at least. She was the sort of audience you wanted to be on your side. I realised I was probably staring, but I honestly couldn't stop myself. Like an exquisitely cut gem or a painting by a master artist, she repaid repeat viewing.

'How is our guest?' she asked, after the hilarity had finally calmed down.

'He is very well, thanks to you and Sollon,' I replied.

'His name is Nicely, Nicely Strongoak,' Sollon added.

She digested this snippet of news. 'You are not Skragsrealm dwarf?'

'No,' I admitted. 'I live in the Citadel.'

She nodded again, 'I have heard of the Citadel. Sometimes Huldre dream of Citadel and wish to go there.'

'Well there are worse places I suppose – it's warmer for a start!'

This didn't get the reaction I had expected; perhaps warmth is all relative.

'I actually was born in New Iron Town. A dwarf place more like Skragsrealm.'

'I do not know of this place, but I will remember it now, Nicely Strongoak.'

'May I ask your name?' I said quite innocently, but it caused Sollon to take a sharp intake of breath and reach into his brightly coloured jacket, presumably not to look for a pocketbook and make a note. The young girl quietened him with a small sign from one hand.

'Nicely Strongoak, does not know our customs, Sollon. It is of no matter.' She smiled again and retired to another platform where she curled into a small ball and seemed to disappear under a whole pile of blankets.

'My apologies, Sollon,' I said, a little confused. 'The last thing I intended was to give offence.'

Sollon thought on this for short while. 'Names are powerful. Not easily given.'

'But you gave me your name, Sollon.'

'I gave you a name, Nicely Strongoak.'

'To find someone's true name is to have power over them.'

'How should I address her then?'

'She is the Winter Queen, the heart of the people – its leader, spiritual core, augur, enchantress and storyteller.'

'I thought the elderly woman I saw last night was your storyteller. She certainly seemed to have everybody engrossed.'

Sollon smiled broadly. 'That was the Winter Queen.'

'No,' I began, 'I meant the very distinguished old Lady, the one with the…' I trailed off as I realised the full impact of what Sollon was saying. He smiled at me as if in confirmation.

'That is why no person should have power over one so full of power herself. It is also why such a person must be of the "purest metal". Do understand that?'

'I think so.'

'A Winter Queen, or indeed a King, can have great influence over the minds of folk of all races, to influence or even control.'

'Right. Sollon, can you tell me – the Winter Queen, is this another name for a Snow Queen?'

'As men call her.'

'But aren't you men, Sollon?'

'We are Huldre. Sleep now, dwarf.' And with that, he got up and went to the platform next to the Queen's and curled up on it in a similar fashion. I decided then that whatever else Sollon may be, he was certainly as inscrutable as a wizard in a steam-room.

I lay there for a while and gave some more thought to Snow Queens and Winter Queens and the sorts of enchantments that can make you think a young girl is old – or maybe that an old woman is young. Tricky difficult to pull off, that, whatever the face-cream sellers may want you to believe.

I thought for a long time in the warmth of the Huldre toopuk, surrounded by these strange but remarkable welcoming folk. There were certain thoughts and ideas – pieces of a puzzle that was much larger than I could have ever believed, slowly coming

Dwarf Girls Don't Dance

together in my mind. I wasn't sure what the picture on the box was yet, but I had an uncomfortable feeling that I wasn't going to like it when I had the pieces put together.

Outside, the wind blew and more snow fell up against the Huldre's cosy retreat, while inside I slowly put together my jigger puzzle. Then, just as the picture slowly began to form, I fell asleep again.

26

Captain Royalwench

The sudden storm lasted most of the next day and the one after. I spent it in the company of the Huldre in a sort of daze. I was conscious that I was experiencing a way of life that had changed little in generations – an existence as old as anything that Widergard could still throw up. It was pleasant, warm and cosy, inside the toopuk, while outside the wind still blew and blew and eventually blew itself out.

Songs were sung, and other verses read aloud. Many were performed by the elusive young/old Winter Queen and I couldn't take my eyes off her. Neither could anybody else, to be fair. Such was the spell she could weave. I thought of Luce, he would have fitted right in here.

Filling, tasty food was passed round often enough, and calls of nature were carried out swiftly and efficiently. Sollon asked me some questions about Skragslanding and Kellisgrund, but showed no interest in the Citadel – a strange world where snow was such a novelty that it became a talking point for weeks and folk complained if they had to put a coat on. I slept again and dreamt of the Winter Queen and then again and then it was time to go.

We were to travel by uskhal cart – a strange two-seated affair with blades instead of wheels and pulled by two large beasts that thankfully seemed to be completely well disposed towards the task. The Snow Queen bade me goodbye, looking deep into my eyes as we parted, before bending close to whisper.

'There is an enchantment upon you, Nicely – a good thing.'

'A pixie's kiss perhaps?'

'Yes,' she smiled, 'that could be it. It will help you should you need it.' Then she looked serious before speaking again: 'But there are other bad enchantments at work around you, powerful charms that seem almost familiar to me. I have done my best to address them. Beware, you have a powerful enemy.'

'That's just my luck,' I said. 'I never get the hopeless enemies.'

She took my hand and pressed something into it. I looked. It appeared to be a simple necklace with an animal tooth attached. Wulsk, maybe?

'Wear this close to your heart and if you have the need grasp it and say my name.'

Just as I was about to ask the obvious she locked eyes and a voice I didn't so much hear as feel said: 'I am Niejte.'

I got something in my eye, and before I had finished wiping it away, she had gone, and life was much diminished.

It was an interesting journey to Skragslanding, and I even opened my eyes for some of it. Just the bits that didn't involve frighteningly scary drops to the jagged rocks below, poking evilly out of the snow like the broken fangs of an ice giant.

Sollon dropped me off in Skragslanding by a large public building called the Skragsmetheldheimforg that I didn't recall noticing before. With a name like that, I'm sure I would have remembered the name post. Skragsmetheldheimforg housed, I was assured, a whole array of speech horns that could be used for calling anywhere on Widergard – even the Citadel. I got off the sledge, grateful to be in one piece. We said our goodbyes. I wished I could think of something to pass on to the Winter Queen, but I didn't have the words. Sollon just smiled, as if sensing my inability, clicked his reins, and the usk trotted off down the wagon-filled road without a care in the world.

I shook my head and came round, as if from a very long dream. Which it wasn't – again.

I went in the Skragsmet-whatever, found a booth with a free horn and took out a pocket of change. I got through to my number straight away and recognised the slightly sleepy voice at the other end: 'Red Sylvester here – whoever you are it's too early.'

'Hi, Red. You on your own or is Blondie around?'

'She's away, Nicely. On a boat, would you believe – somewhere warm.'

'How's your diary?'

'Free for a few days now.'

'Well, sort out something warm for yourself to wear, will you? I've got a little job, and you're going to need your furs.'

'Now, Nicely! You know I don't agree with killing animals purely for decorative purposes, only to eat, and I can't eat fur. Anyway, how cold are we talking?'

I told her.

'Hmm', she relented. 'Maybe I'd better pack my long winter woollies,'

'I'll provide you with plenty of insulation when you get here.'

'You will indeed do that, Master Detective! I charge double when it drops below zero.'

'Don't worry, Red. Our client has just become a very wealthy dwarf, as long as we can stop the locals trying to stretch her.'

'I'm packing as we speak.'

'Thanks, Red. I'll leave a number at the Kellishaldt train station for you to call. It'll probably be a man called Lippy who picks you up. And he is just going to love you!'

'Oh? What else should I pack then?'

'Running shoes.'

After speaking to Red, I dug out the number for the Kellishaldt Keep.

The horn barely tooted once. 'Detective Analyst Grundrund here.'

'Detective Strongoak here,' I replied.

There was a pause.

'And might Detective Analyst Grundrund ask where "here" is exactly?'

'A very large new building with a very long name that I can't pronounce in the centre of Skragslanding.'

'The Skragsmetheldheimforg?'

'That'll be it.'

'You do realise that half of the local Watch and most of Kellishaldt's have been looking for you since your abrupt exit from the Torfull Dollund retirement party?'

'Well, you know what it's like when they serve up the wine at just the wrong temperature. What's a body to do?'

'And no trace of your wagon has been found.'

'That's because it's half way down a ravine with the brakes cut.'

There was a silence at the other end of the call, and I could almost hear Grundrund processing the information.

'I think you had better wait safely there while I drive across town and collect you,' she said, finally.

'I think I had better wait in the nearest place that can roast a bean without killing it!'

'Nicely!'

'Don't worry, I'll leave a message at what appears to be the Skrags-whatever information desk. No need to hurry, but very pleased to see that you do care!'

I put the horn down in time to miss the string of goblin expletives that were heading my way from Kellishaldt.

It turned out that I was just around the corner from the Wisklehald, and I was soon holding a very hot cup of the largest stranger's coffee that they made. The Huldre were lovely folk, I would be forever grateful to them, and their Winter Queen, but they did not even know about coffee. And boiled tree-bark is not something I would recommend to anybody.

I took the time to try to get a better idea about the lid to that jigger puzzle that I was still piecing together. Who would have wanted to cut the brakes on my wagon and why? Was it connected to the death of Duffy's father? It couldn't go back any further than that, surely?

So engrossed was I that Grundrund nearly crept up on me. I was practically the last one to notice her. A six-foot-plus, blonde-haired, blue-eyed female, goblin law-enforcement officer, can still turn a few heads in Skragslanding.

'Nice togs,' she said, sitting down.

I had forgotten what I was wearing.

'The other suit's in the wash.'

'I am glad your hat made it through.'

'It takes a lot to part a dwarf and his hat.'

'It is not a good match.'

Dwarf Girls Don't Dance

I took the Hat off and put it on the table. 'Better?'

'Much. So, somebody has tried to kill you at last?'

'It happens,' I admitted.

'Why am I not surprised?'

Not a lot I could add to that. A young bar help came over. I think he had drawn the short grass. Timidly he asked what Grundrund would like to drink. Grundrund pointed to my coffee. 'I will have whatever he is drinking, but larger.'

'We don't do a larger one,' the bar help replied, now really nervous.

'Then give me two.'

'And another for me too. Put them on my slate, thanks.' The young man walked away, relief not so much etched into his face as carved with a hammer and chisel.

'Any suspects?' Grundrund continued.

'Let me think – well, just about everybody I know or have ever known in Kellishaldt and Skragsrealm seemed to be there, so I guess there may have been a few.'

'And any reason why they should have wanted to put Dollund senior into an early peat bed too?'

'And the answer to that question, my dear Detective Analyst Grundrund, will win you the treasure chest and all of its contents.'

We brooded on this while the stranger's coffees arrived. Grundrund swallowed her first cupful in one go – not worried by the heat. She wiped her mouth with satisfaction.

'That is good. Why have I not had that coffee before?'

'Maybe you've just not been enough of a stranger?'

Grundrund looked at me, not understanding. I rubbed my face. I badly needed a shave and a hot bath; a back rub probably wouldn't go amiss, but I kept that to myself.

'It's just a name, Grundrund. It's what they call a decent cup of coffee hereabouts.'

'Ha! Good name! Now, what next?'

'I feel,' I had to admit, 'like going to bash a few heads together until I get some answers.'

'No! That kind of thinking has got goblins exactly where they are today, which is at the bottom of the heap.' Grundrund said, picking up her second coffee and savouring this one before speaking: 'Goblins think they are cleverer than other folk, they think they are stronger than other folk and they know they are better looking and they, therefore, believe that they are entitled to more than their share. This is not the case. The truth is that forces that play to their weaknesses, their own greed and sense of being hard-done-by, have always manipulated them. Goblins need to stop looking for the easy options, of finding ways to cheat the system. They need to learn the rules and apply themselves and then within a generation they will be running this country – for the good of all, of course. Do not behave like goblins always have done.'

She put her coffee down in the saucer with a surprisingly gentle *clink*.

'Is that really true?' I had to ask.

'Yes,' she answered, straight-faced as ever. 'Goblins have great intelligence and strength.'

'No, I meant that goblins really believe they are better looking?'

'Of course,' said Grundrund. 'Who else possesses such fine fighting teeth?' She bared hers in what just might have been a smile. An elderly couple got up and left quickly.

'I have to agree with you there! As aggressive dentition goes, goblins are way ahead.'

'Very, very far ahead. So, we do this by the books – agreed?' She lifted her cup.

'Agreed,' I replied, with only a little reluctance.

'And if that doesn't work, then we go and bang a few heads together and kick a few folk in their most sensitive parts too!' Grundrund banged her cup down now with more enthusiasm.

'Oh, yes!' I finished my coffee in a similar fashion.

Grundrund stood up and stretched; the remaining customers edged back in their seats.

'But first, we have a little chore to do.'

'Oh, yes?' I wondered what this might involve.

'The good people of Skragslanding's law enforcement community have been particularly concerned about the absence of one dwarf Master Detective. All leave cancelled, and Chief Royalwench apparently has been moving mountains to find you.'

'Chief Royalwench? What, really?'

'Yes, she is well thought of, as I believe I told you.'

'Isn't it great to find out that somebody, somewhere, loves you?'

'Oh yes, so let us go say our "thank yous" for their efforts on your behalf.'

I left some extra corn on the table for the bar help to peck at; after all, between the two of us, Grundrund and I had managed to empty the place of customers.

Skragslanding had built themselves a nice new cosy keep since my last visit all those years ago. My welcome was a lot warmer too. Detective Analyst Grundrund flashed her shield and briefly filled the desk officer in on the details. He blew the horn upstairs, and we were escorted by a scout to see Captain Royalwench, a name that left me considerably puzzled.

There was a small reception area, but we only had to wait a moment before we were shown into the office.

You have to admire a woman in uniform, and this one looked really good. Mind you; she had always looked really good, in everything and nothing. The uniform just added a certain thrill, especially as I could still see her large shining bracelets sticking out at the cuffs.

'Hello, Princess,' I said, smiling at the woman seated behind the large oak desk.

'Hello, Nicely. I am so pleased to find you safe and well,' she said, getting to her feet. The years had hardly touched her. Perhaps a touch more steel to the backbone and a harder glint to the eye. Plus the black ironwood truncheon hanging at her side was new. She moved lightly around her desk and to my slight embarrassment, planted a kiss on my forehead.

'I take it, you two have met?' said Grundrund, with just the right amount of peeve. Any more peeve might have sounded angry, and less would have been pointless. 'Are you going to keep doing this, Strongoak?'

'Honestly, Grundrund, I'm fresh out of surprises.'

The former Warrior Princess turned to my companion.

'My apologies, Detective Analyst Grundrund, I am delighted to meet you too. I have heard very good things about you. She reached out to take the goblin's hand, and the two of them shook. They made an interesting pair. The former Warrior Princess, born into a life of luxury and potential carnage and now charged with keeping order in the busiest port of the North and the goblin that had rejected villainy and the worse elements of her race in order to maintain the law.

Dwarf Girls Don't Dance

The dark-haired woman and the blonde-haired goblin, with barely an inch in height between them – so different but so much the same. I'd take either of them for my team, thank you. If the ravening hordes ever came ravening near me, boy, would they regret it.

'Might I have a word with Detective Strongoak in private, Detective Grundrund? Nothing to do with your case, and we won't take long.'

'It's your keep, Chief Royalwench,' said Grundrund. She left quietly, although I, for one, saw the eyebrow being raised.

'Law enforcement, Princess?' I asked, after the door was safely closed. 'I mean, real honest to goodness law enforcement?'

'Your doing, Nicely. After Mansel's murder, I thought about how I could best contribute to making Widergard a better place. This seemed the obvious answer.'

'And you end up becoming Captain of the Keep, of course?'

'Something of the discipline and order appealed to me here. I respect the hierarchy, and I don't mind taking orders.'

'But prefer giving them?'

She smiled and twenty years dropped off her. She put her truncheon on the desk, as if putting her position aside.

'Well, I've had more practice at that side.'

'I didn't think you were returning, not after you disappeared back to your parents' place so quickly – with no word.'

'Yes, I'm sorry about that.' She did sound genuinely apologetic. 'I really had no choice.'

'I had to hear it from Duffy.'

'When I said I had no choice, I meant it, Nicely! A troop of the royal guard appeared at night, drugged me and carried me off in a horse-drawn carriage of all things. I hate those contraptions.'

'What?' I exclaimed.

'Oh yes, very "old-palace" my parents. It took me six months to escape and get back here, and by then, of course, you were long gone.'

'Hey, parents, eh? Give them a couple of crowns and look how they behave.'

'Yes. My parents expect to be obeyed, and when I wouldn't, and I didn't, I was duly cut from the royal line.'

'Princess!'

'No longer royal and without gold for the first time in my life. I had to get a real job. I did want to find you, but had no money for the fare to the Citadel.'

'Duffy?'

'Nobody knew I was here. I wanted it that way. To succeed or not on my own terms.'

'I get it.'

'I knew you would. And then one case led to another. Promotion and men to command, I'm sure you understand.'

'Of course, Princess. Or should I call you Zella now?'

She raised an eyebrow. 'Am I right in assuming you have spoken to Sansire then?'

'Just briefly at Duffy's father's vigil.'

'A very bad affair this,' she said, her face clouding over. 'I wanted to attend, but even as a private individual, it would be seen as undiplomatic with the case in progress, especially as I am not exactly unknown to many of the folk involved.'

'And any ideas of your own about what happened?'

'I did promise Detective Analyst Grundrund that I would not discuss your case.'

'Yes, sorry.'

'But I can tell you this, as it is not directly related, that over the last few years we have something of a crime wave in Skragslanding.'

'That sounds worrying. Is it?'

'It is. To be honest, it is one of the reasons I have been promoted – to bring some fresh thinking to the problem.'

'And the attempted theft of the Heartstone and the Dollund killing could be involved? A crime wave spreading across the Eskrag?' I scratched my head and tried to think through the ramifications.

'I couldn't say that with any certainty, Nicely. But gems seem to be particularly targeted at the moment.'

'Interesting. Perhaps including an attempted theft of just about the most famous diamond in Widergard?'

'Yes, and this isn't the goblin gangs of old – we cleared them out. This is more organised. It is like there is a central intelligence organising everything.'

'Organised crime?'

'Very much so.' She sighed and tapped a quill, irritated and vexed in equal measures. 'And they do not object to using violence – killing; even torture.'

'A Dark Crime Lord?'

'As good a name as any I suppose.'

'The sort of crime that became so prevalent in the Citadel a few years ago?'

'So I hear.'

'At least until we got people like Kingley under lock and key.'

The Warrior Princess was now fully the Captain of the Skragslanding Watch again.

'Kingley?' she said interested.

'A very nasty creepy bit of work, connected with this case only in the sense that the whole affair resulted in Diamond leaving the Citadel.'

'The dwarfess accused of the murder?'

'Yes. The dwarfess I represent.'

'And?'

'No "and" – just the dwarfess I represent!'

'Only asking, Nicely.'

'Apologies, but I get that question a lot.'

'Only natural, Nicely. I mean, I can see no wedding ring and no addition to the family knots.'

'Full marks, detective.'

'Now, Nicely – no call for that.' She looked genuinely upset.

'Sorry, Captain – it's been a strange few days, but having my wagon brakes cut and almost getting eaten by wolves will do that to me.'

'And I'd like a full statement on that. I need to justify the search operation after all.' She smiled with something of the warmth of the woman I knew all those years ago.

'Of course, and thanks for coming to look for me, Princess,' I said sincerely.

'As if I would let you die out there in the cold.'

'Well, thanks anyway. It matters.'

She coughed a small business cough, not like she had a lump in her throat or anything.

'So, this client of yours…'

'Now I think we are definitely impinging on Detective Grundrund's territory.'

'Forgive me. Shall I call her in?'

'Allow me.' I got up to fetch my colleague. 'And I still don't know what to call you, Princess!'

She laughed again before sitting down back behind her desk.

'I think we had better keep it formal when in public.'

'Certainly, Captain Royalwench.' I paused on the way to the door. 'And don't think I've forgotten where that came from!'

'Well, I could hardly use my real name any more, Detective Strongoak.' She shuffled some papers around. 'And please do still call me Princess – when in private.'

I briefly thought through the implications of that, but decided I had better concentrate on the matter at hand.

'Detective Analyst Grundrund,' I said, opening the door. 'Captain Royalwench would like to talk to the two of us.'

'A pleasure,' said Grundrund, walking back in and keeping her face suitably straight. The Captain picked up her truncheon again and clipped it to her belt – back to business.

The three of us sat round the big desk, all on best behaviour. I brought them up to date with my adventures with the Huldre, which raised a few eyebrows. We traded notes and considered the wider implications of what might be going on in Skragslanding and Kellishaldt and the likelihood of there being one all overseeing Dark Crime Lord. I mentioned the possibility of interrogating Torfull again, this time with the weight of the Skragslanding Watch behind us. Captain Royalwench agreed. Captain Royalwench, in fact, would go with us. Captain Royalwench would kick some dwarf backsides if required. It was all very amicable, serious and adult, until after we had said our goodbyes and Grundrund and I were back into her Gaddergast 4-0-2 and on our way to Kellishaldt.

'A kiss from the Captain of the Skragslanding Watch. There is more to you than meets the eye I think, Detective Strongoak,' said Grundrund.

'Ancient history, Detective.'

'You have had sex with this woman, I think?'

'Axes and blood, Grundrund! Could you please not mention out loud everything that comes into your head! Yes, you're a good detective, I admit it, but please just let this one drop!'

'All right, I will' she said, pumping some steam, 'but I think you would perhaps still like to have sex with her?'

'Grundrund! Enough!'

She drove off, voicing that infuriating goblin chuckle.

'Good choice, I think.'

'Enough Grundrund!'

It was after normal visiting hours by the time we got to Kellishaldt Keep. Grundrund pulled a few strings, and I got to see Diamond, but she had to be in attendance with me. This wasn't awkward at all, but I did at least get to reassure Diamond that we were making progress. Nobody had bothered to tell her I was missing.

'The arbiter of yours is useless,' I fumed.

'What's a girl to do?' Diamond quite rightly pointed out.

I couldn't get to tell Diamond everything about what was on my mind because, at the moment, I couldn't tell Grundrund everything either. Hopefully, Diamond was reassured.

'You have not had sex with the dwarf woman,' observed the goblin detective.

'Grundrund!'

'But you would like to I believe.'

'Leave it alone!'

'What a complicated life you lead, Master Strongoak,' she concluded.

I didn't argue with that one.

I managed to meet up with Lippy later, after Grundrund dropped me off back at the *Skragshelder Inn* and I'd cleaned up and changed. I bought the old fellow a few drinks. I didn't progress the case one inch, but sometimes the only answer to a question is beer.

27

Answers

There had been a minor thaw, and Grundrund and I made very good time across town and through the bridge back to Skragslanding. We stopped there long enough to change wagons into an official Skragslanding Watch wagon driven by Captain Royalwench herself.

'Now we shall get some answers,' she said, determined.

For appearance sake, as I was still only a consultant, I sat in the back. With Grundrund and the Princess seated up front, I didn't think I was in any danger, so I did what I normally do under such circumstances and had a nap.

Halfaxen Deep was looking very familiar by now, but this time we weren't kept waiting. The Princess made her way straight to where Torfull was ensconced with his books, next to the large fire in a private hall. This room was designed for winter comfort, not to impress the guests, and the elderly dwarf didn't welcome the interruption, especially when he saw Grundrund and me.

'You two!' he spluttered. 'I thought I made it clear that I do not welcome goblins to my hall! You have impinged on my tolerance for long enough.' He reached for a bell, but the Princess did not give him time. She showed him a gold badge that complemented her uniform beautifully.

'Torfull Halfaxen, I am Keep Captain Royalwench of the Skragslanding Watch. I am here to question you on a number of matters, not least the attempted murder of Master Detective Strongoak, who is here as the representative of the defendant in another important case – namely the murder of Danwright Dollund, the co-owner of your company Dollund and Halfaxen. Your assistance is requested. This can be carried out here or, officially, at the Skragslanding Watch.

'At the Keep!' Torfull spluttered, even more irate. 'Do you know who I am?'

'I think I just made that perfectly clear, didn't I?' said Captain Royalwench. 'Now are you willing to answer some questions, or would you like me to get your coat. It is a cool day, and I understand you have not been in the best of health.'

Torfull had finally found his bell, and he rang it loudly as he shouted: 'Fastspade! Fastspade, where are you? Get rid of these fools for me immediately!'

'I am afraid that won't be possible,' said the former Warrior Princess. 'He is detained.'

That wasn't technically correct. Fastspade was actually hanging by his belt from a large, ornate, but very sturdy, lighting sconce.

Torfull sat back in his seat, his face reddening, on the verge of some sort of fit.

'Young woman! I know all the White and Wise of Skragsrealm! Let me tell you…'

'No, let me tell you.' The former Warrior Princess said, squatting down by Torfull's seat. 'I am the Captain of Skragslanding

Watch. In Skragsrealm and Skragslanding, we are facing a period of particularly violent crime. I have been appointed with the full co-operation of the Dwarf Permanent Committee to address this problem. If I find you are obstructing this investigation, I can and will, have you keeping us company in the Skragslanding Keep. Is this clear?'

At this point, the best Torfull could manage was a nod. I would have felt sorry for him if he weren't such an annoying example of everything that was bad about my race.

'Good,' said Captain Royalwench, straightening again. 'Then my colleague Detective Analyst Grundrund from our friends in Kellishaldt, and Master Detective Strongoak will ask you some questions. Please answer them as if it is me inquiring. Understood?'

One more nod. I looked across at Grundrund, and she motioned me to start. My question took everybody by surprise, not least Torfull.

'Torfull Halfaxen, can you tell me, please? How long were you in love with Talensia Dollund?'

'What rubbish are you talking now, Iron Town dwarf?!' Torfull spluttered.

Captain Royalwench gave him a look to chill the marrow in your bones before speaking very quietly: 'Just answer, please.'

'I have never heard such…'

'Then let me repeat the question,' I said, equally serious. 'How long were you in love with Talensia Dollund, Duffy's grandmother? I mean, was it love at first sight? Was she already seeing Danwright and you just couldn't help yourself? Or were they married by then and you had to keep it a guilty secret?'

'I resent that, Strongoak!'

'Resent away, Master Halfaxen! I've found over the years that I've never lost sleep over other folk's indignation.'

'You are rude, ill-mannered and discourteous, "Master" Dwarf!'

'And I just don't know how I am going to manage when it comes to writing up my life story, but then again I won't have to mention that I slept with my partner's wife!'

To my surprise, a tear trickled down the old dwarf's cheek. 'I didn't... I never did. Honestly, I didn't. It was love at first sight, on my part, anyway,' he said in a quiet, almost trembling voice. 'I was the first to meet her, you know?' He looked up, appealing for understanding.

He didn't get any, so he continued: 'She worked for us, for Halfaxen's I mean. I just saw her in the office one day. She was working as a translator – some of our more traditional client still like contracts to be drawn in dwarvish or elfish or whatever. She had a natural aptitude for languages, I think because of her mixed race. She never went into too much detail about that side of things – there was certainly some elf, you could tell that, and her father was a Woodsman, but I like to think there was dwarf too.'

'I'm sure of it,' I agreed.

This seemed to please the old Dwarf. 'So, I liked to think there might be a chance – for us, I mean, although I knew my parents would be firmly set against me marrying out. If I could confirm some dwarf blood in Talensia – well, I had hopes.'

'And then along came Danwright?'

Ok yes,' he sighed, 'Danwright! Danwright with his great idea. And it was a great idea, no doubt – to join our companies together. To combine what we were best at. And I thought that if we were successful, my family would forgive me anything.

Allow me anything! So I hired detectives to look into her family and kept hoping.'

'But in the meantime?'

'I missed what was happening under my own stupid dwarf nose. Danwright was what they call "dashing" I believe. Tall, athletic and… you can guess the rest.'

'And you had never said anything, so Danwright didn't know about your feelings?'

'No,' he sighed. 'Even worse, my parents were continually putting forward eligible candidates from the most suitable of dwarf families. Including Heldwide's eventual mother.'

'And you gave the Heartstone to Talensia?'

Grundrund really picked up her ears at this question. The former Warrior Princess was engrossed too.

'Yes,' Torfull said finally. 'As a wedding present, but I said she had to keep the information quiet. I made them both promise.'

'Which is why she hides it in the portrait of her I saw at Skavernslager Cottage?'

'Of course,' he said, tetchily.

'Which is why you built them the cottage as well? The official present?'

'That's right. Talensia loved it there. She'd often visit for the summer.'

'Which is why it has a similar floor to that of Dollund House where you installed the coffer for Danwright, to hide the Heartstone safely.'

'Yes. You can't take a chance with a gem that valuable.'

'And you built yourself a secret stairway all the way down from Dollund Hall to Skavernslager Lake? To visit?'

Dwarf Girls Don't Dance

'It wasn't secret,' Torfull said defensively. 'Well, not until I was married and Heldwide was born. Then it had to be more... secret.'

'Of course.'

'Heldwide's mother, my wife, she would not have understood. She is not the understanding sort. She is not fond of... other races. She is from a very old dwarf family and prefers the old ways.'

'I've met the sort.'

'Now, go, please. I do not feel well.'

I could see the others about to disagree, but I shook my head. I had got what was needed. It was time to go and leave the old dwarf to his memories.

'Strongoak!' Torfull called out, as I reached the door. 'I would not have killed young Danwright for all the gold in Widergard. He was Talensia's son when all was said and done. I watched him grow up. I loved him like a son as well.'

We left the old dwarf by the fire, unasked questions still on both the women's lips. Grundrund was the one who remembered to take Fastspade down.

I changed seats with Grundrund when we got back to the wagon, so that I could give the Captain directions.

'I'm still not sure why we are doing this,' the goblin complained.

'I made a promise to another law enforcement officer, and I intend to keep it,' I told her curtly. 'And you're not about to stop me, Grundrund.'

'Give the dwarf his head,' said Royalwench.

Grundrund sat back with a sigh before speaking: 'I do not see what all this talk of old love affairs has to do with our case. This death surely has nothing to do with love?'

331

'Oh my dear Detective Analyst, I do believe that this is where you are wrong! It's all to do with love – it always was.'

The former Warrior Princess looked over at me with a strange glint in her eye, but she kept on driving. Soon we were in Skavernslager. The former Chief Reeve of Skavernslager had himself a nice little house just outside of town. It wasn't built in the dwarf style.

'I'm too old to go back underground now,' he explained. 'At least not before the big one that comes to us all.'

Personally, I just think he didn't like to be too far away from the town's centre of activity – his old office. The young dwarf Todderam who had done the thumb fonts all those years ago was running the show now. He was driving behind us. The former chief, who still answered to the title, made it clear that he was going in the wagon with the new Captain Royalwench. He was sitting in the front, and I was in the back with Grundrund. No way was his vintage of dwarf going to actually sit next to a goblin; I believe it was something of a triumph to get him in the same car.

'Skavernslager cottage has been closed since that poor woman's death, all those years ago,' Delvedeep went on to explain. 'A young dwarf couple rows over every week or so and makes sure it doesn't fall into disrepair.'

He looked across the water at the dark building just visible on its hill at the centre of the island. 'But I'm supposing nobody actually wants to live there.'

'And no unusual events in the district since?'

Delvedeep shook his snow-topped head. 'No, we've kept an eye open for any rogue trolls that might have come this way again, but no luck there. The most we see is an occasional one of

Dwarf Girls Don't Dance

those Huldre, but they're peace-loving folk with those big beasts of theirs.'

'Usk,' I said. 'They're called usk.

'That's right, usk. See more of them than you used to now.' The chief stroked his long silvery beard, lamenting how times had changed.

Nothing on the island had changed at all.

Grundrund, who had expended some of her pent-up energy on the rowing, took me quietly aside as the Princess led the others to the cottage.

'This is where the treasure-trove heiress murder took place, yes? Very young woman – what was name?'

'Mansel,' I replied.

Her eyes lit up with a new understanding. 'We studied scrolls of the case – there was a dwarf involved. He found the body.'

'He did, and he's never forgotten it.'

'I am letting you run with this, Strongoak.' she growled. 'Especially as the Captain trusts your instinct and I appreciate your need to find…' She stopped abruptly. 'The Captain? Surely not the Warrior…?'

I put one finger to my lips. 'Come on, Grundrund, let's not miss the fun.'

Todderam had inherited a key to the cottage along with his position. He opened up the double doors leading to the entry room with its beautiful wooden 'sunburst' floor.

'Your call, detective,' said Todderam, turning to me.

'Look familiar, Grundrund?' I asked the goblin.

'The floor over the coffer, in Dollund House – very similar.'

'Give the goblin a pickle.'

I bent down and touched the intricate design. It really was a lovely job of work. Just like Dollund House.

'It can't be the eldest son's birth date this time – let's try Talensia's.' I explained.

'Have you memorised the birth dates of all of the Dollund family, Detective Strongoak,' Grundrund commented.

'Yes,' I replied simply. 'When coffers are involved, it's the first thing I do.'

I pressed the sunbeams in the appropriate order, and there wasn't even the slightest 'click' as the wooden panels opened up in the sunburst pattern to reveal—

'Stairs! Well, burn my boots and blunt my axe, it's a set of stairs!' The former Chief Reeve Delvedeep was suitably astonished.

'What does this mean, Nicely?' Captain Royalwench looked down into the dark.

'Some long overdue answers I hope,' I replied.

Grundrund squatted by the hole. 'Not much space down there.'

'There doesn't really need to be, detective,' I said, and lit up my torch. 'Not for a dwarf.'

I was right; there wasn't a lot of space. I mean you couldn't hold a party down there, but you could certainly be comfortable for a week or two if you were a dwarf, especially not a large dwarf. It was even divided into small rooms, and in every one there was an observation point that, via a clever array of mirrors, afforded views of just about every room upstairs.

'This is not good, not good at all, said Delvedeep, who had joined me at the bottom of the steep stairs.

'Very much, not good,' I echoed. I shone the torch in all the corners, but there still didn't seem to be anything labelled "clue".'

'I'm going to try coming down,' the Captain shouted.

'It'll be tight – better let Chief Delvedeep back up first.' I turned to the old dwarf.

'Could you ask Todderam to check the boathouse, please. There was a skip in there.'

'Yes,' said Delvedeep, 'I remember – a small pleasure boat.'

'Would you check if it's still there?'

Delvedeep nodded and carefully made his way back up the stairs, allowing the Princess down. It was cosy, but we'd been cosier. She shone her own torch around, her face grim.

'Is it possible, Nicely? Could somebody have been down in this rat hole all the time we were here for the Longest Day festival?'

'It's certainly got to be a possibility, Princess.'

'And then they just creep out, kill Mansel on the lake and then hide again? Why would Torful do such a thing?'

'Why indeed would Torfull do such a thing?' I bounced back at her.

The Princess's face took on a look of horror.

'You don't mean…?'

Her sentence was interrupted by a call from up the stairs. Chief Reeve Todderam shouted down: 'The skip, it's not there!'

We all reconvened in the boathouse next to the wharf. It looked the same as we had left it twenty years before, although the hampers had been removed at least. The old boxes, including the ice ball hoops and catchers' gloves, were still there.

It's a strange thing to do – stare at an empty space, as if you suddenly expect whatever was there to appear back again. The small boat had long gone, of that I was sure, and no way was it coming back.

'We knew it was there after the murder. I should have checked this out when we both rowed back over after the inquest,' Delvedeep said in a very annoyed tone.

'It didn't occur to me either, Chief,' I admitted. 'And you, reasonably enough, were looking for somebody driving along the road, not rowing back across the lake.'

'And we weren't looking for somebody still on the island. We had searched thoroughly.'

'We'd all searched.'

'But not well enough, it seems.'

'Don't beat yourself up, Chief,' I consoled. 'None of us had considered this possibility.'

Grundrund cleared her throat before speaking: 'You will excuse me, but perhaps an outsider's eye might be helpful.' Grundrund looked at Captain Royalwench for authorisation.

'Please do, Detective Grundrund,' she replied. 'I think we would be most grateful for your contribution. Let us do it outside. I have had enough of this place.'

We left the gloomy boathouse and walked back to the cottage where we found some garden chairs, last used on that fateful day a lifetime ago. We sat in a circle and let the goblin speak.

'If I am remembering correctly, it was twenty years ago on Midsummer Eve. A group of nine friends had spent the day celebrating, and some time after Mid Watch six had gone to various beds, while three – Berger the gnome artist, bard Luce, and the Lady Mansel – continued to celebrate?'

The Princess and I both nodded, and Grundrund continued.

'Sometime during night, or early morning, Mansel – who was dressed to resemble the Lady Willow – was lured, or carried, to lake where she was strangled and the string of Greenwood emeralds she wore stolen. As all folk present on the island could account for whereabouts, and had corroborative testimony, it was assumed that somebody chanced on the island. Carried out affront and escaped without being seen?'

She looked around the group, and we all nodded.

'And now it seems that all time there may have been somebody else here, hiding in secret room, who could have got out during the night in question…'

'Or earlier, and just lurked in the trees,' added Delvedeep.

'Very true,' agreed Grundrund. 'And then after carrying out the homicide and robbery, they returned to the hidden room along with gems while investigation took place above. Escaping at unspecified time later in the small skip.'

'Probably on, or after the day the inquiry into Mansel's death was reported,' I added.

'How so?' asked Grundrund.

'I came over with the chief soon after. We'd both had our suspicions that the emeralds were still on the island.'

'Gem sense?' Grundrund asked.

I nodded. 'We thought so, but it wasn't clear,' I explained.

'It was like something else was masking everything at the time,' Delvedeep added. 'But when we came back later it was clear then that something had changed – that the gems had gone it now transpires.'

'A troll was suggested because of the size of the bruises on the dead woman's neck, I believe,' said Grundrund. 'I don't think a troll would have found that a comfortable place to live, for a fourteen-night. Neither would a goblin.'

Chief Reeve Todderam stroked his beard, not fully convinced, 'whoever it was still had to get out of the valley and there is only the one road.'

'The one road, yes. But it seems not the only way out,' added Captain Royalwench.

'Ice ball gloves!' I interrupted – a feeling very much like Rage beginning to bubble up inside of me.

'Your pardon, Detective Strongoak?' Grundrund queried.

The Princess realised almost immediately.

'Of course!'

'Ice ball gloves. There's a box of them in the boathouse,' I continued. 'They are reinforced to play the game and effectively enlarge the hands.'

'Of course,' said Delvedeep. 'We missed that too. We'll need to send them for analysis, Todderam.'

'Of course,' the new chief replied.

It could have been almost anyone, any race then?' asked Delvedeep.

'Anyone who knew the room was there,' Grundrund stated correctly. 'And fit in it.'

'Halfaxen,' said Delvedeep sadly.

'He had a secret passage from his hall down to the lakeside,' the Princess shook her head sadly, thinking back over the years.

The local law enforcement officers exchanged amazed looks.

'Nobody knew about that,' said Todderam, with something of an air of accusation.

'We only just found out,' Captain Royalwench added diplomatically.

'Torfull Halfaxen,' said Delvedeep, shaking his head. 'A dwarf I have known all my life.'

'No,' I said. 'Not Torfull.'

28

Red

'Buns!' the Princess exclaimed, almost beside herself with indignation, which considering the speed she was driving was not a good idea. 'I cannot believe this!'

'I'm sorry, Princ— Captain, but it's the only option that makes sense. There was no way that Torfull Halfaxen was going to be able to disappear for that sort of time! Buns, that was a totally different matter back then.'

The argument had been going on since we he had dropped the current and former Chief Reeves back at the Skavernslager station with requests to carry out discreet inquires into the whereabouts of Heldwide Halfaxen – some twenty years ago!

'And he could easily have discovered his father's secret route down to lake,' Grundrund quite rightly observed. 'And once he had committed one killing, well, they say second is easier. He could have known about the Heartstone and Dollund's coffer – at least the first one.'

'But why, Officer Grundrund?' What's the motive?' She looked across at the goblin detective. 'You don't know Buns!'

'Didn't you tell me that he had the hots for Willow?' I asked.

'Yes, he had the "hots",' the Princess replied. 'So what?'

'He thinks it is her that he is luring out,' Grundrund said. 'Mansel sees her old friend Buns and goes with him. When he realises it is Mansel, not Willow, he loses it – as I am told Dwarves can,' she finished diplomatically.

'No! Then why steal the necklace? I can't believe this is the answer.' The former Princess shook her head defiantly.

'I don't think it is, Princess – at least not the whole of the answer,' I confessed. 'The rest should hopefully be supplied once we get back to Kellishaldt.'

The two of them took turns firing questions at me all the way back, but I refused to be drawn any further. The picture was almost all there – just a few more pieces to fall into place.

It was getting late by the time we made it back to Skragslanding to pick up Grundrund's wagon. The town was beginning to take on a peculiar aspect: strange and familiar at the same time. These dwarf halls, gnome burrows and tall men's wooden buildings all seemed to belong to another world – one I was told about in a book maybe. Yet I knew that if you walked down the passage next to that cheap three-story lodging house, you would find a small street called Middle Row where there was a fine gnome eatery called Protillo's, which cooked the best fiery red bean stew imaginable, or use to be at least.

'Hey, Captain Royalwench – is Protillo's still there?' I asked.

'Best fiery red bean stew you will ever eat!' she shouted back.

'Good,' I concluded. I wasn't sure why, but the knowledge gave me great satisfaction. I was probably finally managing to integrate difficult parts of my past with my present, which all the head specialists say is a good thing, especially for handling anger issues. I still wanted to kick some other heads in.

Dwarf Girls Don't Dance

We picked up the Gaddergast 4-0-2 and dropped the Princess off. She was to organise things on her side of the bridge, for after my plan swung into action. Grundrund would have no authority there. I knew she was itching to be in on the action, but she had bigger responsibilities now. She'd get to play her part too.

'You have changed, Nicely,' she said to me, quietly, as we stood outside the keep entrance doors, waiting for Grundrund to drive her wagon around.

'Have I? Hat size is still the same.'

'As are many of your jokes.'

'Ouch, Captain Royalwench, you can sure cut a dwarf down to size!'

I was conscious of her staring down at me. 'That has never bothered you has it, the height thing?'

'What, me being the tallest in my class?'

'Were you?'

'I was, but I never picked on the smaller guys. That's the sort of consideration I think is important in life and I expect to see it in others.'

'Absolutely.'

'And you also have to remember that scholars have now shown that dwarves can be up to one and a half times as strong as other races – including goblins.'

'Which I imagine dwarves were pleased to hear.'

'Oh, yes! It's all to do with levers and muscle development and bone density and such.'

'I would say that there has probably been a lot of muscle development with you, yes?'

'Working in a slave mine will do that for you.'

'What... really?'

'Long story, Princess. So we don't get too worried about us dwarves not being able to get the pots off your top shelves, not when we can pull your arms off.'

'There it is again – that harder edge – the change I mentioned.'

'It's been twenty years Princess. Even in us longer lived folk, that's a fair chunk of change.'

Grundrund came into view, the Gaddergast 4-0-2 steaming like a wild beast in the cool air. I was steaming too.

'Here's my ride, Princess.'

She gripped my arm tightly. 'We will get him, whoever is responsible—even Buns—they will pay.'

'Oh, they will Princess. We will make sure of that.'

We kissed like companions do. There might be time for something else later. Not now, maybe never. I had changed, and so had she.

'Oh, Princess,' I added as she walked off. 'I have an associate coming. I think you should meet them.'

'Of course, Nicely. Any friend of yours.' She hurried off and through the entrance to her keep.

I got into the Gaddergast 4-0-2 next to Grundrund.

'I like her,' Grundrund said, pulling out. 'There is steel in her.'

'Oh yes,' I agreed, 'and not a trace of rust either.'

We completed our plans during the ride through the bridge. I mentioned my associate, who I described as a specialist, less Grundrund get too suspicious. We then thought about contingency plans and contingency plans for our contingency plans. I just hoped we wouldn't need them all. I can only plan so much before I need to hit something.

Grundrund took me to the Kellishaldt Keep where she had arranged for another wagon to be waiting for me.

'A Gaddergast. I think you will like it, Nicely'

'Yes, thanks Grundrund,' I said without much enthusiasm, knowing what the local wheel situation was like. 'I appreciate it. I'm sure I will.'

We pulled up in the parking circle where I was interested to find a low-slung two-seater wagon waiting for me. It was in midnight blue and... it had six wheels, four small ones at the front, and two normal-sized ones at the back. This was – something else entirely.

'Grundrund – six wheels! It's got six wheels!'

We both got out of the Gaddergast 4-0-2 to admire its younger sister. 'Yes,' she explained. 'The six wheels have two effects: it lowers drag and improves speed on straight, while the four wheels on front improve handling on corners in snow. This will not come off-road!'

'Not my fault!'

She ignored me.

'It is called the Gaddergast Sprint; it reminds me of you somehow.'

I walked around the wagon and admired my new wheels – all six of them.

'Grundrund,' I said. 'I could kiss you!'

'No you couldn't,' she replied.

I found Red Silvestral waiting for me in my bedroom at the hotel. She was dressed in what I would have to call custom combat style – lots of leather and lots of buckles and belts. Grundrund would approve. I've come home to more disagreeable circumstances. Unfortunately, I also came home to Lippy, who was keeping her and a bottle of my drink company.

'I thought I had better take care of her, Master Dwarf,' he confided. 'Her being a nice lady alone in a big city as it were. A very nice lady.'

'Down, Lippy,' I whispered back. 'She could eat you up and pick her teeth with your collar bones.'

Lippy did not look convinced.

'Just like she did her last four husbands.' Lippy drunk up and was out of there before you could say widower.

Red was busy looking out of the window to where Kellishaldt was being pebble-dashed with a form of sleet that was probably technically different from one of the other forms of sleet that had been assaulting me since I had been here. Like who really cares, as the result is misery in every case.

'My, but you take a girl to some interesting places, Nicely.' She pulled the curtains tighter and went across to stoke the fire higher.

'Didn't you know that Kellisgrund is the largest shipping nation in Widergard now?' I said, stifling a yawn.

'I didn't! Well, that makes it all worthwhile!'

'And they are Widergard's biggest importer of gravel.'

'It keeps getting better.'

'Like gravel, do you?'

'Fascinated by it!'

'Excellent, because you would not believe the party we are going to tomorrow. Everybody who's anybody in Kellisgrund – and into gravel and conglomerates – will be there.'

'My,' said Red, 'I just hope I can find something to wear. I didn't pack my hard hat.'

We went and found beer. We both needed it.

29

The Boscomere Feast

Grundrund had not been wrong when she said gravel was big business in Kellisgrund because the Boscomere Feast was indeed a major event. It was held in the Kellishaldt Hallow Hall, which was fully decked out in extra gnome lights for the occasion. If everybody who was anybody wasn't there, it must have been because they were required elsewhere to keep the lights running and the roads to the hall clear.

First, Red and I had a quick clandestine meeting with Captain Royalwench just this side of the Bridge. She ran quickly out of her wagon to where I drew up in the borrowed Sprint. She opened a rear door, letting in a blast of cold air, both from her and the weather.

'I hope this is important, Nicely. Law enforcement agencies can get rather cross about the unscheduled arrivals of neighbouring officials.'

I ignored her in the nicest possible way. 'Princess. I want you to meet the associate I talked to you about. Red, this is Captain Royalwench. Captain Royalwench, Red Silvestral.'

Red turned, the two shook hands, and the Princess said quietly: 'Nicely, do you not know any unattractive women?'

'No such thing in my book, Princess.'

The former Warrior Princess tutted as I looked across at Red.

'She's clean, Nicely.'

'Good, I had to be sure.'

'What is she talking about, Nicely? What is "clean" before I forget my official's oath and hit you heavily with my truncheon?'

'Red is an enchantress, Princess – works for the Filth Fellowship in the Citadel and helps me out when she can as well.'

'Enchantress? And you thought I was…'

'Had to check.'

'Oh my – that means… enchantment is involved?'

'I suspect as much,' I said grimly. 'We'll know later, and then you'll know.'

Grundrund was next. We met her outside Kellishaldt Hall, now dressed up in all its finery, as was Grundrund.

'Looking good Detective Analyst,' I complimented her. 'Any trouble getting the invitation?'

'Strangely, they assumed that as you were going, I should be at your side.' She tried hard to sound aggrieved, but I know it would have been impossible to keep her away.

'And this is the "specialist" you mentioned, Detective Strongoak.' She eyed Red, unsure of what to make of her.

'I am indeed the specialist, Detective Grundrund,' Red said, holding out her hand, and they shook. 'And it is my great pleasure to confirm that, as Nicely suspected, you are not enchanted.'

'Not enchanted?' said Grundrund, generally taken aback.

'That's what the lady said, detective. And she should know, her being an enchantress.'

'I have never heard of such thing in Kellisgrund.'

'That's really strange, detective, because you have one of the most natural race of enchanters living over the bridge from you.'

'Dwarves?' she said, surprised.

'Try further north.'

'Ah, the Huldre!'

'Give the goblin a pickle!'

We let Detective Analyst Grundrund enter ahead of us, so as not to cause too much talk. I knew Red would cause plenty enough of that as it was.

We handed in our coats and capes, and I have to give it to the attendant, he didn't drool too much at what Red was wearing.

'I didn't have much room for extra clothes,' as she had explained to me earlier when revealing the scraps of various coloured silk that she assured me would assemble themselves into something that resembled evening attire. It did, and beautifully so. I just worry about all these young women wandering around without a vest on. I wore midnight blue, and the Hat was staying on tonight. Kellisgrund manners allowed that.

Kellishaldt Hallow Hall was buzzing. Red and I seemed to be amongst the last arrivals. We joined a queue to meet the host and hostess: Cannly and Pallis. I used the time to quickly scan the room. It was hardly recognisable from before, very jolly as it happens. Lots of lights and spinning mirrors and a large platform curtained off at one end.

I spotted the Chief Arbiter in earnest conversation with Arbiter Skunglard, which must have been exciting for them both. Duffy was there talking with his brother Hass, and a woman I didn't recognise but assumed was Hass's companion for the evening by the way she was climbing all over him.

Passaloll was also there, but she seemed to get everywhere in Kellishaldt. She had a crowd of admirers, including High Captain Gobblod, of all folk, and the leader of the company council I had seen at the bequest. Sansire and Osk were talking with a round, prosperous-looking, elegantly turned-out gnome that it took me a moment to recognise as Berger. Besides them there was a grey-haired bearded older man, leaning on a stick. He had the aspect of a wizard about him, in which case he was to be watched carefully.

Of Heldwide Halfaxen, there was yet no sign.

'Well, well, well,' I muttered under my breath.

Red must have thought I had been asking her a question because she murmured back: 'Not well at all, Nicely! There is so much charmwork in action here that I feel almost physically ill.'

'Not good?'

'Nicely this is so far over onto the "not good" side of the scale that the needle is threatening to break itself against the glass.'

Before I could get more detail, we found ourselves in front of Pallis and Cannly.

'Master Strongoak, so pleased you could make it,' said Pallis, who was obviously well practised at this sort of thing.

'And who is your delightful companion?' said Cannly, looking by far the most animated I had seen him unless gravel was in the conversation. Red had that kind of effect, even when she wasn't trying.

'Master and Mistress Boscomere, this is my business associate Red Silvestral,' I introduced her with a small bow. Red put her hand out in the required fashion.

'Please do call us Pallis and Cannly,' said Pallis.

'And I do have a proper name, Nicely,' said Red, looking intently at me, with a shake of the head that wasn't to chide but to indicate that these two were also clean. Much to my relief, I hate getting the host beaten up or arrested.

'Oh no, you must let us call you Red! It sounds so glamorous,' pitched in Cannly, now totally won over. 'What is it that you do exactly? Or would you have to bury me alive with hill-wights if you told me?'

'Not necessarily alive,' Red countered, and the temperature dropped a degree or two.

Red then did her professional laugh to break the atmosphere she had intentionally just created. It is a thing of wonder – her more natural expression of mirth being something between 'filthy' and 'raucous'.

We all joined in – she is that good.

'Perhaps, Cannly,' she continued, 'you would be kind enough to introduce me to a few people? Nicely is hopeless at that kind of thing. I must meet all your lovely guests.'

'Delighted, Delighted!' Cannly was away with Red on his arm with barely a look at his wife. She seemed more amused than upset.

'Well, perhaps you would be kind enough to escort me into the hall, Master Strongoak, as my husband seems to have deserted me?'

'My pleasure, and please do call me Nicely.'

'Yes, of course.' And most regally she did enter too. I turned a few heads myself. One of them was Sansire's, but from the look on her face, I don't think she was admiring my dress sense. The last time I had seen an expression like that was a long time ago and in another country.

'Is Red really your associate, Nicely?' Pallis enquired. 'If it's not too crass to ask?'

We took two drinks from a passing gnome who was doing a brisk trade with his tray.

'She is indeed, Pallis – I even pay her stamp. A dwarf can generally get a seat at a table anywhere, with the high and low both. However, there are places habitual trouser wearers cannot go and conversations we are not privy too.'

'I see.' Pallis nodded. 'I think that is the kind of job I would have enjoyed.'

I was taken aback and must have showed it. 'What, do you think so little of me, Master Detective and us only having just met?'

'I have concluded no such thing, Pallis I assure you – after all, you are Duffy's sister for a start.'

'Yes,' she said, eyeing her brother. 'And that's the problem.' She then looked directly at me.

'You've probably heard that I don't get on with my brother, Nicely.'

I shrugged, then said, 'Folk will talk.'

'It's all right; I know what his friends think – what Mansel used to say.'

I was surprised by the mention of the dead woman, and again Pallis picked up on it.

'Yes, the late lamented Mansel. Do excuse me, I'm not speaking ill of the dead. It was a terrible, evil thing that happened to her, but she wasn't quite as simple as she made out.'

'I didn't think she was simple. Far from it.'

'Then good for you, Nicely. She always pretended that she didn't care about losing my brother to the elf Willow, but I wasn't convinced.'

'But Luce – I saw Mansel with him; her feelings.'

Dwarf Girls Don't Dance

'Oh yes, I believe she genuinely fell for him. But I also believe that if Willow hadn't come on the scene, Luce wouldn't have got a look in. All this "we're like brother and sister" was so much hogswash. She would have bounced his armour quicker than a gnome up a fir tree!'

'Colourful, Lady Pallis, but hardly relevant, given the circumstances.'

'Of course.' She laughed. A professional laugh, not as good as Red's, but not far off it. 'A long time ago – another world, one might say.'

She looked at her brother again. He was unaware of Red standing right behind him while supposedly being introduced by Cannly to another guest and was now casting glances in our direction. 'Shall I tell you why I disliked my brother, while still loving him, of course?'

'Please do?'

'Because he got everything.' Her face looked harder now and a lot, lot older. 'He was male and the oldest, so he got the whole pot! Everything I wanted as well. Leaving me to marry Cannly. Lucky me.'

She turned, switching on her best smile again.

'Do excuse me, Master Strongoak. I mustn't keep you all to myself.' She excused herself and joined a nearby group of the White and Wise.

Duffy joined me, repentance written large across his face, which is a neat trick.

'Nicely,' he said, with no preamble. 'I've been an absolute git. The only thing I can say in my defence is that my father's death has not only been a huge personal blow, it's dragged up the Mansel tragedy again and my losing Willow too. But when I heard that you had gone missing – well, I felt awful! I didn't want to lose you… lose track of you too – not after your arrival back here after so many years.'

'That's all right, Duffy. I know it can't have been easy, the last few weeks.'

'It's not, I'll be honest. But that is no excuse. You have a friend in desperate trouble, somebody I am personally fond of too, and I have been no help whatsoever. I feel ashamed of myself.'

I glanced across and managed to catch Red's eye and inclined my head towards Duffy. She gave a quick shake 'no' before moving on. I felt a surge of relief.

'Let's get ourselves a couple of drinks, Duffy.'

I led him to a quiet alcove where a gnome in a smart weskit offered us a couple of beazer teasers. I checked out who might be interested in our conversation. Passaloll seemed to be taking everything in, her eyes sweeping the hall floor like fell-lights.

'Duffy,' I said, leaning back in my chair. 'Try to keep a smile on your face will you please – like we're just catching up?'

'Aren't we?' he replied, the required smile now all over his face.

'I need you to know something. I haven't been able to be completely honest with you.'

'How so?'

'I'm not just looking to get Diamond out of your very fine new Keep; I'm hoping to put to rights another very long overdue violation.'

A look of uneasiness crept over Duffy's still handsome features. 'Nicely, are we talking about Mansel's murder? If that's the case, I hope you are serious because…'

'I am very serious, Duffy. There is a secret room in Skavernslager Cottage.'

His surprise couldn't be faked.

'There can't be! I'd have known!'

'Nobody knew, Duffy. Not your parents, nor your grandparents.'

'But in that case – you have to tell the local law. That Reeve, what was his name?'

'Don't worry, Duffy,' I said placating him. 'It's all under control. I'm telling you now – and I do need you to keep a lid on this – I'm telling you now, because if anyone, and I mean anyone, comes asking for help, don't give it to them!'

'But Nicely…'

'Trust me on this, just for tonight, at least. Nobody, not even an Idler'.

Red Silvestral was getting close, Cannly still in tow. She gave me a certain look, while indicating our host with her eyes.

'Do me a favour, please, Duffy, take Cannly off our hands.'

Duffy nodded.

'Ah, Nicely!' said Red, now approached at speed. 'This must be your handsome friend Duffy you told me about! How very wonderful to meet you.'

Duffy took the proffered hand and kissed it lightly before speaking: 'The pleasure is all mine, but you will have to excuse me now as I must steal our host away for a moment, as there is an introduction I need from him.'

'Duffy Dollund!' blurted Cannly. 'And I was enjoying the party so much!'

'I'm sorry, brother-by-law. Tedious, isn't it?'

Duffy took the heart-broken Cannly by the arm, but only after the host had extracted the promise of a dance from Red.

'Phew,' said the tall enchantress, dramatically opening a small hand fan from her vanity bag. 'That one has not been fed recently.'

'I think perhaps his wife is mean with the rations.' I smiled broadly, because we were having such a good time. 'So, what's the tally?'

'A lot of people have been touched lightly. Not under any influence, but enough evidence to show that somebody has been looking at the possibility.'

'And more directly?'

'Your Arbiter Skunglard – big time.'

'Blood and dust, I feared as much.'

'And the Chief Arbiter, but not as deep.'

'A small mercy.'

'And you are going to need them too, because I have to inform you that High Captain Gobblod has been got at as well.'

We smiled broadly. What a good time we were having.

'Well, doesn't this get better and better, Red! How about the rest of Duffy's crowd? Sansire, Berger, Osk?'

'Clean.'

'That's a relief!' I managed a more genuine laugh. 'I really hoped not.'

'Not so the blood relatives, I'm afraid.'

'Who?' Panic gripped my gut and gave it a playful twist.

'The stepmother Passaloll. She is "charmed-up" to the back teeth. I am surprised she can get up by herself in the morning.'

'Which confirms a few of my worst fears.'

'However, nothing really explains the enormous levels of charmwork I'm feeling.' Red looked around, all senses reaching out.

'Do you think the enchanter is here, Red?'

Dwarf Girls Don't Dance

'Not necessarily.'

I glanced around as unobtrusively as possible. Of course, the one person I really wanted to see wasn't here. Then I heard a small gasp from Red, beside me.

'The bull's eye!'

I turned, and there was Heldwide Halfaxen, coming back into the room with High Captain Gobblod.

'That dwarf, Nicely!' Red continued, breathing hard. 'I don't think I've ever come across anybody under such levels of enchantment.'

'His name is Heldwide Halfaxen, Red.'

'His name is whatever he is told it is by whoever is pulling his strings; such is his degree of enchantment. They could call him Primrose the Pixie, and he'd try to fly to the nearest flowerbed.'

'Any idea how long somebody could have been manipulating him like that?'

'Years – decades even! I really don't know.'

'Oh, dear, Red. He, you see, is the heir to the Halfaxen share of Dollund and Halfaxen.'

'But not the Heartstone?'

'No. Which might be really annoying somebody who likes to pull strings.'

Buns had now joined the bearded man with the cane I had seen earlier. They seemed to know each other well. I looked around for Grundrund. She was in a serious discussion with her boss. I needed to tell her the latest on Gobblod.

'Something is afoot I do believe, Mistress Silvestral!'

'I love it when you go all Master Detective on me,' she replied, her voice breathy.

'Go train me a dragon, Red. I've got me some dwarf business to attend to.' I walked across to where Buns was still deep in conversation. As I approached, I studied him as close as I could, short of opening his mouth and counting his teeth.

How could you tell what enchantment looked like?

Could it allow you to function all day like a normal member of the community, yet the next moment murder your friend? Wouldn't that leave some sign on you – some mark? Yet Heldwide seemed to be what he had always seemed to be, the affable, prosperous, well-groomed dwarf with the ready smile and the easy manner. That's probably what should have made me suspicious in the first place: how many dwarves did I know that fitted that description?

'Do excuse me interrupting, Heldwide. I was just needing a word.'

'Not at all, Nicely, in fact we were coming to see you. You remember, Luce, don't you?' he said, indicating the greybeard leaning on his stick.

'Luce?!' I managed, the word barely escaping my lips.

'It's been a very long time, Nicely. It's good to see you.' He put out a hand that he must have borrowed from somebody twice his age.

'Why, yes, Luce – of course. A very long time.' We shook hands. I tried not to stare at the lines and hollows that had ravaged the face of the once beautiful Luce. I was suddenly back on the lawn outside Skavernslager Cottage, on the Longest Day, looking at a man in a wizard outfit and wondering about farsight.

'I'm sure you must have so much to talk about,' Buns said, with a small clap of his hands. 'I will leave you in peace for a while and go work the room, as I believe they say.'

Buns left, leaving me to collect my wits, all without me having had my urgent word with him either.

Dwarf Girls Don't Dance

'Luce – my apologies for not recognising you. It must be the beard.'

'Don't worry, Nicely. I could say the years haven't been kind to me, but in truth, *I* haven't been kind to me. The years do what's in their contract to do.'

'It's understandable. Mansel's death – it was a terrible thing. You were bound to take it hard.'

'Was I?' Luce said. 'Yes, I suppose I was?'

'I don't think any of us were the same afterwards. I know I wasn't.'

'And where did you go to, Nicely?'

'The Citadel. I joined the Guard.'

'The Citadel?' Luce thought back. 'I think I may have gone there. I probably encountered your Guard too – that was usually the case before I was moved on.'

'You weren't to blame, Luce.'

'No? After all, if we hadn't kept on drinking, if me and she had been in bed as Mansel wanted, then this "terrible thing" would not have happened.'

'And why may I ask, Luce, was that? How come you didn't succumb to the midsummer madness like the rest of us?'

'Because I wasn't in love with Mansel.'

'I see.'

'Probably not, Nicely.' He sighed, the long sigh of a man at the end of his life, when he should have been in his prime. He continued in an even quieter voice: 'I was in love with Duffy, of course.

'With Duffy?' I said, taken by surprise.

'What's the matter, Master Detective? Didn't you know some elf doors swing both ways?'

'Sure,' I began, but Luce interrupted.

'I suppose we all were, a bit, in our own way. Weren't we? And so Mansel dies, because I wasn't the man she thought I was, or she wanted me to be.'

I didn't know the answer to that one, but I did feel a deep wave of sympathy for this still grieving, tortured, wreck of a man – the one who once had a golden voice.

'So, how come you turn up now, Luce?'

He smiled for the first time. 'It was Heldwide, of course. Always thinking of others. He tracked me down – persuaded me to show my face again, "start my rehabilitation", as he put it. Good old Buns.'

Yes, 'good old Buns'. I wondered what he was after. I saw Red beckoning me, out of the corner of my eye.

'You must come and meet my associate, Red Silvestral. You'll like her.'

'Will I really, Nicely?'

'Yes, you will – all else aside, I suspect you still have a weakness for good-looking people of any sex or race.'

'Perspicacity, Master Strongoak? My, how we've grown.'

I introduced Luce to Red. She looked him up and down.

'Lose the beard, get a decent haircut and use some face cream. I'll give you some exercises to do mornings and night and a least a dozen full breathes per hour – you'll be back and able to charge the boys top gold down at the dockside.'

Luce let out a roar of laughter that I think surprised even him.

'Associate, Nicely? Are you not sure that it is not you that works for her, not the other way around?'

'That's what I tell myself.'

Red leaned forward to whisper in Luce's ear: 'My sister and I let him believe it to keep him happy.'

'A sister,' said Luce, in apparent disbelief. 'There's two like you?'

'The other one comes in blonde – we like to provide choice as well as quality. Now, Luce why don't you sort us out some drinks and I'm going to find me scissors and a razor.'

Luce was hurried off to find a drinks trolley with one wave from Red's perfectly outfitted hand.

'Somebody is operating on your friend Luce, Nicely,' she confided. 'Only recently, but they are leaning heavily. I don't know what they are after, but I doubt it's good.'

'Could it be Buns?'

'Come on Strongoak, get with the route map!' Red tutted. 'Buns is enchanted, he is not an enchanter! Charmed up, not charming. It's somebody else, and you had better find him, or her, fast. They are not taking prisoners now.'

'That's the idea, Red.'

'Now, where can I find some scissors and a razor?'

'Are you serious, Red?'

She gave me a look straight from the old scrolls.

'Of course, I am serious. This is a body in real torment here. I do not abandon such people. If we don't step in somebody else will, and the results will not make Widergard a better place. Now go!'

I went. I didn't find scissors, but I did find Grundrund.

'Nicely, some interesting news for you.' Her smile pulled up tight against those fine goblin gnashers. Whatever was coming next, I wasn't going to like one little bit.

"My boss tells me that the Heartstone is to be given into the custody of Heldwide Halfaxen who, as the maker of the best coffers in Widergard, is in the best position to ensure its safety.'

'Grundrund, your boss has been sprinkled with more magic dust than the piss pot at a Pixie's partnership party.'

Grundrund looked around; smiling fit to scare children. 'Excellent, Master dwarf! What a colourful way you have to present more truly appalling news.'

'Even better, our lad Buns seems to be totally under control of personage unknown who might very well be the Dark Crime Lord plaguing Skragslanding and now here.'

'And I have just been ordered to deliver the Heartstone to his plaything,' she took a large drink from the big beer pot in her hand. Goblins don't sip fancy drinks. 'This gets better and better. Anything else you've forgotten?'

'Duffy's sister-by-law is involved too… as well as the chief arbiter and the man who should be getting Diamond off the hook.'

'I do not normally drink while on duty,' she said. 'Tonight, I am making an exception.' She took two more drinks from a passing gnome and downed them both.

'Now, Master Detective – what is the plan? Because, at the moment, I can't think of anything better than bashing heads.'

Whatever plan might have been forming was interrupted by the large blast of a horn and the platform curtain being pulled back as the band behind it swung into action with considerable skill and enthusiasm. The folk all moved to the sides to free up the floor for dancing, and I lost track of everyone I wanted to keep tabs on.

'Blood and axes, Grundrund!' I swore. 'This is just what we don't need. Can you see Passaloll?'

'No!'

'Buns?'

'Same answer.'

'Curses! Vanished like they'd just subscribed to Magic Rings Monthly. You look for Passaloll, I'll check for Master Heldwide.'

Grundrund lit off, but was back almost immediately. 'I've just seen her queuing for her wrap.'

'Follow her, but not too close. Try to make it back here for Midwatch. I'll keep looking for Buns.'

This was harder than it should have been. Side-chambers full of food had been opened up for those not wanting to dance and too peckish to wait for the feast proper. The side chambers had smaller rooms running off them too, and in one of them, I found Berger, with Sansire and Osk. She was seated, looking pale, her husband and the gnome in attendance.

Berger hurried over to meet me. 'Nicely, old chap – wonderful to see you again! We were all quite worried after you left Torfull's party.'

'Thanks, Berger. But you really have to excuse me now. Important matters I need to attend to.'

'As is this: Sansire's gift, it's returned.'

'What!'

'And she needs to talk to you – now!'

'It was after we met at the Vigil,' the seer confided. 'I wasn't sure at first; it seemed as if it was just my dreams misbehaving, as they will. But when you walked into the Hall this evening, I knew. I am whole again.'

'This blue suit will do that.'

'This is serious, Strongoak!' Osk almost yelled, concern for his wife written large all over his face.

'I know it's serious,' I replied, trying to be more diplomatic than I felt. 'Sometimes there just aren't the words.'

'Nicely,' said Sansire, certainly somewhat more her old self now. 'Another one of us – one of the Nine Idlers – is going to die, and another one of us is going to do it.'

'Not this time, Sansire! Not this time! I promise you that much!'

I discovered Red with Luce in a bathroom, where to the amusement of other guests, she was giving Luce the promised haircut. His beard had been trimmed right back to a fashionable stubble, and he was already looking years younger – less decrepit, more rakishly wasted.

Red took me aside while Luce admired his reflection.

'A word please, detective.'

'He looks so much better, Red.'

'Yes,' she dropped her voice. 'I have been working on the enchantment at the same time. It was worming its way into him, going fully against the person he is instead of working with his desires and corrupting them as is the usual way. Very bad news.'

'Were you in time?'

'I hope so.'

'Could something similar be done for Buns?'

She shrugged. 'Give me and Blondie ten years, then maybe, but no guarantees.'

'Take care of Luce, Red, and don't let him near the other Idlers, especially Duffy'.

I checked the wagon circle and was just in time to see Buns pull away in his wagon – a yellow '52 Dragonette, curse him for his taste, but yellow, honestly? Grundrund's Gaddergast 4-0-2 had gone, but the Sprint was waiting ready-primed. I jumped in and reversed, only to have the passenger door flung open, and Duffy leap in after me.

30

Kellismarsh

'Nicely! What is happening here?' said the agitated Danwright Dollund the third. 'Sansire is predicting murder, and Osk is blaming you! While Luce looks as if he has returned from the dead. What is going on?'

I swung the Sprint out of the circle and poured on the steam, racing after the speeding Dragonette.

'Hold on, Duffy!'

'I am holding on,' he replied.

'I am not just talking about the drive,' I said, and then told him all that I knew: 'Buns murdered Mansel, dominated by an evil enchanter who worked on his love for Willow. He hid in the secret room in the cottage his father had built to spy on your grandmother, who Torfull had secretly given the Heartstone to as a sign of his devotion. So great was the enchantment around him that Buns was capable of obstructing Sansire's far-vision and my dwarf gem sense.'

I moved the wagon up a gear while Duffy sat, his gob well and truly smacked.

'Buns also killed your father. He wanted the Heartstone back; it would have rankled him that he had the gem that he believed belonged to him.'

'Flying worm scat, Nicely!'

'Exactly.'

'But Buns – he was our friend; one of us?'

'Don't think of it as Buns. He's just a cat's paw.'

'But when Sansire had her premonition, he went away to ensure it didn't happen.'

'He went away to take instructions I'm guessing, while the puppet master considered how to use this turn of events to his advantage.'

'This is incredible.' Duffy shook his head in disbelief, not able to take it all in.

'I'm afraid your father's second wife is involved too.'

'Passaloll!?'

'Oh, yes. I just hope the daughter is unaffected.'

'Semeline, the poor girl, we must get her to safety.'

'We will, Duffy.'

I hadn't gained on the Dragonette in the town, and we were now heading into the country and traffic was thinning and the Dragonette was accelerating, but at least it was still in sight.

I hoped the Sprint would catch up on the icy roads.

Suddenly Buns' Dragonette took a turning right ahead of me, at speed.

'Where does that road lead to, Duffy?

'That is the main road to Kellismarsh –where Passaloll lives!'

'And unless I am mistaken that is Grundrund's 4-0-2 parked opposite the turning.'

Dwarf Girls Don't Dance

We pulled up with a six-wheeled slide next to Grundrund's big black lump of steaming metal and joined the goblin as she watched the empty road.

'A nice night for a solitary surveillance, Detective Analyst,' I commented.

'That road only goes to Kellismarsh: one way in and one way out. Passaloll went down it some fifteen minutes ago. She is not going anywhere. It is convenient that you turn up now. Master Halfaxen is in the pus wagon, yes?'

'That's a Dragonette, Grundrund!'

'It is still the colour of pus. We will take my wagon.'

We joined her. Speed would not be of the essence now.

She let the brake out on the 4-0-2 and drove quietly down the road to Kellismarsh. The houses on either side were isolated, very large but gloomy, what light the thin moon provided was being swallowed quickly. Beyond the boggy gardens, the marsh spread out unbroken into the darkness.

'Passaloll's property is the fourth on the left further down here,' said Duffy eventually.

'Thank you Master Danwright,' Grundrund said, taking out a shooter and checking the chamber. 'I think it will be for the best if you stay here.'

'Oh, really?' Duffy replied. 'In that house is my half-sister, my step-mother and the dwarf I trusted like a brother who may just have killed one of my best friends. How exactly were you thinking of making me stay?'

'He has a point, Grundrund. We don't want him kicking up a fuss, do we?'

'No, but it's the type of statement I am legally obliged to make.' She handed the shooter to Duffy and retrieved a pelleter from under the driver's panel guard. She filled her pockets with more shells. It was going to be a busy night.

'So, Nicely – what exactly do you think we are about to face here?'

'An enchanter, that's for sure – and not an everyday one. The Dark Crime Lord of Skragslanding probably. A nasty piece of work undoubtedly. I don't think he will have many grunts with him, not his style. Prefers manipulation to the physical stuff.'

I passed Grundrund a spare spray bottle of the mixture I had got made up and delivered to my rooms earlier.

'That's juice from Protillo's spicy five-bean stew. First chance you get, spray it in his eyes and don't listen to his voice either of you.'

We all quietly decamped. The lights were on in Passaloll's house. The front room had the curtains closed, but there was a gap.

'Anything you can tell me about Passaloll's new bed-warmer, Duffy?' I whispered.

'Not much. I only saw him the once – at an event to do with Semeline,' Duffy whispered back.

'Any thoughts?'

I could see Duffy struggle. 'None really – to be honest, I can't remember that much about him at all.'

That didn't sound like the Duffy I knew. I didn't imagine he had forgotten by accident.

I indicated for the others to stop and then crept up to the window. Through the gap, I could see Passaloll and Buns standing next to a roaring fire. They were talking animatedly to a seated figure with his back to the window and a screen to one side. I could just catch a glimpse of a blond head.

Dwarf Girls Don't Dance

More hand language and then we were heading to the back entrance.

It was a good lock, but it wasn't a dwarf lock.

The door opened onto a passageway. I could hear Passaloll and Buns; voices were raised. We followed the passage to the entrance hall proper. The front room opened off it – door ajar.

'We are in trouble,' said Buns. 'This Strongoak has brought an enchantress from the Citadel. He is not stupid.'

'Our position is weakened; we will be found out!' insisted Passaloll.

'They're not wrong,' I shouted, bursting into the room with Grundrund and Duffy close behind me.

Hey, you can't pass up on a line like that!

'Now, nobody move a muscle, say a word, or even think of casting a spell. You in the seat, get yourself up and turn around very slowly – eyes to the ground.'

The seated figure did as requested and turned to face me.

'Pixies piddle—I have never seen you before,' I was bound to admit.

'Of course not fool. Now all of you be still!'

A figure moved out from behind the screen. His voice had more power than I could ever have imagined. It had such authority, such strength, and such force. It was impossible to resist.

'Everybody put your weapons down.' We all obliged.

'And thank you for walking into my trap. I thought to catch the dwarf and goblin, but I have the golden boy as well to later make mine.' His voice was like a living being in my head. And I recognised it. With a supreme effort of will, I moved my head to survey the figure that was now standing by the fire.

'Autumn!'

'Troublesome Strongoak, Master Fool,' he spat out.

'I thought as much.'

'I said, be still!' The voice now was a weapon, a whip that could cut the flesh from your body. I winced under it as if beaten.

'You knew nothing, dwarf.'

'Kingley was your cat's paw,' I struggled to articulate.

'Of course, he was! I do not make myself a target. I do not need the trappings of power, just the power.'

'The power of... Snow King of... Huldre?' I managed to say.

'Huldre?' he sneered unpleasantly. 'I am glad to be done with them! A tribe of peasants scraping a living in the frozen wastes, living on lichen and dreaming of their glory days, when they could be lording it over all you inferior degenerate folk.'

'Harsh... Autumn.' I struggled to say anything more as my mouth now didn't belong to me. 'Nothing... degenerate like wealth?' I added after an ice age or two.

'Oh yes,' Autumn laughed – a sinister, but also sensuous sound that sent a shiver through me. 'I do have a weakness for the shiny stones. But they are useful as well, far easier to move than gold. The Greenwood emeralds got me out of that frozen wasteland and this midge-infested swamp!'

'All... way to... Citadel.'

'Yes.' Autumn came closer to examine me. He hadn't changed a jot, except to loose all appearance of servility. 'To the Citadel, where my plans were working out very well, until you and that stunted peeler come along and ruined everything.'

He looked deep into my eyes.

'I was so pleased that day in Kellishaldt when I saw her deformed frame. So perfect for my plans for Dollund the Dullard, with the added bonus of seeing her swing, which she will of course. My arbiters will see to that.'

Dwarf Girls Don't Dance

'Master,' Heldwide began urgently.

'Shut up, Buns! Do not interrupt here! Can't you see I am examining your kinsman?'

Autumn got even closer. I could feel a chill from his skin.

'This dwarf has resisted me; he should not be able to resist me. Drop the shooter.'

I tried not to comply. I tried with every fibre of my being.

'Drop the shooter,' he shouted, and it was like being hit by a wall of sound.

I fought to not drop the shooter.

'How does he do this? The others cannot resist me. How do you do it?'

I flicked my eyes left and right and saw that Grundrund was indeed completely incapacitated; the sweat was breaking out on her forehead as she struggled. Duffy was completely immobile; the only thing that had changed about him was the hate I could see growing in his eyes.

Autumn walked around me like I was some kind of exotic specimen he had found.

'I was... kissed by... wild... pixie,' I managed to say, feeling the first return of control to my trigger finger as I fought the enchantment.

Autumn laughed from behind, which was as disconcerting as it gets.

'Very funny, dwarf. A wild pixie – as if!' He paused to think. 'Actually, pixie magic just might be capable.'

All the while, the hand not holding the shooter was moving slowly towards my neck. I felt for the usk tooth on the chain there, and holding it murmured, 'Niejte.'

Two beautiful blue eyes looked at me from across the miles, and life returned to my trigger finger. The shooter barked. I missed Autumn by a mile, but he was now rather preoccupied ducking and totally missed the ironwood truncheon that came swinging down on his head.

He fell to the floor, pole-axed. Captain Royalwench stood over his prone body.

'I will not shoot a man in the back, no matter how much he deserves it,' she said darkly. 'I hope you don't mind me following you beyond my jurisdiction, Officer Grundrund. This one will be tried and will hang in Skragsrealm.'

Grundrund let out a roar as Autumn's hold finally lost its effect. Duffy slumped, and Passaloll fell like an axed tree, but Buns had been under the enchanter's influence for a lot longer.

'Master!' he screamed, pulling out two old-mine hand pistols and blasting at the room.

The Princess was his target; she barely had time to put up her hands, and then he just continued spraying bullets around like so much Pixie dust.

I leapt to the Princess's side, but she was already falling. Grundrund fired as she sought cover, but the enforced immobility had spoilt her aim. The pellets blasted the wall where Buns had been standing, but he was now behind the very solid desk and still firing.

'Oh Princess,' I groaned as we rolled behind a day bed, convinced that she must have been hit.

'Captain, while we are on duty please, Nicely,' she said.

'You're not hurt? You're really not hurt?'

She held up her arms where the chewed up ends of her uniform now showed considerably more bracelet.

'You stopped bullets with bracelets? I can't believe it!'

'Warrior Princess, Nicely. That's how you earn the big buckskins.'

Dwarf Girls Don't Dance

Grundrund's pelleter roared again.

Captain Royalwench rolled onto her side and shouted: 'Buns this is me, the Princess! Stop this immediately. This isn't you! This worm has burrowed into your mind.'

'You speak of things you cannot understand, Princess,' Buns screamed back, now definitely not the full treasure chest. The Master is wise, the Master is glorious, the Master has true majesty – go now, and the Master in his mercy may yet let you live.'

'Oh Buns,' she said sadly, before shouting: 'This is your last chance, Buns!'

His answer was another round of shots.

The Princess got up, and in one move, jumped the daybed and leapt onto the desk behind which Buns still cowered, and then she shot him.

'Farewell Heldwide Halfaxen, though we lost you so many years ago.'

'Strongoak!' Grundrund shouted, getting up to one knee and ignoring the blood splattering her best tunic, 'the enchanter!'

Somehow Autumn had recovered enough to stagger out of the door. If he had hopes of driving away, they were soon shattered, along with the front room's window. Grundrund elbowed this in, and her pelleter spat again, shredding the tyres on his waiting wagon.

I ran out of the room and was following a trail of blood leading to the back door, when I realised what was happening to me. The Rage was taking me. Something about fighting Autumn's control had done this.

Not that it mattered now. I welcomed the Rage.

This was the creature responsible for Mansel's brutal death at the hands of somebody who had once loved her. And for poor

Duffy's father's grizzly end, and for framing Diamond for a murder, and tonight he would die. The Rage would be fed or I would die; it was too late for anything else.

I realised Duffy and Princess were running behind me now; I could smell the anger in their sweat. The Rage does that to your senses.

'Nicely!' shouted Duffy.

'Don't get in my way, Duffy. I am killing him. Don't try to stop me either Princess. Where is he?!'

'That's what I'm trying to tell you,' shouted Duffy, pulling me to a halt. 'He's headed into the Kellismarsh.'

'He must know a path,' the Princess spat out.

'No,' I screamed, 'he's Huldre!' I spotted the blond figure in the moonlight, sprinting across the swamp. 'If they can run on snow, he can run across this – but he won't escape me!'

I was away before they could stop me. It was easy at first. I jumped from tussock to tussock. I could do this. I could do anything! I would break his bones. I would suck them! He would know pain before he died. My legs could carry me anywhere; they were dwarf legs! They could run for miles, climb mountains, a marsh wouldn't stop me. A marsh couldn't stop me!

The marsh stopped me.

Suck muck pulled on me, hindering my every move! I could see Autumn running easily ahead. He turned, laughing at me.

'Don't think you have won, dwarf! I will be back again for you and your friends!'

No, no, no! This could not happen. I fought against the suck mud and fought and fought, but I might as well have tried to beat up a snowstorm.

'Nicely! Grab the rope! Grab the rope!'

Dwarf Girls Don't Dance

I became aware of voices, and then felt the rope hit my shoulder. This was not a good situation. Autumn was getting away, and I was in danger of dying for nothing. This was not good at all.

I grabbed the rope.

The Warrior Princess and Duffy pulled with all their might and even that wasn't enough. It took a wounded Grundrund to add the strength of her one good arm to eventually free me, and drag me back to dry land.

I was exhausted but still fuming.

'He can't escape, not now! Not now!' I beat the ground in anger until my fists bled, fully consumed by the Rage.

Grundrund expressed it better. She let out a roar that was as loud as anything I have heard from any creature, on two legs or four. It was the cry of a wounded beast, born of agony and frustration – the cry of a creature that had wandered onto the swamp and was now caught, sinking and flailing.

Autumn stopped. He must have found solid ground. He cupped his hands and shouted at us. 'I will have my revenge on you all, goblin, man and dwarf! One night I will be there by your bed, whispering in your ear, and you will be mine! Then you will know agony the like of which you cannot imagine, and what is more, you will thank me for it.' He laughed. As evil a laugh as I have ever heard.

And something moved behind Autumn.

It was just a dark shadow at first – no real shape or structure. But, as it reared and slime and water slid from the terrible form, a frightening head became obvious and it propped itself up on the overlarge front limbs that it required to swim the thick swamp waters. Enormous jaws opened below pale uncaring lights. The jaws gaped, wider and wider, and then with a clash of primeval teeth shut tight.

Before he was probably even aware of what was happening, Autumn was gone and the marsh closed up again over the both of them.

'Mud dragon,' said Grundrund conversationally. 'A large one too. They prey on wounded creatures that get caught in the marsh. Beasts that shout like I shouted. Good.'

She spat at the mud and then added: 'Enchant that.'

She turned and limped back into the house. Duffy and the Princess helped me up, and we followed her, my Rage all spent.

31

Goodbyes

Various calls were made on the horn, and a lot of very official people began to appear. Quite a few of the local White and Wise arrived from the Boscomere Feast and went into council with Detective Analyst Grundrund as she was patched up. The talk at the feast was all about the sudden collapse of the Chief Arbiter and his former apprentice, Arbiter Skunglard, as well as the head of Kellishaldt Keep, Captain Gobblod.

I'm sure Grundrund was giving them a whole lot more to talk, and think, about.

The physics came and took Passaloll. She didn't know what day it was. Neither did the real Fullerall, who had been held captive while Autumn took over his life. That seemed to be his way. Never throw away a cat's paw that could prove useful in the future. Even Kingley paid his upkeep for Autumn in the end. A great investment that made us believe we had caught the real villain. I should have suspected something when it was Kingley who rowed across from the island with the Grunt, leaving Autumn with his feet up in the middle of the lake.

For poor Heldwide Halfaxen, there was no help available.

'I should feel worse,' the Princess said to me. 'But I think there was nothing left of the Buns we knew.'

Duffy nodded his head, exhausted. 'You're right, Princess. And even if he'd regained his senses, I don't think he would have wanted to have lived with the knowledge of what he had done to Mansel.'

'All that time, in a room beneath our feet, waiting to come out and steal the Greenwood emeralds. It's hard to believe,' said Duffy.

'I'm not sure,' I felt forced to contribute. 'I think the plan was always to kill Willow.'

'Really?' said the Princess.

'As far as I know, that's how enchanters work. They take some real and heartfelt emotion and twist it and corrupt it. By the time Autumn finished with poor Buns, if he couldn't have Willow, no one would. He would hardly have been aware of the jewel theft.'

'Then he just handed the emeralds over to this Autumn creature?'

'Yes. Not being able to sell them locally, I imagine Autumn left there pretty quickly and set himself up in the Citadel.'

'Where he found another creature to be his cat's paw and became this underworld figure with a bad reputation,' the Princess finished for me.

Duffy sighed heavily.

'Willow blamed herself so much because she had made the last drink and Mansel had changed her outfit to look like her. She should be told the truth at last, though it won't be easy.'

'Which is why you should tell her, Duffy,' I said.

'Me?' he replied in surprise.

'Of course! The Citadel isn't the other side of the world, and it's not that scary. But if you need a Shield, I could recommend one.'

Duffy smiled.

'Maybe I will at that. Maybe I just might.'

Grundrund joined us from her council.

'How are we doing, Detective? Ten years apiece in the Kellishaldt Keep?' I asked. Or can we all go home and drink a large amount of something sticky? Which is what I intend to do whatever you say.'

'It really depends on what the new Acting Captain of the Kellishaldt Keep says,' Grundrund said solemnly. 'But as that appears to be me. I think we can certainly set the glasses up.'

'Excellent!' I said. 'Thoroughly deserved, of course.'

'As I seem to be the only one with any grasp on what is going on, I don't think they had any choice.'

'And my shooting of Buns?' asked the Princess. 'What does the acting Captain say about that?'

'I have informed the council members here of the close work we were carrying out with our Skragslanding colleagues. Especially how this was vital to the solving of not one, but two murders, of prominent members of the Kellisgrund community and they were delighted to hear of such "close co-operation" between the law enforcement agencies.'

The Princess nodded.

'And of course, Buns was a Skragsrealm native, which leaves me with the sad duty of informing his father.'

'Who I don't imagine will be that surprised.' I added.

'Really?' said Grundrund.

'I think he must have realised something was amiss – subtle changes in Buns. His absence during the time of Mansel's murder for a start. That might even be why he never told Buns about the second coffer.'

'It's possible,' said the Princess.

'But he was too attached to the secret love he still held for Talensia Dollund,' I continued, 'that he didn't want this memory violated, or the secret of his visits to come out.'

'Hmm,' said Grundrund, in that strange Goblin way. 'There is news about your friend Luce. After the creature Autumn died, he had something like a seizure, screaming that he had to kill Danwright Dollund.'

'Oh, Luce,' muttered Duffy. 'Not you as well?'

'Don't worry! With Nicely's friend Red there, he was able to come out of the fit, and he seems to be recovering well with, hopefully, no lasting effects. It might even have been of long term help to his mental health she has suggested.'

'All Autumn's work again!' I said angrily.

'Of course, to throw us off the scent.'

'And what of my client, Acting Captain Grundrund?'

'There will be some scrollwork, but tomorrow as soon as possible, she will be set free without a blemish to her name.'

'That is what we like to hear.'

'And of course, with a very valuable jewel to assist in her integration back into the community.'

'Which I am sure we can assist her with,' added Duffy.

'Sounds good!' I said. 'Now, where is that bottle with my name on it?'

Later that week Diamond and I went a fine gnome eatery called Protillo's in Skragslanding for our celebratory meal. Skragsrealm offered a little more in the way of anonymity. The fiery red bean stew was as good as I remembered. Diamond tried to insist that it was her treat.

'After all, Nicely. Somehow I seem to have gone from keep fodder to wealthy dwarfess, and I'm not sure I feel comfortable about either. But I wouldn't be anywhere without you.'

'I know what you mean, Diamond. Apparently, Mansel's parents were still offering a reward for the apprehension of her killer. They're trying to give it to me. Not really what I was searching for here.'

'How are the others now – all those that fell under Autumn's spell?'

'It's variable. Red is working with them.'

'How I disliked that man! Kingley wasn't actually that bad a lot of the time, but when Autumn came around, all the girls just felt uncomfortable. Even his girlfriends.'

'And you think they had a choice in the matter?'

Diamond shuddered. 'I didn't think about that! I was lucky he didn't try it on me!'

'Lucky, maybe? Remember, he really needed to find a body's weakness to exploit it. Like poor Heldwide's love for Willow. Anyway, I've asked Grundrund to contact the Huldre and see if the Snow Queen can help those affected as well. Red has got a job after all.'

'What about those gloves they found in the study?' said Diamond, still not really believing she was free. 'This secret evidence they were always about to reveal.'

'There was never anything conclusive from the tests they carried out. Any small dwarf hand could have fitted that glove, and Heldwide was quite slight, another reason for him using the iceball catcher mitts when he killed Mansel. Besides Acting Captain Grundrund has deemed the evidence tainted because of Gobblod's involvement.'

'Good, I'd hate to have that hanging over my head. Snow Queens and enchantresses, what an exciting life you do lead, Master Strongoak!'

'There's just one more thing.'

'What's that, Nicely?' She looked at me, suddenly unsure. I hated what I had to do next.

'They aren't the only gloves, are they?'

'Sorry?'

'The gloves that they found at Dollund's place.'

'Well,' she said, 'I have other gloves.'

'Yes, like the gloves you used to wear dancing at the *Hungry Hippo* in the Citadel, Diamond.'

'Oh.' She went very quiet.

'The gloves you were wearing on the night Roli Seneschalson died.'

'Those gloves.'

'Gloves which really would have done an awful lot to protect an individual's intricate nail job. As I was reminded recently.'

Diamond moved her food around her plate before speaking: 'I don't know is the answer, Nicely. Before you ask the question, I really don't know. That's what the Rage is like isn't it, when it takes over. The drink – well, it did taste strange.'

'But you arranged the glasses like that. You knew I would pick up on it. The conclusions I would come to.'

'Does it make a difference, Nicely?' Diamond asked, looking at me straight with those big wonderful, soulful, very dwarf eyes of hers.

'Yes, it makes a difference.' I hated myself for saying it, but I had to. I hope I didn't live to regret it.

She was sad as she asked: 'Do you think we would have worked, Nicely? Me and you?'

I smiled before answering, like I hadn't considered the idea before.

'Yes, we could have worked – but it would have meant going the full fellowship: half a dozen mine rats crawling around in the

Dwarf Girls Don't Dance

hearth, a little place in New Iron Town perhaps, and two weeks at a Time-off Haven each year. Maybe I could have got a job in security for a big company. Maybe you could have entertained the local old folk. It could have worked, but I don't think either of us was quite ready for that then, or now, and perhaps we never will be.'

She nodded quietly. 'Maybe you're right at that.'

She lifted her glass. I did the same.

'Thanks for saving me, Nicely. Here's to Master Detective Strongoak, defender of lost causes.'

'Here's to you, Diamond. May you always make the heart beat faster.'

We chinked glasses and I toasted her: 'Keep shining, Diamond.' This time I knew we wouldn't meet again.

Lippy drove me to the station when it was time to go. I wanted to ask about his mother. I almost hoped to see her again, perhaps with a new piglet. Lippy had a new Heslington. Apparently, it wasn't as good as the last one.

'I will get it sorted, you see.'

I had said my goodbyes to Sansire and Osk. The return of her Gift that seemed to coincide with my arrival was going to take some sorting out for the both of them. And it certainly was back; she had predicted the death of one of the Nine Idlers at the hand of another after all. The Princess didn't feel good about that, but she had a job to do, just like we all have.

We knew we had both changed, and we left it at that. There wasn't really an appropriate goodbye to be said it seems, as she hadn't tried to say one.

Berger, I would be seeing a lot more of, now that he was such a name in the Citadel. Duffy had already been on the horn talking to Willow. She was also living in the Citadel. I would be seeing both of them very soon. Luce was a changed man, or much more himself. Red was actually staying around for a while to work with him. That seemed to be making them both happy. Maybe he was more adaptable than he realised.

I didn't exactly expect a big send-off from Kellishaldt station. I certainly didn't expect to see Acting Captain Grundrund waiting for me in the rain.'

'Captain Grundrund.'

'Master Detective Strongoak.'

'Nice day for a funeral.'

'Yes, the bodies will sink quick today.'

I turned the collar of my coat up. 'It's being so cheerful that keeps you Kellisgrundians going.'

'Our humour is perhaps an acquired taste.'

'Like your coffee.'

She did her little goblin chuckle.

'Anyway, thanks for coming, Grundrund.'

'It is my pleasure. I also had a last question for you.'

'Fire away.'

'I can understand your distrust of Arbiter Skunglard, but what made you suspect Captain Gobblod had been influenced in some manner?'

I looked at the goblin, towering way above me. 'Because of you,' I told her.

'Explain please.'

'He gave me you, expecting that you would be an encumbrance – hinder my investigation at every turn. Assumed we would never get on.'

'I see.'

'He wanted me to fail; there had to be a reason. I could tell pretty much straight off that you were an efficient law enforcement officer, with great insight and a top detective to boot – and therefore a very useful asset.'

She shifted a little on her large boot-shod feet.

'For a dwarf, you sometimes show excellent observational skills and very good deductive power.'

'For a dwarf.'

'Naturally.'

'Don't get all mushy on me, Grundrund.'

'It's the approaching steam train. I think a smut has got in my eye.'

'Yes, I get that problem sometimes.'

We both stamped our feet in the cold air.

'And what of your dwarf friend?'

'My client?'

'If you wish to continue with that pretence —yes, your client?'

'The job is done. Case solved, two cases solved.'

'I see. That's it?'

'That's it.'

I heard the train whistle blowing now, some way down the Eskrag still. It sounded lonelier than unrequited love.

'I think Diamond might give Skragsrealm a try now. I think she'll like it there,' I told the goblin at my side.

'I think you need to spend more time with your own kind, Nicely Strongoak – especially women.'

'And what kind would that be, Captain Grundrund?'

'With dwarves, of course. Too many tall women in your life – you will get neck ache eventually.'

I had to laugh at that.

'What did you think I meant?' she continued.

'With officers of the law. Aren't they "our kind" now? For the both of us.'

'I socialise with goblins still,' Grundrund insisted.

'In the *Mud Dragon*, which I am guessing is not exactly goblin High Society?'

'I do not think I belong in High Society. I don't think they'd be interested in what I have to say. I don't imagine they listen to you much either. I just believe in society, like you do.'

The steam train pulled up to the platform. Folk got off, folk got on. I hefted my trunk. 'I'd best be going; it looks busy.'

'There is a seat reserved for you in the last carriage, Nicely.'

'That's very kind of you, Grundrund. I really appreciate that.'

She walked along and opened the door of the last carriage. 'Goodbye Nicely Strongoak. Until the next time we meet.'

She bowed her head as I got on. Then she stood on the platform and waved as the train pulled out.

'Hey Grundrund,' I shouted back at her with a smile. 'You never told me your first name?'

'No, I didn't,' she said, laughing back at me.

I struggled along the carriage with my trunk. She hadn't reserved me a seat. She had reserved me a whole compartment: a sleeper, blinds down, looking very cosy.

I was struggling with the door latch, when it opened from the other side.

'Hello Princess,' I said to the smiling woman waiting there for me.

'Grundrund said you never listen to her advice and I had some leave owed.'

'Delighted to hear it.'

'Let me help you with that case.'

The train whistle blew, and this time it didn't sound lonely at all.

www.ingramcontent.com/pod-product-compliance
Lightning Source LLC
LaVergne TN
LVHW041739060526
838201LV00046B/866